ALSO BY

DIEGO DE SILVA

I Hadn't Understood

MY MOTHER-IN-LAW
DRINKS

Diego De Silva

MY MOTHER-IN-LAW DRINKS

*Translated from the Italian
by Antony Shugaar*

Europa
editions

Europa Editions
214 West 29th Street
New York, N.Y. 10001
www.europaeditions.com
info@europaeditions.com

Translation by Antony Shugaar
Original title: *Mia suocera beve*
Translation copyright © 2014 by Europa Editions

Library of Congress Cataloging in Publication Data is available
ISBN 978-1-60945-232-2

De Silva, Diego
My Mother-in-Law Drinks

Book design by Emanuele Ragnisco
www.mekkanografici.com

Prepress by Grafica Punto Print – Rome

Printed in the USA

I try to keep my nose out of my own business.
—Vincenzo Malinconico

CONTENTS

MY MOTHER-IN-LAW
DRINKS

WHY IT'S A BAD IDEA TO ASK THE FIRST QUESTION THAT POPS INTO YOUR HEAD

I f there's one thing you should absolutely never do when storm clouds are gathering over your relationship, it's ask your girlfriend if there's something wrong.

Because if you thought that with that question (which among other things is an ambiguous question, and like all ambiguous questions it tends to elicit an answer that is, in turn, another question) you were going to get the lay of the land and maybe even start a conversation that might solve a problem that was sitting there quietly bothering no one, a problem that would have taken care of itself if some idiot hadn't come along and riled it up, then it means that you don't even realize that the idiot in question is you.

Would you care to know just how the conversation is going to unfold, and I mean line by line, if you're reckless enough to light that fuse? Then please, read on.

You: Is there something wrong?

Her: What kind of question is that?

You: It's just a question.

Her: It's just a question.

You: Right.

Her: That's not just a question.

You: If you say so.

Her (coming after you, because by this point you're probably already hurrying out of the room): What, are you saying you think there's something wrong with our relationship?

You: I didn't ask if there was something wrong with our relationship.

Her: Then what *did* you ask? If there's something wrong with me?

You (already starting to get a little hot under the collar; a detail she picked up on right away, because she knows you): There's nothing wrong with you.

Her: Then what the hell *did* you mean by that question?

By this point, it's guaranteed that the two of you will break up within the next two or three months.

It goes without saying: it's a question I've asked.

A Common Sense of Aesthetics

For starters, I need to learn to mind my own business and not to open up to strangers. My grandma was 100 percent right, and that's a fact. You can't fool grandmas, they're not like so many of the moms you run into nowadays, who don't even realize that the children living under their own roofs are torturing their schoolmates until they see it on YouTube. If my grandma is looking down on me now, I'll bet she's delighted. She's probably invited a couple of her girlfriends over (I could even tell you which ones) and she's just sitting there, watching it all on a celestial TiVo, savoring how right she was, and on her own viewing schedule (which after all is the only truly satisfying way to enjoy being right).

I mean, after all, I'm not an especially outgoing person, so I shouldn't have any trouble keeping my thoughts a little more to myself. If it were entirely up to me, if the sidewalk stanchions of everyday wisdom weren't always tripping me up, I'd gladly abstain from doing lots of things, such as passing the time of day with other people.

It's not that I'm stuck up. It's really just that, if you think about it, idle chitchat is demanding. You have to get yourself into the frame of mind to simplify to an extreme extent, treat things dismissively that actually matter to you, look your conversational partner in the eye now and then (some people are simply incapable of doing this and offer only a three-quarter view of their faces the whole time you're talking to them).

It's the same kind of awkwardness you experience, only to

a slightly lesser extent, when you ride the elevator with a fellow tenant and you feel duty bound to say *something* even though you have less than zero interest in talking at all, much less with that particular fellow tenant (who, now that you come to think of it, is one of those tenants who never even say hello), so you always wind up coming up with stupid topics such as it's about time the weather made up its mind to really get chilly, no more of this namby-pamby weather where if you dress light you catch a cold but if you add an extra layer of T-shirt you break into a sweat.

To say nothing of those times when you have to stand there and listen to opinions that leave you openmouthed, like this one I heard a while ago from a character whose name I can't even remember (it's incredible the way certain people will confide in you first thing) who opined that squeegee men at traffic lights would rather kill time all day long than work a real job: Just try to get them to show up at five A.M. tomorrow morning, this guy said to me, at this or that building site and break their back the way that Italian construction workers break theirs— try it, and see what they say.

"Legal pay, minimum wage, tax withholding, and full benefits?" I asked.

This was followed by a painful silence.

". . . Sure, withholding, and benefits," he said vaguely, his voice trailing off.

Now, I don't want people to take me for a sociopath, but when you come away from a conversation like this one, even if you didn't totally cave in to the asshole du jour, you feel like a bit of an asshole yourself. As if you'd just sold the guitar you owned when you were a kid, if you know what I'm saying. Because that's how idle chitchat works. Conversation, when it's, shall we say, free and easy, unassuming, without pretenses and, especially, without an audience (which is exactly the kind of conversation in which people tend to say what they really think) impoverishes our language and, to an even greater extent, our thoughts. When you have an audience listening to everything you say, you have to take responsibility for your statements. You can't just cheerfully opine that squeegee men don't like to work. In a public forum, the common sense of aesthetics, by which I mean that all-powerful social inhibitor generally filed under the vague but unmistakable heading of "Just Doesn't Seem Right," prevails.

The funny thing about Just Doesn't Seem Right is that it manifests itself without warning in the form of misgivings, so that something (an act, a statement, a question), even if it's not wrong just yet but there's a faint chance that it might turn out to be, automatically makes you refrain from it.

It's an extremely vigorous aesthetic canon, this Just Doesn't Seem Right. Nobody knows exactly what it consists of, but damn if it's not effective. Let's take making out, for instance. You're energetically rubbing up against your girlfriend; at a certain point you really feel like grabbing one of her ass cheeks and giving it a squeeze, or even both of them, which I guess is a little truck-driver-ish but *what fun*; and she might not mind it a bit either (right then and there she could probably go for a good hard spanking), but you hold back because it Just Doesn't Seem Right. And so you go home doubly dissatisfied, first because making out can have painful aftereffects (and at your age you ought to know it), and second because you denied yourself the pleasure of a moment of butt-grabbing, which now that you think about it wouldn't have been at all a bad thing.

So that's the way Just Doesn't Seem Right works. It's a kind of invisible censor, and it does its best to save you from embarrassments that wouldn't have been such a big deal after all.

To simplify, Just Doesn't Seem Right, also known as the common sense of aesthetics, could be defined as the fear of doing or saying something you might later regret. If you want to stand up to its dictatorial influence, you need to have style and know it. In other words, you have to have tremendous self-confidence.

I've just explained the reason why I'm unable to stand up to the tyranny of Just Doesn't Seem Right.

A little less than half an hour ago, when the civil engineer who got me into this fine mess first intercepted me among the shelves filled with canned tomatoes and ready-to-eat pasta sauces as I hunted for a jar of Buitoni Fior di Pesto, saying, "Pardon me, but aren't you the lawyer Malinconico?" I ought to have simply asked how he happened to know me, let him explain that a few years ago I had brilliantly argued the case of an old friend of his who'd been crippled in a workplace accident, and then made my excuses, whatever popped into my head, like maybe that my car was double-parked. But the thing is, it's such a rare experience to encounter someone who says he's happy with my professional services that when it does happen, I luxuriate in it. Frustration makes us vain.

As soon as I heard the name of my former client I mentally glimpsed the cover of the case folder, and after that, remembered every detail of the case.

"Comunale, Vittorio, of course, of course," I confirmed, nodding my head yes over and over, like the little rag dogs people stick to the rear windows of their cars.

Italian lawyers remember their clients by their surnames first. It's a way to make them anonymous, to focus on the problem facing them. Vittorio Comunale is a person. Comunale, Vittorio, is the title of a story.

"You heard, right?" said the gentleman I didn't yet know. A distinguished individual, maybe fifty, with nice manners, extremely skinny, in fact undernourished, a face so steeped in suffering that it made me cringe to look at it, as if there were some chance of him infecting me with his torment.

"Yes, I did, but too late. I'd happily have attended his funeral, that is if going to a funeral is something you can do happily."

He smiled. In the background the radio was playing "Montagne verdi."

"Vittorio told me you were a nice guy, Counselor."

"So was he. He was one of those people who seem incapable of becoming embittered, I don't know if that makes any sense to you. Even in the state he was in, I never saw even a shadow of indignation on his face."

I was genuinely taken by the topic, but my eyes kept trailing after "Montagne verdi" (once you recognize a tune, you tend to follow it through the air as if it were an insect). The lady who cleans house for me always sings it, that's why. And she's not the only one. My friends and I conducted a little survey among ourselves and we came to the irrefutable conclusion that housekeepers in their fifties sing "Montagne verdi" while they work, and not some of them, *all* of them. As if they came with some sort of preinstalled software that automatically starts them singing that song the minute they pick up a bucket and a broom. As if the sentimental evocation of peasant society contained in those verses, that Heidism for grown-ups, in contrast to the repetitively cloistered nature of modern housework, somehow made the mopping of floors pleasingly nostalgic.

There are other songs (all of them strictly seventies or, at the very latest, early eighties standards) that seem to be real crowd-pleasers on the housecleaning circuit: for instance, "Che sarà," the Ricchi e Poveri version (identifiable by the imitation of Angela Brambati's trademark yelp—you remember her, the brunette), "Se mi lasci non vale" by Julio Iglesias, and "Maledetta primavera" by Loretta Goggi; but none of these songs has ever come close to challenging the supremacy of "Montagne verdi" (the secret of its lasting popularity, in my opinion, lies in the "black-nosed bunny," an image that's practically impossible to get out of your head).

My interlocutor stood silent for a long time, while I speculated mentally on the whys and wherefores of that inexplicable phenomenon. At last, he broke the silence.

"No, I think . . . I think that makes perfect sense, really." He wasn't having an easy time of it though, because his voice broke on the last couple of words in the sentence.

So I brusquely interrupted my metaphysical pursuit of Marcella Bella and turned my eyes back to him. He looked pretty beat up.

"Listen, I'm sorry, I didn't mean to upset you."

"No, no, you didn't," he hastened to reassure me, squinting as he shook his head. "What you said was really nice."

"Well, I'm glad to hear that, Signor . . ."

"Sesti Orfeo. Engineer Romolo Sesti Orfeo."

And that's where I sort of got hung up for a second.

For a working professional to introduce himself with his official title is, all things considered, a perfectly normal thing to do. But when I heard the way he underscored his credentials (with that surname that smacked of fallen nobility, moreover), who can say why, it just gave me a strange impression immediately. As if the guy was up to something. Which he was.

"For that matter, Counselor, you'd never have been so intransigent in the negotiations over damages if you hadn't taken his case to heart," he added, throwing me offstride, so much so that I paused a moment to look him in the eye.

"If it had been up to me, I would have taken it to trial," I said, puffing out my chest.

And the guy nodded, even tossing in the faintly virile smile of a man admiring the balls another man has shown in his decision making.

I'm not a tough guy. I never have been. If you want to know the truth, I doubt I've ever made a real decision in my whole life. I don't much like making decisions. To make decisions you have to be sure of yourself, and I'm hardly ever sure of any-thing. I'm more of a multiple options kind of guy, really. Here's a for instance: I've never broken up with a woman. That doesn't mean I haven't offered my passive cooperation in letting a relationship waste away and die. In fact, when it comes to the failure to render emotional aid and assistance, I'm a repeat offender, if I'm really being brought to book for my transgressions. But standing by and watching as a relationship goes under for the third time isn't the same thing as stating openly: "Look, I don't want to be with you anymore, and that's that."

This is the thing: I don't want to take responsibility for los-ing something important. I don't see why I should. If I'm going to have to lose something important, I'd rather have someone else take the blame for it, truth be told.

Same thing goes for my, shall we say, professional life. I'm not going to knock my head against the wall over matters of principle. Because, obviously, if you're going to make a big deal about matters of principle, you need to be able to rely on a working system of justice.

If there's any chance of sparing a client the ordeal of a law-suit—and I'm not trying to brag here, but I've never swindled a client—I choose that option. I hate protracted negotiations that drag on so long that you almost forget about them, law-suits that last seven, eight, ten years. Nothing turns my stom-ach like a case file yellowing away in the filing cabinet, dates of hearing that when you reread them it dawns on you that your oldest child wasn't even born yet (even though, Jesus Christ, the whole thing's about nothing more than a miserable fucking patch of damp wall in a relative's kitchen). I find it debilitating to be involved in something where if you happen to run into a client on the street, he doesn't even bring the topic up, he just gives you a look steeped in compassion that seems to have been put on just to say: "It probably isn't even your fault, but Counselor, what a fucked-up profession you're in."

The worst thing is you can hardly blame them. These days—there's no point trying to be all juridically correct—we're all pretty much resigned to the idea (a little facile, yes, but still applicable in the majority of cases) that bringing a lawsuit is the one sure, patented way of ensuring that a dispute seizes up and remains disgracefully insoluble.

Modern lawyers are a little bit like psychoanalysts, in that certain people continue going to them for years even after it has become abundantly clear that they'll never solve their problems. (I know a couple of people who've told me that they can't even remember why they went into analysis in the first place, and they weren't kidding when they said it.)

Consider people who don't pay their bills. They've found a fail-safe method for getting by: they just sue. They use time as a form of currency. And they eventually wear their creditors down to the point where they're happy to take pennies on the dollar just for the sake of getting shed of the whole goddamned dispute and never having to think about it again.

All this is just to illustrate that—to return to the moment in which I was about to reply to Engineer Romolo Sesti Orfeo—I'm usually not so strict if there's any chance of resolving a case amicably.

But when Vittorio Comunale's employer asked to meet me in his lawyer's office to settle the case out of court, the offer that fell on my ears was so shamelessly stingy that I got that mocking grin on my face that you see in the movies when somebody openly provokes a serial killer (a silent smile that says: "You haven't got the faintest idea what kind of trouble you've just landed yourself in"), after which I turned on my heel and left, muttering a quiet "*Arrivederci,*" and maybe not even that.

The next day, they called me to quadruple the offer, but by that point I had become intractable, and I was even starting to enjoy myself. Listen to me, I told my colleague, if your client really thinks he made a reasonable offer, why don't you have him come repeat it in court, then we'll see just how much the shattered leg of a forty-year-old construction worker is really worth; and that's just limiting ourselves to the leg, since the pillar that fell on him did plenty of other kinds of damage, as I'm sure you're aware.

So he says: I swear to you that I had no idea he'd offer you that figure.

So I say: Are you telling me he made an idiot out of you?

So he says (after a pause during which he must have been wondering if he'd heard me correctly): Thanks for the professional solidarity, Counselor, but these things happen. Haven't you ever had a client put you in a difficult spot?

So I shoot straight back at him: Not to this degree, but sure, every once in a while.

I was instantly reminded of a nightmarish moment of embarrassment, one of those scenes where reality itself fades away as everyone turns to stare at the one individual still picked out in high definition: that is to say, you.

Filippo Sciumo, that was the ogre's name. He liked to go around town stealing car radios by smashing in the windows with his knee, the idiot, until one night he happened upon a vehicle with windows made of bulletproof glass, after which he'd fallen to the asphalt howling so loud that the carabinieri themselves came galloping to his rescue (apparently—according to Sciumo—they never once stopped laughing the whole way back to headquarters as he sat handcuffed in the backseat of the squad car).

At any rate, my job was to obtain a plea bargain, and knowing his tendency to take offense at trivial slights, I'd told him over and over again to keep his mouth shut and let me take care of it (especially because I'd already struck a deal with the prosecuting magistrate: all we had to do was fill in the form), but instead, that lamebrained ape, that dangerous moron, may the devil screw him on his afternoons off, one second after the reading of the counts of indictment, had the brilliant idea to loudly dry-gargle and then spit on the floor.

I've had tough moments in my life. But none of them compare to this one; I swear, I wished that a natural catastrophe of some kind would swoop down and strike the part of the world I occupied at that moment, eliminating all forms of life (first and foremost my own) that might possess memory of what had just happened.

"Hey, Malinconico, are you still there?" my colleague had asked me, since I'd stopped speaking entirely, horror-struck as I was at the resurfacing of that bloodcurdling memory.

"Yes, sorry, I just got . . . distracted there for a second."

"Well, what are we going to do?"

So I said (rocketing back to reality): "I'm not even going to discuss it."

Just like that, cut and dried. Absolutely sure of myself. And I'd have toughed it out, too, if Vittorio Comunale hadn't insisted on getting it settled immediately ("Just get me a reasonable sum, Counselor, all I want is to put it behind me").

When you think of the victims of workplace accidents and you try to put yourself in their shoes, or in the shoes of their families, you imagine them as combative, spirited, determined to carry on the battle to the last breath. That's not how they are. People who are injured on the job come out of it as debilitated as if they'd had open-heart surgery, and the same goes for the family ("Counselor," Comunale's wife once told me on the phone, "my husband is *broken*").

"Forgive me, I didn't mean to pry."

Those were the words with which Engineer Romolo Sesti Orfeo commented on the decline and fall of my warlike intentions concerning his old friend's lawsuit.

"No, not at all, I apologize if I seemed a little combative," I replied, placatingly, in my turn. "Evidently, I still haven't entirely gotten over that epi . . ."

And there I left the sentence unfinished, because the attention of Engineer Romolo Sesti Orfeo, from one second to the next, had been totally captured by one of the closed-circuit television monitors that dotted the supermarket's ceiling: specifically the one directly behind me, some six feet overhead, perched directly above the boxes of egg lasagna (and who can say why they always put the egg lasagna on the uppermost shelf).

Whereupon I turned to look myself, expecting to see some jaw-droppingly hot babe or at least an armed robbery in progress, but there was nothing on the monitor that justified the distraction, aside from a guy with a ponytail wearing a trench coat straight out of *The Matrix* nodding in the general direction of the automatic swinging entry gate, as if it had opened because it realized who it was dealing with.

"Something wrong?" I asked, turning my disappointed eyes back to Engineer Romolo Sesti Orfeo. I was starting to get sick of this conversation.

"What? Ah, no, sorry," he said, emerging suddenly from his trance, "it's just that that monitor seemed to me to, how to put this . . ."—and here I got the impression that he was improvising—". . . to be taking its sweet time."

Whereupon I must have seemed even more confused than before, because he immediately hastened to explain what the hell he was talking about.

"The video security system is operated by the central computer. When a customer comes in, the sensor on the video camera captures the face and automatically transmits it to the monitors; then the computer records everything on the hard drive. Sometimes it happens that a monitor stalls for a few seconds, as if the system had taken too big a bite out of something and were bracing itself to swallow it all down, I'm not sure if that's clear."

I nodded generically, to convey that I thought I'd grasped the concept, though I still failed to see the connection between that brief treatise on video security and the relative stranger who suddenly seemed so eager to lay it out for me. But he went on, in a hold-on-and-in-a-second-you'll-see-what-I-mean tone of voice.

By that point I didn't really give a damn about seeing what he meant, since I'd already been standing there talking to this gentleman I didn't even know for a good fifteen minutes (moreover it was ten in the morning and I was considering the possibility of swinging by the courthouse, just to see what was going on), but I stayed put and kept listening, more than anything else because It Just Didn't Seem Right.

"Now. If that sort of spell extends even by the slightest amount of time, I'm talking microseconds here, I'd notice it immediately, because it might be an indicator of the onset of a technical glitch of some kind."

As he was finishing his sentence he pulled out of his jacket pocket a gizmo that looked very much like a remote control and aimed it at the monitor which, according to him, had just malfunctioned. Only he didn't push any buttons, and I could see that clearly.

"Then I suppose that would make you . . ." I said, with a rhetorical flourish.

"The computer engineer who designed the video security system," he finished, underscoring the words ever so slightly.

"Ohh, I see," I said (by which I meant: "At last, we can go").

The truth was that—aside from my complete lack of inter-est in the topic at hand—I didn't really believe what he was saying. That is, it's not that I thought he was making it up (though I did have my doubts about the idea that the system had problems swallowing its mouthfuls of data), but it seemed to me that the object, or perhaps I should say, the subject of his interest was not the supposed malfunction of a television monitor or anything like that, but more likely the guy dressed like a character from *The Matrix*, whose movements in fact he went on tracking on the monitor while speaking to me. He reminded me, to return to the subject of elevators and the grimness of the temporary relationships established therein, of the Falsely Nonchalant, that is, those people who talk to you about the weather, all the time taking sidelong glances at themselves in the mirror, because they just find themselves so irresistible and delude themselves into thinking that you haven't noticed a thing (just like the people who pick their noses during a conversation, confident that they're fast and clever enough to be able to extract the booger and easily roll it between thumb and forefinger without your catching on). All the same, the detail left me absolutely indifferent: if he liked *Matrix* characters with ponytails, that was entirely his business.

So I extended my hand and assumed my customary stance of departure (leaning slightly forward from the waist, standard businesslike smile, right leg just starting to lift into a step, vaguely reminiscent of the actor Alberto Sordi).

"It's been, ahem, a pleasure to meet you, Engineer, but now I ought to be . . ."

"Do you handle criminal cases as well, Counselor?" he asked me in reply, as he stood staring (by now openly) at the video monitor behind me.

Whereupon I just stood there stupidly, hand outstretched, which by the way is a position I detest because it creates a panhandling effect that increases with the fury of an avalanche.

"I . . . sure, when it comes up," I said, but in the quizzical tone of voice that comes naturally when someone asks a question out of left field.

And at last I withdrew my hand, which by now had become a sort of prosthesis.

"When it comes up," he repeated, leaning on the four words and staring at me as if to say that he really intended to remember that. This last bit of ambiguity really plucked my last nerve.

"Listen, you're acting kind of strange, you know that?" I told him flat out, somewhat rudely. In fact, my jaw had set firmly.

Engineer Romolo Sesti Orfeo once again fixed his gaze on the monitor. Behind him, at the end of the aisle, Matrix appeared, coming toward us with the brisk step of someone who knows exactly what he's looking for.

"Yes, I know," the engineer replied at last, his voice dropping an octave. "But there's a reason for it, believe me."

I instinctively shot a glance over at Matrix, who kept coming closer, even though he seemed entirely indifferent to us.

"Don't look at him, please," Engineer Romolo Sesti Orfeo begged me under his breath.

Whereupon I replied, whispering in turn out of an automatic instinct for imitation:

"Hey, listen to me, I don't know what you're up to, but whatever it is, I want nothing to do with it."

And he replied, still under his breath:

"In that case, get out of here now, Counselor, because something's about to happen that you might not want to see."

Hooooold everything.

You've just heard the kind of phrase that basically leaves you without any alternatives.

If someone tells you to leave because any minute now something's going to happen that would be better for you not to see, do you leave? Of course you don't: you can't. Because by that point you're already in. And the worst part of it is that you have no idea in what. Maybe it's a tragedy that you have a chance of preventing. Perhaps someone's about to die and you could save them. Or else nothing could happen at all (in which case it was theoretically possible that all Engineer Romolo Sesti Orfeo wanted to do was pick Matrix up and take him back to the privacy of the stockroom): and in that case you'd enjoy the benefits of courage without having to lift a finger.

One alternative would be to run off and call the police: but what if the tragedy occurs just as you're rushing to get help? Tragedies, it's well known, take place in a matter of seconds. What are you going to do, miss that crucial instant? The carpe diem ethos works in tragic proceedings as well. It's far too convenient to trot it out only when you're trying to get someone into bed. Your conscience would torment you for the rest of your life, and it would be right, of course. You might try to tell it, "I couldn't have done anything about it anyway," and it would reply, "Sure, but you didn't know that when you took to your heels."

The fact is that there are situations in which you have to stay, even at the risk of getting involved in something inconvenient. It's no fun to say it, but that's how it is. From outside the situation it's easy to shake your head no. But just find yourself in the midst of things happening all at once, then come talk to me about it.

Just to give an example, I know some people who, a few months before getting married, used to go out walking with their doubts in tow (there was no mistaking what was happening because when you ran into them, you'd see them arm in arm, the doubts), and these people, even though you could see it on their faces that all they wanted to do was cancel the wedding, you understood just as clearly that they were absolutely incapable of mounting that revolution, so all that was left for them to do was to go out for a walk in the early afternoon.

One huge lie that we have inherited from the rhetoric of liberty is that when it comes to the important decisions in life there's always time to go back and make a change. But it isn't true. Because time passes, and it's not willing to cooperate with anyone or anything. Time has no patience for ignorance. Just like the law. It's no accident that the whole concept of the statute of limitations is based on the passage of time. And if legislators (which is more or less like saying God, in that field) based such a nitpicky mechanism on the passage of time, there must be a reason. Time has a compromising effect, no doubt about it. And those who jilt their fiancées at the altar (I've never heard a story in which the opposite happens), even if their deed, in the accounts of subsequent generations, tends to be regarded as a masterly blow that few on earth have ever had the nerve to strike, are individuals who turn their backs on time, and their reputations as free men should be reevaluated once and for all, because there's nothing praiseworthy about humiliating a woman in front of her friends and family after the corsages have all been chosen, unsightly though they well may be.

F rom what I know about myself, walking into a supermarket in the middle of the morning on a weekday is
never a good sign. Especially if the supermarket is on
the far side of town.

What happens to me when something starts to go wrong,
especially in periods when it seems like everything's going just
fine, is that a kind of frenzy, a frustration, a jumpiness comes
over me, so that I have to go out wandering, as if I'm looking
for something I've lost.

And since I can hardly wander around looking for nothing in
particular, and given that I have no idea what it is I need but nevertheless feel a sense of disquiet that prevents me from going for
an ordinary stroll (because an ordinary stroll requires a clear
conscience), I invent nonessential errands for myself, such as, in
fact, in this case, buying a jar of Buitoni Fior di Pesto.

The fact is that since Alessandra Persiano has come to live
with me, a few things have happened.

The first thing is that a number of my fellow lawyers have
stopped saying hello to me.

The second thing is that many other fellow lawyers who never
used to say hello to me have started saying hello to me now.

Obviously, there isn't a bit of difference between the former
and the latter: in both cases, the motive is envy.

There's one (he's called Massimo Corrente, though I really
shouldn't name names) who's become a real problem. He waits
for me outside the hearing rooms, shoots me defiant glances in

the hallways (at times he even puts his hands on his hips, so that the only thing missing is for him to say, "Excuse me, would you mind looking somewhere else, thanks"), he walks past and lightly grazes me when I stop to talk with a colleague or (less frequently) with a client, he harasses me with anonymous phone calls, all silent, except for those times when he abandons himself to guttural panting.

One night when I just couldn't take it anymore I shot back, "Come on, you animal, tell me what you're wearing, I'm already in my underwear," and that put an end to that. But if he doesn't stop persecuting me I'm going to report him for stalking.

Anyway, this whole thing with my colleagues who, one way or another, can't seem to wrap their heads around my new love affair has turned into a pain in the neck. Not a serious one, granted, but still equipped with all the essential features that characterize a genuine pain in the neck: frequency, persistence, monomania.

Now I'm not trying to say that this is the reason for my recent problems with Alessandra Persiano, but the fact that a small army of obsessives like the one I just described should be hard at work injecting poison into my daily existence has its inevitable consequences for my life as a member of a couple.

Okay, at first success is extremely gratifying. The fact that the public recognizes your better qualities is obviously something that brings pleasure. Especially if those qualities are confirmed by a hot babe who makes people (let alone lawyers) turn around in the street. And even more so if you're completely fucking worthless as a lawyer.

All right, let's tell it like it is: the best thing about success is detecting that sense of inferiority in other people's eyes.

It's a deliciously vulgar sensation, and no one will ever admit to it, but it's just to experience that feeling that everyone wants to be successful. After a little while, though, things start to get complicated. In the sense that every so often you're tempted to stop one of them, one of those loser doormen who shoot you glances as you walk past, and say to him, "So tell me, you think I'm so repulsive that I couldn't possibly be with a beautiful woman? What did you expect, that she'd shack up with you? Have you taken a look at yourself in the mirror lately?"

In short, when you're being observed to the point where you feel like you're posing for a calendar, after a while the suspicion starts to set in that you've wound up in someone else's place sheerly by accident, and that just when you least expect it he will return to reclaim that place and send you back to the losers' quarters, where in fact you grew up and where your old friends will be waiting to welcome you back with open arms.

Which is precisely the kind of dilemma these vultures are trying to push you into.

At first, when I confided in Alessandra Persiano about this sort of persecution, she would say, "Just enjoy it."

And then I pointed out that it wasn't becoming to pay yourself compliments.

"Pay myself compliments? I'm paying you a compliment, you idiot," she would reply.

And I didn't know what else to say.

The third thing that's happened to me since this truly beautiful woman has come to live with me is that my ex-wife has started asking for the alimony check that she used to refuse categorically in a display of the compassion she's always shown for my miserable income.

And when I asked her if she didn't think that becoming such a stickler immediately after a woman other than her moved in with me didn't seem at least slightly suspicious as far as coincidences go, she replied in no uncertain terms:

"Oh, certainly I'm doing it on purpose, I'd have to be a weasel to deny it. I need to punish you, and this is the only method I have at the moment for processing the pain that you've caused me by letting another woman into your life."

"It seems to me that I ought to remind you that you lived with that gigolo of an architect for two and a half years after you dumped me, Nives. Was that just a way of processing your pain, too?"

"Don't you dare try it, Vincenzo. I'm not going to let you manipulate me with your chronological evaluation of events. I'm mad at you, I have to find an outlet for my aggressive impulses, and the way things stand now it doesn't do me a bit of good to worry about whether it's wrong or right."

"Christ, Nives. You're a psychologist."

"Now don't start referring to our roles as a way of making me feel guilty."

"What are you talking about roles for, Nives, I was referring to income. It takes me three months to scrape together what you earn in one."

"So? You can't lean on the idea that the costs of our divorce are a burden to be borne only by me."

"But you broke up with me."

"At first. But after that I wanted to get back together."

And so we went back and forth like this for a good half hour, with me pacing up and down the hall of my apartment sweating like a moving man, trying to talk some sense into her, and her trying to explain to me that there was nothing objectionable in her behaving like an asshole.

In the end, I shouted at her to go get screwed by a cooperative of unemployed butchers, but not before telling her I hoped that all her patients, every last one of them, would commit suicide en masse, thus providing an excellent advertisement for her practice.

She must not have cared for this last line, because she hung up without another word, and when I called back to tell her that I had only been kidding it went straight to voice mail.

Then there was what happened with her mother, which helped us get things back onto an even keel somewhat.

L isten, I think that I'd better . . . call the police," I stammered, in the pathetic hope that such a clumsily expressed threat might dissuade Engineer Romolo Sesti Orfeo from his intentions, whatever they might be.

"There's no need, they'll be here before long. Now if you'll excuse me," he replied with the mechanical calm that comes an instant before launching oneself into an undertaking whose outcome is unforeseeable.

And he finally strolled off, nonchalantly trailing after Matrix, who in the meantime had reached us and walked past without so much as a glance, turning down the next aisle, where on the near side was stationed the refrigerator case full of dairy products and fresh pasta, and on the far side there was the fruit and vegetable section, with the self-service scales, the plastic bags, the cellophane gloves, and all the rest of the necessary equipment.

I stayed put, between the canned tomatoes and the boxed pasta, enlisted in spite of my own intentions, cursing the moment I decided to walk into that supermarket (where it was fucking freezing, moreover) to buy a jar of Buitoni Fior di Pesto, and anyway, I must already have at least eleven jars of Buitoni Fior di Pesto at home; in fact, Alessandra Persiano makes fun of me every time she opens the pantry and finds them lined up like toy soldiers, Look at this, you still shop like a single man, she says, and she laughs, Ha ha.

As if ever since she moved in all we'd been eating were delicacies from the hands of Chef Gianfranco Vissani.

And now I knew that the police would be coming. At least, that's what I'd been told. Perhaps Matrix was a wanted criminal and Engineer Romolo Sesti Orfeo was an undercover policeman staking out the supermarket on a hunch that sooner or later his man would come in so that he could arrest him? That would explain the sketchy lesson on the operation of the video security system, to say nothing of the farcical move with his finger on the remote control: truly pathetic.

So was this a long-planned police operation about to be set in motion? From one minute to the next, would the supermarket suddenly be filled with cops, pouring in through the side doors with bulletproof vests and submachine guns, and would they haul off Matrix as he smiled, the way notorious wanted criminals always seem to do at the moment of their capture, at the photographers and television crews who promptly materialized?

It was a plausible hypothesis, but I didn't believe in it past a certain point. A policeman with that kind of priority on his mind is unlikely to waste a lot of time chatting with people about his dead friends—at the risk of involving them in the operation, for that matter.

At that point I started taking under consideration competing possibilities, such as, for instance, that this was not a police operation at all. That it might be about an old settling of accounts, a private dispute, a retaliation between rival gangs, even. In that case, the arrival of the police foretold by Engineer Romolo Sesti Orfeo took on an entirely different connotation: the police would be coming, sure enough, but only to collect a dead body.

The more solid the alternative hypotheses became, the more I wondered whether the wisest thing might not be to rush out of the store and call the police myself. But by now Engineer Romolo Sesti Orfeo had almost drawn even with Matrix, who was coasting along the dairy case without paying him the slightest attention (something that only confused me further, because a fugitive, or in any case someone involved in dodgy or criminal matters, ought to be suspicious of his fellow man by definition, especially when his fellow man is following him), and I felt called upon to stay there, even though I didn't know what was going to happen, much less in whose defense I was supposed to intervene. Among other things, at that hour of the morning the supermarket was practically deserted, so that, if needed, I wouldn't have been able to turn to any volunteers for aid and assistance.

The thing that got on my nerves the most was the fact that Engineer Romolo Sesti Orfeo (if in fact that was his real name) must have figured out what kind of person I was, otherwise he'd never have been able to drag me so successfully into that fucked-up situation in the first place.

That's why he'd gone to all the trouble of complimenting me on my inflexibility in negotiating his old friend's settlement, and I, like a prime sucker, had gone along with it. Obviously I couldn't take to my heels now—not after allowing myself to be praised as a man of principle.

In the meantime "Montagne verdi" had finished playing, and a few yards down the aisle there was a little old lady who kept shooting me glances, because she'd already tried three times to reach a jar of cranberry beans, without success.

I wondered: all those people who are always sticking their noses into others' misfortunes—the rubberneckers who always cluster around when public disasters occur; those who, when a fistfight breaks out, don't think twice about risking their personal safety just to elbow their way into the front row; the people who, when they hear two cars crash into each other, even if they've been standing in line for forty-five minutes at the post office, will happily give up their turns to run outside to enjoy the show live—where the fuck were they all right now, why didn't they come nosing around, prying into the sinister intentions of Engineer Romolo Sesti Orfeo?

Now Matrix was moving along the metal rail running along the front of the dairy and fresh pasta case with the step of a prison guard inspecting cells on death row during evening shakedown, scanning the yogurt section with particular severity. Engineer Romolo Sesti Orfeo was little more than a yard away from him, but unlike Matrix, he had his back to the dairy products, because he'd pulled the remote control out of his jacket once again and was now pointing it at two other monitors with the nonchalance of a technician testing an electrical system.

After the engineer had been playing around with the remote for a while, Matrix turned his head and looked him in the face (Engineer Romolo Sesti Orfeo gave him a perfunctory smile, which he did not return); then Matrix looked down at the hand that was holding the remote control, and from there back up, at the two monitors, after which he made a sort of approving expression with his eyebrows (kind of like: "Oh, I see"), and then went back to hunting for yogurt.

"Young man, excuse me," the little old lady had, so to speak, asked me, seeing as her ocular solicitations hadn't had much effect. And she tipped her head in the direction of the cranberry beans, which were in fact on a shelf too high for her to reach, short as she was.

That's what old people always do when they need something: they mobilize you even before you realize what they want done. You have to make yourself useful without explicit guidance from them.

"Ah, certainly," I replied, and I headed over to help her.

It was just as I was on tiptoes trying to reach the jar of beans for her (how long could I have taken, five seconds?) that I recognized the nearby voice of Engineer Romolo Sesti Orfeo as he said simply, in the calmest possible tone:

"Freeze."

I turned around and saw, first, Matrix's arms rising slowly over his head as if in response to a divine convocation, then his head with the ponytail, then a pistol aimed roughly at his temple, and then a hand gripping that pistol, in turn connected to an arm that ran straight into the side of Engineer Romolo Sesti Orfeo.

That's exactly how I saw it, step by step, working backward, the way it looks when you hit REWIND on a camcorder without first hitting STOP. It's incredible how fear circumscribes and amplifies one's perception of events (which is why many witnesses, even when testifying under oath, will insist that they never saw the one specific thing that the judge keeps asking them about, because at that moment, even though they were right in the middle of what was happening, fear had selected certain details for them while canceling out all the rest).

In a situation like that, one thinks, who knows what speed the brain is operating at. How much instinctive philosophy it produces. What intelligent thoughts about the provisional nature of life, the discovery of what truly matters, and so on.

But the only question that kept drilling into my head as I was standing there was this: "How the fuck does he keep his hand from shaking?"

Get it? Not: "Where did he pull that gun out from? I didn't notice any bulge in his jacket when we were talking before"; or else, following a slightly more paranoid line of argument (justified, I think, given the circumstances): "Now he's going to shoot him and, while he's at it, he'll turn around and take me and the old woman out, too."

Just, you know.

No: "How does he keep his hand so still?"

That's all.

As if this were some tremendously important question. As if its answer would determine all further developments.

Okay: it was bullshit. One of those senselessly obsessive thoughts that you cling to in extreme situations.

But you should have seen Engineer Romolo Sesti Orfeo in

action. He moved competently, calmly, as if he'd never done anything else in his life but throw down on people in supermarkets. If he wasn't a professional, he'd at least practiced that operation down to the very last details.

Matrix, for that matter, now that I had a better look at him, was much younger than the engineer (at a glance he might have been somewhere between thirty and forty), wiry but brutal-looking, like an Extreme Fighting lightweight champion. The kind of guy I'd say "Sorry, my mistake" to if he cut in front of me, just to be clear.

"Excuse me young man, could you give me those?" said the little old lady, clearly out of patience by now. She was referring to the jar of beans that I was clutching by the lid with all five fingers of my left hand. She still hadn't realized what was happening right behind her (which was a relief, because I was afraid she might scream).

I'd heard her, but my body was in standby mode. If I'd been able to move, I'd have handed her her inopportune jar and then urged her to get out of there as quickly as she could, perhaps making my escape with the excuse of ensuring that she reached safety.

Instead I stood there, incapable of tearing my eyes away from the scene that, just a little more than ten feet away, continued to intensify and deteriorate in that surreally deserted supermarket which people seemed to be consciously avoiding rather than coming in and buying groceries (and to think that I could hear the attendant at the deli counter rustling around in back doing something, just a short distance away), even though it would have taken practically nothing, a trifle (a child on the run from his mother suddenly appearing at the other end of the aisle, a slightly louder than average noise, any of an infinite number of microevents) to violently alter the progression of developments and unleash tragedy.

Pure pornography, clearly. Because when reality starts putting on a show, that's the effect that it achieves. That's why reality shows, which constitute only the feeblest attempts at imitating reality itself, are as successful as they are.

In fact it was not only my fear of the worst that kept my attention so riveted. The truth is that, although admitting this is not exactly a testimony to my integrity, a part of me wanted to know how it was going to end.

Matrix remained obediently motionless awaiting further instructions from Engineer Romolo Sesti Orfeo as if he were accustomed to this sort of contretemps.

"Turn around," he ordered, moving the pistol barrel from his temple to his cheek. "Next to me. Slowly. Without lowering your hands."

Matrix complied, but he came dangerously close to snorting in annoyance.

"Feh," said the old woman, deeply annoyed that I still hadn't made up my mind to give her her fucking cranberry beans.

Engineer Romolo Sesti Orfeo took a step back, continuing to press the barrel of the pistol into Matrix's cheek.

"On your knees."

For an instant Matrix hesitated, as if that order somehow deviated from police protocol for that kind of operation; then he put on an expression of visible tolerance for a rank beginner. He was probably hoping to make Engineer Romolo Sesti Orfeo nervous and provoke him into doing something stupid, so that he could take advantage and pull a counter-maneuver of some kind. But if that was his plan, it wasn't working.

Once his kneecaps touched the floor, the next command was issued.

"Hands behind your back. Crossed. And lower your head."

Matrix shot him a glare, as if to say that now he was taking things too far.

The only reply that Engineer Romolo Sesti Orfeo offered was to shove the pistol barrel a little harder into his cheek.

It must have hurt, because Matrix pulled his head back and emitted a moan that was immediately silenced, the way you pull away from the dentist's drill at the first stab of pain.

"Move it," the engineer commanded, with glassy indifference.

That was when the old woman realized that something was happening behind her that might be worth seeing and finally she turned around.

"*O Maronna*," she said in a faint voice. And she covered her mouth with one hand (I wonder why, I thought to myself, people always feel a need to censor themselves when something scares them).

Whereupon I had the impulse to give her the beans, just like that, for no good reason, but this time she was the one who refused to cooperate.

Matrix crossed his arms behind his back and bowed forward. Engineer Romolo Sesti Orfeo followed his movements by moving the barrel of the pistol from his face to the back of his neck. With his free hand he lifted Matrix's arms to the height of the metal rail that ran along the front of the dairy case. The leverage forced Matrix to bow even lower, as if he were supplicating the linoleum floor.

Now it looked like a wartime scene. A prisoner awaiting execution, kneeling before his executioner, deprived even of the right to look at him.

Matrix's face, what little I could see of it, seemed to have lost the careless confidence it had worn until just a minute before. A loss that by rights I ought to have noticed with some satisfaction, considering how obnoxious I'd found him up to that point; but instead I was having a hard time accepting it. Seeing someone fall completely under another person's control always has a unpleasant effect on me.

The old lady grabbed my arm. She was squeezing it.

I came that close to saying "What about the beans?" but I managed to restrain myself.

Engineer Romolo Sesti Orfeo pulled a pair of handcuffs out of his pocket. The appearance of such a distinctly police-related contraption reassured me of his intentions. In fact the old woman immediately asked me, "So he's a detective?" as if I ought to know.

What I found most unsettling about that masterfully executed operation was the fact that, in spite of appearances, it still didn't look like an arrest. At least, not an ordinary arrest. The impression one got from watching Engineer Romolo Sesti Orfeo at work was that he'd been waiting for that moment for some time. There was something excessively calculated, something . . . personal, in that display of bravura. That's why I continued to refer to him mentally by the name and title with which he'd introduced himself. In other words, I didn't believe (and hadn't believed from the beginning) that he was a cop.

Matrix's breathing was labored, defenseless and uninformed as he was with regard to his own future prospects. Engineer Romolo Sesti Orfeo snapped a handcuff around the first wrist, ran the chain around the metallic bumper that ran along the front of the dairy products case, and then proceeded to cuff the other hand.

Having successfully partially hogtied him, the engineer withdrew the pistol and, with the ultra-nonchalance of a consummate professional, turned on his heel and started walking calmly down the aisle, leaving his hostage behind him, as if he were done with him.

I was still standing there with the old woman clutching my arm, as if we were a pair of extras dressed for a film, waiting for the unit production manager to tell us whether we should stay or were free to go.

"Did he arrest him?" the old woman asked me.

"What does it look like to you?" I replied.

Engineer Romolo Sesti Orfeo looked me right in the eye and nodded, just once.

The old woman immediately released my arm and stared hard at me, just inches away from my face.

I started covering my ass like an idiot with such pathetic phrases as "Hey, surely you don't think that . . ." and "Look, I have nothing to do with . . . ," the end result of which was only to reinforce her suspicions of some association (whether of a criminal or law-enforcement nature was unclear: from the way she was looking at me I doubted that there was any difference between the two for her) between me and Engineer Romolo Sesti Orfeo.

After blundering along for a bit, I blurted out a generalized "Aw, fuck it" under my breath, and even took a backhanded swing at the air between me and the old woman; then I made a point of putting her damn-it-to-hell cranberry beans back on the top shelf (now you can climb up there yourself if you want them so much, you mistrustful old biddy).

She threw her head back in reverse, visibly horrified, and finally cut out the ocular inquisition she'd been conducting.

Having resolved our personal problems, we went back to our consideration of the hostage situation in progress.

Engineer Romolo Sesti Orfeo, with surreal nonchalance, had gone back to fiddling around with the remote control, once again aiming it at the two overhead monitors across from the dairy case.

Matrix, meanwhile, still down on his knees, finally managed to swivel his head in the direction of his handcuffer in search of some indication of what his fate would be; when he saw him madly engaged in what appeared to be a generic operation of product testing, an expression of genuine confusion came over his face.

I too had begun to wonder if Engineer Romolo Sesti Orfeo might not be slightly cracked.

I think I read somewhere (or else I'm completely making it up, who knows; regardless it strikes me as logical and even vaguely scientific) that when you really and truly screw up, whether involuntarily or intentionally, it sometimes happens that your brain is unable to come to grips with the immanence of your actions; in other words, your brain refuses to tell itself the story of what you've just done. The result is a temporary *vacatio mentis*, or perhaps we should say fugue state, after which for a short while we behave incongruously, just as, sure enough, once happened to me when it was handbags, so to speak, between me and a sort of girlfriend, and I ended up ordering her out of my car in a part of town that was clearly unsafe for a young woman on foot. I took off, tires screeching (I still remember the sight of her disbelieving face in the rearview mirror), but as soon as I had swerved around the corner I completely forgot where I lived and after driving around at random for a while (which was a real nightmare, now that I think back) I went back to where I'd left her, not so much to make up for what I'd done but rather because I hoped she'd give me directions, or at least to get her to say to me, "Where the fuck do you think you're going? That way, you idiot!" (I don't know how germane this example actually is; but anyway.)

"Nice work," Matrix said. Referring to Engineer Romolo Sesti Orfeo.

The engineer didn't bother to reply; instead he set down the remote control on one of the shelves where the fruit was displayed across the aisle, and appeared genuinely curious to see what was coming next. Matrix must have interpreted his silence as a sign of weakness, because he immediately launched into a crescendo of threats intended to win his release, like in a cop movie where coolheaded veteran detectives detect a hint of hesitation in the bad guy, so they walk toward him, unarmed, urging him to shoot as he backs away, trembling, until he collapses, breaks into tears, and hands over the gun.

"As long as you just handcuffed me, okay . . . but this,

here," and he clarified by shaking his hands and rattling the handcuffs against the metal rail of the dairy case, "this is taking it too far."

What struck me was the way he managed, even from his helpless, hunched over position, to be so brazen, and clearly very confident that before long their roles would be reversed.

Engineer Romolo Sesti Orfeo must have thought the same thing because he immediately turned to look at me, flashing me a mocking smile that more or less translated as: "You hear this guy?"

Why the hell he kept shooting me those looks of connivance was beyond me; and aside from being intrinsically objectionable, it was starting to worry me, because the last thing I needed was for Matrix to think that I was in cahoots on this thing and come looking for me once the whole business was over.

"Tell me," Matrix went on, "are you by any chance hoping that this will get you a promotion?"

Short pause, after which he got to the point, lowering his voice slightly and putting on a friendly smile.

"Tomorrow morning I'll get out of jail, then I'll come find you, wherever you might be, and first I'll shoot you in both hands, and then in the face, you can count on it . . ." But he said it in the tone of voice of an old uncle who, upon running into the little nephew he hasn't seen in forever, crouches down and says, "You've gotten so tall!"

Now then. I don't know what sort of impression words like these make when they're written down on a sheet of paper; but I guarantee that when you hear them live they induce the same kind of nausea that would beset you if, without any advance notice, they were to take you away and force you to witness an autopsy. Because they do more than just promise death: they give it shape and presence; they bring it close; they show it to you.

"And remember," Matrix added, just to make sure he'd covered all his bases, accompanying his words with an obscene leer, "I'll make sure and come personally; that way you'll be able to introduce me to your family."

It was after this abominable kicker that I felt certain that Matrix must be a camorrista: and not just a two-bit gangster, a heavy hitter. Not so much because of the tone of voice but because of the expressive power of his words, their ability to conjure up such frighteningly vivid images.

Camorristi are past masters of the art of ambiguity, expert communicators, ideal ad men. The messages they send do much more than merely intimidate their recipients: they take them straight out of a state of law. Their messages suggest a throwback to an earlier society, where justice has no power because the strongest make the rules. It is this authoritarian subtext that offends us so intimately, because it turns back the clock with such rude certainty that we question what century we're in. It's the possibility of going so far back in time that throws us off balance.

The Camorrese language is a reactionary form of Latin, as in ancient Rome, that sends us back to a world that we thought we'd left behind us forever.

I had a hunch that this threat of a transversal vendetta would send Engineer Romolo Sesti Orfeo over the edge. And so it did, in fact. Don't ask me why, I couldn't say. Sometimes you just get lucky and nail it, right when you're on the precipice of a world of pain. As if the motives that two or more people might have for slaughtering each other, when it comes down to it, had somehow acquired an aesthetic all their own.

When Engineer Romolo Sesti Orfeo lunged at Matrix I almost missed it; that's how fast he was. He grabbed him by the hair and yanked him to his feet, jamming the pistol in his face again with such fury that I was afraid that I was about to see Matrix's head turn into a New Year's Eve fireworks display any second now. In the scuffle a half-liter bottle of yogurt tumbled off a shelf, cracking open on the floor and whitewashing a section of tile. The old lady once again dug her talons into my arm. Matrix was unable to keep his balance on his knees and instinctively pulled up his right leg so that he could brace himself against the floor with one foot. Interpreting that move as a potential attempt to fight back, Engineer Romolo Sesti Orfeo slammed his knee into Matrix's ribs, simultaneously pulling him toward him and forcing his leg to bend awkwardly. Matrix squeezed his eyes shut and clenched his teeth to keep from screaming and bent forward even deeper, crawling on his knees, sucking air and coughing. I—or rather, we, since the old woman was basically attached to me—we both recoiled in empathy, taking part in a simulation of the pain that Matrix must have been experiencing.

Now he was panting and biting his lips, perhaps suffering more from his helplessness than from the actual pain. Still holding him by a hank of his hair, Engineer Romolo Sesti Orfeo jerked Matrix toward him forcefully, claiming him as his personal property. Matrix made an attempt to say something, maybe an oath, or another threat; but all that came out was a grunt, something incomprehensible. The old woman was squeezing my arm at regular intervals, like a girl when you take her to see a horror movie (which in fact encourages physical contact), and any minute I expected her to throw her arms around me. Engineer Romolo Sesti Orfeo resumed his close-quarters battle with his prey, and now seemed intent on communicating something especially important to him.

I hadn't imagined him like this. While he was immobilizing and handcuffing the man, he'd behaved like the suspect-apprehension equivalent of a dental hygienist. Now he was pure rage.

"Unfortunately for you, I'm no cop," he said into the guy's ear. But since he neglected to lower his voice, we heard it too.

Bingo, I thought to myself.

Ignoring the pistol barrel jammed into his cheek so hard that he was forced to keep his jaws open wide, and even though he was half-blinded by the extreme closeup of his captor's face, Matrix stared right back at Engineer Romolo Sesti Orfeo, though he could hardly have expected to see anyone else at this point.

But perhaps he did see someone else. A tremendously unhappy person (just for an instant, an abyss), then a horribly empty one.

"Well, you've already taken my family away from me, piece of shit."

The old woman turned toward me, to share the dramatic intensity of that moment.

A wince registered instantanouesly in Matrix's glistening eyes, like a momentary drop in the tension. I thought I saw him hold his breath for a microsecond.

Finally Engineer Romolo Sesti Orfeo let him go. Matrix's head seemed to rejoin the rest of his exhausted body, with a sort of rebounding motion. The, shall we say, poor man coughed convulsively, partly suffocated by the quantity of saliva that had flooded his mouth on account of his gaping jaws, and zigzagging aimlessly around on his knees he tried to hoist himself upright in order to make up for the constriction of his arms.

The engineer slapped at his clothes haphazardly, as if he felt it were important to straighten up his appearance before returning to check on his audience, which consisted of the old lady and myself, the latter even more aghast than the former. He then picked up the remote control and once again pointed it at the two monitors in front of him, pressing a series of buttons sequentially, or at least that was my impression.

A moment later an image of Matrix appeared on the two television sets, on his knees, his wrists handcuffed behind him to the metal rail of the dairy case. It looked like a video clip from Al Jazeera.

Engineer Romolo Sesti Orfeo shot me another one of his canny little glances.

I must have responded with an especially baffled expression, because a tiny oblique tremor in the old woman's eyebrows gave me the distinct impression that she was revising her opinion of me. For that matter, all it would take was a smidgen of logic to see that if I had been in cahoots with Engineer Romolo Sesti Orfeo, at the very least I ought to have given him a hand instead of standing there watching while he handled everything on his own (okay, maybe that was too sophisticated a thought process for the old biddy).

I instinctively turned to look at the monitor behind me, or rather, above me, expecting to see a screenshot of Matrix done up as a hostage there too, and that is precisely what I saw.

At that point, my confusion began to dissipate.

Matrix hawked and spat some more. When he was breathing more or less regularly again and looked up, the first thing his eyes lit on were the two monitors looming over him on the facing wall. He looked puzzled, almost as if he'd seen someone he thought he knew.

At first he must not have believed his eyes, because he first looked down at his body ("Wait, is that what I'm wearing?"), after which he craned his neck like an expanding telescope toward the monitors, a move he accompanied with a quick right-left-right shimmy of the shoulders (a little like what boxers do when they're sizing each other up during a match).

Once the movement test had chased the last of his doubts from his mind, he started grinding his teeth and hyperventilating, as if only then had he really begun to feel trapped.

At that exact moment, I recognized the voice of a female cashier in the distance asking generically, "What on earth is going on over there?" and then another voice, also female, perhaps a little younger: "Franco, Franco, did you see that?"

Then another. And another. And another one still.

"That's impossible. Look, he's on that other screen, too!"

"Oh my God, but where is he, inside the store?"

"Mamma, why do we have to leave?"

The populace of the supermarket had lifted their eyes to the closed-circuit television sets.

At last I started to feel a little less alone.

It All Stems From Infancy
(Including an accelerated course in not-especially-creative writing, with examples)

"What, your mother couldn't have bothered to tell me herself?" I said to Alagia when she came to give me the news, acting as deeply resentful as I could manage. Her response:

"Oh, I knew it. You're such a pain, Vince'. When are you going to quit taking offense all the time? You're always going on about all the slights and neglectful treatment you have to endure instead of just listening to what people are trying to tell you. I just informed you that Grandma has cancer; don't you think you should be focusing on that?"

Whereupon I was left more or less speechless. It's true, I like to take offense, I like to point out shortcomings in the manners of others, especially when their mishandling of personal interactions is directed at me. I gloat when people fail to behave the way they ought to, because that gives me an opportunity to say so, to manifest my icy disapproval. Acting offended is the work I was put on this earth to do, truth be told.

"Let's just recapitulate for a moment, okay?" I replied, with just the right amount of indignation to keep her from realizing how pissed off I was. "As usual, your mother benefits from every mitigating circumstance; but what am I saying, mitigating circumstances would already represent progress. It never even occurs to you and Alf"—our nickname for my son, Alfredo—"to question anything she does or says. If she so much as spits it's gospel truth. But when you two turn in my direction you suddenly discover the joys of parent-child dialec-

tics, am I right? So true is this that it strikes you ‹
normal to read me the riot act if I so much as dare tc
the childishness of Nives's behavior toward me."

"Oookay," Alagia said, liquidating my diatribe with ¬ pause
that was not exactly brief and served to say: "I acknowledge
that you've done your best, and I'll also be so kind as to sus-
pend judgment, which means you get to land on your feet,
provided you agree not to drag it out any longer than you
already have," whereupon she continued, "So, can we talk about
Grandma now?"

"Of course, of course," I replied, promptly accepting the
compromise. I can't hold my own with this girl: she's practically an optimized, turbocharged version of her mother.

We gave ourselves a few seconds of silence to alleviate some
of the argumentative tension. I put on a show of pacing medi-
tatively around my kitchen table (because that's where we
were) and then I made my way to the simple question I had
culpably overlooked at the outset.

"Where did you say she has it?"

"How would I know? From what I understood, it's some
kind of leukemic lymphoma. One of the pretty rare kinds,
too."

"Jesus fucking Christ."

"The really funny thing was the way she treated the doctor."

"Why, what did she do?"

"You had to be there. He was this smooth operator; he'd
clearly spent some time at the tanning parlor, and he was wearing a pair of orange Crocs with his lab coat, convinced he was
God's gift. He'd called us into his office for a private conversation, all like: 'I need your help with this; we shouldn't deny
anything, just obscure the truth, unveil the actual situation little by little,' 'It'll do us more good than it will her,' and so on.
The whole thing in the damned first-person plural. In other
words, a lesson in sheer humanity that I couldn't tell you, with

Mamma holding her handkerchief pressed against her nose like a boxer after a match and Alfredo who was on the verge of pulling out a pad of paper and jotting down notes. Then, as soon as Grandma laid eyes on him, the junior doctor, she looked him straight in the face and said, 'I've got cancer, right?'; and doctor boy just gaped at her like an idiot. You know when a wife waits up for her cheating husband to come home at two in the morning and wrings the confession out of him before he can come up with a good alibi? Like that. You'd have wanted to razz him if he hadn't done such a perfect job of making a fool of himself on his own; anyway the truth was written all over his face. At that point it would have been practically impossible to pull the wool over her eyes."

"Well then it's just as well I wasn't there, or I definitely would have started laughing."

"That's exactly what she said when we left."

Assunta. Assunta Russo, also known as Ass. Alagia and Alfredo's grandmother. Nives's mother. My mother-in-law. That is, my ex-mother-in-law. A piece of work. Probably the only human being on the planet in whose presence Nives sheds her intellectual pretensions, takes her vocabulary down a good ten notches, and suddenly starts speaking in simple sentences composed of subject, verb, and object, even taking care to stay on topic.

Ass (it's just an abbreviated form of her name and nothing else, and those of you who know English can keep your smart comments to yourselves; besides, if there's anything my mother-in-law lacks, in every sense of the word, it would be that) is the exact opposite of her daughter. Pathologically incapable of dressing up an idea. Indifferent to the subconscious. Allergic to complexity.

To take care of Nives and fund her education, she'd worked as a waitress in a restaurant for practically her whole life, a little like Ellen Burstyn in *Alice Doesn't Live Here Anymore* ("Only that prick of a husband of mine didn't get killed in a car crash, and worst of all I didn't meet Kris Kristofferson afterward," she pointed out to me when I suggested the comparison with the Scorsese film), and it's probably from her dedication to earning a living that she developed her idiosyncratic way of dealing with those people who take problematic approaches to the questions of life.

This much is obligatory biography. But since I've known her for a while now, I believe that I can safely say that this tendency to get straight to the heart of the matter is part of her character. In the sense that even if she'd been wealthy enough not to have to work for a living, her hard-assed waitress's pragmatism would still have guided her through her passage here on earth. Among other things, she never made a point of the fact that she'd spent the best years of her life humping trays so that her daughter would never lack for anything. None of us has ever heard her feel sorry for herself, not even once, like those failures who bombard their children with reminders of all the things they had to give up, practically taking them to court over it, accusing them of making them slave away for them without social security and withholding (you wouldn't believe how many people like this there are out there). It's just that Ass just isn't like that. The only way she knows how to think is in terms of cause and effect. That's why she's always fought against Nives's innate tendency to take the long way around when it comes to understanding things. And as if she'd set out to achieve it, she got herself a psychologist daughter.

Nives claims that she chose her profession as a response to the simplified world model that her mother offered her (and I hardly need point out here that from "as a response" to "offered her" are her exact words).

According to her reconstruction of events, it all dates back to a little tantrum she threw when she was roughly nine years old. One afternoon a wave of unexpected sadness came over her, the kind of depression that attacks children for no good reason and turns them into whiny pests, and sure enough she started pestering her mother, crying and complaining over nothing, the way kids do when they're trying to get your attention but they don't know what they want, basically because what they really want is for you to figure it out for them.

Ass let her carry on for a while, hoping that she'd cut it out on her own, but when she realized that at this rate they might still be at it that night, she sat the girl down and delivered a little lecture that more or less consisted of the following considerations:

"You got a good night's sleep. No tummy aches, no nightmares. Yesterday in school you recited a poem by heart; I know that because your teacher told me when I ran into her at the supermarket. At lunch you ate a cutlet, mashed potatoes, and a second helping of strawberries. Then you watched the cartoons you like on TV. You don't have much homework for tomorrow, your forehead isn't hot, and your dog hasn't died. So will you explain to me why I ought to worry about a problem that doesn't even exist?"

And Nives stood there, raptly following point by point that presentation which was impeccable both in theory and in application; then without speaking a single word or shedding another tear, she went into her bedroom and did her homework, dragging behind her a sense of mortification unlike anything she would ever experience again in her entire life.

From that day forward she never misbehaved willfully, terrified by the prospect of a second rendition.

It was that same day that she felt within her the first stirrings of a decision that she would come to several years after that (from "felt within" to "after that," obviously, I had nothing to do with).

"I'll become a psychologist," she said to herself when she

discovered that a scientific discipline existed that dealt specifically with the feelings of sadness that wash over people for no apparent reason. "I'll try to solve the problems that my mother thinks don't even exist, I'll listen to people when they tell me about them, and I'll take them seriously."

"And I will bust Vincenzo Malinconico's balls all the live-long day," I would add.

Now I don't want to come off as a cynic. When Nives told me the story of the minor childhood trauma that scarred her for life I actually felt a twinge of pity, and I took her hand and then we embraced sweetly (okay, at the time I hadn't gotten her into bed yet, but I swear that I was prompted only by a sincere desire to console her). I can see how a little nine-year-old girl experiencing a wave of unfounded sadness would have her feelings hurt by such a show of maternal cynicism. Because there's no doubt that sadness is real. And it comes when it feels like it, more or less like sneezing. Only you can't just put on a sweater to make it go away.

A little girl who suddenly feels sad for no reason one afternoon (and actually, now that I think about it, it would be vitally important to know whether it was a Sunday) ought to have her constitutional rights recognized—and by "constitutional" I mean relating to her biological constitution—namely her right to have her parent explain to her that feeling sad for no good reason is just something that happens, and that there's no cause for despair, because it'll pass soon enough.

But in order to provide this kind of assistance a mother would have to be willing to recognize the cry for help that takes the form of a child's whining about motiveless sadness and, thus, validate it, at least a little. And the problem is that there are people in the world, even people who are mothers, who simply don't believe in motiveless sadness (perhaps because they're all too familiar with the motivated kind). And so they simply ignore the request. And they don't do it out of selfishness or arrogance: it's more that they just aren't willing to consider the larger theological question. Because it's obvious that no one can persuade anyone else to believe in the existence of something. You either believe or you don't, and that's that.

A mother who refuses to take responsibility for her little girl's unmotivated sadness refuses to believe in it. It's a little bit like a doctor dealing with a hypochondriac: he tends to dismiss out of hand any set of symptoms embroidered with a rich array of details.

Now I—in case you're interested in knowing what I think about it—profoundly envy people like my mother-in-law. People who focus on evidence and rank things by priority. People who get things done. Who dismiss the anguish of a depressing afternoon with a shrug of the shoulders. Who believe that the soul may very well exist, but who still prefer not to open that can of worms. Who don't take their own thoughts all that seriously, and thus manage to avoid sitting around constantly rethinking, refining, modifying, and revising them.

Because I, unlike people like Ass, am a perennial victim of the things that go through my head. And if only I could think those thoughts just once and be done with them. My thoughts exit and enter my mind with such freedom, such promiscuity, such grim determination as to prevent me from making so much as a single decision with anything like true conviction, so that it's debilitating to have to interact with them. My thoughts are a bunch of sluts, if you want to know the truth.

I wish they'd stop treating me like a hotel, coming to me for consolation and help after they've been out doing who the hell knows what around town. That for once in their miserable lives they'd content themselves with their owner and just stay faithful to me.

If I were to identify my chief shortcoming, the one that I most often see recurring in my relationships with other people, I'd have to say that it's my tendency to brood over things. I brood over things a lot. When I'm walking. When I'm working. When I'm having fun. When I'm feeling sorry for myself. When I'm having sex. And especially when I'm not having sex. (And when you think about it, brooding is an activity for psychopaths. Because you brood over what's happened, and what's happened—as the word itself indicates—has already happened. So it's clear that fretting over issues that you can't do anything about is a morbid pleasure, a form of intellectual necrophilia, a masochistic indulgence.)

Well, I do something even worse: sometimes I'm so overwhelmed by my broodings that I actually sit down and write. I fill page after page of Word documents in the hope of finding the right words to nail down one point of view, one I can stick to forever. I work deep into the night, when I really get obsessed. And then I say to myself: What, are you stupid? Are you trying to write a book or something?

Certain nights, as a famous Italian singer puts it, I feel as if I've reached conclusions that might be, so to speak, of public interest, and I go to sleep with a sense of satisfaction.

Then, a couple of days later, when my opinions resume their customary vacillation, I turn on my computer, I open the file Brood.doc, I reread it, and I don't find a single convincing phrase. It all seems patched together, phony. It has the look of a falsified account (if I knew how to read a balance sheet). With the various sentence-pipes all screwed together to form a plumbing system, instead of being left free to wander as they will, each with its own shape, likes the branches of a tree. I don't know if that's clear

If there's one thing that I've come to understand by deleting in one moment of lucid irritation long files I'd spent hours and hours on, it's that you can tell immediately whether the person who is writing something is disinterested or is pursuing some purpose of their own. Because in the first case, you'll be able to understand the writing, however difficult it might be. In the second case, however, you'll need to reread it, and even after you reread it you're left with a certain degree of confusion, so you go on reading awhile longer, thinking that it will become clearer to you as continue (the way it is with board games, when at the beginning they explain the rules to you but you don't feel like concentrating so you cut the explanation short and say, "Okay, let's just start playing"), and in the end, when you still don't understand it (or rather, you don't trust that you've understood correctly), you experience genuine annoyance at the effort you've had to undertake, as if you'd tried to do a favor for someone who didn't deserve it.

When you write that way, that is, in pursuit of a goal, stuffing your sentences with synonyms, adverbs, and ideas that are alluded to but never fully expressed, it means that you're trying to fool someone (whether it's yourself or someone else doesn't really matter).

I personally believe that I'm pretty clear on the difference between disinterested writing and utilitarian writing because in my, shall we say, profession, I'm required to make use of the latter, which is inevitably at odds with the former (and it's no coincidence that I do the former kind of writing at night).

Lawyerly writing is in fact a kind of writing that is designed to turn a profit. There's nothing wrong with that, let's be clear. Among other reasons because all sciences consist of languages. And law is a science. That a scientific language should possess a certain degree of incomprehensibility, and that this incomprehensibility should be experienced in a negative manner by those who haven't mastered a certain type of subject, is the most natural thing imaginable.

But if a report from an expert witness, or even an ordinary medical prescription, is perceived by the reader as a text that

is merely difficult to understand without the help of a translation on a facing page (and in fact the doctor provides one by
reading the prescription aloud as he writes it), any legal document, the minute we lay eyes on it, immediately conveys a
sense of falsehood. In the sense that a legal document is by its
own admission inauthentic. And not because it doesn't tell the
truth. It's inauthentic because it is ontologically prompted by a
vested interest, because it is out to achieve a purpose or a
profit and it makes no bones about it. It's this very shamelessness that makes it seem untrustworthy at first glance.

Put any legal document (a subpoena, an appeal, a com-
plaint, a verdict, or even a simple contract) in front of someone
who's unfamiliar with the courts and he'll tell you that: a) he
doesn't understand it; b) he doesn't trust what little he thinks
he does understand.

And then if that person is actually the recipient of the document in question, what he'll do next, and I mean beyond the
shadow of a doubt, is to pick up the phone and call a friend
who's a lawyer and have him read it, in order to find out what
it actually says.

All this just goes to show you that legal writing is not trust-
worthy. And that the mistrust that the average citizen feels
toward it comes essentially from the fact that he perceives it as
a utilitarian form of writing.

In much the same way (otherwise I'll be told that I'm being
unfair to my fellow members of the bar), though to a lesser
degree, the average citizen is mistrustful of journalistic writing
(the kind of writing in the newspapers that he doesn't buy), as
well as of advertising copy (even though—and this is a paradox—he's not all that embarrassed to purchase a product for
which he's seen a commercial that strikes him as overtly dishonest).

Let's take a look at a nice concrete example of utilitarian

writing and disinterested writing. An example that has to do with me, since I am its author; but I'll examine myself the way an entomologist would examine an insect, I promise.

Example of utilitarian writing (source: Brood.doc by Vincenzo Malinconico, hidden in folder "Photographs, Happy Village in Marina di Camerota, July 2004"):

> *Perhaps we ought to begin to consider whether this relationship, rather than improving our lives, isn't simply complicating them. In that case perhaps we should ask ourselves what has broken between us, and why. Then, together, we can find the least painful solution for us both.*

As you can plainly see, the style of writing that governs these phrases slithers along a path of disingenuous hypocrisy of a pretty coarse variety. It's a kind of reptilian writing, which spots its prey from a distance and then draws closer in ever-tightening circles, awaiting the perfect opportunity to lunge and sink its fangs into it.

The author pretends to start from a potential doubt (before even touching down on the verb "to consider"—which already in and of itself suggests no real volition—he covers his ass with a "perhaps," and then further armor-plates himself with a "begin to," as if even that act of considering is an effort he's not completely sure he's willing to undertake), though it's perfectly obvious that he knows exactly what's going on; then, seeing as the responsibility for an eventual separation (which is after all the reptile's real objective) is not a burden he's willing to bear entirely on his own, he cunningly attempts to farm out half of it to the other party in the doomed relationship, venturing so far as to invite her to underwrite a metaphorical protocol of understanding, an emotional briefing intended to explore a problem that in reality he knows exactly how to resolve (which is to say, by dumping the girl while making her believe that this separation is something they actually entered into by common accord).

In other words, despicable stuff.

Now let's try writing the exact same thing (or to be more precise let's treat the same topic of Love Looking Around for the Check) in a more gratuitous mode.

Here's an example of the kind of prose that might come out of such an effort (or perhaps I should say the text that I wrote after the red-cheeked shame I felt after rereading what I'd previously composed in the utilitarian fashion):

> *Accept the fucking miserable reality, Vince'. You're both stuck. Wasting time wondering how and when it happened is futile at best. The truth is that you just look each other in the face and talk about other things. The only question at this point is which of you is going to bring it up first.*

As you can see, the shift in style was so radical and so sudden that the author was made to renounce outright the hypocrisy of the first person singular, going so far as to address himself in the second person. A necessary splitting of the personality in order to suppress the reptilian (a useful lesson to take away at this point might be "If you want to write, then suppress the reptile inside you"), regain control of present events, and finally break the code of *omertà* that governed his utilitarian writing.

From this point forward, it's all downhill: the author seizes the topic by the horns, and without much beating around the bush writes: "You're both stuck": then, in a single line, he dismisses the old chestnut about tracing the problem back to its source, and limits himself to accepting the fact that what's broken cannot be fixed (because first of all there are some things that are just beyond repair; and second, even if it could be fixed, these days it's not worth spending money on repairs anyway). At this point his renewed faith in the truth allows him to serve up a metaphor, cynical but as eloquent as a scene in a movie: "looking each other in the face and talking about other things," which is also a concise description of the awkwardness that arises between two people who have fallen out of love with each other.

Now, even though I realize that it's an inherently unfair question, compare the examples provided above once again and tell me which of the two writing styles you prefer.

If you ask me, all really good books are written in the gratuitous mode.

Take *The Catcher in the Rye*. It's one of the most disinterested books I've ever read.

Which is why it still sells so many copies.

I think.

How did I even work my way around to this topic? Ah, yes, that whole business about the envy I feel for people like my mother-in-law, who enjoy a simplified conception of life, as opposed to us brooders, who poison our lives by brooding and then use writing as a way of recalibrating things.

You want to know why I write? What's the real, most essential, truly indisputable reason, trimmed free of any and all idle chitchat? I'll tell you why: I write so that I have time to come up with the proper comeback.

My problem is that I'm slow on the draw. That's why I hate my thoughts. If only they'd give me a brief summary of the things that happen, instead of getting all twisted up over everything, then I'd have a chance of coming up with something snappy (and, more important, on topic) more or less when needed.

The thing I ought to have said always comes to me when I'm almost home. Specifically, as I'm turning my key in the door to my building. That's when it appears before my eyes, as if I could actually see it, a well-formed phrase, spare, musical, impeccably logical: designed to discourage any attempt at rebuttal. And that's when I could practically kick myself in the teeth. Because the last thing I can do now is pick up my phone, call the person who won the battle of wits, and say to them, "Hey, so, anyway, about that talk we were having, I'd like to add that . . ."

You can't do it. Overtime rules forbid it.

In real life I can't delete, start over, rethink what I said, correct it.

So I write.

To take my revenge on words.

To tell the story of how things would have gone if I'd used the right ones.

ACTION!

It's about time," I was about to say to the deli counterman—a fatty with a soul patch you'd expect to see on a
carabiniere and the same face he must have had when he
was ten (I don't know if you know the kind of guy I'm talking
about, one of those types you're sure look exactly like themselves as children even if you've never seen them before)—
when he came over to me, shop apron all wrinkled and white
cap in his hands, as if he were on a visit to pay his condolences.

"What on earth is going on here?" he asked me, more bro-
kenhearted than worried.

He saw for himself before I could get the words out.

Matrix glared at him as the deli counterman's jaw dropped
at the sight of that surreal scene.

Engineer Romolo Sesti Orfeo stared at him without saying
a word, his arm dangling inert at his side, the gun in his hand.
He'd prudently positioned himself midway between us and
Matrix, facing sideways, so that he could keep an eye on his
prisoner and at the same time stage-manage the appearance of
the new witness.

Instinctively, the deli counterman with the face he'd had as
a boy stepped toward him, though not with any intent of taking
his weapon or trying to dissuade him in any way: he just made
the move, trustingly, as if he could do something to help him.

"Dotto'," he said.

Scandalized, as if he refused to change his mind about the
handcuffed man.

Engineer Romolo Sesti Orfeo snapped his arm straight out into the air in front of him and aimed the pistol on a line with the counterman's broad moon-face.

"Stop right there, Matteo. Don't get any closer."

Calmly, without a hint of menace in his voice.

Matteo the deli counterman stopped short, turned as white as the cap he was clutching in his hand (just one hand, now), and took a step back. The old woman raised both arms in a pugilistic stance of self-defense. I was on the verge of telling her: "Oh, would you stop always thinking it's all about you? He's aiming at him, not you."

"Please," Engineer Romolo Sesti Orfeo added, almost apologetically. "Stay back."

And that's when it became clear that he was a bit of a sentimentalist, because if he hadn't felt called upon to tell Matteo the deli counterman how sorry he was to have to treat him that way, he wouldn't have fallen into the moment of distraction (a classic: and they always seem to fall for the classics) that any self-respecting criminal would instantly recognize and turn to his advantage.

With stunning promptness, in fact, Matrix leapt to his feet and charged head-down like a battering ram, taking along behind him both arms trapped by the handcuffs that screeched along the metal rail of the dairy case, producing a subversive, premonitory sound.

Engineer Romolo Sesti Orfeo was just fast enough to turn and block the impact with his left arm, otherwise Matrix's head butt would have caught him square between his spine and his ribs. He nevertheless hit him hard enough to knock him off his feet, causing him to lose both his balance and his gun in the same instant (the deli counterman Matteo looked down to see the pistol slide to within a yard or so of the tips of his shoes). The old woman was using me as a human shield, and every so often it seemed to me she jumped into the air back there behind me.

Pirouetting in a tight circle, Engineer Romolo Sesti Orfeo windmilled both arms in the air in a wild but ultimately unsuccessful attempt to grab the metal rail that ran along the front of the dairy case; he then tumbled over onto his right side. He immediately tried to reach out and grab the handgun, but Matrix hurled himself on top of him and kneed him hard in the belly, knocking the wind out of him. Engineer Romolo Sesti Orfeo clenched his teeth and squeezed his eyes shut in a deforming grimace and then curled up in a fetal position, as if to gather the pain into the exact center of his body, thereby suffocating it.

Matteo the deli counterman stood staring at the pistol on the floor as if he'd never seen anything remotely like it in his life. Engineer Romolo Sesti Orfeo gathered his strength and threw a punch in Matrix's general direction, but Matrix dodged it easily, and taking advantage of that further loss of balance he climbed onto the engineer's back, wrapping his legs around him to keep him from reaching the gun. Engineer Romolo Sesti Orfeo found himself crushed to the floor with Matrix riding him like a horse, whereupon he slammed both his hands to the ground in an attempt to buck off his jockey: a move that Matrix immediately countered by glueing his torso to his back in order to force him down with every ounce of his weight. It was as if the two were miming intercourse, with the further aggravating factor of the attempted ear bite on the part of the one on top.

Now the situation had been grotesquely reversed. A prisoner who'd been deprived of the use of his arms riding on the back of the man who'd handcuffed him in the first place.

As for us three useless bystanders: Matteo the deli counterman went on staring at the pistol as if it were some sort of alien organism that had infected his psychomotor software; I was tempted to come to Engineer Romolo Sesti Orfeo's defense, but my ignorance of his motives kept pushing back against that impulse; the old woman had regained her voice, and she had emerged from her hiding place behind my back and was now shouting at the top of her lungs, "Police! For the love of God, call the police!" as she watched the fight on the television monitors instead of live in front of her (a circumstance that would later give me food for thought about people's tendency to look to screens for a confirmation of reality).

Meanwhile two female cashiers had shown up, one klutzier than the other, clutching each other by the arms as they took turns stammering *"Maronna mia"* instead of moving their asses and calling the police before we had time to commemorate the day.

At the far end of the aisle, I got a confused glimpse of two or three shoppers (one of whom must have been the afore-mentioned "Franco") who had shown up on set and were watching the writhing bodies struggle from a safe distance and who were clearly as indecisive and frightened as we were (except they had the advantage of having just shown up and thus being exempt from any obligation to take action).

Suddenly one of the cashiers took off running for the exit. Her coworker dashed after her, I suppose in imitation. To my inexpressible relief, the old woman went after them.

Engineer Romolo Sesti Orfeo covered his ears with both hands to protect them from Matrix's gnashing teeth, as his ponytailed opponent went on snarling and drooling on his head like a rabid dog trying to clamp its jaws shut on anything within reach. Every so often he'd lift a foot and drive his ankle into the engineer's belly.

I couldn't take much more of just standing there and doing nothing, and I was about to leap into the fray when Matrix raised his head and called out to Matteo the deli counterman:

"Hey you! Get the gun!"

The counterman responded with the same disconcerted expression that the guys sitting in the back row in school (generally tall, incredibly skinny, with long bangs and turtleneck sweaters) used to put on whenever the teacher yanked them out of their anonymity and called on them by their last names, whereupon they, abruptly rejoining the scholastic community, would point to themselves inquiringly.

They were incredible, those guys. In practical terms, they attended school incognito, camouflaging themselves with whatever organic material came to hand. You didn't even notice that they were in your class at all until February or March. When the teacher managed to track them down, we'd watch them being questioned as if they were fugitives from the law finally brought to book. I can remember a couple of them, but I still have no earthly idea what their names were.

"You understand me, asshole?" Matrix upbraided him, seeing as Matteo the deli counterman was showing no signs of life beyond pure astonishment. "Put the gun to this piece of shit's head and get these cuffs off me, *now!*" he commanded.

"What?" I asked in Matteo's place.

If you were to ask me what I considered to be the low point of that whole absurd episode thus far, I would have to say: when Matrix ordered Matteo the deli counterman to get ahold of the pistol and use it on Engineer Romolo Sesti Orfeo to get him to uncuff him. Worse than the capture itself, worse than the pulling of the gun, worse than the struggle, worse than the annoying old lady, worse than the reality-show ambush. Only if you hold your fellow man in such low regard to the point that you take his absolute obedience for granted could you assume the right to impart such an order. Because to talk to another human being that way, you have to put him on the scale somewhere below shit.

"Do what I tell you, you'll be better off," Matrix added, after letting fly another ankle to the engineer's belly.

"Go fuck yourself," I blurted out, pointing my finger straight at him. And I bent down to grab the pistol, with the vague intent of using it in some way (glossing over the minor detail that I'd never picked up a gun in my life).

Matrix glared back at me, nonplussed, but he didn't have the time to process the meaning of the disruption before Engineer Romolo Sesti Orfeo whipped around and slammed his elbow straight into the middle of his face.

Matrix's nose erupted spectacularly, knocking him backward and roughly unhinging the corporeal structure erected with such diligence atop his enemy's back.

I think that I recoiled out of sympathy. Reaching toward the pistol as I was, in a not-entirely-wholehearted attempt to get my hands on it, I lost my balance. Luckily Matteo the deli counterman was behind me, and he promptly seized both my arms and kept me from falling. Whereupon I released a couple of pathetic kicks into the air, in the instinctive search for solid ground upon which to plant my feet (more or less like toddlers do when their mothers place both hands under their armpits and lift them up to teach them to walk). Finding that attempt unsuccessful (that fucking floor seemed amazingly slippery), I threw my hands back behind me, harpooning the shoulders of Matteo the deli counterman. We remained in that position, each gripping the other, like a couple of drunks staggering to their feet from the sidewalk after the bouncer has done his job.

Even before getting back onto his feet, Engineer Romolo Sesti Orfeo immediately lunged for the gun, beating me to the punch in that respect, wobbly though my attempt had been; then he stood up, waved the weapon around in the air in our direction (and we paid practically no attention to it, so hardened were we to all threats of danger at this point), and returned his attentions to Matrix, who was partially unconscious, semi-invertebrate, dangling from the hand rail of the deli case. But he did so without haste; in fact, with a perceptible and distinctly unsettling calmness of demeanor, almost as if regaining control of the situation had given him a desire to take his time.

He kneeled down in front of Matrix, the pistol pointed right at his face, waiting for his captive to take a closer look at him, just to remind him who was in charge.

Matrix opened his eyes with effort, blinded by his own streaming blood, humiliated by the defeat.

"Too bad," commented Engineer Romolo Sesti Orfeo, "I wanted to leave your feet untied, for all the good it'll do you." Having said this, he hit him in the head with the butt of the pistol.

Matrix didn't even cry out. He made a standing broad jump to the floor, kicking his legs out in front of him pitiably like a fresh victim in a movie when the killer fires one last gunshot just for effect before turning to go; then, moaning, he scraped the soles of his shoes over the floor tiles, following the stations of the pain as it wended its way through his body and smearing his footwear with the yogurt previously spilled.

That was truly nasty.

A smirk appeared on the lips of Engineer Romolo Sesti Orfeo that made him look both pleased and nauseated at the same time, a twofold expression that lingered awhile on his face.

At this point, I decided it was time to leave.

Engineer Romolo Sesti Orfeo turned to Matteo the deli counterman, who was now looking at him with openmouthed bafflement.

"Matte', I need you to do me a favor. Go over to the household goods section and get a roll of packing tape, the brown kind; then come back here and tape this guy's ankles together."

Matteo the deli counterman, whether more upset or disgusted by what he'd seen I couldn't say, shook his head no.

"You'd better listen to me," the engineer admonished him. "Because if you don't do as I tell you, and if you're not back within ten seconds, I'm going to shoot him. And it will be your fault."

It was at that exact moment that I gave up my plan to high-tail it, out of the vague yet compelling need to make myself useful in some way. As if I'd suddenly been overcome by an undefined sense of responsibility, which led me to believe that I was the only person there capable of fending off the worst outcome. Me, of all people.

"Go on, Matte'," I advised, but in a tone of voice that smacked more of "Listen to me" than "You're free to choose."

The guy tried to argue once or twice, then in the end he gave in.

Engineer Romolo Sesti Orfeo picked up the remote control again, aimed it at the monitors, and pressed some buttons. A second later he spoke and his voice was broadcast over the loudspeakers, perfectly synchronized with the live images onscreen.

"Thanks for your collaboration, Counselor Malinconico."

Hearing my name so publicly proclaimed threw me off-balance.

I looked up the aisle. There was no one now.

"I'd like it if you'd stay, too, now that the trial's about to start."

"*Trial?*" I asked.

Matrix straightened his neck. I can guess that this was an unsettling world for him to hear; something like "audit" for a well-paid professional.

"Do you know who this gentleman is?" Engineer Romolo Sesti Orfeo asked me, ignoring my question.

I looked Matrix up and down. As if I hadn't already seen more than enough of him.

"No, I don't know who he is."

"Strange," he replied, sounding a little disappointed.

It's not like the guy was so famous that I was bound to recognize him.

"Then I'll tell you another name," he added, pausing before laying down his ace in the hole. "Massimiliano Sesti Orfeo. Given the line of work he's in, you must have heard of him."

I looked at the floor, muttering that name, which rang no

bells whatsoever, as a wave of embarrassment from my failure to answer him took possession of my limbs.

Considering me to be a full-fledged criminal lawyer, Engineer Romolo Sesti Orfeo must have thought that all it would take was an eloquently stated hint for me to reconstruct the whole chain of events automatically, but that name, aside from the fact that it coincided with 50 percent of the engineer's own, didn't mean a fucking thing to me.

Obviously at that point in the episode the last thing I wanted to do was make the cringe-inducing statement "No, I have absolutely no idea who that is, sorry." So I limited myself to looking him in the face without saying yes or no, leaving him to understand that I might very well have known who he meant.

Sweet Jesus, I said to myself, it feels like this kind of thing has been happening to me for as long as I can remember, I'm sick to death of it. When is everyone going to stop asking me about things I ought to know and reliably fail to have any idea about?

Like the name of the chief justice of a given tribunal, and the exact timeline of appeals to the higher administrative courts, and what exactly is a legislative decree ("As opposed to a decree law, Counselor?"), and how much time has to pass before a legal separation actually provides grounds for a divorce, and just what provisions were made by the Lodo Alfano ("And while we're at it: what on earth is a *lodo*?"), and: "You mean to tell me that this name means nothing to you?" And I could go on ad infinitum.

Christ, I'd like to see how you'd handle it. One of these days I'm just going to answer: "I don't know the name of the chief justice, I've never presented an appeal to a higher administrative court in my life, I don't even know where the higher administrative courts are located: I don't know a fucking thing!!" In other words, I'll tell the truth, and I'll put an end to that line of questioning once and for all.

The embarrassment of being asked questions you don't know the answers to constitutes one of the gravest social costs of being a semi-unknown member of the bar (SUMOTB). While I'm on the topic, I'd like to stop for a moment and consider this unspoken-of matter of routine discrimination. We SUMOTBs—let it be known, at least this once—are subjected to mistreatment on an almost daily basis at the hands of the average citizen, who, inasmuch as he is a potential user of legal services (PULS), feels free to subject us to gratuitous argumentation with the unstated purpose of rubbing our faces in our own lack of success.

It's a discriminatory form of harassment directed at part-time and freelance workers in general and us SUMOTBs in particular, exposed as we are to the psychological bullying of the PULSs.

I invite you to take a look instead at those older lawyers, perhaps not even all that well respected, who always seem to be heading somewhere in a hurry, rushing from one courtroom to another, hearing after hearing, huffing and puffing in exasperation, and exchanging wisecracks you'd expect from truck drivers when they pass each other in the halls. Do you think that those guys ever have to deal with the problem of refining questions to fit a certain line of cross-examination? That they'd allow themselves to be subjected to the barrage of faux-casual tests to reveal their degree of connectedness to the larger milieu of the bar?

The funny thing is that they might not be anywhere near as well informed as they'd like you to think (because after all, let's get one thing straight: just because you get older doesn't necessarily mean you get better at what you do). In all likelihood they're just clever johnny-one-notes who've been doing the same half-dozen things for a lifetime, and they wouldn't stick their nose in a law book even if an exasperated colleague threw it in their faces. And yet no one would dream of pestering them because outside of the tiny bit of knowledge that they manage to get by on, they don't even bother to wonder what's going on in the world of jurisprudence. And even if you ask them questions pertaining to their fields of expertise, they answer only if generously recompensed, and even then after they've had time to gather adequate documentation. And right they are to do so. So a person says, e.g.: "That lawyer over there collects debts for bank X or company Y." Or else: "This one does labor law, that one's an expert on traffic accident liability." And that person never even dreams of going over and asking any of them what a legislative decree is, or to explain how it differs from a decree law, or why on earth they've never heard of Massimiliano Sesti Orfeo.

In contrast, we SUMOTBs, who try to get by on a handful of specializations in the absence of any clearly defined area of expertise, are forced to put up with whatever PULS happens along to question us whenever he feels like it (so when he does, we just end up feeding him a line of bullshit).

Which takes us back to the paradox of the virtual unknown who's expected to know more than the seasoned and respected members of the bar.

Obviously, this is all sheer insanity. But that's the way it is.

"Hey, you," I felt like saying to Engineer Romolo Sesti Orfeo, "let me clear things up a little for you:

1) I don't have the slightest idea who this counterfeit version of Keanu Reeves might be, nor who the hell answers to the name of Emiliano (or was it Aureliano, I've already forgotten) Sesti Orfeo, but I imagine he's some relative of yours.

2) Cut it out with the riddles. Do you have some score to settle with this character? All right, then tell us who he is instead of playing games. Especially since you've constructed this mini television studio, and we've been standing here for a solid twenty minutes taking in this reality show; don't you think it's high time you at least rolled the opening credits?"

As if he'd heard me, Engineer Romolo Sesti Orfeo turned

to look at Matrix and answered the rhetorical question I'd asked him in my head.

"He was my son," he said.

Matrix filled his lungs with air and sighed, like a defendant who's just heard the sentence demanded by the prosecuting attorney after a lengthy summation.

Ah, I thought. Well, so what?

It's not like he'd said Pier Silvio.

Or Lapo, or whatever.

What was I supposed to have taken away from this—aside from the fact that, obviously, he seemed to consider Matrix responsible for his son's death?

Here's another one of the incongruities I run into with a frequency that is surely no accident. I believe that each of us has certain typical incongruities, serial challenges that crop up for him or her alone and recur in keeping with a stated pattern.

My typical incongruity is that I tend to fail to keep up with what's happening around me. For as long as I've been a regular habitué of courthouses (and the plural here is purely rhetorical, because I only frequent a single courthouse, and not all that often, truth be told), I've found that the reality of the place tends to catch me off-guard (which is another way of saying dimwitted and befuddled).

Like for instance the first time I walked into a courtroom to witness a criminal trial, when after five minutes I realized that I didn't have the faintest idea what the hell was going on, and how different an actual trial was from the way trials were described in my law-school textbooks. It was a head-on collision with the truth. It was like growing up in a family where everyone always speaks perfect grammatical Italian, with plenty of subjunctives and all the rest, and suddenly being forced to learn dialect (with judges who roll their eyes and heave theatrical sighs, chronically depressed defendants, and lawyers who think they're hilarious, among others).

What am I talking about? I'm talking about standing still while everything flies past you. About watching without understanding. About not being able to ask someone to explain for fear of looking like a damned idiot. That's what I'm talking about. A little like when you're sitting at a table with a big group of people and someone makes a joke and everyone's falling over laughing and you, who didn't even hear the joke because you were thinking about something else just then, start laughing along with everyone else so as not to feel left out. And after a while all your facial muscles start aching from the effort (because there are plenty of things you can fake in life but laughter isn't one of them), so you pick up a napkin and hide behind it just enough to cover the bare minimum, waiting for the chorus of yuks to wear itself out and for everyone to go back to talking normally. But instead the hilarity skyrockets, and everyone starts slapping everyone else noisily on the back (one guy even sprays the guy sitting across from him with a mouthful of water). So you concentrate obsessively on the scraps of phrasing taken from the unknown wisecrack, repeated between hiccups of laughter, in an attempt to grasp the nature of the joke unleashed by the comic genius of its originator, but in the meantime the collective giddiness has lit the fuse of other comedians, and they start throwing out more witticisms based on the first one that you missed, and more waves of laughter, and even though you're completely in the dark you start fake-laughing all over again, and so on and so forth, until you get to the point where you can't take it anymore. And so, with cramping jaws, you get up and announce that you have to go to the bathroom, and in fact you do, and while you're in there you wash your face three times in a row, after which you look at yourself in the mirror and it seems to you that you're looking at a man on the verge of despair.

I don't know if I've conveyed the idea.

I'm talking about exclusion from context. About alienation

from what's going on around you. About that lucid lack of awareness that makes you feel like a misfit incapable of grasping the mechanisms that count. Someone who'll always talk about done deeds, because although he was there while the deeds were being done he didn't understand what was going on. And so he'll never amount to shit; at the very most he'll be able to add up the damages (if not to be compensated for them), or do a little after-the-fact analysis.

Success, career, wealth, politics: all the areas of life that matter are based essentially on this distinction between those who grasp matters in real time and those who reflect on the aftermath in a deferred viewing. It's a question of the speed and especially the elasticity with which you learn. It's not a matter of hard work, it's about understanding quickly. If you lack this quickness, then you're shut out of the realm in which decisions are made, and you'll have to settle for those made by others.

There was a loud burst of talking from the front entrance. Some imbecile even shouted. There's always some imbecile shouting in the distance when something happens.

What are you shouting about? You're not the one who's in trouble.

Engineer Romolo Sesti Orfeo, with the nonchalance of someone who hears a tremendous crash out on the street and goes over to the window to look down, picked up the remote control and pressed another combination of buttons.

On the screen the supermarket lobby appeared, with a big crowd of spectators beyond the cash registers, and the attendants engaged in a mix of explaining and barring the way to the rubberneckers who always cluster around when public disasters occur, who were trying to get in and reach the epicenter.

Matrix and I exchanged a look of genuine amazement at what at first glance struck us both as a monumental technological innovation.

That two video cameras might simultaneously provide footage of two distant points of the same location ought to be easy enough for us denizens of the third millennium to wrap our minds around. If the television monitors were connected via a network, obviously one could choose them as needed or even all together, thus making it possible to monitor the entire supermarket section by section. And yet at that moment that possibility, relatively elementary though it was, flabbergasted us as though we were a couple of troglodytes gaping at the discovery of fire.

In the final analysis, the brilliance of the idea, its disarming efficacy, consisted in using the technological equipment that the supermarket already possessed without making any substantial modification to it: in other words, using what was already there (there's nothing more astonishing than simplicity).

This video security system, hijacked and turned, in a certain sense, against itself, along with the images of the people gazing as though hypnotized at the television monitor broadcasting the hostage-taking scene, incredibly reminded me of the live feed of the Twin Towers, both in terms of the strategy of attack and the resulting collective sense of shock and devastation, when television, on a worldwide scale, for the first time in history, was swallowed up by the unscheduled programming that invaded its frequencies, holding it hostage, self-broadcasting, destroying all the existing schedules, and taking all the time and space available for itself.

Whenever I'm in the middle of a mess of some kind I become capable of totally inappropriate extemporaneous conjectures (such as this one) that actually make me feel rather intelligent, truth be told.

The only problem is that since I can't stop to think about them right then and there (the point at hand being that I'm in the middle of a mess), what happens is I skip over them. And if I try to conjecture later, after the mess has been straightened out, I find that I'm no longer capable of having so much as a shred of a thought that's on even remotely the same level as the initial conjecture.

Who even knows how many extemporaneous conjectures I miss on a regular basis.

Over the supermarket loudspeakers we could hear the voices of the crowd clearly now. I'm not even going to bother repeating all the idiotic things they were saying (stuff like: "The Taliban": or another one, exquisitely Pindaric in tone: "I know him, he's on *Posto al Sole*").

Engineer Romolo Sesti Orfeo once again worked the remote control, after which he approached the camera that was transmitting from the front entrance, until he had framed himself in a close-up.

"Silence," he thundered.

All pressed up close to the video camera like that, he kind of looked like *The Scream* by Munch.

At the front of the store, the crowd suddenly went silent. We too stood in expectant silence.

Something must have happened, because the television set went dark for a moment. Engineer Romolo Sesti Orfeo clicked his remote control again and the monitor turned back on.

"Here I am again. Look up," he continued, doing his best to recapture the attention of his already wavering spectators, unable to figure out the right direction to look in (it's unbelievable how little it takes to lose an audience).

"No, not that one. That's a video of you. The other monitor, up high, on the right."

Brief pause.

"On *your* right, for Christ's sake. There, that's it. Can you see me now?"

There was a simultaneous alignment of heads.

"Giovanni? Giovanni, can you see me? Yoo-hoo? Don't look at me like that, you know me."

Giovanni (one of the grocery clerks, probably: he was wearing the same apron as Matteo the deli counterman) was staring at him on the screen with the same astonishment that had previously plasticized the face of his coworker (Engineer Romolo Sesti Orfeo must have been known as a mild-mannered father and head of household in that store).

"Have you called the police?" he asked.

Giovanni said nothing. When I looked closer it seemed to me that what had rendered him so thunderstruck wasn't so much the shock of finding himself face-to-face with a criminal version of Engineer Romolo Sesti Orfeo, but rather the fact that someone was speaking to him through a television set. And that sense of unease, if you want to know the truth, then and there struck me as perfectly understandable, because it's hardly normal to stand looking up at a screen to talk to someone. Fine, okay, we've gotten used to it: video intercoms, Skype, teleconferences . . . But a certain cognitive discomfort still lingers, a difficulty that's reminiscent, in a way, of what old people experienced when TV was first invented. In my family there was a story about a great-grandmother of mine who, when they turned the television on at night, would hurry off to change her clothes and do her hair because she was convinced that guests had arrived. And it's not like she was sick in the head or crazy: there was simply no way to make her understand that she could see without being seen.

"Hey, Giova'," Engineer Romolo Sesti Orfeo kept after him. "I asked you a question, are you going to answer me?"

"Yes," the clerk nodded vigorously, abruptly snapping out of his trance. "That is, Marisa called the ca-, ca- . . . rabinieri, I think."

"Okay, that makes no difference. Anyway, there's no need to shout, I installed an omnidirectional microphone in the ceiling. I can hear you perfectly, the same as you hear me."

"Ah," the clerk agreed, even though, to judge from the look

on his face, I doubt that he'd dedicated a great deal of thought to the question of the omnidirectional microphone.

"Now listen up," said the master of ceremonies, finally coming to the point, "I've taken a man hostage, you understand? I've handcuffed him here to the dairy case and now I've got him covered with my gun. No one is to approach us, understood? *No one.* The first person to try it is going to set off a nice little New Year's Eve fireworks display, have I made myself clear? Keep people far away from this aisle. Same thing goes for the carabinieri. When they get here, let me talk to them. After all, I can see them and talk to them just fine from right here. Is all of that understood?"

"Yes, yes, yes," said Giovanni.

Just like that: three times.

"Excellent," said Engineer Romolo Sesti Orfeo. And turned off the audio from the front entrance.

Matrix was motionless, covered with contusions and completely demoralized. The blood, already clotting, tattooed half his face, and his nose, following the impact with the enemy elbow, had roughly doubled in size. All the same, he didn't hide from the monitors; if anything he defied them with his eyes, putting on a show of dignified iciness.

I was reminded of the look that the animals in the zoo gave us during a school field trip once when the class smart-ass spat in their faces through the bars of their cages.

There was an embarrassing silence, the kind that overtakes you when you suddenly find yourself mired in a strange, dense moment of suspense.

"It seems as if we're waiting for someone," I said, just to cut the awkwardness.

"Exactly," responded Engineer Romolo Sesti Orfeo.

"Not the carabinieri," I ventured, since it seemed as if he was finally in a mood to impart some information on the topic.

He stared at me as if to say: "You're good, you are."

"That's right."

"Then who?"

"Who do you think?"

Whereupon I decided he had chapped my ass sufficiently.

"Why don't you give me the first initial, and then I'll try to spell it from there."

He paused argumentatively, but since he'd apparently enjoyed the wisecrack, and had come that close to laughing, he gave me an answer.

"The television crew."

Matrix went into a nosedive.

So did I.

I stopped for a moment to reflect, even though the idea, oddly enough, struck me as anything but unexpected.

"More television coverage?" asked. "Aside from the footage you're already shooting?"

"You can't possibly think that I put all this together for a closed-circuit viewing."

"Earlier you said something about a trial."

"That's right."

"What do you have in mind, your own version of *Court TV*?"

He shook his head.

"That's prerecorded."

Just then Matteo came back with the packing tape. Engineer Romolo Sesti Orfeo nodded to him to come closer; then he finished the thought.

"We're going live."

We all looked at each other.

And it's here that the show begins.

MISUNDERSTANDING

I thought I was being plenty funny by getting her that bottle. You know when you feel irresistibly witty because you've planned out a gag gift for someone, confident that the recipient's sense of humor will win out, like buying an exercise bike for a friend who just broke both legs in a skiing accident, or else (this really happened when I was in high school) a convenience ten-pack of Kleenex for a classmate who was found jerking off in the gym; in other words, the kind of presents that even before you buy them, in your imagination you run through the full sequence of expressions on the recipient's face seconds after tearing open the giftwrap? There, that's the kind I mean.

I assumed that they'd burst out laughing and then tell me to go to hell, that they'd say that I was the same old idiot as ever and that was why they'd always liked me, that I couldn't have come up with a better idea for a gift to bring with me when I went to see her, such a welcome change from the faux-compassionate visits from her girlfriends, all of them basically overjoyed to learn that she had one foot in the grave before they did.

Okay, after the wisecracking preamble I'd see her bite her lips and get a faraway look as she pondered the unthinkable facts of a Timeline Without a Future; I'd take her hand in mine and I'd sit there listening to myself as I spouted off a series of prerecorded phrases like You're-a-strong-woman-and-I-know-you'll-pull-through-this, or else In-certain-situations-you-find-strength-that-you-never-even-knew-you-had, or Look-people-don't-die-of-cancer-the-way-they-used-to, and so on; because everyone knows that when you go to see a sick person—and the sick person is perfectly aware of the reason for your visit—those are nothing more nor less than goodbyes.

I said nothing to my children, who'd both been kind enough to come with with me, at least not until we'd entered the coffee-roaster's-wine-and-spirits-rum-boutique-and-grappa-shop not far from where I live, which is, as an aside, a place I frequent regularly. And when I'd pointed to the Jack Daniel's, and, what's more, asked to have it giftwrapped, they'd exchanged an alarmed glance, suspecting that they knew who the intended recipient of the alcoholic gift package in question might be.

"Do you really think that's a good idea?" Alfredo asked me after we left the coffee-roaster's-wine-and-spirits-rum-bou-tique-and-grappa-shop.

Alagia hadn't said anything, but she was giving me a look.

I felt like a fugitive from the law or who knows what.

"Oh, cut it out, guys. Now we have to sit around a conference table and take a vote to decide what gift to get Grandma?"

"Papà, Christ on a crutch, it's a nutty idea," Alf decreed.

I really couldn't let him get away with that last one.

"Coming from someone who spent his summer holidays in a Rom camp so that he could go on the Internet and talk about his experiences, that sounds a little like a joke to me. What was the problem, didn't you have anywhere better to go on vacation?"

"I was doing an investigative piece and you know it," he replied, already resentful, but also with a bit of a chip on his shoulder. "I met some Roma, we became friends, and I asked them if I could stay with them for a few days."

"A self-commissioned investigative piece, because I don't think that an editor at *Corriere della Sera* or *la Repubblica* assigned it."

"Oh my God, Papà! Do you always have to reduce the things I do to a question of money?"

It was true, he had a point. I never miss a chance to try to tear down his journalistic ambitions, in spite of the high consideration in which I have always held his ideas, and especially the determination he puts into his work.

It's the same thing with his Roma holidays: if you think that the idea of his spending his August vacation in a gypsy encampment to provide live coverage of the life they lead didn't tickle me, you're wrong. I absolutely loved it. I find it bold and unabashed, indicative of an intelligence that refuses to settle for secondhand information. I'd happily buy a newspaper just to read an article like that. So it's obvious that I ought to be proud of this son of mine. And in fact I am. It's just that I'm so completely fed up with this young man's intellectual honesty. I find my admiration of him to be exasperating. I hate to see his wasted efforts, which no one pays him for. I detest the websites to which he makes a gift of his original and invaluable articles. I'd like to see him get what he deserves, because that's the way his mother and I always told him things would go. And he believed us, he took us at our word. I can't go back on my promise. I shouldn't educated him, shouldn't have instilled in him the importance of hard work, of empathy, of having an inquiring mind—that's the fact of the matter. Every time I see him come up with a new project, and complete it without getting anything in return, and with a smile on his face too, a wave of frustration washes over me, and then I direct it straight at him, the last person on earth to deserve it. And instead of cheering him on, which is what I'd like to do, I wind up demotivating him.

"Christ, Alfre', you work yourself so hard. And you pay the price; we're always coming to pick you up in the emergency room, and all this for what?"

"Please, Papà. Let's not start this again."

"Fine, then let's make a deal: I won't start on that again and you won't break my balls if I want to take a bottle of whiskey to your grandmother."

There ensued a silence of compromise, and we started walking again.

Alagia must have been feeling quite hoity-toity just then, because she was unable to resist the urge to return to the topic, remarking that my idea struck her as "very kitschy," which already was an opinion that made me hot under the collar.

But the thing that pissed me off most was that in order to bestow that pearl of wisdom on me she actually stopped in her tracks, while Alf and I went on walking to the end of the sidewalk: a bad habit (I'm referring to the habit of coming to a halt in order to emphasize a point) that I've never been able to put up with, if you really want to know.

For instance, you're walking with someone. You're talking about this and that (actually, let's be honest: most of the time you're listening apathetically to an account of generally insignificant events). At a certain point you realize that the guy you were talking to isn't there anymore. So you turn around and realize to your astonishment that you've left him a good ten or fifteen feet behind you. But he's still prattling on, ignoring with stunning nonchalance the distance between you.

At this point there are really only two options: either you stop and wait for him to catch up with you (and you'd have every right, since he stopped without telling you) or else, as is more often the case, he just stands there (and he has the advantage, since he stopped a while ago) and you go back, immediately attracting the attention of everyone in the vicinity (because of course, since the other guy stayed behind but hasn't stopped talking, in order to make himself heard he's had to raise his voice, and as a result the one who most stands out in this piece of open-air theater is you as you hurry toward a man who is yelling at you).

The best part is that when you finally come face-to-face with the guy who's monologuing in your general direction and get a chance to hear what was so tremendously important that he had to come to a full and gratuitous halt to say it to you, you're ready to punch him in the nose.

"Did you hear what I said?" Alagia asked, already a considerable distance behind me and Alf.

"Hey . . ." blurted Alfredo turning around, only then realizing that his sister had lingered behind.

"We're crossing!" I said, polemically raising my voice in Alagia's direction; then I grabbed Alf by his right wrist and we took off, heading for the sidewalk on the opposite side of the street, taking advantage of what was left of the yellow light.

My son went along with this lightning-quick abduction with a considerable degree of bafflement (as I dragged him along he never once took his eyes off his sister, who in the meanwhile was hurrying pitiably to cover the distance between us, but by then it was practically impossible for her to make it before the light turned red, ha ha ha) but, with the exception of a couple of good hard tugs that he forced me to impart toward the end of the crossing, he didn't put up any genuine resistance.

When we reached the other side (scant seconds before the stoplight turned green for the through traffic), I uncuffed him.

Back on the sidewalk where we'd left her, Alagia seemed furious. The traffic that was zipping past, fading into automotive evanescence,, between us (I've always been struck by the way that cars seem to dematerialize once the road clears up and they start chasing along after each other) made the space between us even more definitive, and highlighted in particular the marginalization that I had imposed upon her. I found myself thinking about how impeccable my timing can be when I decide to make a point of a matter of principle that basically leads nowhere.

In any case, we stood there waiting for her: me staring at a manhole cover and bracing myself for the dressing down I was sure to get as soon as she made it across, Alf shooting her glances of self-justification alternating with little shrugs as if to say: "What do you want from me, he's the one who did it."

"When did you turn into such a rude oaf?" Alagia practically screamed in my face like five minutes later, that is to say, the time it took for the traffic light to turn green (stoplights, as everyone knows, gauge the time required to turn from one color to another based on a scale that is inversely proportional to the impatience of those observing them: which is why, where I come from, people regularly run red lights).

As she crossed, she was so pissed off that she walked as if she were wearing a back brace.

"Don't stop when you're talking to someone while walking," I told her, preparing to go head-to-head.

"What?" she asked, confused.

"Come on, let's go," I added, trying to grab Alf's wrist again, but this time he was quick enough to elude my grasp.

"Do you mind telling me what's gotten into you?" Alagia asked, baffled by my lecturing tone.

Alf added nothing, but it was clear that he would have countersigned his sister's question.

"Nothing's gotten into me. Ask me anything you want, but just keep walking, all right?"

"Is someone following us by chance?" Alfredo asked.

"Ha ha, funny guy," I said.

"I wasn't kidding. Why do we have to keep walking, exactly? I don't understand."

Whereupon I said nothing, afraid that I'd stumbled into a—as people like to say when they really want you to know that they customarily speak English—*misunderstanding*, if you're one of the Italians who know what that word means. It's when a person says one thing and the person who's listening justifiably understands something else, at which point the first person registers the second person's bewilderment and immediately says: "Sorry, there's been a *misunderstanding*"; and the other one says: "Oh, yes, of course": or else the second person is quicker on the draw and says to the first: "This must be a *misunderstanding*," and finally—but only then—do they clear things up, happy not so much to have cleared up the confusion but rather to have both used the word *misunderstanding*.

"It's a long story," I dismissed the matter brusquely.

"What is?" he asked, genuinely perplexed.

"Ohhh, Alfre'. Please."

"Vincenzo," Alagia broke in while Alf gave me a worried look, "now I need you to explain why you left me standing like an asshole on the other side of the street."

I flared my nostrils and sucked in a lungful of air like a bloodhound on a trail, then I exhaled loudly, immediately provoking a dizzy spell from hyperoxygenation, and then settled on a kind of hooded-eye paternalism along the lines of: "I'm going to teach you something that you won't understand here and now, but it will be useful to you someday."

"If there's a habit you need to be careful not to fall into," I decreed, though I lacked the courage to look my daughter in the eye as I assumed my posture as a professor of Just Measures, "it's the habit of walking and then stopping while you go on talking while the other people keep walking."

This statement was followed by a dead silence.

I went into the kind of trance a soccer player experiences after kicking one into his own goal.

In order to restore that demented statement to something resembling a clear meaning I attempted a conceptual autoreverse, a little like what you do with one of those Russian-nesting-doll-style sentences that contain several people identified by their ties of kinship, such as: "Aldo is the husband of Luigi's wife's sister," which in order to understand them you have to run through them in the opposite direction and think to your-self: "Luigi has a wife; his wife's sister, that is to say, his sister-in-law"—and already the concept of "sister-in-law" begins to sweep away some of the clouds—"is married to Aldo" (and at this point you contextualize Aldo within his family and you almost feel as if you can see him); but even this procedure failed to produce any concrete results. I'd uttered a sentence that could have been conceived by a goat, and that was that.

As my son and daughter burst out laughing right in my face, spraying saliva and slapping each other on the back like a pair of marionettes in a Ferraiolo Brothers' puppet show, I found myself thinking that it's only when you try to improvise a con-cept that's just a little bit complicated that you realize how much you tend to overestimate your own powers of expression.

A person thinks: "This is something I know," and believes that that settles the matter. He couldn't be more wrong. Until you find the right words, you don't know anything. You really ought to do some test runs before you open your mouth. If, when you see highly intelligent guests on television shows expressing themselves in a series of impeccable metaphors and armor-plated turns of phrase, you assume that they're impro-vising, you're mistaken. Those people write out the things they're going to say beforehand. No more nor less than actors working from a script. Words must be chosen carefully, and then some.

"Both of you can go fuck yourselves," I told those imperti-nent louts. "And you," by which I meant Alf, who was laugh-ing so hard he'd almost hit me with a piece of flying snot, "blow your nose, goddamn it."

At that point I turned and walked away, inoffensively offended.

"Come on, Papà, come back!" Alfredo shouted after me, making me feel the way I used to when I was seven years old or a little younger.

That imbecile sister of his, however, wouldn't stop laughing.

"Choke on it," I silently wished her.

They caught up with me about fifty feet on, surrounding me like a couple of hoodlums looking for trouble.

"Well?" I said.

I felt like laughing.

I don't know if this will make sense to you, but we all loved each other very much in that moment.

"What was it exactly that you said?" Alagia said, breaking the silence with all the delicacy of a hippopotamus. "'Get in the habit of stopping to walk when other people are talking and walking while stopped?'"

"Has anyone ever told you what an asshole you are?" I replied, blushing.

She looked her brother in the face and they both burst out laughing again and, before long, I was laughing along with them.

As we were walking toward the apartment building where Ass lived, I linked arms with Alagia and reminded her, as long as she was behaving like an editor of the Accademia della Crusca Italian Dictionary, that, when she was in second grade I think, she once wrote "un'altro" instead of "un altro" in a composition.

She gave me a juicy kiss on my right cheek and told me I was an idiot.

As for my mother-in-law, just as I'd imagined, she had a good hearty laugh when she unwrapped my present.

For me it was a moral victory.

What I didn't realize was that she would actually open the bottle.

REALITY SHOWS ARE NOTHING MORE THAN AN EXTENDED MICROPHONE GAFFE

L ook at me, not him," Engineer Romolo Sesti Orfeo orders Matrix, who starts staring Matteo in the eyes as soon as the deli counterman approaches him with the roll of packing tape.

Matrix turns his head in the engineer's direction with scientific slowness, in such a way that his gaze remains fixed in a menacingly sidelong glare at the poor counterman, and in fact within seconds Matteo has turned pale and stopped cold just a few feet away from them, the roll of adhesive tape in his hands as if he no longer knows what to do with it.

I look at his terrified silhouette in the monitor above me, and I feel a surge of compassion that for a moment clouds my vision.

Furious at the snag, Engineer Romolo Sesti Orfeo grabs Matrix by the hair and yanks him toward him, jabbing the pistol barrel under his chin.

Matrix closes his eyes, clamps his lips shut, and inhales loudly, the way certain sick people do as they brace themselves to withstand with dignity an oncoming attack of the recidivistic pain that afflicts them.

"So you want to keep playing games, eh?" Engineer Romolo Sesti Orfeo warns him. "All right then. Why don't we see what happens if I shoot you right in the legs, that way I won't even have to bother tying you up."

"So you want to keep playing games, eh?" I parrot him mentally, resisting the impulse to emit a loud and mocking

Bronx cheer. I mean really, is it possible to utter a line like that with any real conviction?

Matrix opens his eyes, but refuses to give him the satisfaction of a response.

Anyway, he's bluffing, I think to myself.

"Come on, Matteo, get moving," said the engineer, with considerable nerve: the poor guy was standing there like a coatrack.

"To hell with this," I blurt out. And with two impatient strides I reach the useless deli counterman and grab the adhesive tape out of his hand. "Give it here."

Matrix opens both eyes wide straight at me with a look of perplexity seasoned with something like an overtone of familiarity, wondering who is this guy who has stood by doing nothing from the start except to take the occasional initiative that unfailingly leads nowhere.

Engineer Romolo Sesti Orfeo, on the other hand, flashes an appreciative smile at my unasked-for intervention (and I'm really starting to wish he'd stop flirting with me, because he's been semi-molesting me for the past two hours).

Without wasting any time, I kneel down in front of Matrix, unroll a length of tape, stick it to the left leg of his trousers (as I do so I notice that he's wearing a very nice pair of boots that my friend Paoletta would probably swoon over), and then I windmill the roll repeatedly around his ankles, overlaying ascending spirals of tape until I reach his knees, packaging his shins and calves together; then I yank it tight, pull the roll toward me, lift the strip of tape to my mouth, and tear it sideways with my teeth, declaring the job complete.

I stand up. With contemptuous eyes, I look both the hostage taker and the hostage up and down, the two of them pressed up against each other like a couple of lovers in amorous transport, then I raise my right arm and throw the roll of adhesive tape over the head of Engineer Romolo Sesti

Orfeo, just grazing it, so that he's instinctively forced to duck for fear of being hit; after which he stares at me in astonishment.

At this point I really shouldn't say a word, and in fact I remain silent, symbolically intensifying the dramatic quality of my gesture, which then and there (in part due to the presence of the video cameras filming us, most likely) makes me feel particularly theatrical, I have to confess.

Shortly thereafter, in fact, I realize that I've aesthetically panned the sketch that Engineer Romolo Sesti Orfeo has so painstakingly assembled. By throwing the roll of packing tape in his direction (though not actually at him) I must have metaphorically denounced him for the menial nature of the task he'd obliged me to perform (on a purely substitutional basis, to top it off, since that knucklehead Matteo the deli counterman was too petrified to lift a finger).

I take a look at my image on the monitor and my takeaway impression is that I am now running the show (it's incredible how television manages to liberate the overweening jackass that lives inside us all). After all, I've just stolen the scene from the very guy who mounted the show, and put a lot of hard work into it, in the first place. Or rather, I didn't steal it: I earned it. Perhaps this—I conjecture extemporaneously—is the true meaning of the expression "steal the show." It's incredible how often we use an expression to indicate its opposite. The Italian language truly is awash in amnestied crimes of grammar.

Matteo continues to stand there, his mouth hanging half open. Suddenly I'm fed up with his ineptitude.

"Hey," I say to him, "what is it, did your water break?"

His eyes reveal that the wisecrack has gone over his head.

"I just got you out of a jam, unless I miss my guess," I continue. "You can cut it out now."

At this point he snaps out of it, probably realizing that I'm right. And he takes two steps backward.

I turn to the engineer.

"Happy now?" I ask, in brazenly rhetorical fashion.

A brief but significant silence ensues, after which a burst of applause can be heard coming from the front entrance.

I become a statue.

Matrix, Engineer Romolo Sesti Orfeo, and the knucklehead immediately register the applause, turning to me with a new expression in their eyes.

My self-esteem skyrockets, causing a delightful moment of vertigo.

I feel like a tiger.

I'm a revelation. A rock star.

I'm Bruce Willis in the first *Die Hard*.

I'm the man for the job.

I have the situation well in hand.

I love myself.

Engineer Romolo Sesti Orfeo seems saddened and disappointed.

Disappointment is the most open-captioned emotion of them all. Nine times out of ten when you look at a disappointed person you can immediately guess the reason. It's easy enough to conceal the causes of envy, jealousy, or rivalry. The same even goes for anger. But with the captioning they have for disappointment, there's not much to be done: they're easy to read.

At last we hear the siren of the carabinieri. Even though this is an intervention that we'd fully taken into account (perhaps it would be more exact to say that we've been expecting them), I heave a sigh of relief. The arrival of law enforcement, even if it fails to solve the problem, instantly makes you feel relieved of the responsibility to deal with it yourself. It puts into effect a sort of subcontracting of responsibility for whatever is going on. In certain situations it's a panacea, because it frees you from prudence. And that is why people often become uninhibited pottymouths when the police show up (e.g., at the scene of a car crash).

Some time ago I witnessed a fender bender between a car and a scooter from the window of a friend's apartment. The rear-ender: an older woman. Rather elegant too. The rear-endee: a guy who looked about twenty, maybe twenty-five. The face of a nice young man. They both park their vehicles (he gets off his Vespa; she gets out of a Smart car). The young man neither raises his voice nor makes recriminations; he just requests her insurance details and leaves it at that. She acts mildly exasperated, tries telling him that it's just a scratch, he replies that the owner of the body shop he goes to has been able to buy plenty of real estate with just scratches; in other words they trade sharp words but keep it just within the union regulations for the dialectics of friendly differences, after which the matron resigns herself to her fate, gets back in her car, pulls out her license and registration, and is about to hand them over to the young man, who is legally entitled to peruse them.

At that exact moment, however, a pair of traffic cops walking a beat in the neighborhood happen upon the transaction in progress and come over as duty requires, completely unsuspecting of the fact that they are the full moon that is about to unleash a werewolf.

In fact, the woman not only tears her documents out of the young man's hands with admirable dexterity, but unexpectedly treats him to a gale of filthy insults as personal as they are gratuitous, clearly showing herself to be a pedigreed habitué of some of the more down-at-the-heels taverns of a bygone era.

The two traffic cops exchange looks of astonishment, then set about trying to make her see reason, but the lady, to use what is perhaps a misnomer, shrills at them to keep their paws off her (something those unfortunate civil servants certainly had every intention of doing), and she then lunges at the guilt-less young man with a rage so disproportionate that one of the two police officers instinctively puts his hand on the butt of his pistol.

What left us speechless, me and my friend (or really I ought to say just me, because by now that idiot was rolling on the floor in helpless laughter, and at a certain point he even had to hurry into the other room to keep from suffocating), were not so much the obscene imprecations, the variations on the exclusively scatological and sexual themes that poured out of her mouth, as the *voice* itself. A monstrous, vicious, guttural sound, intolerable to the human ear, broken here and there by hawks of spit and grunts, a harbinger of calamities and disasters. I swear, the first thing to do was summon an exorcist. And when she finally left (I don't even know how) and was pulling away in her car (obviously without having supplied the details of her insurance policy), she even stuck her head out of the driver's side window and went on shrieking, the harridan. Such a scene that the traffic cops and the young man stood there comforting each other for a good ten minutes afterward.

"All right, thank you, Counselor Malinconico," says Engineer Romolo Sesti Orfeo again, raising his eyebrows and making my surname echo over the vegetables and the mozzarella (he must have diligently miked the entire supermarket, to obtain such a roundly stereophonic effect).

"Thanks for dick, Engineer," I retort, still giddy from the homage paid to me a short time ago.

"What?" he replies, pretending to find me amusing.

"You heard me," I repeat, just to eliminate any doubts.

And I place a hand on the knucklehead's shoulder, in an instinctive yet incomprehensible urge to express my solidarity (and in fact he goes: "Mhm!" even accompanying the sound with an affirmative nod).

"I'm not offering you my cooperation," I say, articulating the idea more fully. "I'm just trying to limit the damage. So please refrain from thanking me. I don't approve of what you're doing."

"Ah," he says.

"Right," I say back.

For a little while it's as if there was nothing left to say (which is what happens when you realize that the other person's point of view is exactly as valid as your own. It's as if both parties were getting in each other's way).

I think I hear a faint rumble of applause from my fans back at the entrance. But it might just be my imagination.

"Well, I don't give a shit," the engineer says brusquely. "I'm not here to win anyone's approval."

I didn't expect him to use that kind of language. It disappointed me a little, truth be told.

"Okay," I say, blushing (because we always blush a little when someone speaks to us rudely), "if you're going to put it like that, do you mind if I leave?"

"Then you fail to understand. This is a trial, and we need a lawyer."

"Hey, you know something?" I say, warming to the topic. "This whole thing is starting to turn into a . . ."

". . . comedy sketch," I'm about to say; but I never do, because we're distracted by the commotion that suddenly reaches us from the main entrance, where the carabinieri have just started dispersing the crowd.

Whereupon we all look up at the monitors, having by now become accustomed to the idea that they're our window to the outside world.

The language employed by law enforcement in these types of situations, consisting largely of imperatives ("Keep moving, people"; "Clear out: no blocking traffic"), is usually even more modular than a Billy bookcase (no matter how you arrange the words, the meaning remains the same), and yet it is certain to achieve its intended disruptive effect.

There are a few acceptable variations on the theme, but they too verge on the rhetorical (e.g.: "Let us do our job here," words often pronounced the minute they arrive on the scene, and therefore long before they've had a chance to do anything) or else—even worse—they border on morbid curiosity, which has the sole effect of stoking that curiosity to a raging flame (thus the celebrated "Nothing to see here": which is absolutely guaranteed to nail a crowd to the spot).

Usually, anyway.

Times must be changing, because things seem to be going differently.

First of all, the carabinieri summoned to investigate the foul deed are two in number: nothing out of the ordinary thus far. But the two carabinieri are a man and a woman, and this takes some getting used to, considering the fact that carabinieri teams have long been—misogynistically—made up of men only.

Another thing is that they're both young and even pretty athletic—already something that smacks of a TV show—and since she, important detail, is a redhead, I automatically associate them with Fox Mulder and Dana Scully, the two FBI agents from *The X-Files* who, in spite of the attraction constantly buzzing between them, in nine seasons spent tracking down aliens never—how to put this—closed the deal (an omission to which the series owes a considerable part of its success).

Third, she's the one keeping back the crowd, and she does so without using a single regulation cliché. All she says and repeats is: "*Per favore*," "Please," with a technique you'd expect from a unit production manager on a film set, using her arms as movable police barriers to indicate the imaginary perimeter of the area that is off limits.

Fourth, he doesn't have a soul patch. He's the kind of tall

that during introductions normally elicits the regulation question: "Hey, do you play basketball?" (in the mind of the everyman, basketball is the masonic order to which all tall people belong), and he displays an admirable composure during this preliminary inquiry into what's happened. In spite of the fact that he's already glimpsed the situation in the television monitor overhead (and in fact he never takes his eyes off it), he listens closely to what Giovanni the grocery clerk, having been prepped in advance by Engineer Romolo Sesti Orfeo, has to tell him.

The deus ex machina himself must be feeling somewhat overlooked, because he suddenly bursts into the monitor, filling it with his face.

"Buongiorno," he begins, immediately silencing all voices below.

Mulder puts his cranium into reverse and looks at his close-up, without losing his composure (I'm guessing this young man must do yoga, given the way he responds to external events with such a phlegmatic demeanor).

Scully too, caught off-guard by the noise from the television speaker, turns around.

"Buongiorno," the carabiniere replies, calmly. "I can see you. And I hear you. I imagine the same is true for you."

"Precisely. We're both miked, Captain Apicella."

Mulder arches his eyebrows.

"Do we know each other?"

Engineer Romolo Sesti Orfeo takes a step back to allow the captain to admire him.

"You ought to still remember," he replies, "even though it's been a while."

The carabiniere narrows his eyes, circumnavigates the oval of the engineer's close-up, then his spine stiffens, and he turns to his colleague. When he resumes his conversation with the screen, his tone has changed.

"Of course I remember."

The engineer bites his lip, as if this confirmation has stirred some old pain.

"You were the first to arrive."

"That's right."

A meditative silence ensues, and both men seem to reexperience the memory together, no doubt sharing stills from the past.

"How are you, Engineer?" Captain Mulder-Apicella resumes.

The most conventional question possible, and slipped into what we can only call an inappropriate context, but asked with such authentic interest that I'm moved to wonder whether I've ever said it in that tone myself at some point.

"Well, you can see for yourself, no?" he replies, spreading his arms just barely to present the scene of the hostage situation (a little bit like a circus artist who gesticulates at the end of the routine toward his fellow performers, so as not to hog the applause all for himself), as if the evidence of what he has done is a faithful depiction of his state of desperation.

"I didn't know you worked here," Mulder remarks.

Matteo and I exchange a look of confusion (he even goes so far as to shrug his shoulders and twist his lips into a frown: the conventional stance for expressing a giant question mark), amazed as we are to hear these two men shooting the breeze.

"It's a job I sought out deliberately."

"I thought so. Engineer?"

"Yes, Captain."

"I need to know if anyone's been wounded, please."

Ohh, at last a topic that concerns us all, I think to myself. And Matteo must have thought the same thing, because I see his shoulders relax. Mulder just took the long way around to get to the matter at hand, I now see.

"Only him," replies Engineer Romolo Sesti Orfeo, indicating Matrix with a jut of his chin, "and that's just a nosebleed. For the time being."

Matrix offers no response except to retract his neck and lower his head, hiding himself from the monitors.

"No one else?" asks Mulder, skipping over the "for the time being."

"No one else."

"And those two I see standing next to you, who would they be?"

"Next to him, huh?" I object inwardly. "We're a good ten feet away from him."

"One of them works at the deli counter, the other one's a lawyer."

"A lawyer?" Mulder asks with some confusion, and immediately scrutinizes the television set with an almost paleontological interest, as if the professional guild to which I belong had gone extinct several thousand years ago.

"That's right."

"Are you saying he's *your* lawyer?"

"No."

"And what is a lawyer doing there with you, if you don't mind my asking?"

"Good question," I agree mentally. In fact—without the slightest idea of what I could say on the subject—I lift my little forefinger like a third-grader, but Engineer Romolo Sesti Orfeo shoves ahead of me.

"I asked him to stay."

"So he just happened to be passing through and you made him a court-appointed lawyer?" the carabiniere observes.

Too bad, Mulder, I say to myself, and you were doing so well until a few seconds ago.

"Ha, ha, that's funny, Captain," I butt in.

"Excuse me," he says, trying to act superior in spite of the fact that his face is turning red, "what did you say your name was?"

I look around, as if to enlist those present in helping me to remember whether I might have forgotten something by chance.

"I didn't say," I say.

"He didn't say," Matteo backs me up.

We all take turns looking each other in the face (including Engineer Romolo Sesti Orfeo, while Matrix, at the risk of having his neckbones seize up, goes on staring at the floor tiles to conceal himself from the monitors), as if to underscore just how gratuitous the carabiniere's question really was.

"Ah, yes, in fact I didn't think I'd heard it," he says.

The whole group hovers in an awkward state of apprehension.

"What was that, another joke?" I ask.

I don't know if you've noticed, but I start coming out with snappy answers when an argument really catches my interest.

Mulder scowls.

"You know, I'm not having any fun here, Counselor."

"Well then just imagine how I feel. I've been here from the start and I can't even leave."

He ignores my comment and passes over me entirely, being intentionally disrespectful, and goes back to speaking to Engineer Romolo Sesti Orfeo.

"Engineer, would you please tell me why you want Counselor . . ."

"Malinconico," Engineer Romolo Sesti Orfeo replies on my behalf.

"Malinconico?" Mulder repeats.

Scully smiles in amusement.

"What, you don't like it?" I intervene, in annoyance.

Obviously the one I have it in for is Mulder, not her. She's actually not bad.

"No, it's kind of cute," he says without deigning to look in my direction.

Cute! A totally dismissive adjective, spritzed about like an urticating toxin with slightly delayed effects by full-fledged human jellyfish, who practice the undermining of other people's merits as a way of life.

The best part is that then they accuse you of being touchy (jellyfish always make sure they have an alibi ready before rubbing up against the epidermis of their intended prey) if you lose your temper and tell them that "cute" is a term that, if they really insist on using it, they're welcome to go say to their maiden aunt's toy poodle.

"Well, I think your *Happy Days* haircut is cute, Captain," I counterattack. "Maybe I'll ask you for the number of your hairdresser later on."

The funny thing is that Scully, without even realizing it, cranes her neck, looks at his head, and stifles a grin.

And sure, I said "*Happy Days* haircut" because it was the first thing that popped into my mind. If someone asked me out of the blue what a *Happy Days* haircut looks like, I wouldn't have the slightest idea what to tell them.

We remain in a silence poised between the tense and the ridiculous, until Mulder opts to continue with the line of questioning, forcing himself not to take the bait.

"May I ask," he resumes, once again addressing Engineer Romolo Sesti Orfeo, "why you asked Counselor Malinconico to stay, Engineer?"

"Because I'm the prosecution and he's the defense."

"You're the prosecution and he's the defense," Mulder restates the idea, with some skepticism.

"That's right."

"It sounds like a trial."

"That's right," Engineer Romolo Sesti Orfeo confirms.

"It seems to me that there are quite a few other things you'd need to put on a trial, Engineer."

"You mean a judge, a courtroom, a jury, a stack of legal documents thousands of pages long, evidence in favor of and against the defendant, witnesses who make statements and retract them, extenuating formalities, one adjournment after another, lawyers who nitpick all day long, prosecuting attorneys who just shuffle papers instead of moving the trial forward, and so on and so forth?"

Hey, not a bad summary, I say to myself.

Sure, a little cynical. But still.

"More or less," Mulder tosses back.

"Well then, I don't know what planet you live on. That's nothing but a museum a few visitors venture into every now and then."

I'm starting to like this man.

"And who exactly do you expect to venture into your so-called trial?" Mulder objects.

The same question I would have asked myself, if I didn't already know the answer.

Engineer Romolo Sesti Orfeo dismisses the question with a chuckle.

"Well, how about . . . everyone in Italy?"

For a moment Mulder's head is clearly spinning. He understands perfectly well (that's obvious), but he plays the fool to keep from taking in the reality all at once (I trick myself with the same method whenever my nose slams up against a lack of alternatives).

"I don't follow you."

Engineer Romolo Sesti Orfeo looks a little annoyed (he must hate having to explain something that seems so obvious to him) and comes straight to the point.

"Do you think that the television networks are going to turn up their noses at my monitors? That they're going to turn down a chance to broadcast a show like this?"

"Ah, so that's what you're after."

"I have the format ready to go, Captain. And I'm not even

asking anything for it. Think of what a bargain this is for a TV network. All they have to do is drive over, train their cameras on my monitors, and broadcast it on the national news."

Mulder looks around, trying to catch his colleague's eye, perhaps because he doesn't know what to say at this point (and I understand him, because the engineer's line of argument is technically impeccable).

In fact, she's the next one to speak, as soon as the engineer finishes.

"We aren't authorized to permit that kind of filming."

"Well then you'd better get authorization. Because if you even try to prevent the cameras from filming us, I'll put a bullet right in this guy's forehead."

I look at Mulder and realize that his yoga-induced equilibrium is growing wobblier by the minute.

"Who is that man, Engineer?" he asks.

"About time," I'd like to say.

"You mean you don't recognize him?"

Come onnn, we're finally getting somewhere, I think.

"How do you expect me to recognize him if he won't look into the camera?"

"Not to mention the fact that you've puffed him up like a balloon," I'd be tempted to add.

As if he were suddenly inclined to accommodate the request, Matrix slowly lifts his head and stares into the camera again.

There's a gleam of superiority in his expression, a quickening of pride and defiance. He even seems a little taller than before, like someone who feels called upon to prove he's worthy of his name.

After hamming it up with a dramatic pause, Engineer Romolo Sesti Orfeo takes a deep breath and finally introduces him.

"Gabriele Caldiero."

The silence that falls over the front entrance can be heard from here.

Matteo the deli counterman and I both turn to look at the hostage as if the name we just heard ought to have somehow altered his facial features.

Captain Mulder-Apicella practically recoils from that image. His neck stretches out, lengthening by a good five inches. His eyes, which are very light in color, narrow. Scully immediately draws near him. He whispers something into her ear. She goes back to the people she just shooed away, who now seem even more frightened, and orders them to leave the supermarket. Then she pulls a two-way radio out of her pocket and pushes a button.

I haven't the foggiest idea what plague or catastrophe is attached to that name I've never heard before (at the very most, I could make an educated guess), but my heart rate increases with such uncalled-for intensity that I'm having a hard time breathing, even though I'm standing perfectly still (I believe it when people say you can't tell your heart what to do: it doesn't understand a fucking thing you say).

"Engineer," Mulder calls out.

"Yes," he replies.

"Let us take care of him."

"Not on your life, Captain."

"This isn't something you can deal with."

"Nor can you, it seems to me, given the fact that this gentleman was free to come in here undisturbed whenever he pleased."

Mulder turns to look at his colleague and sees his own consternation mirrored in her face. Then he lets fly another question. And this time it's as if he's vaulted up to another, more technical level of conversation.

"Do you have any other weapons, aside from the pistol I can see in your hand?"

The engineer gathers his thoughts, then replies.

"Are you asking if I've planted a bomb in the laundry detergent section or the frozen foods aisle, for instance?"

"That's always a possibility," he acknowledges.

"In effect, it's always a possibility," the other man agrees.

My gaze meets Matteo the deli counterman's again. "Uh-oh," our eyes seem to be saying.

"I don't believe you," says the carabiniere in an attempt to call his bluff.

"Well," Engineer Romolo Sesti Orfeo rebuts effortlessly, "if you recognize the possibility that I might have planted a bomb, then you'll just have to take that into account. Which means that whether you believe it or not doesn't make a bit of difference, as far as you're concerned."

Impeccable.

"You wouldn't hurt innocent people," Mulder ventures, grasping at straws.

"Don't give me too much credit."

A rather grim silence ensues.

"That remote control you're using, does it do anything else besides control the television monitors?"

This question is so academic it almost leaves me speechless. In the sense of elementary, if not nursery school.

"Give it a rest, Captain. I wouldn't tell you even if it did."

Scully walks over to her colleague and whispers something into his ear.

"Speak louder, young lady," the engineer thunders, primarily to remind her who's in charge.

"She was just informing me that reinforcements are on the way," Mulder explains on her behalf.

"Reinforcements? It's not like you're resisting a military attack."

"This is standard procedure, Engineer."

"Captain, I'm warning you. From here I can see everything,

absolutely everything. None of you can enter or exit the super-market at any location or move around inside the building without being seen on the monitors. If you even try to move in on me, you'll have the first blood on your hands. And don't even think of blacking out the monitors or keeping the cameras away from them when they get here, do I make myself clear?"

Mulder lets the phrase hover in the air for a few moments, then replies, "You've made yourself clear." He pauses for a moment. "But now you need to let me in to see if there are any shoppers who didn't make it out. I believe it's in your interest as much as ours to make sure that no one's remained behind."

It looks as if the captain is regaining ground.

The engineer furrows his brow, then accepts the request.

"I can spare you the inspection, and show you the whole supermarket aisle by aisle. From here, with the remote control. Look at the television set up on the right."

"Please, Engineer," Mulder promptly contradicts him, in the most reasonable tone of voice he can muster, "this is some-thing I have to check in person. I need to look under the lower shelves too. A little kid could be hiding under there. This is a routine police operation, it won't take long at all. Don't worry, I'm not thinking of doing anything rash."

"You couldn't if you wanted to," Engineer Romolo Sesti Orfeo retorts.

"That's true," Mulder agrees. "Look," he says, unfastening his holster from his belt, "I'll leave my pistol with my col-league."

Engineer Romolo Sesti Orfeo puffs up, then slowly exhales. Perhaps the prospect of a child huddled under one of the lower counters really has upset him.

"All right," he says, finally putting aside his reservations. "Then I'll act as your navigator. Follow the itinerary I give you."

"All right," says Mulder, hopefully.

"Take the left-hand aisle, go past the bread counter and continue at a steady pace, keeping to your right. When you bend down to look under the shelves and counters, keep moving, unless there really is a child hiding underneath, as you suggest. Don't take any detours and don't retrace your steps. Once you reach this aisle, come over to where Counselor Malinconico is standing," and here he points to me, as if telling me to stay at the end of the aisle to act as his lookout (whereupon I look at Matteo and think: "Why me? Why not him?"), "and stop there. Do exactly as I say. I'm going to be keeping an eye on you on the monitor. Is that all clear?"

"Perfectly," says Mulder.

And he sets off.

"Captain," Engineer Romolo Sesti Orfeo stops him immediately.

"What?" he asks.

"The gun."

I observe this end-of-scene exchange and wonder: "Is that a classic or a cliché?" Sometimes it's hard to see the difference.

Mulder puts one hand to his forehead.

He seems sincere.

He hands Scully his pistol.

"I'm sorry," he says, "I didn't do it on purpose."

"It wouldn't have done you any good anyway. Get moving."

THAT'S NOT HOW THINGS WERE
(But It Doesn't Matter)

The realization that my crisis with Alessandra Persiano had not only begun but was actually halfway complete came to me one morning in court, as I was exiting a courtroom—which was crowded with colleagues who were not exactly sweet-smelling—where a civil claim hearing had been in session after successfully obtaining a postponement of something like eleven months in a case of mine (as you no doubt know, bringing a civil suit down in Naples almost routinely involves requesting a postponement at some point. There are more than five million civil suits pending in Italy. Oh, I know, that number doesn't strike you as all that astonishing; but I assure you that until you enter into the realm of statistics you can't grasp just how seriously messed-up the Italian justice system is).

It was a vision in the form of an awareness, a déjà vu from the future, the perception of an irremediable loneliness that you have no choice but to face up to, as if in that very instant I had already gone home and found the little sheet of notepaper folded in half on the kitchen table. It was so palpable that right then and there I felt the impulse to grab my balls to ward off the impending disaster, in keeping with the superstition, and I would have done it, too, except that I was busy at the moment trying to squeeze between the fat bellies of two commuting out-of-town lawyers dressed in caramel-colored suits, who were completely indifferent to my repeated attempts to wedge myself between them, busy as they were exchanging patently puffed-up accounts of their recent professional successes (it's incredible how we men, even after reaching respectable ages, still stand around telling each other tall tales for the simple love of bragging).

Don't ask me how such a thing could have happened to me, nor why I immediately took that odd sort of premonition so seriously, nor why I took such great fear. I don't know why. What I think I've learned, in my not-even-all-that-memorable romantic career, is that when we grow apart from someone we've loved (or still do), we leave lots of evidence behind us around the house. Little messages of inattentiveness and dissatisfaction that we scatter everywhere, and we even do it intentionally. We amass piles of discourtesies, omissions, unreturned gazes, words that no longer mean anything. And when we get out on the street, back among the crowds, and we lose the reassurance of the presence of the person who is usually alongside us, even though we feel we don't love her the way we used to, all of this accumulated distance catches up with us among the noises and voices of others, and it becomes loneliness in its purest form.

Once I'd escaped, instead of hurrying off and finding myself a cozy little place where I could settle my accounts with my panic and try to analyze it in some way, I went off to freeze my butt on one of the marble benches not far from the main entrance to the courthouse, and there I started watching the passersby, wondering what it was they possessed that I lacked.

Sitting on the next bench over, in the role of Forrest Gump, there was a homeless man with a carton of Tavernello red who kept shooting me sidelong glances as if he was wondering whether we hadn't met somewhere before. I came this close to asking him if he'd let me have a swig of his wine.

That was when my cell phone rang. I pulled it out of my jacket breast pocket, cursing myself for having forgotten to turn it off or at least silence it (which is what I always do, by the way, on the rare occasion that I actually attend a hearing).

I was in no state of mind to answer my phone, much less to talk to Nives, who in all likelihood was calling to dress me down for giving whiskey to her mother; so I just sat there staring at that plastic leech that kept crying out in my hand, throwing a fit and shrieking as if it were possessed, while my wino neighbor nodded in solidarity, as if he too had recently experienced that same annoyance.

I did my best to resist, but since that fucking cell phone wouldn't stop denouncing my inaction (it's incredible how many times a phone will ring before putting itself to sleep on those occasions when you just wish it would shut up), I finally had to give in, but only after stocking up on oxygen first.

"If this is about the Jack Daniel's," I say, opening with a frontal attack, "I'm stupid, infantile, and inappropriate. If there are no other recriminations, shall we just end the call there?"

The ensuing pause must have lasted, I don't know, a solid minute.

"This is Alagia, Vince'."

Her tone was absolutely commiserative.

Whereupon I had a vision: me in a theater, center stage, caught in a cone of harsh light; out in the orchestra seats and up in the balconies, a packed and sadistic audience pointing at me and laughing (a couple of them were even people I knew).

"Would you tell me why the fuck you're calling me on your mother's phone?" I retorted, pathetically aggressive.

The *tavernellista* turned to look at me.

I must have been shouting.

"Because the battery in mine is dead," she said, maintaining her cool.

My eyes narrowed. All around me things had gotten blurry.

"And you couldn't have called me from the landline?"

Alagia let out a faint sigh before answering.

"Vincenzo."

Calmly, as if there were no reason to get worked up.

"What do you want?"

"You're an idiot."

I couldn't have agreed more.

"Listen, little girl, this isn't the day for it."

"You can save the 'little girl' for your girlfriend."

Provided she's there when I get home, I thought to myself.

"I thought it was your mother calling, all right?"

Another sigh. She seemed worried.

"She's exactly who I wanted to talk to you about."

"Why are you whispering?"

"Because she's in the other room, and I don't want her to hear me."

"Has something happened?"

"Grandma doesn't want to see her."

"What?" I asked, jumping to my feet, both because of the harsh nature of the report and because the bench had anesthesized my butt cheeks.

The *tavernellista* shot me a worried look.

"You heard me. 'Don't bring your mother here anymore.' Just like that. Verbatim."

"But why? Did they have a fight?"

"Of course not. Why would they fight at a time like this?"

"Then what the hell's come over her?"

"We have no idea, Vince'. She doesn't want to listen to reason. Worst of all, she won't tell us what her reasons are. If Mamma shows up at her apartment, she won't even speak. Or else it's like yesterday, when she just locked herself in the bathroom until Mamma left. It's uncomfortable, I assure you. And Mamma's heartbroken."

"Sure, I believe you. Jesus, what a situation. Did you talk to her doctors about it? You don't think it's Alzheimer's, do you?"

"She's fine, Vince'. From that point of view, I mean. She's

sharp as a tack. You should hear how much Romanian she's picked up, with all the practice she gets with Miorita."

Miorita would be Ass's caregiver.

"That's just crazy."

"There's another thing."

"Now what."

"She's always asking about you."

"About *who*?"

"Apparently you're the only person she has any interest in seeing, besides me and Alfredo; and she's not even all that interested in seeing the two of us, if you want to know the truth. That is, she has nothing against our coming to see her, but it's not like she's all that thrilled either. But she never stops talking about you."

"It must have been the Jack Daniel's."

The reference made my bench neighbor swing around.

"You know, I thought the same thing? All right, but in any case you've always been her favorite."

"Okay, you can stop buttering me up, I get it."

Meaningful pause.

"Mamma is really depressed, Vince'. I wouldn't have asked if it weren't truly necessary."

"Hey, I can't force Assunta to see your mother if she doesn't want to, okay?"

Silence.

Cue the sense of guilt.

"Hey," I said, promptly assuming the form of a doormat (a metamorphosis that comes to me very easily, since I perform it on a regular basis in my interpersonal relationships), "are you still there?"

"Yes," she replied, appropriately overwrought, the little shit.

"I meant to say that I'll do everything within my power, okay?"

"Okay. Thanks."

Pause. At the end of which I got the urge to make a voluntary statement.

"Still, go fuck yourself."

For a moment she seemed really hurt.

"Why?"

"Because you really know how to make me feel I'm in the wrong. You're almost even sneakier than your mother. By the way, is she aware of the project?"

"Of course not. You know she can't stand mediation."

"Ah, right. I had forgotten about her bedrock principles."

"I need to ask you one more thing."

"And that would be?"

"We ought to try to keep her from finding out that you're going to see Grandma."

It took me a minute or so to take in the concept.

"Oh, really?" I blurted out. "Now I'm supposed to carry on a clandestine relationship with your grandmother to keep from offending your mother's rigid beliefs? Listen here," I piled it on as I got excited, "you're already asking me for a favor: I'm not going to do it on the sly on top of that!"

It took her a moment to launch her counterattack.

"Christ, Vince', put yourself in her shoes: your mother is dying of cancer and you can't even comfort her because she doesn't want to see you, but at the same time she's constantly asking after your ex (and let me emphasize, *ex*) wife. Wouldn't you be depressed? Don't you think it would be more noble of you to do your best to fix this absurd situation without bringing it to your ex (and let me reemphasize, *ex*) wife's attention, rather than boasting about it?"

Shit, I thought.

I hate it when my interests and considerations are rendered null and void by those of other people. Because it's obvious that when other people's interests prevail objectively over your own, you have to give in. And you have to do it in spite of the fact that, when all is said and done, you might not give much of a damn about those other people's interests; after all, you have problems of your own, and it's not written in stone that you always have to take on the problems of other people, who enlist you in their causes with the flimsy excuse of being in the right. It's not as if just because someone's in the right they can go around intimidating their fellow man and handing out to-do lists. A person ought to renounce the privileges that come with being right in order to be considered truly right in the eyes of others. But no, all those people who are in the right simply use the fact to their own advantage. So that, at the end of the day, they aren't really all that right, if you ask me.

Take right now. You were just sitting there on a bench making yourself feel miserable about your own problems and not bothering anyone else by doing so. At a certain point someone calls you, gives you this long list of information about your ex-mother-in-law who's about to start chemo and who has inexplicably declared that she no longer wishes to receive visits from your ex-wife, and you, who weren't even aware of the situation, and whose only crime it was to have answered your phone, find yourself from one moment to the next with a job to do.

And the best part about the whole thing is that you're in the wrong, to top it off.

Doesn't it all seem like a little much?

"Hey," I shot back, verging on exasperation, "why is it that one way or another I always have to catch a dressing down? Why do you always have to make me feel like a crook, even when you're asking me to do you a favor? I mean, what the fuck!"

Silence.

Ahh.

That shut her up.

Just for the moment, of course.

"Sorry, I didn't mean to be unfair. It's just that we're very worried about Mamma, Alfredo and I."

"All right, listen, forget about it. I'll see what I can do."

And we exchanged our goodbyes.

See if you can guess the word I said when I hung up the phone.

The *tavernellista* shot me another look of solidarity, then he hoisted his container of wine into the air, as if dedicating it to me, and took a long swallow.

I nodded to him as if to say: "To your health."

And that was it. I went for a walk around the neighborhood in order to mull over the potential developments of the events currently under way, when unexpectedly, as in a vision, I glimpsed Alessandra Persiano intently tapping away at her cell phone about fifty feet away from me, as the crow flies.

For a moment, I swear, I didn't think she was real, so light and luminous was she, so perfectly attired (one of the things about her that really drives me crazy is that even if you see her in an article of clothing that she's worn like four hundred times before, it always looks as if she just bought it), nonchalant in her loveliness, inexplicably sexy as she looked down at her cell phone screen with a faint expression of disgust on her lips.

As my cowardly heart flung itself against the bars of my rib cage, consuming in just a few seconds at least a couple of hours' worth of fuel (to the point where I wanted to say to it: "Why don't you sit still, don't you know who that is?"), I registered the symptoms of a very specific cognitive delusion that I've only ever experienced when I've run into famous people, for example this one time with Sting.

I don't know if you've ever noticed, but when you happen to run into famous personalities on the street they always prove a little disappointing. And not because we like them less than we remembered or less than we thought we would if we ever came face-to-face with them: quite the opposite. What disappoints us is how comfortable they seem in their own skin, the way they do just what they want to do, the way they act more or less like anyone else. It's their autonomy with respect to what we expect of them, their right to be ordinary people if they feel like it, that brazen freedom to enter and exit their characters, that suddenly liberates them of all the things that we've projected onto them without their even knowing it, so that we somehow feel stupidly cheated.

Though it's embarrassing to admit it, we don't acknowledge their right to brazenly spoil our imaginary world by doing what they please with themselves. We don't like to see them operating with such freedom. We'd prefer them to live in seclusion, far from the hellish realms of ordinary life. They ought to stay put where we left them, rather than wandering around freely (if you're going to be so damned important, do you have to be free as well?).

I'm beginning to believe in the existence of a perverse law of conservation that forces us to pay for success by depriving us of freedom. Take Roberto Saviano. For the people who love him, the knowledge that he can't move around freely is a form of insurance for our imaginations. The public preserves him aesthetically intact in the cloistered existence of an armor-plated, bodyguard-protected life. They won't run into him on the street; they have to wait to see him on TV. They can't ask him to autograph their copy of *Gomorrah* the way they could with a book by any other writer; they'd have to get past the officers of his police escort. And if they want to chat with him for a moment, they have to take advantage of the few minutes available before he is whisked off again. But can you just imagine how depressing it would be to be standing next to him at a nightclub while he (perfectly justifiably) chatted up some chick, who wasn't even all that pretty, because maybe he'd had too much to drink (that is, the exact same thing you would do, if you could). Of course it would disappoint you. You'd think to yourself (even though it's none of your fucking business): "Oh, Savia', seriously?"

In short, having gotten over (as it were) the shock of this vision of Alessandra Persiano, I fanned myself with my hand for a moment, stopping dead in the middle of the street, waiting for her to notice me.

She didn't notice.

I'm not exactly stunning, after all.

"No, you certainly aren't," my guardian angel immediately confirmed (though let me point out that I wasn't the one who hired him).

"Do you really have nothing else to fucking do?" I replied.

And I started waving my hand like one of those automatic mannequins that raise and lower their arms to signal a detour on the highway.

Finally, the woman who I was starting to doubt was actually my girlfriend spotted me. The expression that appeared on her face, and I'm not exaggerating, was the expression she might have had if she'd entombed me the day before.

"Am I already a zombie?" I wondered as I walked toward her with a sense of resignation very much like what I used to feel when, as a boy, I got up from my desk and approached the blackboard knowing I was unprepared (if you want to know the truth, those moments are pretty nice).

"Come on, it's nothing," said the bastard assigned to my guardianship. "The worst will come later."

"Ah, thanks, you're an angel," I shot back.

In the all things considered very brief distance that separated me from Alessandra Persiano, I ran down a short list of the formulas of dismissal that she could have chosen to employ in a circumstance such as this:

a) Please, don't make things any harder than they have to be;

b) I'm glad I ran into you: it's better to talk in a neutral setting, I don't think I could have handled this kind of anguish at home;

c) I don't want to lose you as a friend;

d) The keys are on the front table. Don't try to get in touch with me, please. I'll call you;

e) I need to try to understand what I'm feeling, and I can't do that unless I get some distance from you;

f) Shall we find a place to sit down in a coffee bar around here?

When I reached her, prepared as I was to be executed by a firing squad right then and there, the astounding sight of her face lighting up, smiling, as if she was as surprised as anyone by the happiness that had overtaken her, so wrong-footed me emotionally that I actually thought I'd heard the sound of a little chime in my ears, like when cartoon characters fall in love.

"You just got a text," she said.

"Eh?" I said.

Completely thunderstruck, I'm sure.

"A text," she said again; but since I just kept staring at her as if this were the first time I'd ever heard that particular word, she started jabbing at the air with her forefinger in the general direction of my jacket's breast pocket, then she restated the concept slowly and carefully, even raising her voice a little.

"You just received a text message on your cell phone."

So that was the little chime I'd heard.

"Ah," I said, returning to the three-dimensional world.

And I pulled out my phone.

As if I gave a damn about a text message in that moment.

I recognized the phone number of the sender. I broke out in a full-body sweat as if I'd been flash-frozen. I didn't have the faintest idea how I was going to get out of this one.

"It must have been me calling you a minute ago," Alessandra Persiano said, pulling me out of my quandary without knowing it.

I half closed my eyes, moved practically to tears at the thought that my vicious guardian angel had finally remembered to do something on my behalf.

"Oh, really? What happened, were you not getting any reception?" I replied, raising my voice as if I were particularly fascinated by the lack of cell phone service in that part of the city (when you're caught red-handed, you always express great interest in insignificant details), and at the same time I took a look at the text, pretending to check to confirm that it was in fact a message alerting me to the missed call from Alessandra Persiano (I know that I could have waited to read it at a more opportune time, but pretending to check for her call while I was standing there seemed less conspicuous).

More than reading the text, I stared at it.

Why do you all say "I'll call you" when you have no intention of doing so? You're so predictable. VFCL

VFCL? I thought; and then, a second later: Ah, right, *vaffanculo*. Fuck off.

I instantly pushed the home button and shot back to the main menu, and then I slipped my cell phone into my breast pocket, as clumsily as back in the days when I used to shoplift ballpoint pens from the Upim department store.

"What's the matter with you, Vince'?" Alessandra Persiano asked, drawing closer and pumping my sweat production up to a terrifying level.

"Nothing, maybe it's just that, well . . ." I replied, amazed that she should mistake the chip on my shoulder for timidity.

"Well lookee here," she broke in, flirtatiously; only to add, caressing my forehead in a motherly fashion, "You're sweating."

And if you just knew the reason why, I thought, shriveling inwardly.

Nearby that winged viper of a bodyguard was practically rolling on the ground laughing.

"The only reason you intervene is to get your kicks, eh, you filthy piece of shit?" I messaged him telepathically.

Every time I'm on the verge of changing my opinion about him, he always manages to restore my original attitude. There's no two ways about it.

"Hey. Hey now," Alessandra Persiano went on in her Nurse Persiano mode (one of my personal favorites). "Calm down, okay? Nothing's happened."

It had been a long time since she'd been so sweet to me.

"Nothing's . . . happened? Because I had the distinct impression that . . ."

"Shh."

She placed the tip of her left forefinger on my lips.

I stood there like that, my lips sealed by her magnificent pinkie finger, incredulous in the face of this reversal of fortune, amazed that I was out of the doghouse without having done practically anything, baffled at the rapidity with which my cast-iron certainty that our relationship was about to come to an end had just crumbled into dust.

Alessandra Persiano had now gone all doe-eyed with me, flirting so relentlessly that I was tempted to remind her that we were on a public thoroughfare.

Seen up close, her beauty ravages me like nothing else on earth. And if you want to know the truth, I don't especially like this feeling. For a while now, I haven't really been comfortable with the lowering of defenses that comes with love. The feeling of being so disgustingly vulnerable and open to any and all kinds of compromise in the presence of a pair of eyes, the curved lips that make up a smile, the unutterable rotundity of a tit.

Maybe it's because I'm no longer (even) forty years old, but I think that type of ineptitude is acceptable when you're young, when you have, as the saying goes, your whole life ahead of you. Because when you already have a good portion of your life behind you—and quite a bit more, let's be honest, settling around your waistline (I think you know what I mean)—you can't handle that kind of happiness. When it comes to love, happiness is costly, no kidding around. They don't give it out free of charge, that kind of happiness. In fact, if you really want the whole story, no happiness ever comes free of cost. Happinesses are tremendously expensive, and if you take out a mortgage on them, it's even worse.

And let's not go any further with this. That would be the wise choice.

"I'd forgotten how handsome you look when you're scared," Alessandra Persiano purred, brushing her lips against mine.

Whereupon a hot flash of enthusiasm came over me (I felt it spread out from my spine, the sort of instantaneous inflammation that's gone as quick as it comes: this is something that's happened to me since I was a kid), and right then and there I regained my sense of humor. Because the first thing I want to do when I'm happy is crack a joke.

"You see," I said, "that's how it is with us semi-ugly guys. We need specific planetary alignments of the emotions to make the most of our looks: embarrassment, shyness, disappointment, failure, illness, mourning . . . in other words, you need to pity us a little in order to find us alluring, if you see what I mean."

She half closed her eyes as she shook her head no (that's her way of enjoying the crap I say), then she remarked, with a phrase that I'm hearing entirely too often these days:

"You're such an idiot."

"I love you too."

She grabbed me by the tie and pulled me toward her, with the insolence of a two-bit street thug trying to start a fight.

There are kisses that are given to remember what kissing was like once upon a time. To understand whether they still have that flavor that you used to like so much. When they work, those are the best.

This was one of those.

In fact, my boxer shorts were suddenly too tight on me.

"Guess the idea I just had," Alessandra Persiano said immediately after, nibbling her lower lip.

"If it's the same idea I just had, we'd better hurry home."

"I don't think I can make it all the way home."

"Excuse me?"

"Plus I don't feel like it."

"I was pretty sure you did."

"I meant the going home part."

"Well . . . then what?"

She smiled, craftily.

"Then come with me."

She took me by the hand.

"But, what . . . ?" I tried to ask as she dragged me along with her.

"Shut up."

I stand there uncomfortably at the end of the aisle, waiting for Mulder as ordered, while Engineer Romolo Sesti Orfeo, a short distance away, follows his every step on a monitor that he's conveniently split up into six panels, mapping the entire supermarket, including the emergency exits.

Watching a miniaturized version of the captain moving quickly down the aisles, bending over continuously to check even under the lower shelves, immediately makes me think of Pac-Man, that old video game in which a bulimic ball moves through a maze gobbling down a long line of pills until it runs into certain colorful little ghosts that kill it, putting an end to its pig-out. From the familiar little smile that appears on Engineer Romolo Sesti Orfeo's lips, I guess that he must have just made the same connection.

Matteo the deli counterman nonchalantly twists open a bottle of mineral water and is about to tip it up and take a swig. Engineer Romolo Sesti Orfeo promptly looks daggers at him, freezing him to the spot with the bottle just inches from his mouth, forcing him to look inside it like a pair of binoculars.

I witness this wordless ocular tongue-lashing and for once I have to agree with the boss. It's not as if you can just start nonchalantly popping open bottles of mineral water in this kind of situation. You can't act freely if you're in the same room as someone holding a gun. The first rule of power is that when you're in its presence you have to ask permission.

Every now and then Matrix kneels down and then gets back up. His legs are probably falling asleep on him. The engineer shoots a discreet glance at him from time to time between one screen of Pac-Man and the next.

"Hey," Matrix suddenly says to Matteo the deli counterman, "splash a little water in my face."

"Say what?" Matteo asks.

Matrix snorts rudely through his nose.

"What were they even thinking when they hired you?"

Got to agree with you there, I think to myself.

But a second later I add (still in my thoughts): "But that doesn't mean that he ought to be working for you instead, asshole."

"Hey, you," the engineer shouts at Matrix, "you need to ask me, not him."

"I beg your forgiveness with my face pressed to the floor," Matrix replies, sarcastically self-flagellating. "Could that guy splash a little water in my face, because I hate the taste of blood, pretty please?"

"And by 'that guy' I assume you're referring to Matteo?"

"Yeah."

"Then repeat your question."

Matrix sighs and makes the correction.

"Could *Matteo* splash a little water in my face?"

Engineer Romolo Sesti Orfeo makes him wait awhile before responding.

"No."

Then he turns his back on him, refocusing his attention on Pac-Man.

Matteo the deli counterman sports a double chin of gratification.

Matrix clenches his jaw, capitalizing his rage. I'll bet any amount you like that right now in his head he's storyboarding a video clip of the various forms of torture he'd like to personally inflict on his captor before sending him to meet his maker, should he manage to get out of this situation alive.

Here comes Mulder.

I wait for him, motionless, without the slightest idea what I'm supposed to say to him (the best I've been able to figure out is that I'm supposed to serve as a sort of barrier, keeping him from nosing around on set), when the voice of Big Brother thunders over the loudspeakers.

"Stop right there."

Mulder stops short.

I turn to look at my commander as if to ask why he would appoint me bailiff and then do everything himself.

Mulder is just a few steps away from me.

I look at him.

He looks at me.

Oh my God, why?

"What are we doing?" I ask the engineer, turning my head in his direction.

"Nothing is what we're doing. Captain, your inspection is over."

"Can I come closer?" he asks, speaking to the monitor.

"What now, do you want to check to see if there are any children hiding here too?" Engineer Romolo Sesti Orfeo replies.

"No," he replies, with a regulation smile, "on the contrary, I thank you for having allowed me to venture this far to check. I'm only interested in seeing whether the prisoner is injured."

"I've already told you he's fine," the engineer replies. "Am I just wasting my breath, or is it a simple matter of you not believing me?"

At this point I count to three, confident that Matrix is going to try to take advantage of the situation in some way or other (and in fact that's exactly what he does: I know them, these kinds of people).

"He broke my nose," he tattles, in a whiny voice. "Help me, I'm hurt bad."

The voice of someone with a terminal illness, slightly hoarse: the kind of full package of victimhood you'd expect from an appeal to Amnesty International.

Criminals are always eager to turn to institutions when they're the target of some injustice. They have a fine-honed sense of legality. They adhere to the values of civil society with the timing of a conscientious taxpayer.

Truly a stupid move, on Matrix's part, to stage that pathetic bid for pity. Engineer Romolo Sesti Orfeo, in fact, is quick to swat it down.

"Oh, what a pity," he remarks. "Did you hear that, Captain? He hurt his little nose."

And with these words, he aims his pistol straight at him.

"You think he'll start crying if I shoot him in the foot?"

His arm held out straight and stiff as a rod, an icy gaze, the pistol ready to fire, like a snarling dog driven into a rage by a leash holding him back just inches from his prey.

We all look each other in the eye, stunned at the speed with which he's moved from rhetorical irony to cold menace.

In that moment I catch myself thinking that if there were a director running this thing instead of the stinking fixed video cameras, he'd probably zoom in on the barrel of the pistol and from there do a slow diagonal pan toward Matrix's feet and then pan even more slowly up toward his terrified face and just hold that, leaving all of us in suspense, waiting for the gunshot, creating that secret rooting for tragedy that always drives a blockbuster. After all, suspense—I conjecture extemporaneously—is nothing other than the awareness that there's nothing you can do but sit back and watch things happen. It's a welcome state of powerlessness. When you buy your movie ticket, when you invest in emotions (because, let's face facts, emotions are for sale just like everything else), the fact is you're commissioning a hypocritical state of anxiety into which a director places you and from which he then plucks you with the sleight of hand of a movie camera. You're the passive paying subject of an agreed-to masochism, made possible by a work of art.

Now Matrix is afraid. He's pissed off the boss, and he knows it. The problem with criminals is that they always want to land on their feet. They're even arrogant when it comes to acting. They don't hope even for a second that you're going to eat up the song and dance about their struggles and/or repentance: with much deeper duplicity, they chip away at your sense of personal dignity. So you wind up going along with them just to protect that value of dignity that you can't stand to see betrayed. It's sort of like they're asking you to buy the ticket so you don't have to see the show.

Matrix's problem, the way things stand now, is that Engineer Romolo Sesti Orfeo has no intention of buying that ticket.

Mulder gets a whiff of the potential bad outcome and hastily runs for cover.

"Engineer, that's enough, I think."

The funny thing is that he looks at me while he says it.

Engineer Romolo Sesti Orfeo's hand begins to shake. Which doesn't strike me as a good sign for Matrix. Who in fact begins to salivate excessively, all of a sudden.

"Have you noticed how quick these bastards are to take up the mantle of victimhood, Captain?"

I can't help thinking of the movies again. When you're watching a film, if someone with a gun starts spouting all kinds of theoretical nonsense while holding someone else at gunpoint (think, for instance, of Samuel L. Jackson reciting from the Book of Ezekiel, or at least so he says, to his victims in *Pulp Fiction*), you can pretty much be sure he's about to shoot.

"I know, I know, you're right," Mulder replies, trying to

seem as accommodating as he can, "but there's no reason to make things more complicated than they have to be."

He puts both hands in the air and takes a few steps back.

"All right, I'm leaving."

Engineer Romolo Sesti Orfeo says nothing. He probably didn't even hear him, drunk as he is on the feeling of power that he gets from holding his finger on the trigger. Look at him: he has all the trappings of a dirty old man with his eyes glued to the ass of an underage girl, who only realizes what a creep he's been after getting thrown off the bus.

At this point I really ought to do something; so I do.

"What's the matter with you, Engineer? Are you trying to ruin everything?"

Like a bucket of ice-cold water. Engineer Romolo Sesti Orfeo turns to look at me, blinking his eyes twice, as if he didn't recognize me.

The effect I was hoping for.

"What?"

"I thought you wanted to put this guy on trial," I say, looking disappointed. "That's why you asked me to stay, right?"

"That's . . . right."

"Then don't do anything stupid. Even if you just shoot him in the foot, he could die from loss of blood."

He looks up into the air. He registers the concept. He lowers the gun. He runs his other hand over his forehead.

"Yes. You have . . . a point, Counselor."

"Good," I say.

We all heave a sigh of relief. Especially Matrix, but I immediately shoot him an icy glare to make it clear to him that I've just saved his ass (forget about his foot), just in case he missed the point.

Matteo the deli counterman puts the bottle to his lips and takes a long drink, permission be damned. For that matter, Engineer Romolo Sesti Orfeo's reflexes are still too sluggish from the emotional roller coaster for him to scold Matteo over this minor oversight (actually I think that if I wanted to I could probably even disarm him: but there's no way I'm going to make things hard for myself just to do Matrix a favor).

Mulder reappraises me with his eyes, almost as if he'd just promoted me to the rank of fellow cop, thanks to this latest dramatic twist. I gesture to him to make himself scarce, seeing as his presence has produced undesired results. He complies, backing away, turning around, heading back down the aisle, and disappearing. I watch him turn into Pac-Man again on the monitor as he retraces his steps back through the grocery-store labyrinth.

"I believe I owe you my thanks, Counselor," says Engineer Romolo Sesti Orfeo, who has in the meanwhile completely regained his mental clarity.

"Actually," he corrects himself, speaking to Matrix, "you're the one who should thank him. If it wasn't for him, you'd be walking with a limp by now."

But Matrix, as I would have expected, just stares at the floor.

"Hurrah for gratitude," I observe.

Whereupon Matrix starts to say something, but I steal the ball.

"Ah, no, eh? Not another word out of you. Christ, they make you all with a cookie cutter, don't they, all you targets of the Anti-Mafia Law. You're professional criminals, you spend decades running from the law without being caught, they make movies about you and everything, and then the next thing you know you take a bullet to the forehead because you don't know when to keep your fucking mouth shut."

"But I . . ." he tries to object.

"That's enough. You've already caused enough trouble."

Engineer Romolo Sesti Orfeo smiles contentedly.

"You see why we needed a lawyer here?"

I say nothing, realizing how right he is. I just spoke to Matrix the way a lawyer speaks to his client. And to think I'd promised myself that I'd never defend these people again as long as I lived.

I'm about to try to justify myself somehow when on the monitor showing the front entrance a dramatically familiar figure appears, accompanied by an assistant equipped with a video camera.

The instant I recognize her, I swear, my heart stops; and at the same time I swing around, aghast, and stare at Engineer Romolo Sesti Orfeo, as if to ask him if this was the "television coverage" he was hoping for.

He looks at the screen, and then at me.

"*Mary Stracqualurso?*" he says in horror.

Now *that's* a name that we all know.

A silence of solidarity ensues.

Engineer Romolo Sesti Orfeo, with a heartbroken gesture signifying both total despair and complete resignation, picks up his remote control and activates the audio from the entrance.

Mary, in the meantime, has completed her negotiations with Mulder and Scully to start reporting, and she already has her microphone in hand, while the cameraman positions himself at the appropriate distance, first panning over the surrounding monitors and then focusing on her.

"*Buonciorno,*" she begins in a thick Neapolitan accent.

All four of us look exchange a look.

It's miracle I don't burst out laughing.

T
he guy at the reception desk must have thought he was making quite the impression of the sophisticated hotel clerk by not looking either of us in the face at all as we handed over, respectively, my driver's license and Alessandra Persiano's state ID card.

From behind her incredibly cool passion-violet-orange Alain Mikli glasses, Ale shot me a sidelong glance captioned: "So get a load of this guy."

"He must be a conscientious objector," I commented aloud.

Alessandra Persiano emitted a raspberry of a snicker confined entirely to her nose. For a moment the receptionist remained motionless, then he started up again, completed the necessary series of steps to assign a hotel room, and finally handed over the electronic key card, though not before he'd informed us (with his face turned in the opposite direction) that the *card* (that's right, he used the English word, with a pretentious mushy French *r* in place of a proper trilled Italian one) also turned the power in the room on and off, so we should be sure to remember to insert it in the appropriate slot.

This wasn't the first time that I'd encountered this misguided sense of discretion on the part of hoteliers. As if there were a rule book somewhere that stated that couples without luggage asking for a room must necessarily be having some kind of illicit affair. Maybe it's the time of day that arouses suspicion; who knows. But the reception desks of the world are crowded with clerks who act all discreet while ushering you through the check-in process, so that when they're done with you, you head for the elevator with your head bowed, perhaps with your wife hurrying after you, asking what's your rush.

Just in case you're wondering whether I didn't feel like a little bit of an idiot for agreeing to the idea of going to a hotel to rub up against each other when we could have just as easily holed up at home (and, as we say in Naples, enjoyed ourselves on the cheap and cheerful): yes, in fact, I felt like a complete idiot. In part because the room cost something like 190 euros, with breakfast included, one of those rooms with satellite TV that welcomes you by name when you walk in and a pseudo-Montblanc pen on display on the nightstand, the kind that the minute you see it you say to yourself: "I'm taking that with me."

But Alessandra Persiano had decided to indulge in a naughty whim to place a narrative seal on our recovery as a couple (you would not believe the emphasis that women put on narrativizing the events of their love lives), so there was no way I could safely object. Among other things these kinds of hotels, where they're always holding conferences on topics like *The Consequences of Secondhand Smoke on the Pathologies of the Middle Ear*, or else *Repersuading the Badly Advised Client: What Investment Scenarios?* with that distinctive patented technoluxe gloss, always get on my nerves after a while. Because instead of putting you at your ease, they force you to act like a government official traveling on business.

When you walk into those earth-tone rooms, where there's a button for everything and the piped-in chill-out music that you'd expect from a CD that comes free with a shrink-wrapped newsweekly like *L'Espresso* follows you into the bathroom along with the pervasive scent of lavender, you inevitably begin to assume certain preprogrammed behaviors, like taking off your jacket and rolling your shirtsleeves halfway up your forearm, brushing back your hair, and loosening your tie, even if you don't wear one.

It's a typical example of environmental mimicry, the kind that can temporarily turn you into a total asshole, so that if you don't take a moment to get your head screwed on straight again, you might end up walking into an elevator a short while later and running into an old childhood friend, who you haven't seen in thirty years and who now works there as a bell-boy, and pretend not to recognize him, just for instance.

Still, I have to admit that the sexual benefits obtained in return for the investment were well worth it, and then some.

The minute we shut the door behind us, Alessandra Persiano wrapped herself around me with such greediness that I didn't even have time to slip the electronic key card into the slot to turn on the electricity, and so, not knowing what to do with it, I held it in my hand for at least the first five minutes of copulation, until she noticed it, tore it from my grasp, and threw it over her shoulder with a defiant and ultra-erotic back-hand that seemed as if she'd done it just to say to me: "You poor middle-class idiot imprisoned in your minor-league insignificant preplanned mediocre life, in this moment of total spontaneity, what are you doing, clinging to reality? You're worrying about the key card for the light? What are you think-ing, that you might not be able to find it when we're done (i.e., you're already thinking about afterward)? Forget about the details, to hell with them, ignore them, they don't matter: we're about to destroy all that pointless nonsense right now."

A very nice speech, no doubt about it (at least I assume it was: because all Alessandra Persiano actually did was throw the key away, if we're being honest); in response to which, nonetheless, it would have been child's play for me to say: "So did we really need to spend 190 euros to perform this fabulous iconoclastic act?" But the sex was going so remarkably well that not even my dialectical autism could spoil it.

The really memorable thing is that, once we were done with the first session, and I mean immediately after, like maybe a minute later, not even enough time to go freshen up a little, Alessandra Persiano had already climbed back in the saddle on top of me (just for fun, really, playacting at being the insatiable nympho, I'm guessing) and I, thinking that I would need at least a couple of the delectable gianduia chocolates available on the nightstand to recharge my batteries, felt myself practically respond on command, astonished (because I'm astonished every single time) at how my old playfellow had just confirmed himself to be a stubborn freelancer, refusing to accept full-time positions and always doing more or less what he pleases (and in fact when she felt herself suddenly tipped off-balance by the upstanding handbrake, she commented, her eyes widening: "Oh, Vince', holy crap").

So anyway, if the purpose of that impulsive nooner was to capture and preserve the love that we'd rediscovered on the street and perhaps persuade it to stick around (because love, by its very nature, is something that comes and goes freely: the challenge is to trust it to return, and not pull any stupid-ass moves while it's away), I'm not saying we nailed it, but we were close.

But before delving into the story of the incident that just a short while later came close to sending everything to hell in a handbasket without any hope of remediation, I think it's appropriate to report the text of the postcoital conversation that began after the regulation five minutes of depression that overtakes virtually every woman after her second orgasm (when she turns over on her side with her back to you as if you'd somehow offended her, or else lies flat on her back staring at the ceiling, catatonic, and you lie there, waiting for who knows what, without any idea what the fuck to say now).

Ale: You know what just occurred to me?
Me: No, can I think it over for twenty minutes or so?
Ale: Idiot. Something that my mother told me a while ago.
Me: It's all fine, as long as it's strictly recreational.

Ale: You'll like this.

Me: If you tell me, I might.

Ale: All right then. When my parents met on the street, I mean whenever they ran into each other by chance, they'd fall in love all over again.

Me: Get out of here.

Ale: Really. And I'm not talking about who knows how long ago, they'd already been married for twenty-five years, give or take. They practically lived separate lives, at home they didn't pay all that much attention to each other, they talked no more than the union minimum required, they squabbled over trivial matters, the way people do when they can't stand looking at the same damned face day after day. And yet, this miracle would happen: all they had to do was meet by chance in the street and they'd start courting like a couple of kids. Mamma told me that a thrill would sweep over her, an urge to go somewhere and have lunch together, to have him take her to pick out a dress, to go back home and get along.

Me: What about your dad?

Ale: Same thing! Mamma says that he got all awkward and funny and clumsy; he'd ask if he could walk with her, if she had any other plans for the day; if he had plans of his own, errands or appointments, he'd immediately cancel them . . . in other words, he became heartbreakingly solicitous and loving, like a young man courting and afraid he'll be told no.

Me: Hey, your eyes are starting to glisten.

Ale: It's just that it strikes me as so . . . rare. Like a blessing reserved for the two of them alone.

Me: That's true. But did they run into each other by chance all that often?

Ale: Well, I don't know about often. It happened occasionally, I guess. But it was something completely spontaneous, you know what I mean? Not only did they fall in love, they acted as if they'd just fallen in love for the first time.

Me: So what you're telling me is that you and I just made a remake of the way your parents used to fall in love in the street.

Ale: Well, yes. More or less. But I only realized it just now, when I saw you on the street before I wasn't thinking about it at all. And . . . and there's something about it that I like. It's like a bridge between me and my folks. That is, I meant to say, between my folks and us.

Me: Eh, I'm pretty sure that if my father had run into my mother in the middle of the day, the most he would have said to her would have been: "Are you sure that Vincenzo went to school today?"

It was at that exact instant, just as Alessandra Persiano—after the moment of astonishment that always comes over her after I've spouted one of my more memorable pieces of bull-shit—was about to burst out laughing, that the sound of another text message coming through on my cell phone greeted our ears.

Uh-oh, I thought.

I lay there frozen, stretched out on that fucking 190-euro-a-night bed, mentally kicking myself for having forgotten once again to turn off or silence that miserable fucking spy of a phone, while Alessandra Persiano's profile took on the suspicious angularity of solid evidence.

"Message for you," she said, definitely hostile. "Another one."

"Eh?"

"What's wrong, didn't you hear the chime?"

"Ah, my cell phone, you mean? Sure."

"Well, why don't you check and see who's writing you?"

"I don't feel like getting up."

Wrong answer: because immediately, as if I'd spoon-fed her the answer she'd been waiting for, she started to get up herself.

"Okay, I'll get it for you."

I promptly grabbed her arm.

Another obvious screw-up.

She dropped her gaze to my offending hand, then looked up at my face and stared at me, glassy-eyed.

"Come on, who gives a damn about that," I said, trying to pull her toward me, but I must have seemed absolutely ridiculous in that attempt to sidetrack her. "It's so nice to just lie here together."

She pulled away, with a studied slowness, even.

"Do you not want me to know who's texting you?"

I faked a weak, ambiguous laugh, then answered like a certified moron.

"What are you talking about?"

Silence.

Then I tried stroking her hair.

She jerked her head to one side.

There are various types of disdain. But the kind that sneaks into lovers' arguments I consider to be the most detestable of all.

"Hey," I said, with a pathetic smile. "I didn't know you were so suspicious."

She went on staring at me, chilly and inquisitorial, kneeling on the bed, wonderfully indifferent to the nakedness of her magnificent breasts which were now facing me like two no-entry signs.

At this point I had no option but to bluff.

So I bluffed.

"Okay, Detective Persiano: would you mind getting my cell phone out of my jacket, and while you're at it, could you also read me the text message that just came in, just to save me the trouble?"

You know when you put a DVD into your DVD player to watch a certain scene and you hit fast-forward and click through to 32x to zip straight to the point in the movie you want?

Well, that's the exact speed at which my whole life passed in front of my eyes as Alessandra Persiano pondered whether to take the high road (the option I was hoping for) or to put me to the test.

"You're such a child," I shamefully stammered when, a second later, she went for the second option.

I came close to begging her not to do it, as she stood up and grabbed my jacket.

She pulled my cell phone out of my jacket pocket.

She flipped it open.

Stretched out on that bed, I was already a dead man.

So I couldn't believe what I was seeing when she narrowed her eyes, opened them wide, went momentarily apneic in disbelief, and then exploded in laughter so hard that she practically folded over in half.

"What's gotten into you?" I asked, sitting up straight.

But she couldn't stop. She went on reading and laughing as if the cell phone were showing a comedy. She'd entered into the usual endless loop of interactive hypnosis for the sake of ha-has in which the more you look at the subject of the ridiculous situation, the harder you laugh, as if you somehow couldn't wrap your mind around the fact of its existence, and so you go on staring at it to fix it in your memory before it vanishes.

I almost had to shout to make myself heard.

"Who the fuck is it from, if you don't mind my asking?"

She replied by sort of spitting and grabbing her belly with one hand.

"I don't . . . know . . . pffh . . . it's a number without a name . . . hee, hee, hee!"

With tears streaming down her face coming dangerously close to falling with every step, she came over to me and held the phone scant inches from my face.

Don't ask me why, Filippo, but I need to see you tonight. Please, come by whenever you're free. No matter what time it is.

It was as if someone had turned the air conditioner up as high as it would go.

Probably the biggest piece of dumb luck of my whole life.

I could hardly believe it.

I blessed my innate laziness for not having put that idiot woman's name in my directory.

I looked around.

No sign of the angel.

"*Filippo?*" I said, playing the part (I suspect badly, partly because I threw in a little fake-baffled smile; but Alessandra Persiano was too red in the face from laughing to catch me).

Even I felt like laughing at the thought that that idiot had been so simpleminded in her attempt to make me jealous that she'd actually included the name of her imaginary (or perhaps real: fat lot I cared) lover, thus unintentionally rescuing me.

Taking big gulps of air between the hiccups that were finally subsiding, Alessandra Persiano got back up on the bed and dragged herself on her knees to my side, wiping away her tears with her pinkies.

"Hey, Filippo, how's it going?" she said, intending to milk a while longer the effects of what she thought was a misunderstanding.

"Ha, ha, funny you," I replied, with a barefaced nerve that on its own deserved a Nobel Prize.

"What are you doing tonight, hee, hee, hee, are you going to come by?"

"Sure, sure, go ahead and joke about it," I added, in a hypocritical crescendo that makes me shiver just to think about it. "But what if I'd really just gotten a text message from my lover instead of an obvious wrong number? Eh? Then what would I have told you? Ah?"

"What an idiot you are, Vince'."

"No, what an idiot *you* are, to think another woman was texting me."

At that point, the angel appeared. Right there, between the curtains and the TV. Arms crossed and right foot tapping on the hardwood floor.

"Jesus God, you really are a filthy pig," he said.

"Nice hotel, eh?" I replied telepathically.

"Well, if you want to know the truth, it seemed like you were acting a little defensive, earlier," Alessandra Persiano admitted.

"Just because I wanted to stay cuddled up with you in bed? You're so dishonest, you women."

The busybody angel slapped a hand to his forehead and shook his head in disgust.

"Oh. But wait," Alessandra Persiano said at a certain point, suddenly very serious.

"But wait what?"

"Nothing, it's just that . . . I was thinking about that Filippo. I wonder what kind of stallion he must be for her to be begging him like that."

"What?"

She didn't answer. She was smiling, as if she'd just had a clever idea.

"Hey, Persiano," I scolded her in feigned horror, "I don't even know who you are anymore."

"You know what we should do? We should call up the girl right now; that is, I'll call her, which works better, and I'll say: Listen, I just got this text message, would you mind giving me the right number for Filippo? No, you see, it's just that you texted my boyfriend by accident, and he's the opposite of Filippo, as far as those things go he's not exactly a . . . Get it? Hee, hee, hee."

It took me a few moments for it to sink in that I'd actually heard her right.

"Get what? Fuck you!"

"Come on," and she tried to grab my cell phone (which at that point I wouldn't have surrendered even under armed threat), "can't you imagine how funny it would be?"

Ooooh, we'd die laughing, I thought.

"Just forget about this brilliant idea, okay?"

"But why? Come *on*!"

"Because number one, it's a prank only an asshole would pull; two, it's in bad taste; three, I don't see why you have to call from *my* phone, if you don't mind."

During the pause that followed, I realized I'd just put my foot in it.

"You're right. I'll call from mine. Come on, give me the number!"

And she stood up to get her purse.

Jesus, what an idiot I am.

I'm absolutely positive that just then my temperature must have been 103 degrees.

"Listen, just drop it, okay?"

"But why do you want to spoil my fun?"

"You want to know why?"

"Right. Why?"

I didn't have the slightest idea what the fuck to say, but suddenly, in the midst of complete darkness, I glimpsed a shaft of light (later I understood why: the angel, nauseated by my lackluster performance, had left the room).

"Because . . . Sorry, what makes you think the text was necessarily sent by a woman?"

Her expression suddenly changed.

"Oh. I hadn't thought of that."

Then she went into a trance.

At that point I realized I'd gotten off scot-free. The mere

thought of hearing a male voice answer the call, of intruding on a form of intimacy she knew nothing about, was enough to dissuade her from her planned prank.

Like many other members of the female sex, Alessandra Persiano tends to be very considerate of gay people. She's horrified at the idea of seeming indelicate.

And so, problem solved.

Later I decided to go by and see my mother-in-law (as long as Alagia had roped me into becoming her home caregiver, I might as well start right away).

We were in the kitchen, me, her, and Miorita (her caregiver), when another text message came in.

Text messages are always suspicious if you fail to read them right away. In fact Assunta and Miorita exchanged sidelong glances. Whereupon I let out a pro-forma sigh of annoyance and pulled out my phone (though I'd have gladly ignored it, considering all the cell phone trouble I'd had to deal with over the course of that day).

I read it.

I probably betrayed a slight sense of panic, but the text was far too demented not to prompt at least some minimal facial twitches.

Instead of putting the cell phone back in my jacket pocket, I laid it down on the table, facedown.

Then I sat there for a little while, waiting to decide what to do next.

"Your problem," Ass said, catching me off-guard (which is something I've always hated because, no matter how you look at it, it's not fair play to catch someone off-guard like that), "is that you're still trying to have a sex life."

"Eh?" I asked, with the astonishment of someone caught red-handed.

"Just think of it as a routine, a grind," she argued, completely nonchalant, taking it for granted that I knew what she was talking about. "After all, that's the movement in question. You'll see how much easier it comes to you."

"I don't see what you're basing this fine piece of advice on," I retorted while mentally treading water. "Leaving aside the fact that sex and life are two very different concepts."

She smiled.

"You need to use the bathroom, don't you?"

"What?" I replied, truly caught off-guard now.

"Well, don't you?"

"Umm . . . actually, yes, but how did you know that?"

"Because you have a burning need to write back to whatever young woman just wrote to you."

I blushed.

"Who are you, my jealous girlfriend?"

"Oh, don't be ridiculous. It's just that I can't stand seeing people make fools of themselves."

"It's not what you think."

"Then let me read it."

"Sorry?"

"I'm not your girlfriend, right? So you have no reason to make up stories."

"All right."

I grabbed my cell phone, opened my text messages, and handed it over to her, like a robot.

Even now I can't believe I did it.

She read the text.

No expression whatsover.

She handed me back my cell phone.

I reread the text, as if I couldn't remember it.

Well? You're not going to say anything about the "wrong number" message I sent you on purpose?

We sat in silence for something like a couple of minutes.

Two minutes without talking is a long, long time when you're in the same room as another person.

"How long has this been going on?"

"Nothing's going on."

"Then I guess now you're going to tell me that it only happened the one time."

"That's right."

Silence.

"Okay, three times."

Silence.

"Five, maybe six, okay?"

"Was it really necessary?"

"These things are never really necessary. They just happen."

She looked at me as if to say: "Huh."

"Now you must be feeling pretty full of yourself, having discovered you're so intelligent without even knowing it."

I came that close to blushing.

I told you, this woman is embarrassing.

"A little."

Pause.

"You're a dickhead."

"You think I don't know that?"

"No, but world class, seriously."

"What makes you so sure of that?"

"Because only a world-class dickhead would be sent a text message like that."

Truer words were never spoken.

I was about to tell her how right she was when, looking around (since I couldn't bring myself to look her in the eye), I happened to spot a bottle I recognized.

"That's the one I gave you, if I'm not mistaken."

"Mm-hm."

"Well, there's quite a bit missing."

"So?"

"So I'm a dickhead and you're some kind of genius?"

She thought it over for a moment.

"Am I supposed to be saving my virginity for the chemo?"

I stared at her, not knowing what to say.

Then, as if on a delayed fuse, I burst out laughing.

And so did she.

After we'd been sitting there for a while wiping away our tears, I felt obliged to point out to her that concerning the matter of one's so-called sex life, I'd actually spent a lot of time thinking about it, and I'd come to the self-taught conclusion that they really were two entirely different concepts, that they really didn't play well together.

She told me that that was fantastic, that she'd been losing sleep over that question for years, and that she had absolutely wanted someone to explain it to her before she died.

The Banality of Dogs

I n a way—which I'll explain later—I like Mary Stracqualurso. Anyone who's encountered her unmistakable
prose even once in his or her life will, I believe, be able to
sympathize.

When I'm channel-surfing through the local TV networks
and I run into her in the middle of a guest spot on a news
broadcast or in the act of bestowing a pearl of wisdom on a
working beat reporter, who extends his microphone to her in
the belief that he's drinking at the fount of a venerable old
glory of Italian journalism, there's nothing I can do, I have to
listen right through to the end.

I delight in her goatish ignorance, the way she's chronically
misinformed on any and all subjects, the inurbane diction that
is so distinctly her own, the chilling nonchalance with which
she says *d* when she means *t*, *c* when she means *g*, *f* when she
means *v*, *p* when she means *b*, and *z* when she means *s*.

I am filled with an unidentifiable but pleasant lassitude in
the presence of the disarming obviousness of her opinions, the
mediocre moralism, the baseless conceit with which she will
pontificate on any topic without knowing anything about it,
the saliva-sprays that accompany her bilabial occlusive conso-
nants, often forcing her interlocutor to move out of their range
with cranial jerks that are as sudden as they are ridiculous (she
has certain unresolved issues with her dental adhesive), the fact
that she thinks herself irrestrainably amusing and wise (a conviction that she bases essentially on the fact that when she

makes a wisecrack she laughs at it herself, often even before saying it), the congenital cowardice, the way she never speaks the name of anyone powerful, unless it's to kiss an ass that may one day prove useful to her.

And for the five minutes following her performance I sit there crying crocodile tears in front of the television set, satisfied and responsible for the harm I do to myself, a little bit like a diabetic secretly binging on Nutella.

The constitutive torment driving my perversion is the fact that I can't understand such a phenomenon. I watch Mary Stracqualurso to figure out if she really exists, and how she interacts with reality.

But beyond (and even more important than) the metaphysical inquiry, there's a part of me (of all of us—and there are many of us—who are incapable of resisting the fascinating impunity of the illiterate), more instinctive and immediate, that responds symptomatologically to the Stracqualursian stimulus. All it takes for me is an "In that gase," an "Exacdly," an "Obfiously," and I'm glued to the screen and turning up the volume, dropping everything else I might have been doing at the time.

Don't think I'm an impassioned fan of trash TV. I hate trash TV. I don't have a taste for bad taste. I'm clear-minded enough to realize that if, the minute I come across Mary Stracqualurso on TV, I stop watching any other program and stick with her, it must mean I like her.

Even those who are sublime connoisseurs of trash TV actually like trash TV, but they just won't admit it. They're like closeted gay guys who pretend they like to watch mainstream porn films but concentrate on the cocks.

Now, if I don't like something, I just try to avoid it. The sublime connoisseurs of trash TV, the ones who systematically critique the contestants on *Big Brother*, are transformed into editors of the Accademia della Crusca Italian Dictionary as soon as the moderator of a talk show hesitates in his use of a subjunctive, issue report cards on the etiquette of the rich and famous, judge the way they hold a fork or match the colors of their clothes—those are people I consider assholes.

Let's be perfectly clear: if I hear a public speaker slip on a verbal banana peel, I'm the first one to laugh. But I'm not an illiterate-hunter; I'm not that sadistic.

Among other things, if we're being completely honest, if you want to critique someone—even if it's a contestant on *Big Brother*—then you have to have accomplished something in your own life. And if you take a look at the average profile of a fan of trash TV, nine times out of ten you'll find a frustrated member of the petty bourgeoisie, with a family that depends on him but who is in turn dependent on his family (frequently on his wife), devoid of talent but generically cultured and educated, with artistic and/or intellectual aspirations that were predictably shipwrecked, and who, in response to the question: "I'm sorry, but what work is it that you said you do?" plunges into a tragic, dazed silence that he immediately however overcomes, piling on self-definitions that leave the hapless listener in the most claustrophobic state of awkward embarrassment.

Like a maniac throwing open his raincoat to offer unfortunate passersby the unasked-for spectacle of the pitable attributes he possesses, the impassioned fan of trash culture will demonstrate a thorough expertise on the topic of bad taste (especially with regard to television), in a desperate attempt to avenge himself on his biography. In other words, he suffers from a bad case of failure mange. Even though the facts (and especially his vital statistics) tell us the opposite, he is convinced that he is artistically gifted. A little bit like old people who feel young inside. He's attempted various careers, always keeping one in reserve as an alibi (politician and, in second rank, journalist; rock star and, in second rank, music critic; poet and, in second rank, author; director and, in second rank, TV writer; and the list could go on and on), but the truth, pure and simple, is that he doesn't know how to do a blessed fucking thing.

And it is precisely when faced with this elementary discovery that those suffering from failure mange perform their most memorable acrobatic moves, narrating their own failures as a demonstration of multifaceted artistic versatility, a generic aptitude at a Little Bit of Everything; much like those talentless musicians who appear each time with a different instrument but don't really know how to play any of them.

As a result of this unfounded belief in a talent waiting to be specified, the object of fame to which those afflicted with failure mange aspire becomes practically incidental. They'd do anything—from neorealist film to cabaret—if an offer came in.

From this point of view, between them and a modern *velina*, or showgirl, for whom a bit part in an Italian-made Christmas screwball comedy and a cabinet-level position as a head of a ministry are equivalent career objectives, there is no difference. But a modern *velina* has recently turned eighteen and can afford to sport a miniskirt: not so for those suffering from failure mange.

Those afflicted with failure mange wind up spending their lives waiting for the opportunity that will change everything. They think that, if they were just given a chance, they could take on the world. But because the world shows not the slightest interest in them, they attack the world on the Internet, publishing (that's exactly what they call it, when they pontificate on an online message board, convinced that that is the appropriate verb to describe the activity to which they devote themselves with such passion) pitiless reviews on topics having to do with every realm of human knowledge, from movies to television, from poetry to literature, from politics to everyday life, from techno to opera, and interior decorating to youth fashion (those with failure mange declare themselves to be formidable experts in this field in particular, even though they never spend any time with young people, and for that matter why on earth would young people ever want to spend time with them?); but given the fact that their desperate attempts make no impression save in the fraternity of online losers, each of whom they know individually (because those who have fallen into disgrace always seem ready to underwrite pacts of entente), the only option left to them is to go in search of wingnuts who at least, in comparison with them, have the defect of not speaking the Italian language correctly.

When we speak of Mary Stracqualurso, on the other hand, we must move past the mystifications of trash TV and the pathological deviations of failure mange and instead delve into a phenomenon that, as I said at the outset, truly smacks of the inexplicable.

Maria Antonietta Stracqualurso (stage name, Mary Stracqua) is a masterpiece of evolution. A contemporary classic. Living proof (complete with a speech impediment) that it's possible to carve out a niche for oneself (or in her case, actually thrive for years) in the garden of local journalism and culture, even if you're functionally illiterate.

Because Mary is not merely ignorant in this day and age, a carefree era that has by and large dismissed ignorance as an issue. She was already ignorant—and this is what counts most—in a time when being ignorant counted. When culture had a shared meaning. When the inability to speak proper Italian constituted a stumbling block that kept people from teaching, running for elective office, speaking in public, and writing.

Even in those times, she managed to infest newspaper city rooms, imposing her terrifying syntax on the reading public without anyone raising their voice in objection, without a single self-proclaimed public intellectual making the slightest effort to halt her misbegotten plans for expansion; even then,

I was saying, she managed to make her presence felt at any public occasion where she could make her hulking, ill-clad figure known, in the self-engineered role of social crusader, blazing a shining path for later generations of illiterates who justifiably wondered: "If she can be a journalist, why not me?"

From this point of view, Mary Stracqua was an early pioneer of the modern shift with regard to the very concept of the career path, whereby, as we now realize, it is possible to establish oneself as a prominent public figure even in the complete absence of talent or skill.

Now, however, if the winner of *Big Brother* steps onto the public stage on a strictly prospective basis (many of the competitors on that immensely popular show, in fact, get nothing more than a walk-on role on a TV series or two or perhaps an appearance on a talk show, and most of them are quickly forgotten), Mary is an example of how one can exercise the noble profession of journalism without having even the vaguest notion of what a news story is, how to put one together, and how to broadcast it.

Today, Maestra Stracqualurso has decades of experience behind her, and she still wields considerable power in the cultural circles—and I use the term "cultural" with scare quotes and due reservations—of this city (in part because, obviously, not only is she a journalist, she is also a playwright, a poetess, a novelist, and no doubt other things as well—it's odd that she hasn't yet been given a tenured professorship at the university, now that I think about it), and she does so with impeccable frequency.

There's not a local television news show or radio station that doesn't reach out to her at least a couple of times a week for her commentary on current events. And she promptly responds, with a paternalistic egotism that she doesn't even bother to conceal, interlarding her bloodcurdling pronouncements with such violent attacks visited upon the proper use of mood, tense, and agreement, with such a cascade of adverbs chosen and employed with ham-handed incompetence, that you ask yourself—but seriously, almost hoping for an answer, since this is something that matters to you on a personal level—for what un-fucking-fathomable reason does such an obviously inept and unlettered donkey continue to enjoy the use of public forums, where she is allowed to offend the intelligence of her fellow man with complete impunity.

Show up at any academic conference ("*gonference,*" she'd say), lecture, exhibition, paid author appearance, election campaign dinner, or press conference, and there you'll find Mary Stracqualurso.

Little does it matter whether or not she actually received an invitation (if she did not, she will take umbrage and invite herself, and you can rest assured that she will always find someone happy to give up his or her front-row seat for her): she'll be there no matter what, it wouldn't be the same without her; Mary Stracqua is the city's historical memory, a city that will never be able to separate her from itself (another of her rust-proof convictions is that nothing happens without her knowing about it).

But the most deeply inexplicable mystery concerns the atmosphere of collective intimidation and *omertà* that Mary has managed to create around herself, nipping in the bud any possibility of dissent. In this city that always looks the other way there is not a journalist, university professor, doctor, lawyer, engineer, or even failed artist who's had the nerve to tell her to her face what everyone thinks, and that is that she's an illiterate bum, incapable of stringing together three coherent words (much less of putting together an actual news story), organically servile with any representative of actual power with whom she comes into contact, whether it's her condo board or the city council in town hall, and moreover that the news guild membership card that she carries with her says a great deal about the usefulness of what we smilingly call professional orders. Everyone, formally, respects her. And everyone, pragmatically, condones her. They all let her live, make her appearances, offer her commentary. Occasionally (even now), they let her write.

I know a couple of managing editors of local papers who, after being subjected to her weekly barrage of phone calls requesting publication of an editorial she's scrawled, organize collective newsroom readings of her articles, where the staff split their sides with laughter for days at a time (some jot down the finest savagings of the language and then send them out by email, chain-letter-style); after that, however, once the great author's spelling has been cleaned up and her ideas organized into something resembling a coherent whole, obviously, they always publish it.

See the way it works? We laugh at Mary Stracqua, and at the countless small and mid-sized parasites like her who infest the newsrooms of our nation's press, the political secreteriats, the ministries, the television stations, the universities; but the truth is that we are all accountable for their survival. We allow them to set an example, instead of quashing that example. We perpetuate this collective intellectual conformism, this cultural hypocrisy that allows us, like the little professors of trash media, to point and jeer at the ignorant when they can't hear us. We're tolerant and accommodating. And when we stand by and watch them, we are taking part in an interactive spectacle. We're tacitly approving a disgrace.

Look at what we've done, in our small way, to ruin the world.

My mother-in-law, and who could blame her, enjoys making fun of me, but I really had given some serious thought to the whole issue of sex and life.

And since the last thing I want is for anyone to think that I'm a person who says things just to hear the sound of his own voice, I think it's best to take a few moments right now to clear up my point of view on the topic.

If anyone ever asks you a question that contains the phrase "sex life," what you're going to think they've asked you, regardless of how they put it and even of their actual intentions, is: "How long has it been since the last time you got lucky?"

And right after that: "Do you think there is any real chance that you'll get lucky within a reasonable period of time, starting now?"

The immediate problem posed by questions about one's sex life is disarmingly materialistic: Do you have sex? Do you not have sex? How often?

In the presence of sex, we become disgustingly quantum, and that's that. And when sex is followed by life—forget about it.

Sex isn't a form of life. It's a kind of heart attack (and in fact sometimes you die having sex; and there are people who hope that's how they'll go, if they have any say in how they're going to meet their maker).

Having a sex life means, if we're being completely truthful, dying every so often.

*

One of the last times I ran into Nives, at a parapharmacy downtown (she was right there when I walked in, or I would have avoided her like the plague, since I was already something like two weeks behind in my alimony payments), I was with a female friend of mine who needed to buy I can't remember what (by the way, it's unbelievable how many parapharmacies there are around the city these days).

Let me point out immediately that there's never been anything between me and this female friend; in fact, she's just a friend who happens to be female. But she's one of those female friends who, when they're with you, behave as if they were your girlfriend, you know the type? Like they'll walk along beside you hooking pinkie fingers with you, they'll brush the crumbs off your lips after you've gone to get breakfast in a café and you've had a croissant, they give you a quick kiss when they show up and another one when they leave.

It should also be noted that these female friends, when they're having trouble with their husbands or live-in boyfriends, are likely to be willing to have sex with you (three times, tops, otherwise you ruin the friendship), but this wasn't the case here, in part because I was (more or less) with Alessandra Persiano (who, if you know what I mean . . .), and my female friend had been in a happy relationship with some guy for a couple of years now.

And Nives, who has busted my balls as long as I've known her with this piece of mythology that when two people are in the same room she can instantly tell whether or not they're an item, even if they don't so much as say a word to each other, these things ought to be obvious to her trained eye, she is a psychologist, after all.

But the minute my friend and I walked into the parapharmacy, she flew into a veritable rage of jealousy and put on a display of boorish behavior so callous and offensive that even now I blush in shame at the thought.

Like the very first thing she did was to snicker openly and allusively in a really repulsive manner, cc'ing everyone present, then she said hello to me but not to my friend, and before leaving she brushed a little dandruff off the shoulder of my jacket (as if she were still free to indulge in such personal and intimate gestures), and finally took her leave with a phrase so corrosive that the Mafia could use it to dispose of corpses, which ran verbatim:

"I see that your sex life is enjoying a sharp uptick, my compliments."

And I, in the presence of this masterpiece of gratuitous commentary (do you by any chance see a connection between my sex life and the fact that she ran into me in a parapharmacy in the company of a female friend? I mean, it's not as though we were buying condoms: but then, so what if we were?), instead of retorting that upticks of that kind had long since ceased to be any of her business, and that in fact it was no concern of hers with whom I had said upticks, I found myself, incomprehensibly, reflecting, then and there, on the spot, on the nature of the phrase "sex life," as if it were more than I could do to overlook its fundamental inaccuracy.

These unscheduled insights into words or groups of words do occur from time to time; from one moment to the next they mistake you for an Italian language detective and just throw up their hands and turn themselves in, reporting themselves for their inadequacies; and you just stand there looking at them, thinking to yourself that people, yourself included, on the whole just operate on trust when it comes to everyday language: especially when dealing with concepts in common (ab)use that sound particularly chic, such as for instance the much-discussed "sex life."

What makes the two concepts incompatible—if you're

interested to know the conclusions I came to in the parapharmacy while my ex-wife was harassing me and my friend with her illegitimate jealousy—is that sex, unlike life, always entails an elevated degree of awareness, for as long as it lasts. Life, on the other hand, is something we enjoy by and large unconsciously. In the sense that it's something we take for granted until something happens that threatens it. Like the first law of motion, also known as the law of inertia (or Newton's first law), which states that a body will remain in its state of rest or uniform linear motion as long as external forces do not intervene to modify that state.

The fact that an external force can modify a body's state of rest or uniform linear motion (which are both states that closely resemble life itself) doesn't mean, as far as the body knows, that it won't maintain that state for all time, because as long as that state persists, it will have to tolerate it, waiting for it to come to an end.

You can't exist in a given state (in other words, you can't live your life) if you're continuously worrying that from one moment to the next an external force might very well intervene and modify that state. In order to live (that is, to maintain a state) you need to cultivate the illusion that the state in question will last for all time, or else be unaware that the state is temporary (which amounts to the same thing).

To accept the provisional nature of all states, then, means, in point of fact, to use another very chic transitive verb (one that my ex-wife in fact uses frequently), that one must suppress it, that is, behave as if you've forgotten that life (that is, the state of rest or uniform linear motion) is provisional; which is to say, hold infinity in the palm of your hand (I think I must have heard that somewhere).

In other words: we take life for granted. And if there's one thing we never take for granted, on the other hand (and when I say never I mean *never*, not even during times when it seems like you might finally be able to stop worrying about it), that would in fact be sex.

Sex—let's not act jaded about it—is always an event. It is to life as the external force is to the state of rest or uniform linear motion in the first law of motion. It modifies a body's condition (it's better if it's more than one; but two bodies is definitely the minimum for any serious consideration), it throws it into turmoil and regenerates it. Most of all, it cheers a body up. Which is the reason there are so many grouchy people out and about.

What makes people who aren't getting laid resentful and intractable (people who are always pissed off at everyone, who snap at you even if you just ask them what time it is) isn't even the lack of sexual activity per se, but the fact that, by not getting laid, people who aren't getting laid remain irremediably identical to how they always are, and they can't reconcile themselves to this continual unchangingness. Because after all—let's admit it—sameness is a condition that works fine when it comes to egalitarianism and equal rights, but when applied to oneself it's a tremendous pain in the ass. So much so that sex, even if you always do it in the same way (leaving aside eventual variations), is never the same. There is no such thing as reproducible screwing. The screwing may be better, the screwing may be worse (even screwing that doesn't turn out well is never the same from one time to another), but you'll never be able to produce an instance of screwing that is identical to another one.

Among other things, there are tons of people who aren't getting laid at any given time. But, really, a *lot*. In fact, as far as I know, they constitute a majority. Which strikes me as another excellent reason for rejecting the theory of the sex life, which at this point would become a privilege accorded only to the few, while the great thing about life is that life is a right accorded to all.

In other words, there's not much to be done about it: if you want to keep from being the same as you always have been, what is required is the intervention of an external sexual force, which from an organic point of view also serves a literally Newtonian purpose. In fact, the immediate and most unmistakable symptom of sexual desire, especially male sexual desire, is the interruption of that state of rest (so much so that on those occasions when that state is not interrupted, you're sure to remember the day).

But it's clear that women have their own ways of being roused from a state of rest. And it's a wonderful thing when they are. Because after that it won't be long before the motion begins, a motion that, while uniformly sussultatory instead of rectilinear, is still perfectly acceptable.

When we left the parapharmacy, I explained all these considerations to my friend, because I was afraid that unless I repeated it all aloud I'd probably wind up forgetting it.

She listened to every last word, nodding with conviction at the crucial points.

Then she told me that she couldn't understand how I could have thought such a thing while my ex-wife was treating me in that abominable manner in the parapharmacy, and in any case it seemed to her that I did the right thing by divorcing her, because there was no doubt about it: she was a tremendous asshole.

Whereupon an enormous wave of sadness washed over me at the thought that Assunta, by refusing to see Nives during such a difficult phase in her illness, had in fact expressed an opinion very much in line with my friend's view of her.

And as far as I'm concerned, no matter how many excellent reasons you might have for refusing to see another person you've known all your life—in this case, a mother and her daughter—there's always something about it that doesn't really add up. A faint whiff of bullshit.

The kind of bullshit that saddens everyone's lives a little.

Never Judge an Amateur Game by the Positions Assigned To The Participants

The attire that Mary Stracqualurso chose for the special edition broadcast: a mutt-colored light-wool skirt suit; a patterned blouse with an unwatchable slit between the buttons right in the middle of the tits (through which, even from here, you can just make out a hint of lace); an Hermès scarf wrapped around her neck loosely like a tie, as if she'd just reported a two-hour piece from Baghdad; a bad dye job with visible roots; pearl earrings; ballet flats that a teenage girl might wear; and a fountain pen poking out of her jacket pocket.

From the controlled excitement she adopts as she reports the news she must feel very CNN right now. And, in fact, once—I swear—I actually heard her say on TV: "My colleague Peter Arnett" (who is, for those who might not remember, the journalist who not only won a Pulitzer Prize in 1966 for his reporting in Vietnam, but became very famous twenty or so years ago for his coverage of the Gulf War for, you guessed it, CNN).

"We interrubt our reculARLY zcheduled procramming for an extraordinary edition of the news," she announces; and then a dramatic pause ensues.

"'Our regularly scheduled programming'?" I dismiss the phrase mentally with the speed of an old maid commenting on the courtyard below. "Our normal home-shopping shows, is what you mean."

God, I can be cutting when I want to be.

"I'm sbeaking to you from the vront entrance of the Migliaro subermarget," the dean of local reporters says, finally getting to the point, "on the wesdern outsgirds of the zity, where, as var as we gan dell, a gitnabbing appears to have daken blace a short dime aco."

Engineer Romolo Sesti Orfeo, Matteo the deli counterman, and I turn to look at one another, wondering just what the "wesdern outsgirds" might be (mouthing the question just slightly out of sync), and then almost immediately exchange an "Ah, yes," nodding our heads.

"Thus var," Mary goes on, accompanying herself with the leer of the incorrigible joker who can't keep herself from getting off a line, even when she knows it's out of place, "nothing particularly oritchinal, if you forgive me the choke, ha ha."

We are all thrown into a state of bewilderment similar to that caused by minor earthquakes, when you look around in search of other eyes that might share your suspicions (in the monitor, in fact, I lock eyes with the scandalized visages of Mulder and Scully).

Matrix stares at Mary Stracqua on the TV screen, his face twisted and his distress showing in every fiber of his body, as if he was having a tremendously hard time translating, or else simply couldn't believe his own ears, or else was mortified at the realization that the story of his first (I'd have to guess) live onscreen capture should have been entrusted to the specimen in question, or perhaps all three.

I sympathize with his dilemma, and I have to remind myself how much I hate him in order to tamp down a feeling of fellowship.

We hardly have the time to recover from our astonishment before TeleCessPool's Pulitzer Prize–winning reporter goes on to finish her thought.

". . . If it weren't vor the vact," she goes on, savoring the imminent scoop, "that the gitnabbing is still under way, and apove all that we can actually proadcast it live, since it was gap-tured from the very beginning by the subermarget's system of videosurfeilliance."

Look at her: her nostrils are flaring with satisfaction.

"In this kind of store, as you know, the glosed-circuid monidors are gondinually vilming: which means that the gitnabbing was regorded by the system, and so it won't even be necessary to infesticate to find the griminals, and the bolice will vind that half their work is already done, ha ha."

In the glacial pause that follows I find that thus far, all things considered, aside from that masterpiece of fine taste concerning the lack of originality of this hostage taking, the ridiculous diction, the wisdom of the closing statement, and the accompanying side dishes of idiotic giggles, she has not yet said anything inaccurate, journalistically speaking.

Instinctively, I triangulate once again with Matteo the deli counterman and Engineer Romolo Sesti Orfeo, finding confir-mation of my impression in their faces. And so, when Maestra Stracqua resumes, we find ourselves all a bit more willing to lis-ten to what she says.

"It cives the imbression of peing in an American mofie, with the pankrobbers locked inside the pank and the bolice outside necotiating to free the hostatches."

"Oh, how Pindaric," I comment inwardly.

If we were in an American movie, by now the building would be surrounded by dozens of police cars, with sharp-shooters posted on nearby roofs, black-and-yellow police tape cordoning off an extensive surrounding area, a screaming crowd split up into sympathizers and those who would like to see the hostage takers locked up, and the most popular TV net-works of the country competing for live coverage, and Engineer Romolo Sesti Orfeo would already be negotiating with a hard-bitten cop played by someone like Harvey Keitel or Tommy Lee Jones, who would have already told him to remain calm more than once, and made a certain number of fairly compromising personal commitments in exchange for a rapid and bloodless resolution.

But this is reality (which is like a movie with poor production values and a screenplay written by dilettantes), and so all we have to entertain us, at least for the present moment, is a pair of carabinieri awaiting reinforcements and Mary Stracqua behind the microphone.

"The divverence," Peter Arnett's Neapolitan colleague continues, carefully lowering her eyelids to half-mast (I know that inspired hesitation: she's preparing to deliver an authorial insight!), "which chust coes to show how reality always outsdribs the imatchination . . ."

Wooow! I say to myself.

I practically burst into applause.

Engineer Romolo Sesti Orfeo (I'm not kidding) mops his forehead, as if listening to this idiot talk were physically exhausting.

". . . is that in this gase we gan follow in real dime what's coing on inside the store, so it seems reasonaple to think that this is politigally motifated."

. . . Oookay, I think to myself, with a sigh of relief. Once again, she just made it.

Jesus, that was hard. Like watching a depressive go for a walk on a ledge high up on the side of an apartment building. I can't wait for some other television station to show up, depriving Mary (at least) of the exclusive live feed, and freeing us from this torture.

I take a breath, look around, and the faces I see look as exhausted as my own. Matrix, on the other hand, has become completely expressionless. Up until now his expressions have ranged from lèse-majesté to impulses toward revenge, but what I see on his face now is a blank slate, a horrendously placid surface.

I'm reminded of those TV shows set in hospital emergency rooms where the doctor steps away for a few seconds only to find upon his return that the wounded patient is already as stiff as a board. Mary Stracqua's reporting from the front entrance must have stunned him, that much is clear.

I try to put myself in his shoes, recapitulating the events, and I think to myself: Now then. I'm handcuffed to the metal rail of a dairy case in a supermarket on the outskirts of the city; there are a dozen or so television monitors showing me in this humiliating condition; I'm probably going to die, because the guy who set up this whole prank doesn't exactly seem interested in letting me leave except feet-first; I still don't know why all this is happening to me, and to cover the live broadcast of my ultimate misfortune they've sent an aging bumpkin of a TV journalist from a local network who can't speak proper Italian and gets off an idiotic one-liners.

At the conclusion of this sort of train of thought, as is only natural, my emotions are all in turmoil. And this undermining of the defensive impulse, this apathetic surrender to whatever the future may bring, is a typical product of the state of confusion that Mary Stracqua seems to cause in anyone who listens to her.

When you find yourself forced into a corner, the only tool at your disposal that can possibly get you out of that situation is a clear head, the ability to make the most of even the faintest glimmer of a chance you have. You have to think fast, and you must be rigorously selective in the steps you take.

Mary, however, compromises all strategic and, more generally, all intellectual activity. She draws you out of yourself, she hijacks you, making you worry about her instead of yourself, leaving you with your heart in your throat every time she starts a new sentence and, especially, every time she finishes one. I can't imagine that there's a human being on the planet capable of withstanding the stress of these continuous acts of transference.

I include Matrix's reaction in the general symptomatology common to anyone who has undergone this surreal experience, and I come to the surprising conclusion that, when it comes to Mary Stracqua, even the Camorra is powerless.

"The store," Naples's own Oriana Fallaci continues, "has been evacuated" (this one, by dumb luck, she pronounces perfectly), "the situation is already under gontrol, the puilding is about to be gordoned off, and vurther reinvorcements are on their way. No demands have yet been issued for the liperation of the hostach who, as these sequences show, is still in the gitnabbers' hands."

From this side of the Stracqua Reality Show we remain mystified, but we don't even have the time to process this last phrase before the mental defective completes her defamatory tour de force, delivering a final, fatal blow.

"Here," she says, pointing to the monitor being filmed by the video camera held by her unfortunate cameraman and assistant, "as you gan see, it's bossible to clearly see the outline of a man with his hands behind his back, and three other intifichuals, all without masks."

There must be something intrinsically ridiculous about the dismay that suddenly appears on all our faces; otherwise I can't explain the hint of a smile that has just appeared on Engineer Romolo Sesti Orfeo's lips.

I don't know what the hell I'm feeling: something like the kind of muttering sound your computer makes when you're sitting there waiting, starting to suspect that okaying that automatic update was a big mistake.

"Hey," Matteo the deli counterman says, breaking the silence, bright red from the seriousness of the accusation, "what the hell is this woman saying?"

Then he turns to Engineer Romolo Sesti Orfeo, conferring upon him directorial authority, as if to say: "What, you're not going to speak up?"

The engineer, contrary to my expectations, keeps his cool in the face of the gross libel perpetrated by the cretinous newscaster. If anything, he seems determined to have some fun with her.

A masochistic pleasure that, all things considered, I'm equally eager to enjoy.

"As you gan imatchine," Mary Stracqua barrels on, "we are in the bresence of an anomalous case, goncerning which there is zdill a great teal to be dedermined, but bersonally, considering the nature of the agtion, I wouldn't rule out the hybothesis of a derrorist oberation."

Whereupon Matteo the deli counterman waves his little hat like a white flag, calling attention to the harmlessness of his uniform; sort of like saying: "Hey, take a look at me, does this look like a terrorist's outfit to you?"

I scan the monitors for Mulder and Scully, and they seem to be just as disconcerted by the shamefully irresponsible information that Mary Stracqua continues to spout, ravaging that minimum of journalistic ethics that even an illiterate like her ought to be conscious of, if only from having heard others refer to it.

The two of them stand there, exchanging off-kilter glances, focusing on the idiot like two hunting dogs, driven by the impulse to tear the microphone out of her hand and at the same time restrained by the risk of being accused of infringing on the freedom of the press on live TV.

This further, perverse combination of circumstances that conspire once again in Mary Stracqua's favor, allowing her to spew her bullshit with impunity, with no objections from anyone, triggers an irrepressible rage within me.

I break in, and it feels as if I've just shattered the blank wall of *omertà* that has protected this living disgrace for far too long. The feeling that I'm taking the law into my own hands, seeing that justice is served retroactively, fills me with a sublime dizziness. If this is what cocaine is like, I understand why so many people snort it.

"Listen, Signora Stracqualurso, there's something I'm dying to know."

She looks around, disoriented. I doubt that Mulder and Scully failed to inform her of the presence of the microphones, but, impatient to blurt out the news and self-centered as she is, she probably didn't take the time to add two and two.

"Here, over here," I come to her aid.

I mean the monitor in front of her, which I'm speaking to her from and in which she can see me.

"I'm right here. Don't you recognize me? You just pointed me out to your audience as an alleged terrorist, why would you look at me now with that bovine expression?"

She turns salmon pink, as she struggles to comprehend the technological wonders of the new millennium.

The monitors show new arrivals among the rubberneckers crowded just outside the door: a large band of hooligans elbowing their way into the front row. They don't even know what's going on yet and already they're commenting. Unemployed hyenas, it's clear. The kind of guys that wander the streets in search of somebody else's business to stick their noses into (preferably of a catastrophic nature). But nobody beats them when it comes to stadium waves, there's no doubt about that.

"So tell me," I ask, doing my best to look sincerely interested, "do you pick your clothes out on your own, or do you have an ill-intentioned girlfriend giving you advice?"

She looks at me in confusion. Matrix and Matteo the deli counterman also seem somewhat baffled. Engineer Romolo Sesti Orfeo, on the other hand, opens his eyes wide and then puts his hand over his mouth.

Deep down, we understand each other, this guy and me.

"You know what really mystifies me about you?" I resume.

"The way you manage to bring together a total lack of good taste with an obsessive pursuit of that touch of class. Have you even looked at yourself in the mirror with that jacket?"

And she even takes a look at it. As if she didn't remember which jacket she was wearing.

At this point little seedbeds of laughter start to spring up around the entrance (there's one—super-contagious—who sounds like a seal).

The great part is this is all going out live.

"You look like an old Fiat 128. My grandpa had one that was that exact same color."

After rounding out the idea, I pause and look around, waiting to enjoy the fruits of my performance.

The hyenas begin cackling unrestrainedly. The seal gets to work too, making converts along the way. Engineer Romolo Sesti Orfeo presses his hands against his face, doing his best to silence a burst of convulsive laughter, but it overflows laterally, turning into ridiculous snorts, sobs, and groans. Matteo the deli counterman puts on an empty smile, the kind that means you didn't get the punch line. Mulder and Scully turn beet red in their effort not to piss their pants laughing. Even Matrix emerges from standby mode, raises his head, looks at the monitor to verify the similarity between the color of the jacket and a Fiat 128, and then abandons himself to a series of labial firecracker pops, which seems like a watered-down version of the belly laugh he'd no doubt have let loose if he didn't have much more serious problems to worry about.

At this point I believe that Mary is coming dangerously close to having a stroke. In the meantime she presents a striated version of her face to the live broadcast, accompanied by a faint tremor of her jaw.

If you want to get some idea of the level of self-satisfied ecstasy I'm experiencing right now, try to think back, if you've seen the movie, to the scene in *Witness* where Harrison Ford (who's playing a cop, and a pretty rough-and-ready one, who infiltrates an Amish community to escape certain crooked colleagues of his who'd like to take him out) breaks the nose of this asshole who's been mocking his Amish friends for a good five minutes, counting on the fact that the Amish never react to provocation.

True of the Amish; not true of Harrison Ford undercover.

Especially if you go right up close to him and make faces.

"And don't grind your teeth," I dig in, "since it's clear you have problems with your dentures. How would it look if they popped out on live TV?"

Laughter breaks out again, in a crescendo of raucous coarseness fueled by the sheer gusto of cruelty. One hooligan shows off a piercing whistle that would have done honor to a goatherd. On one monitor I see a thumb jabbing skyward repeatedly as if to say: "Way to go!"

I think of all the people watching at home, who knows how many there are, watching us live, of all the years they've waited for this moment, and I'm practically moved to tears.

This one's for you, boys.

"Who are you, how dare you?" the poor woman finally counters.

"Boooo!" the hyenas comment in chorus.

I may have also heard an: "Aw, go fuck yourself," but that may just be wish fulfillment on my part.

"What do you mean, who am I?" I reply, disappointed to find myself so quickly defrauded of my identity as an alleged terrorist.

I'm on the verge of adding a little something extra (like, say: "My God, Mary, can't we even rely on the bullshit you spew out anymore?"), when unexpectedly Engineer Romolo Sesti Orfeo breaks in, in an exceedingly calm tone of voice, instantly dousing the brushfire of excitement.

"You're a cretin," he launches in Mary Stracqua's direction.

She retreats into her shoulders so abruptly that her neck practically disappears.

"Hey," I say, looking at Engineer Romolo Sesti Orfeo.

Which stands for: "You took your sweet time."

We all shift our attention to our leader, in unison, waiting for what comes next. Which, in fact, comes next.

"Do you realize that that's a microphone you have in your hand? That you're actually speaking on live television? That the people who are listening to you will take seriously the false and above all completely baseless news you've just reported?"

Jesus, boys. This must be Judgment Day.

"I thought you were just a comedian, a sketch artist, and in a sense I even found your imitation of the Italian language droll. But now I see you're a genuine con artist, a dangerous ignorant fool. What were they thinking when they gave you a press card?"

"That's right, go fuck yourself!" a loyal hyena shouts in solidarity.

"You asshole!" another hyena adds. But it's not clear who he's yelling at.

Whereupon Mulder and Scully lunge into the fray, arms outstretched, to prevent a riot.

The poor woman tries to launch an indignant counterattack.

"Listen here, I won't permit you . . ."

"Shut your mouth," Engineer Romolo Sesti Orfeo promptly annihilates her with an abrupt, masterly transition to a disrespectful use of the "*tu*" form. "You don't give orders," he goes on, switching back to the "*Lei*" form. "You don't even understand what's going on in here and yet you act all hurt: learn your profession, you utter donkey."

"Waaah!" one hyena howls.

"Outstanding!" shouts another.

Then they start clapping their hands (some stamping their

feet as well), laughing, and shouting filthy words without subject or predicate.

Scully and Mulder don't know whether they should feel
embarrassed or join in the laughter with the rest. Matteo the
deli counterman sports a happy face of Satisfaction Obtained
(on this occasion I learn that contentment too can cause blushing).

As for me, I have to summon every ounce of my self-control
to keep from punching the air in joy.

"Captain," Engineer Romolo Sesti Orfeo calls out, in a tone
of voice that seems intended to reestablish the level of drama
that the situation had attained before the arrival of this charlatan.

In fact the hyenas, eager for fresh carrion as they are, immediately pipe down.

"What," he replies.

"Would you please take the microphone away from her?"

Mary stares at Mulder, scandalized, as if to say: "You're not
dreaming of obeying him, are you?"

"Did you hear what I said?" Engineer Romolo Sesti Orfeo
asks, seeing as Mulder is just standing there, conducting an
ocular consultation with Scully.

"Don't you dare," Mary Stracqua says, trying to intimidate
him.

"Captain," Engineer Romolo Sesti Orfeo resumes. Calmly,
unruffled. "That cretin has already done enough damage." He
snaps off the safety, aims his gun at Matrix, and reiterates the
concept: "Take that microphone away from her. Immediately.
I'm not going to tell you again."

We all stand motionless, petrified.

Even the hyenas seem to huddle together.

Matrix grinds his teeth.

Mulder takes a step toward Mary Stracqua and holds out
his hand.

She looks him in the eyes, hesitates, then slowly hands him the—and this is what technicians call it because of its shape—ice-cream cone, with a pained sequence of broken gestures, like Clint Eastwood tossing away his pistol in compliance with the orders of the bank robber du jour, who just threatened to murder the hostage (usually a woman, preferably a blonde) unless Clint does as instructed.

An intolerable scene.

I can't stand watching it any longer.

"Just give him that fucking microphone!" I finally blurt out in exasperation.

I catch her so completely off-guard that the poor woman practically capsizes, leaping up awkwardly and making one of the hyenas guffaw. The ice-cream cone flies out of her hand. Mulder lunges and catches it in midair, keeping it from crashing to the floor.

There follow machine-gun bursts of laughter. Mary turns angrily toward Hyena Central—which has by now developed an insatiable appetite for mocking her—but all she's met with is a chorus of: "What the fuck are *you* looking at?"

Mulder gets back to his feet, bright red from the unplanned rescue operation and furious with Mary Stracqua for having indirectly made him part of her foolishness (it's typical of foolishness to extend its effects to everyone who happens to be in the vicinity, even if they've done nothing to deserve the embarrassment and have in fact gesticulated wildly to mitigate its effects).

Continuing to look the mental defective in the eye and counting to ten to suppress the homicidal impulse surging through him, Mulder, with all the nonchalance of a surgeon in the OR, hands the ice-cream cone over to his colleague.

Scully takes it with some bafflement, as if to say: "And what am I supposed to do with this?" Then she hands it to the cameraman, who grabs it one-handed, turns it off, and stuffs it into the back pocket of his jeans, while with the other hand he holds the video camera in place between his shoulder and his neck.

"Now, please, put down the gun, Engineer," says Mulder to the monitor.

"*Engineer?*" Mary Stracqua repeats, flabbergasted.

Engineer Romolo Sesti Orfeo snaps his pistol's safety back on and sticks it into his belt.

"Now what?" asks Mulder.

"Now nothing, Captain. I have no need of moderators, much less incompetent ones. All I need is for the cameraman to aim his video camera at the monitors and film everything that happens. Nothing more."

Mary Stracqua attempts a soundless objection, but Mulder isn't putting up with anything else from her: he places the palm of his right hand a couple of inches from her face and with his left hand grabs her by the elbow, pulling her to his side and holding her still, determined to keep her from causing any more damage, like an elementary-school teacher with the worst-behaved students.

For the cameraman, the fact that Mary Stracqua has been silenced is manna from heaven, hoped for but unlooked to for who knows how long: it seems to have put a bounce in his step, such is the ease, if not the gracefulness, with which he finally conducts his camerawork, moving here and there, dropping to his knees and standing up again, shooting sections of the supermarket, patches of crowd and grimacing hyena faces, and then focusing directly on one of the closed-circuit monitors.

"My name is Romolo Sesti Orfeo," says the engineer, looking straight into the camera, "and I'm a computer engineer. I'm the one who designed the video security system for this supermarket, and I'm the one who organized the hostage taking you're watching right now."

He speaks without hesitation, with the calm, unhurried

tone of someone who knows exactly what they want to say and takes all the time necessary to say it; and yet—and this is really an odd impression, like when you're about to choke back a tear but you're not sure why—it's as if his voice had aged a little bit. As if the weight of the topic had forced it down an octave.

"Let me begin by begging the pardon of those who know me and especially of those who love me, because I know that I'm not appearing here at my very best. For that matter, I myself never would have believed I'd come to this point. I've always been a peaceful man, a father and a husband, a hard worker. I had a simple life; I expected normal things from it. I had a son. Until one day"—and here he turns to look at Matrix, pointing his finger straight at him—"this man came and took my son away from me."

Matrix lifts his eyes to look at him, and in this moment it's as if my mind resets itself, a fortuitous and completely automatic reanimation of facts that were destined to be forgotten— and suddenly I see everything. I see the headlines from that day, the few columns of newsprint I read, possibly while waiting outside a clerk of court's office.

Massimiliano Sesti.

The newspapers must have shortened the surname when they reported on the murder. They'd killed him along with a friend outside a pastry shop at dawn. A Camorra execution in the classic style, carried out with exemplary ferocity. The only problem was that Massimiliano Sesti's criminal record was spotless, unlike that of his friend, who'd had one minor run-in with the law for drug possession. A minor infraction, but enough to shroud both deaths in an intolerable ambiguity.

Even a hack reporter, with the life stories of both victims in hand, would have come to the conclusion that this was a case of mistaken identity. Two young men out roaming the city after a night of club hopping, with an unfortunate resemblance to the killers' intended targets. But when the Camorra kills so openly, people tend not to bother delving very deeply. The collective memory is uninterested in making the effort to believe in innocent victims. Deaths like these don't elicit pity, or even indignation. They're just never mentioned again, fundamentally because there's always a tinge of suspicion.

So this is the purpose of the live show: to remove the mark of infamy from the reputation of a murdered son.

Engineer Romolo Sesti Orfeo starts telling his story. He reports the details of the slaughter; he accuses the mob boss by his first and last name; he shows that he knows a great deal about him, offering a brief summary of his criminal biography, and then identifying him as the one who ordered the death squad out that night. Every time he says his son's name, his voice cracks, and each time with effort he picks it up, reassembles it, glues it together as best he can, and continues.

And as he proceeds with his heartbreaking closing argument, I'd like to tell him that I know this story, that all a person had to do was to read that one column to know that his son had nothing to do with it.

Read it, that's all.

I should tell him not to bother, as far as I'm concerned.

That I already know. I have proof.

I don't need a trial.

Instead I remain silent, like everyone else, and I let him speak.

Because you can't interrupt a person who's grieving and who's right.

THE PROGRESSIVE DISAPPEARANCE OF MEANING

Have you ever felt a lack of desire to express youself? I don't mean a lack of desire to talk: to express yourself, specifically. To express feelings, tastes, attitudes, ways of looking at life. No, eh? Well, that's how I've been feeling, ever since I left that supermarket.

Let's be clear: I'm not depressed. I'm not a shut-in, I don't walk for hours at random (which in the end is the same thing as being a shut-in), I don't drive around aimlessly, I don't ruin dinners I'm invited to, I get normal amounts of sleep on a regular schedule, I don't do drugs, I smoke and drink in moderation.

And it's not even that I'm not interested in what I would have to say. It's that I don't feel like making the effort of seeking out a form to give my thoughts in order to make them accessible. Reaching out to others has its cost, that's the thing.

But in private I produce lots and lots of material that some might even go so far as to describe as intelligent. There are times, in fact, when I'm astonished at certain intuitions that come to me when I'm just walking down the street or eavesdropping on snatches of the conversations of the people who walk past me.

Take the day before yesterday, for instance. I was walking past a hoity-toity wine bar, a place that only opened recently. Just then I remembered that when I was a boy that building was an art nouveau movie theater, and a really nice one. This theater, since it was on the outskirts of town and had a clientele that was not particularly well-to-do, showed discounted movies. That is, it showed films that the movie houses in the city center had just stopped showing. In other words, it was a secondhand movie theater; they weren't even really second-run movies, or reruns, that's not the right term; they were new movies set aside on layover, and the deferred projections, which we enjoyed once the theaters in the center of the city were done with them, corresponded to the class divisions of society, which in those days were much more clearly drawn than they are today.

During the times of year when the first-run movie theaters shut down for the holidays, and there were no leftover films to offer us, the discount art nouveau movie house showed some films that were truly unbelievable (and lowered its ticket prices even more); I can't imagine where they found them. Like that one whose title I've never been able to forget, *Tarzak Against the Leopard Men*. (Tarza*k*, you get it? Isn't that *k* a master-piece?)

When this movie theater folded, in the sense that the owners just gave up running it because it was no longer bringing in satisfactory receipts, it had an afterlife straight out of the hand-book: first the city took over its operation, transforming it into a sort of art house theater, then that folded too, and so they shut it down again and after that it reopened as a porn theater.

This phenomenon, typical of the outlying parts of the city, this downward spiral that unfailingly leads to the porn indus-try, which expropriates a resource once intended for the pub-lic and assigns it a use diametrically opposed to that which had inspired its salvage, has always had a slightly neorealist effect on me. Porn thriving where culture fails, and even showing culture how wrong it was. Decadence sets its seal, certifying the final act of surrender.

And so, as I walked past the former art nouveau discount movie house, which then became something of an art-house, indie cinema, only to become a porn theater and, in its present incarnation, a wine bar *con cucina* (that is, basically, a restaurant) frequented by young urban happy-hour militants who leave home dressed as if they were going to an audition for the dating show *Uomini e Donne*, it occurred to me that porn, at least until the advent of the Internet (which once and for all shifted the channels of consumption to home viewing, a transformation that had already begun with the spread of videocassette players), had unfailingly performed the distinctive function of propping up movie theaters that were running in the red. Porn put them back on their feet when it seemed like there was nothing left to be done, inevitably showing up at the end of a degenerative process, like a hyena rooting around in search of carrion.

And at that point I also realized that porn always comes after something else. After the death of Eros, after a bankruptcy, a business failure, the end of a dream. To celebrate itself, porn needs uninhabited, deserted spaces. The only concept of development driving it as an enterprise is profit. And so it takes over a failing business and avoids having to pay any startup costs. It settles the territory for as long as there's money to be made and then moves on to the next operation, since one place is just as good as any other.

But who should I tell them to, thoughts of this kind? My problem is a motivational deficit when it comes to the effort of transmitting them. It's sort of like when you sign up for a gym membership, and you start out with the very best intentions, and for the first few weeks you don't miss a single day; then the motivation gradually begins to subside until one day, as you're lying there on your back on a bench hoisting a couple of dumbbells, you suddenly stop and ask yourself: "What the fuck am I even doing this for?" And you stop going.

The only person I seem able to talk to these days—aside from Espedito Lenza, the accountant/financial adviser and cotenant of the office space we theoretically both work in (though I'm not sure that "talking" is the right word to describe the verbal activity I engage in with him)—is my mother-in-law.

I know that technically I ought to say "ex-mother-in-law," but I just can't seem to do it. In part because it has never even occurred to me to consider Assunta as belonging to my past. And then also because the concept of "ex" is already implicit in the concept of the mother-in-law, in my opinion.

The in-law, as a category, is by definition someone who *has been*: worker, husband or wife, mother or father, plus a whole multitude of secondary positions and lieutenancies and prox-ies of all sorts occupied over the course of a lifetime. Such a person has performed so many different jobs that once they attain the status of father- or mother-in-law it's a little bit like being made senator for life. They're an ex inasmuch as they're a father- or mother-in-law, in other words. So true is this that their highest (and last) aspiration is to become a grandparent (which in turn means telling their grandchildren the story of their life and therefore, once again, behaving like an ex).

The nice thing about talking with my mother-in-law, I was saying, is that with her you never have to justify anything you've done. I know that sounds a little odd, but if you think about it, the majority of human interactions is to a very large degree made up of justifications.

Assunta, on the other hand—either because she's allergic to extra verbiage, or because she has an extremely prehensile intelligence and is very quick to grasp concepts, or because she can't stand people who piss and moan (and also because, let's be frank, when she wants to she can be a bitch on wheels)—has this prerogative that is entirely her own, i.e., she never expects anything from other people, and I mean nothing from nobody, and since she communicates this from the outset, this complete lack of interest in profit, whatever form it might take, this predication of the relationship on a totally gratuitous footing, she puts you wonderfully at your ease. Because it's wonderful to interact with someone who asks nothing of you (which is after all the founding contract of all friendships, as well as the reason that friendships break off).

Make no mistake: she's not an easy woman to get along with, Ass. It's not as if she behaves this way with everyone. This is how she makes friends. It's a special treatment, reserved only for those she likes.

The really remarkable thing (and it astonishes me, because you'd expect it to be the other way around) is that, even now that she's sick, *she's* the one who keeps *me* company. Who raises my spirits, even.

I drop by to see her every night (after seven, when I leave my office; you can easily imagine the wisecracks I get from that idiot Espedito), and I really believe that if my list of appointments for the day didn't include a short visit to see my ex-wife's mamma, these days I'd be short on meaningful human relationships (with the exception, obviously, of Alagia and Alfredo; but the relationships one has with one's children, of course, are not simply human, they're superhuman), and I wouldn't even miss them all that much.

The fact is that ever since I walked away (unharmed, luckily: otherwise I wouldn't be here to tell the tale) from that whole hostage-taking affair, everything has—how to put this— become superficialized. I mean it. It's as if suddenly reality had started to do a shimmy and grind all around me. As if reality were suddenly terribly interested in taking care of me.

Sometimes it's embarrassing how considerate and kind reality can be with me. It invites me places, it sends for me, it sees me home. It gets me things. Special deals. Delicacies. It always puts easy-listening music on in the background (though I could do without that, to be honest).

I don't know if you've ever had reality doing a shimmy and grind around you. I imagine you have. I think that everyone, at least when they were young (between the ages of twenty and twenty-five, let's say), has had their period of social bliss with reality doing a shimmy and grind. Maybe it only lasted a total of six days, but they've had it. And they'll never forget it.

It's the down-home equivalent of the fifteen minutes of fame theorized by Andy Warhol. If it happens to you when you're young, it's wonderful. The kind of period in which you inexplicably move from a condition of semi-insignificance to one of widespread admiration, and suddenly in your little universe you become someone without having done anything to deserve it.

That's when girls all of a sudden notice that you exist. And that incomprehensible phenomenon of emulation and competition is suddenly unleashed among them, whereby they start clustering around you four or five at a time. All you need is for one of them to show some interest in you and the others will imitate her in a chain reaction. Practically speaking, you become a novelty. You become fashionable.

At the same time (in part because of this newly acquired popularity with females) it happens that lots and lots of male friends start to reach out to you. Including those you'd long ago lost touch with. And you go to lots of parties. And people laugh at everything you say. And they ask you where you bought your shoes and the tattered orange sweater you've been wearing for seven years now. And the girl who dumped you last month and treated you like a bathmat is going around telling everyone that she can't understand what went wrong between the two of you (especially now that you're going out with Renata Falci, who's cute as hell), since she was head over heels with you the whole time. And she thinks that by sending you the message via a third party she'll have you running back to her doorstep like a delivery boy (because you're kidding yourself if you think she's going to go to all the trouble of coming to you and crawling at your feet, begging for another chance, like you did at least twelve times before), only of course you never call her (first of all because you're going out with Renata Falci, and second because the last thing on earth you would do is call her, now that you know that's what she expects you to do), and so after a couple of days she calls you (in the early afternoon: she always calls at that time of day, to take advantage of postprandial sleepiness, probably), asking why you called her; whereupon you say to her: "Look, I didn't call you"; and she plunges into a bewildered silence, as if she had no idea what you're talking about (she's very good at conveying this sense of genuine disorientation), then she replies: "Hold on a minute: my sister told me that you called last night looking for me, I thought you wanted to tell me something"; and you say: "Your sister?"; and she doesn't answer, to emphasize the fact that your question was purely rhetorical, then (in a skeptical voice): "Ah, well, okay, in that case, sorry, my sister must have been confused": and you say: "But how did your sister get the impression that it was me, if it wasn't me? Did the person who called say he had the same name as me?"; and she (after counting to five): "Are you by any chance trying to say that I made the whole thing up just to have an excuse to talk to you?"; and you think: Noo, of course not! but instead you answer: "I'm just saying that I didn't call you, that's all"; and at this point she pulls the evidentiary ace out of her sleeve, the ace that according to her lamebrain strategy ought to safely place her above all suspicion and she says, verbatim (in a tone of voice like And-now-let's-see-what-you-say-to-this): "Hey, listen, my sister's right here. Right next to me. Do you want me to put her on, so she can tell you herself?"; and you say (starting to get a little irritated): "I don't have any reason to talk to your sister. Why the fuck should I talk to your sister? So that she can talk me into believing that I called your house when I didn't?"; and she says: "All right, all right, I get it, there's no need for you to shout, there must have been some kind of misunderstanding, sorry for the call"; and you say (coldly, after having made an enormous effort to control the uptick in blood pressure that has pushed you close to nervous collapse): "No problem"; after which a very brief meditative pause ensues, and then she goes: "Are you dating Renata Falci?"

Another typical effect of the period of social bliss that you experience when you're young is this: if you play an instrument (especially the guitar), suddenly everyone's talking about you as if you're really good. And when they see you pluck and strum, like at a party, everyone sits around you and listens to you play in the most reverential silence, as if you were executing remarkable feats of virtuosity, even though the hardest thing you've done has been to play a diminished chord (and even then it took you a full minute to switch from the chord you played before). And there's always some guy who asks if you'd be willing to give him lessons, even though you're totally unqualified to give anyone else lessons, seeing as you've never taken any yourself, having only ever played by ear, and you modestly decline the request, while at the same time letting him think that you could if you wanted to.

In these periods of unjustified overestimation of one's musical talents, it's absolutely necessary to maintain your self-control, because if you let the flattery go to your head, before you know it you're starting to think you're actually that good, and that the stuff you play really is complicated, but it just doesn't feel that complicated to you because it comes to you so naturally. It's a kind of induced autosuggestion that you have to learn to guard against if you have any respect for music and especially for the instrument you've chosen to play, because somebody who plays a musical instrument always knows, and I mean *always*, it's practically impossible for someone *not* to know, whether the stuff he plays is worth something or just a sham, maybe a well-devised sham, but a sham nonetheless. Because after all the real musicians are always there to remind you who they are and who you are, so if you're a guitarist and you like Clapton, for instance, you'd never, never ever, dream of thinking that there's not really all that much difference between you and him (which is the typical self-evaluation of the mediocre): though that's something you might actually fool yourself into believing during those periods of social bliss with reality doing a grind and shimmy; in the same exact way in which you, since by now you're rocking around town with Renata Falci, kissing her in public and so on and so forth, at a certain point you start to suspect you might actually be good-looking and that the reason that you didn't notice you were good-looking before was only because you're a modest young man, without a hint of vanity (but deep down thinking that between you and James Dean there's not really all that much difference), and the very fact that you go along with that suspicion and start to talk in an undertone and put on all sorts of idiot poses, like you start to believe that you have beautiful eyes because this one girl told you you did (and after all, that line about having beautiful eyes is something that girls say all the time, even to guys whose eyes are totally unremarkable), so when you find yourself talking with some girl you immediately lower your eyelids to half-mast, and you think you're bewitching her with your bedroom eyes, and you bring your face closer and closer to hers as if she were literally incapable of keeping from kissing you, even if you just met her, and you're so confident of your allure that you don't even realize that you're coming dangerously close to crossing the line into molestation, in addition to looking ridiculous, and you wonder which side of your face is your good side, and you convince yourself that it must be your left side, so every time you talk to a girl you try to position yourself so that that's the side she sees, and it's a problem if, let's say, you're sitting on a bench and she's sitting on your right, because if you want to show her what you think is your good side you have to twist your torso around into an unnatural position, like something out of yoga, and after a while she's bound to start thinking you don't really like her at all, and wondering what you even brought her to that bench to do anyway (because, it goes without saying, benches are notoriously compromising locations for girls) if rather than giving her a kiss you just keep contorting yourself as if being close to her was something you found repugnant.

In short, even if I'm no longer young, and I haven't picked up a guitar in a long time, and I wouldn't dream of sitting on a bench in a secluded spot in the park alone with a girl at the age of forty-four, still, that's the sort of period I'm experiencing right now. And, in case you're interested in knowing, I'm not even all that sure I'm enjoying it.

Imagine that your phone keeps ringing all day. That in nine cases out of ten a voice you've never heard before says your name, followed by a question mark. And when you answer yes, the voice introduces itself with a name followed immediately by the name of a newspaper or magazine or television network. With the result that you promptly memorize the name of the newspaper or magazine or network, and you automatically forget the person's name.

And imagine that this person then asks if you would be willing to give them an interview about what happened at the supermarket. That you play a little hard-to-get but deep down you're flattered to be asked. That the journalist realizes it and starts to work you. And that he asks you first one question, then another. And he starts pounding away at his computer keyboard while you answer. And you find the sound of his fingers on the keys gratifying.

And you don't speak the way you normally do at all, but instead think carefully about what you say, taking care with how you use verbs, adverbs, and all the rest. And you come up with some good metaphors too, of the sort that you'd never have thought of if there hadn't been someone on the other end of the phone willing to take you so seriously.

Imagine, in other words, talking as if your words really mattered. As if your version of events and the opinions that you express had a worth that was acknowledged from the very start. To such a degree that every so often the journalist asks if you wouldn't mind talking a little more slowly, because he's having trouble keeping up with you.

Then imagine that you go into a café to have breakfast and suddenly you have the impression that someone not far away is talking about you, and they're not even bothering to whisper. That you turn around to look in that direction and in fact there's a group of four people, two of whom are sort of halfway pretending not to look at you while the other two just can't take their eyes off you, even though they seem very embarrassed to be openly displaying so much interest in a person they've never met.

Imagine that you feel terribly ill at ease. That you stir your coffee around with the little espresso spoon fifteen times in a row. That you look down at the croissant on the plate on the table in front of you and think: "Oh well." That you realize that they've ruined your breakfast, since it's impossible to do something like eating breakfast while strangers are staring at you, but that you nevertheless go through the motions, since there's no other way to hide your embarrassment.

Imagine that after a little while one of the four takes the initiative to come over and tell you that they recognize you. That he, and his friends, want to shake your hand, since they absolutely couldn't stand the idea of not doing so. That one by one they take turns telling you that they sincerely admired the way you handled that tragic situation. That they treat you like the star of a hit movie. That they ask what if feels like to be in that kind of a situation. That they want to know if Engineer Romolo Sesti Orfeo has come out of his coma.

Imagine that at that point the other people in the café all look at each other as if to say: "Is that really him?" That they all come over, and a crowd starts to form. That this goes on for a while. That then you have to talk with them all. That then the barista insists that your coffee and croissant are on the house.

That once you finally manage to get out of the café you get this inexplainable lump in your throat. That you feel the compelling need to hear the voice of the woman you love, as if that's a way of remembering who you really are.

And so you automatically reach into your breast pocket, and only then do you remember that from one day to the next your woman left you without even explaining very clearly why. And your hand just lingers there, without grabbing the cell phone or pulling it out, as if it were waiting for you to tell it what to do.

And then you think that you really can't stand these emotional tics that get stuck in the past and pay no attention whatsoever to the way things change, because after all, when reality rejects them and ships them back to you like expired food, how awful that is.

Mulder and Scully's reinforcements arrived a while ago, and from outside you can hear the confused sounds of cars and the voices of people talking over each other, repeatedly telling the spectators to "stay back" because "there's nothing to see here."

They seem to be tremendously busy out there, even though the monitors keep feeding us the same images, more or less, and the sensation that I'm starting to feel as I realize that I'm now inextricably a cast member of this reality show of sorts with a condemned man awaiting execution is embarrassingly familiar: could it be, I ask myself, that we've run through the entire bank of narrative canons available?

At a certain point I think I hear a helicopter coming closer but I couldn't be sure: that too might be just another one of the imagination's ready-made dishes.

Every so often a siren wails, I wonder why they turn it on, by now the building must be surrounded and I can't imagine there's still any need to warn anyone at this point. Maybe it's a way of continuing to attract rubberneckers so the cops can tell them to stay back because there's nothing to see here.

The carabinieri have cordoned off the space in front of the supermarket with their squad cars, but the hyenas have refused to give up their positions and continue to watch over the scene of the so-called trial, although they have been forced to move back, maintaining a safe distance roughly equivalent to that between the audience and the stage at a rock concert. Ever since Engineer Romolo Sesti Orfeo revealed Matrix's identity and announced the reason he'd taken him hostage they'd gathered in a silence that seemed suspiciously like the rumblings of imminent revolt. In all likelihood a faction is being formed to root for the wrong side, and I believe that Mulder and Scully also foresee this same outcome because they look increasingly on edge, and for that matter this would not be the first time that police and carabinieri were attacked by the very people they're supposed to protect.

Not long ago RAI TV also showed up, in the person of a formerly hot female journalist, her hair carefully tousled and unkempt, and as soon as she stepped out of the news truck she immediately interviewed Mulder, who told her nothing more than the bare necessities, summarizing facts of which she was certainly already aware, only to beg off, saying: "Now please let us do our job," after which she attempted to talk to Engineer Romolo Sesti Orfeo in, as they say, real time, but he caught her off guard and explained to her that all he was willing to give her was permission to place her video cameras facing in the direction of the monitors and to broadcast live, otherwise she and her entire news crew could leave. After all, the video up to that point had already been saved to the computer, and that's not all: a local television station that she'd probably never even heard of but which nevertheless existed (because, he was quick to add, local TV stations do exist)—and unless he'd been misinformed, that local station was also carried on a satellite network—was already broadcasting it from the beginning ("Yes, but the reporting was done by Mary Stracqualurso!" I was tempted to say to him), so it was pointless for her to act as if she were getting a scoop, in fact she'd be well advised to get rid of her whole snooty attitude that she was the national journalist who was going to show up and immediately monopolize the news, given the fact that she'd arrived second, and in these cases there's no way of inverting the addenda.

Now I'm not especially fond of the journalist in question, but frankly I didn't see any reason to treat her in that manner, especially given the very real likelihood that that idiot Mary Stracqua might think that Engineer Romolo Sesti Orfeo was taking her side and defending the TV station for which she, so to speak, worked; but that was obviously just my problem.

Clearly Engineer Romolo Sesti Orfeo was nursing some sort of age-old dislike for this woman: one of those dislikes that you just can't wait to express (that kind of thing happens sometimes with television personalities).

To keep from seeming mortified, the formerly hot female journalist put on a formal smile (one of the best ways to defend yourself against embarrassing situations is to pretend you find them amusing), but there was no mistaking the fact that she was really upset about it. There was a look on her face like the one you see on the faces of politicians during the opening sequence of the talk show *Ballarò* when, by regulation, they are obliged to take the wisecracks of Maurizio Crozza, who even calls them by their first names before busting their chops, one by one, methodically, and in order to seem likable they let loose with those bloodcurdling belly laughs, the kind that make it perfectly clear that what they'd really like to do is get to their feet and curse the moderator's nearest and dearest deceased relatives.

And so what the poor RAI television journalist tried to do next was retreat to live commentary, but she almost instantly realized that this was a tactical misstep, because when you're dealing with reality television all comments are like lipstick on a pig, since as a format it's practically self-sufficient (the highest degree of usefulness that moderators of reality shows can attain is when they announce the nominations or introduce the live feed with the father and the mother of the idiot who's on that week and the idiot, from the private booth—that sort of cubbyhole from which the contestants communicate with the studio, with red moquette on the walls like in a bordello—starts whimpering and whining about how he loves and misses them, and his parents, even stupider than him, reply that they're so proud to have a son like him).

Matrix seems exhausted: or, more precisely, disjointed. The fact that he can't move his arms or legs has made him restless, so that he keeps changing position: sitting, squatting, kneeling, on his side, standing.

In spite of everything, he maintains an obstinate combativeness in his eyes and jaws that in a way I even find admirable, and he concentrates as much as he can on his effort to keep from looking Engineer Romolo Sesti Orfeo in the eye. Denying him his gaze is the sole offensive weapon remaining to him.

I review events and reflect.

There are only the three of us left in here (Matteo the deli counterman just a short while ago obtained permission to leave). Engineer Romolo Sesti Orfeo has captured his man and exhibited him before the video cameras exactly as he had planned. He's told his tragic story and delivered it into the public realm. He introduced himself with his first and last name, and then he introduced his prey, also with first and last name. He has attracted the attention of the mass media and compelled law enforcement to intervene. He has succeeded in having the building isolated and surrounded. In mobilizing a daunting array of men, vehicles, and infrastructure. Outside, the usual little knot of pro-mob-boss demonstrators are probably getting ready to make themselves heard, just to throw the sense of solidarity among the crowd back into a minor state of crisis. The video footage that has been stored in the supermarket's central computer and broadcast on television up to this moment alone is destined to become the subject of studies, arguments, and especially media jackals for a long, long time from here on. Even if Engineer Romolo Sesti Orfeo stopped right here, limiting himself to taking this man hostage without going any further, he'd still go down in history. At this point, whether or not he shoots his prisoner is a fairly secondary matter. He's already become an icon of a civil society that has nothing left to lose and is now desperately counterattacking, and he's probably well aware of it (even if this was not his goal). Before long, Mulder has told us, Assistant District Attorney Carlo Alberto Garavaglia will arrive; for years he has been investigating the criminal activities of Gabriele Caldiero (alias Matrix), and he wishes to have a frank and open discussion (that is exactly what Mulder said, verbatim) with Engineer Romolo Sesti Orfeo, in the hopes of dissuading him from taking this all the way, I presume. With regard to which Engineer Romolo Sesti Orfeo merely observed: "I have nothing to say to Dottor Garavaglia, except that today I will do the job he failed to do."

His plan, in other words, putting aside whatever finale may be awaiting us, has worked out perfectly.

And I, now that we're about to get to the (so to speak) good part, have had my fill of the whole thing. Because I'm suddenly filled with an oppressive feeling of self-pity, and I can't stand being here a minute longer.

If you think that self-pity is an inappropriate emotion in this sort of situation, you're quite wrong. I've spent my whole life getting sucked into things that mean nothing to me, spending time in places I want to leave.

How many times have I found myself in similar situations? Sure, without armed engineers, okay, but perfectly identical in essence. Situations in which I could feel someone stitching a role onto me that was not mine, appropriating my life, my desires, and who I thought I wanted to be. I'm all too familiar with that malaise, that wondering, "What on earth am I doing here?" and staying even when all I want to do is go, or, even better, never to have been there in the first place. If I have one regret, it's that I've accepted instead of walking away, that I've said yes to keep from disappointing the expectations of those who have placed their faith in me; and the years have gone by, turning me into that domesticated version of myself that I know I am now.

I see myself, right here and now, not much older than twenty-five, in a courtroom during a hearing in a criminal trial, as a pair of carabinieri escort a sort of CEO of the Camorra into a cage located just a few yards away from the raised podium where the panel of judges presides (a distance that, choreographically as well as visually, has always reminded me of the distance between a baby's crib—which, in fact, has bars—and the big bed where Mamma and Papà sleep), and the guy's attitude is one more of concession than of submission to the legal process, a nonchalance typical of the habitué, as if all that remained to be ascertained in his case was how to conveniently reconcile the various charges and who knows what other debts to society remaining on his account, recalculating a sentence or weighing it and eventually reducing it in light of other sentences; and the only thing I'm thinking about in that moment is that I can't stand wearing a tie, that I've never been able to stand it because it makes me feel stiff and I have a hard time breathing; and yet I've been putting one on every morning for the past six months, and in the past few weeks I've even been successfully tying the knot on the first try, and what's worse is that I'm getting used to seeing myself in the mirror with these clothes on. And then I decide that I absolutely need to find a new café, because the barista at the café I go to get my breakfast at every morning already calls me Counselor, but I'm not a lawyer, I'm tempted to tell him, I only just graduated, I haven't passed the bar, I'm not sure what I want to do, I might not even take the bar exam at all, I don't want your terms of respect, direct your expectations elsewhere and stop filing liens on me, I refuse to sign, I'm not planning to marry your daughter, Signore Barista.

"See you around, Engineer," I say to Engineer Romolo Sesti Orfeo, catching him off guard.

And I start heading toward the aisle.

All outside sounds die away at that exact moment.

You could hear a pin drop.

The impression I get—crystal clear, as if I were visualizing it—is of a wave withdrawing and pausing for a moment before crashing down on the rocks again.

It takes me a minute to remember that we're broadcasting live.

"What?" says Engineer Romolo Sesti Orfeo.

He seems so sincere that then and there I think that he really didn't understand me.

"I'm leaving," I explain, with the same nonchalance that I would have used if he'd asked me what time it was. "I don't intend to stay here."

A half-smile appears on his lips, like an indulgent father who's been disobeyed.

"I don't recall telling you that you could go."

"I didn't ask your permission."

He thinks it over.

"Don't provoke me, Counselor."

"And if I do, what are you going to do about it? Shoot me?"

We plunge into a silence that lingers in the air.

In the monitor I glimpse the silhouettes of Scully and Mulder as they seem to sharpen. Matrix lifts his head and looks at me; I sense his admiration. Then I feel something like a shiver running through an audience held in suspense, emanating either from the monitors or else from the crowd waiting behind a barricade outside, and directed at me personally. There is no doubt that I'm making quite an impression at this point. And it's even likely that I gave my defiant answer for this exact purpose.

If you want me to tell you, the dimension of live TV is not

bad at all. Because everything you do or say automatically benefits from a heightened symbolic potency, which disinhibits you so much that it pushes you to go all the way in anything you've started, even if you're not entirely sure of it (like right now, when I must seem like a very courageous guy, whereas all I really want is to get out of here).

It's the most natural thing in the world, in fact, to feel a surge of pleasure upon seeing reality respond promptly to any input. Because reality doesn't usually let anything shake its foundations so easily. The relationship that reality tends to establish, at least with the human race, is one of delayed cause and effect. I'd even say that, if we really want to tell it like it is, most of the time reality is so lackadaisical that by the time it responds, you're long over it. And so by the time reality is there in front of you, all willing and eager (television perfectly produces this impression of transition-in-process), obviously, you're glad to take advantage of it.

It's a little bit like winning at roulette or craps, actually.

Engineer Romolo Sesti Orfeo continues to look at me without speaking. In a certain sense, I've got him cornered. The most telling detail is the way he keeps shooting glances at the monitors.

"You know perfectly well that I wouldn't do that."

I look at his pistol.

"No, in fact, I don't know that at all."

He stares at me.

In this moment, it seems to me as if I've disarmed him.

So I press on:

"Would you trust me, if I were talking to you with a gun in my hand?"

"You're not the one I'm using it against."

I reply in a stream of words, following the flow of my own arugmentation:

"The mere fact that you have it changes everything."

We stop talking and look at each other. I'm so satisfied with what I've said that I think this really would be the perfect moment to turn and leave. If there's one thing that I really like (this is something I haven't mentioned yet) it's walking off-stage.

When there's no crushing retort, of course.

Engineer Romolo Sesti Orfeo thinks it over, then nods, allowing a hostility that he hasn't shown until now to shine through.

"Do you want to know what you've just made me realize, Counselor Malinconico?"

I say nothing and wait for him to answer his own question.

"If with this performance straight out of an American TV drama you expect to get me to beg you or even force you to stay, you're mistaken. But what's worse is that you haven't understood the way things work. Not just in here, but also outside in the larger world."

Whereupon I have to exercise great self-control to keep from popping him one in the nose. First of all, to hear him accuse me of televised exhibitionism—him of all people!—is at the very least ridiculous. Second, I can't stand these kinds of attempted thefts of other people's dialectical advantages with the aggravating factor of paternalism. We're arguing, I trip you up, and so now you say that I'm the one who doesn't get it? It's an ugly accusation, telling others they don't get it when it's all perfectly clear. What, did you have an ace up your sleeve that you were refraining from using out of chivalry? Fuck you: if you're so smart, how come you didn't say it earlier? Or else, be my guest, let's see if you know how to shake the foundations.

"Oh, really?" I retort, with a sarcasm that gives me a great deal of pleasure, considering that I usually tend not to know how to reply in this kind of situation. "Well, excuse me if I don't understand much about the world, Engineer. Too bad there's not a damned thing to understand here, aside from the fact that you're forcing us all to witness your misbegotten spectacle, which frankly ranks far below a cheap American TV drama."

The hyenas burst into an obscene explosion of laughter that can be heard from here.

"I'm not forcing you in the slightest," Engineer Romolo Sesti Orfeo rejoins with an irritating show of calm. "Do you want to leave? Go ahead. After all, I'm just trying to do you a favor. If you choose not to take advantage of it, so much the worse for you."

This last line sounds even crazier than the one before it. For a moment I stare at him, as if I'd missed something and were trying to figure out whether the atrocity that had just escaped his lips had any foundation in fact. That's what happens when people try to foist the reverse of the facts on you.

"Hey, try not to spout any more bullshit. We've heard far too much of it already today."

And instinctively I turn to look at Mary Stracqua.

Who looks back at me uncomfortably.

More cackling.

And even one who hiccups.

I didn't do it on purpose, I swear.

"Let's get one thing clear, all right?" I continue. "First, I don't need any favors; second, I didn't ask you for any; third, taking someone hostage isn't a favor: ask around."

"I took a criminal hostage, Counselor, not you. I only offered you a case. And the offer still holds, if you're interested. I really don't understand why you're clinging to this stupid matter of principle. After all, all I asked for was for you to do your job, nothing more. And what's more, until just a short while ago, you were doing very well."

Now I lose it.

"It's time for you to cut it out with this buffoonery, Engineer. I'm not working as a lawyer here. I'm just another one of your hostages being forced into a cameo in a television format of questionable taste."

"Exactly. How can you fail to see the opportunity that's just fallen into your lap?"

I'm left speechless.

Some wise guy outside laughs.

"Excuse me?"

"You have a counter-historical concept of your profession, Counselor. Don't you know what kind of world you're living in? Do you still believe that trials are held in courthouses?"

I take a deep breath and force myself to think clearly.

"Oookay. You already said that to Captain Mul . . . you've already said it. And it's an interesting and provocative idea, I won't deny that. But if you expect us to take it literally you really are delirious."

"Then take this literally: who are you? A famous lawyer, by chance?"

My head starts swimming slightly (when people insult me, I generally tend to get dizzy), then I turn red as a prawn and probably start to puff up too.

"You're an asshole."

No reply.

In fact, just a smile.

Outside, the hyenas seem to be having a party.

I look up at the television monitor and see Scully covering her mouth with her hand.

My jaw quivers.

"If you weren't holding a gun I'd punch you right in the mouth."

"I know. I'm sorry."

"*You're sorry?* Go fuck yourself."

"What I meant was simply that I doubt you're any less talented than any number of trained pet lawyers who pontificate on television every other day, and on the odd days too."

That much is true, I think to myself.

"I'm not a TV showgirl, Engineer. I'm a lawyer. I don't need spotlights and I don't need cameras. You can have them."

A few people cheer, while a few others boo and jeer.

"Come on, Malinconico, don't be a hypocrite. There are no lawyers who don't want to be famous. Legal careers are based on success and fame."

"Well, I'm sorry to disappoint you but that's not where my ambitions lie."

"Ah, no? Then what is it exactly that you're hoping for, to remain a supremely talented nobody?"

Well, how do you like that, I think to myself.

"The whole idea of niche professions is out-of-date, Counselor. Get rid of it. Today you have an opportunity to practice your profession at the very highest level, the level that matters. Here, on live television, right now, without having read the files and exhibits, without having prepared your defense, without knowing where to start nor exactly what to say, without judges or court clerks or witnesses or defendants, without any civil rights or due process. We're in the kingdom of approximations, we're on TV, you understand? And not just any channel: RAI TV. *This* is the courtroom that people pay attention to."

I'm left stunned, or perhaps I should say . . . left behind, as if I were unwilling to give him credit for having recovered so quickly. The worst thing is that I can't even motivate myself to come up with a response to his arguments because, however much it annoys me to admit it, they intrigue me. But in any case I couldn't make a retort even if I wanted to, because he doesn't give me the time.

"Criminal prosecutions have become a farce. There's no longer any mystery, there's nothing compelling about them. Can you imagine the look on Kafka's face if he could see what's become of the trial in these people's hands? To get to a definitive verdict you have to go through three levels of courts, which is quite enough to ensure that the crime's dramatic impact thoroughly fades away. And in the meanwhile, television holds a trial of its own, shapes an audience, splits it into those in favor and those against, teaches them all to parrot court-speak, and sees to it that certain laws are passed and others aren't."

He's leaking like a faucet. Clearly he's been pondering these concepts for a long time, and that's why he expresses them with such conviction. For that matter, you can't undertake any sort of armed military mission without some foundation of theoretical preparation.

Keep going, I think. Sooner or later I'll answer you.

"Why would you expect people to care about a case that drags on for years and years, with delays and peevish objections of every kind, only to culminate, when it does culminate, in a cobbled-together verdict that fails to punish the guilty or compensate the victims? The half-baked television version is a thousand times more impactful. It gives rise to ways of thinking, it shapes trends."

At this point I'm getting ready to say something.

He probably realizes it, and drives home his point.

"You might tell me I haven't done much better. That I've put together a vulgar spectacle and by doing so I'm sinking to the same level as the criminal I'm judging. I'll admit that, if it gives you any satisfaction. But try stopping the first person you meet on the street tomorrow morning, and ask them if they know who my son was."

He stops to gather his thoughts while I try to reassemble the different parts of his argument which, while it still fails to convince me, is technically impeccable.

"The trial of the probable murderers of Massimiliano, yes that really was a piece of buffoonery. Two coke-addicted hired killers who've done nothing but lie for the past two years, kicking their criminal responsibility back and forth without naming a single name or admitting to a single juridically useful fact. I wish I could show you the arrogance with which they sit in court and answer the prosecuting magistrates' questions, the barefaced shamelessness of their statements. You ought to come by sometime and see the gall of the witnesses as they retract their testimony. The *omertà*—the code of silence—that you can smell in the air the minute someone mentions this man's name. The judges' powerlessness against a mouth that refuses to open."

A silence of agreement falls.

Even the hyenas are quiet.

I don't know if I'm successful in masking it, but at this point I'm truly impressed.

"I won't tolerate this quagmire any longer, Counselor. This silencing of truths that are evident to one and all. Today I'm speaking my mind, taking the floor, and I'm no longer interested in complying with the rules. I want a kangaroo court of my own, ham-handed and slapdash, a trial held in aisles lined with sliced prosciutto and fresh mozzarella. Look, I fit in perfectly. There's no need to even include a word from our sponsors, no commercials of any kind. I want an audience, a *real* audience, made up of unspecialized television viewers, and I want them to hear about my son, I want them to remember his story, I want them to believe *more or less* in his innocence. That's enough for me. I want to have the benefit of the doubt, but *genuine* doubt, with some who believe and others who don't. I've had more than enough of this culpable ambiguity to which I've already been sentenced, de facto. And look, I'm not even interested in seeing justice served; I don't aim that high. All I want is for justice to be known."

He stops as if to savor the silence after that summation (which, to give him full credit, has left us even more speechless than we were before; who knows whether he improvised it or wrote it out in advance), and that's when—just as I'm making a superhuman effort to come up with an argument that has even a shred of validity to offer in rebuttal to his impeccable populist pragmaticism—an unpleasant and familiar odor reaches us, making us all simultaneously lower our eyes in Matrix's direction.

I say we "lower" our eyes because a puddle of piss is spreading across the floor at the prisoner's feet.

With a by-now well-honed sense of television timing, we raise our eyes and look at the monitors, to see whether the detail in question is also visible in the live broadcast (at this point there's not a gesture, a word, or an event of any kind, no matter how minuscule, that we don't automatically go looking for confirmation of on the television sets: as if reality had moved inside those boxes, and the present moment were on a loop-delay).

Since it doesn't appear to be glaringly obvious (the floor was already smeared with yogurt), we lock eyes and come to an instantaneous agreement to say nothing about the embarrassing spill.

It's a little pact that automatically springs up among us, and to which I adhere instinctively and immediately without even understanding who or what it is we're trying to defend (is it Matrix's privacy, so openly violated by this exposure, or our own images, which we'd rather not see sullied on television, or even worse, the reality show that I'm helping to put together, albeit against my will?).

The only thing I do understand—as I catch Matrix's eye and see that he's now staring at Engineer Romolo Sesti Orfeo and smiling at him with the desperate satisfaction of someone who's finally managed to land a blow—is that he did it on purpose.

When you see a prisoner abandon himself to such an instinctive need, you finally *really* understand what it means

not to be able to use your hands, to be in the hands of someone else. It's almost as if you take part personally in his regres-
sion. And it's hard to take.

By pissing himself, Matrix has upped the ante. He has, so to
speak, reversed the responsibility for his capture. As if he had
turned to the television cameras and said: "Look at me now.
Look at what he's done to me."

And Engineer Romolo Sesti Orfeo, practically from one
second to the next, finds himself cast as a torturer and turnkey,
something very different from the image he had until just a
minute before (at least, it hadn't come through so clearly).

Which, necessarily, changes everything.

THE TELEVISION OF SENTIMENTALISM
HAS NEVER EXISTED

You should see him, Matrix, now that his self-induced incontinence is beginning to become visually recognizable on television—the buzz of the hyenas, in fact, has begun to take on the unmistakable tonality of disapproval (a couple of them are already bickering with each other); Scully and Mulder exchange a glance for the third time; the female journalist from RAI (who strikes me as a fine specimen of a jackal, truth be told) has leapt straight up into the air; Mary Stracqua hasn't noticed a thing; her (ex) cameraman has already zoomed in repeatedly on the trousers—you ought to see, as I was saying, what a face of pure innocence he's put on. What a Christlike position he's assumed (on his knees, his head bent over one shoulder, his sad eyes staring, his mouth half-open). How he's playing the part (badly, but that hardly matters) of the prisoner deprived of his rights. A truly despicable spectacle, a horrifying blend of pity and disgust.

By now we all ought to be able to agree that in order for reality shows to work, they must arouse aesthetic revulsion. Since reality shows are documentaries about human misery made for nonscientific purposes, we watch them to feel superior. And so it's obvious that in such a format a corporeal excretion becomes pure kryptonite.

People have no problem swallowing polemics motivated by relative indignation concerning, for instance, television's humiliation of the body, provided they remain strictly within a cast-iron aesthetic schema (the *veline*, or pneumatic young TV showgirls, showing off their tits and asses, oh what an objectification of the female body); but like hell are they going to put up with the compassion stirred by the sight of some poor man soaking in a puddle of his own urine. The reality show does not admit classical *pietas*. At the very most, programmed emotions.

Let's take, for example, shows designed to resemble shipwrecks: concentration camps surveilled by tyrannical video cameras that save the lives of those who remain but execute the prisoners they liberate. In the concentration camp of the reality show, being freed is like being sent to hell. Whoever is rescued from the island is a dead man.

The apprenticeship of privation created to teach the true values of life does not leave room for personal initiatives or reckless impulses. It's a sort of coercive emotional treatment tested out on the contestants (sort of like the one to which Malcolm McDowell is subjected in *A Clockwork Orange* to eradicate violent impulses from his psyche), who are asked in the final episode the regulation question: "Do you feel like a different person now?" And with tears in their eyes they all say yes.

Imprisonment, exile, loneliness, sadness, distance, the challenges of socialization and adaptation, even hunger and thirst—when placed within that sort of logic all these are nothing but slightly more demanding parlor games in which the contestant never really runs the risk of doing himself or herself any real lasting harm. The safety nets are always carefully strung up. In fact if you feel ill there's a medical service ready to examine and treat you. Death on a live broadcast is not (yet) a part of our scheduled programming. Because clearly the last thing the corporation wants is lawsuits for wrongful death on its docket. It's enough to see the contestant make a little bit of a fool of him- or herself (which is after all a way of winning).

This is why Matrix's coup de théâtre has so irremediably undercut the would-be reality show of his hostage taking.

Because it has suddenly made it very serious indeed. It has engendered a real danger of fellow feeling, which is something that you want to avoid above all else in this kind of program.

Years ago I saw part of a porno variety show that was called, I think, *Provini in diretta.*

This is how it worked: a well-established porn actress agreed to mate without preamble with various aspiring cine-stallions (or rather, ordinary chronically horny male civilians, decidedly unattractive and driven by the desperate ambition to achieve their goal of screwing not so much the woman of their dreams as the woman of their wet dreams) for a preset number of minutes.

The conditions for taking part in the audition: prior authorization to broadcast whatever was filmed, no matter the outcome in terms of performance.

Translation: you want to screw the porn star? Be our guest, she's all yours, you don't even have to pay a cent. But if you can't do it, you'll spend the rest of your life in the public archive of epic embarrassments (which as a poison pill, let's admit it, has more the flavor of a deal with the devil than a mere abusive clause, and moreover without the certainty of benefit that any self-respecting devil is required to provide, in keeping with the minimum demonic contractual standards currently observed).

Now you're probably thinking: "Sure, but at the very worst the only people who are going to know about it are consumers of pornography, whether occasional or habitual: it's not as if I'm making a fool of myself on, say, a prime-time show like *Domenica In.*" Sure but fucking nothing. It's a monumental failure and humiliation, and there's no fixing it. It's a blot on your sexual criminal record that you have absolutely no chance of getting expunged. You can already imagine it, the private showings people would hold just to roll on the floor laughing behind your back.

After three or four auditions, I swear, I had to turn it off. I just couldn't bring myself to watch it anymore. They should have called the show *If This Is a Man*, seriously. A full-fledged celebration of performance anxiety and impotence. There wasn't a single one of those desperately horny losers who came anywhere close to producing even the most timid attempt, and I don't even mean an effort sufficient to cross the threshold, but even just to ring the doorbell.

And it was genuinely heartbreaking to have to watch the puppet show of commiseration that followed, the whining and the justifications, the requests, all rigorously turned down, for a second chance, the contractual courtesy of the porno diva in stiletto heels and fishnet stockings as she consoled the miserable wretch before dismissing him and moving on to the next failure.

As you can guess, the horror show in question dates back to the pre-Viagra years. Considering however not even so much the anxiety as the complete failure in terms of performance on the part of the auditioners, in all likelihood the magic pill of our present age would have had no more effect than a Tic Tac.

The purpose of the program (perhaps not directly pursued by the producers and directors themselves, but still very elegantly attained) thus wound up being to confirm the annihilating power of the video camera. Because it's obvious (though not to the participants of *Provini in diretta*, evidently) that to give a sexual performance under the gaggle of lights on a film set (and moreover with a cameraman right there directing traffic and giving you orders like, I don't know, "Now lift your leg" or "Pull out and then go back in") must be quite a challenge if you're not a professional, or at least a filthy and completely uninhibited pig.

Thinking back on it all these years later, *Provini in diretta* was to a normal reality show what an Ultimate Fighting Championship round is to a normal boxing match. Low blows, in particular, were absolutely allowed. And it was the program itself that administered them.

After all, it too was a reality show (what could be more real than a sexual failure caught on tape?); but the fact that, by exposing the contestant to that emotional massacre, it left the door open to human compassion made it completely unthinkable for a mass audience.

To defend against the risk of sentimentality (which, by creating fellow feeling with the contestant, tend to distance the viewer from the format), the reality show has therefore elevated the art of making an ass of oneself to a core, protected value. It's confined it within certain preset boundaries. It takes extreme care not to arouse compassion. In its universe, there is no such thing.

Exactly the dirty trick that Matrix had just managed to play on the reality show of his imprisonment.

"Hey," I say in a low voice to Engineer Romolo Sesti Orfeo, in the tone of a friend offering advice, "let it go."

"Let what go?" he replies, also in a voice just above a whisper.

I glance down at Matrix's puddle, just to make it clear what I'm talking about.

"It's not worth it."

"What's not worth it?" he asks, pretending not to understand.

I tilt my head toward my shoulder and compress my lips as if to say: "Come on."

"Oh, yes it is," he says.

But he's not really convinced, and it shows.

I'm about to reply when, out of the blue, the formerly-hot female journalist from RAI breaks in from the front entrance, thundering from the television monitors in a piqued tone of voice, like a young schoolteacher disciplining a pair of naughty schoolchildren.

"Can we hear what you're saying too?!?"

Just like that, peremptory, as if we'd just made a rank beginner's mistake.

We all fall silent and turn in her direction, incredulous. In the dramatic pause that ensues she realizes that she's put her foot wrong and starts swiveling her head back and forth, looking first at Scully and now at Mulder as if the two of them were playing Ping-Pong.

I promptly retract whatever blame I was leveling at Engineer Romolo Sesti Orfeo for having treated her preemptively to a large helping of whoop-ass (he must have already known what an asshole she was); then we exchange a glance as if to say: "You first or me first?"

Me first.

"Listen, you," I practically shout at her, "if you want to make yourself useful, why don't you just leave?"

The journalist lowers her sails then and there.

Mary Stracqua's ex-cameraman, now a freelancer, instinctively takes a close-up of her face (at that moment I wonder where *her* cameraman is).

"I only wanted to know what was going on," she explains, her face red as a beet.

"In that case, just watch, and don't bust our balls," Engineer Romolo Sesti Orfeo says, beating me to the punch.

The journalist heaves a sigh and the hyenas let loose. It's all a big collective "Waahh," raucous laughter, and even a few entirely inappropriate offers of sexual services aimed at the poor woman (one, in particular, so horrifies her that she remains wide-eyed as if she'd just visualized the position proposed).

"What I want to know is where's your cameraman?" Engineer Romolo Sesti Orfeo asks like a punctilious director.

Exactly what I was wondering myself a minute ago.

"Ac . . . tually," she stammers, "he just went out for a minute to shoot some footage of the exterior and . . ."

". . . And you don't even know where your cameraman is. Okay, that's all we need to know."

"All right, Engineer," the formerly hot female journalist counterattacks in an upsurge of wounded dignity, digging in for the fight, "you got me. Now do you mind if I ask you a few questions?"

"I'm not here to give interviews."

"Well, you're the one who wanted television coverage, if I'm not mistaken," she retorts, annoyed. "So let us do our job."

It seems she shouldn't have said that, because Engineer Romolo Sesti Orfeo turns ugly again.

"*Your job?* What kind of job did you do for my son? Did your news program by any chance do a piece on him, a feature, an in-depth investigation? Did you talk to me so that I could have my say on the subject? You should have turned this into a cause célèbre, the massacre of two innocent young men: but you aimed low, presented it as a minor news item, one of those tidbits that leave your viewers horrified as they eat their lunch, just long enough to switch over to something completely different, as you like to say in your bland, anodyne language."

Now he's pushing ahead like an express train, and there's no stopping him.

"Well, I have some news for you: I'm here to do your job. The job you don't seem able to do. The job you don't do. In fact, I've already done it, and now I'm moving on to the next phase. You can stay if you want to, you can film everything that happens and broadcast it live, and that's far more than you deserve. Or you can leave; it makes no difference to me. I don't intend to answer any questions."

The journalist tries to say something, but Mary Stracqua unexpectedly intervenes in her defense, entirely unasked and out of place.

"Why don't you leave her alone?!" she exclaims, in an irrepressible outburst of feminine solidarity.

"Oh no, you're not telling me *she's* still here, are you?" says Engineer Romolo Sesti Orfeo, speaking to me instead of her.

And everyone laughs.

In the presence of yet another conversion of tragedy into farce, once again I'm tempted to leave, and I just barely manage to resist the impulse.

"All right," I say to Engineer Romolo Sesti Orfeo, "I'll stay."

He stares at me as if to say: "When did I ask if you would, excuse me?"

I ignore this (especially because he's right), and then I deal a new hand.

"What do you say we restore a minimum of decorum, Engineer? It doesn't seem to me there's anything to laugh at here."

"You're perfectly right, Counselor. Let's get this over with, I'm in full agreement."

And he aims his gun at Matrix.

Who clenches his jaw in an expression of defiance.

I don't know whether he reacts this way because he's not afraid of dying or because his criminal instincts tell him that Engineer Romolo Sesti Orfeo hasn't decided to shoot him yet.

I don't have criminal instincts (at least I don't think I do), but I'm inclined to think it's the latter, right here and now.

Evidently Mulder thinks otherwise, since he addresses Engineer Romolo Sesti Orfeo from the monitor, even putting both hands in the air, as if the gun were pointed at him.

"Engineer, wait!"

"What do you want, Captain?" Engineer Romolo Sesti Orfeo asks without lowering his pistol.

"Don't do it," he whispers, almost as if he were asking it as a personal favor.

And in fact Engineer Romolo Sesti Orfeo hesitates for a moment.

"Why shouldn't I?"

"Because there's no need. Don't you see that you've already done what you set out to do?"

"You think so? Do you know what day it is today?"

Mulder is stumped.

So I answer for him:

"Wednesday."

"That's right, Counselor. And do you know what happens, let's say, every other Wednesday, as regular as clockwork for about a year now?"

A rhetorically inquisitorial question, considering that he's glaring contemptuously at Matrix as he asks it.

"This disgusting bastard comes here, to this supermarket, to buy his favorite yogurt," he says, answering his own question.

Mulder says nothing.

Whereupon Engineer Romolo Sesti Orfeo goes on to detail the charges with an indignation, it should be said, that is rather touching.

"How could you let such a dangerous criminal move around freely in this neighborhood? How could such a thing be allowed to happen?"

"I honestly don't know, Engineer. Believe me," Mulder replies, genuinely overcome. "These things do happen, and there's nothing we can do about them. It sometimes happens that fugitives from justice go on leading ordinary lives, and it might take us years to find them. It's not our fault. We do what we can."

"I have to agree with Mul . . . He's right," I break in. "You can't put the blame on . . ."

"Stay out of this, Counselor," the engineer brusquely interrupts me. "You're here to defend that man over there, not the police."

I'm so taken aback that this time I don't even blush.

"I'm not your henchman," I reply in a chilly tone. "Address me with due respect."

He takes my point and arches his eyebrows in a way that to some extent placates me.

"You're right, forgive me," he excuses himself, shaking his head. "My nerves are shot."

"Engineer," Mulder resumes, "please. You've already taken a hostage; don't add murder to the list. Leave him to us. Let us arrest him."

"So that he can wallow in jail waiting for another trial to start? And who knows when and how that trial will end. Thanks a lot, Captain, but I've already gone through that routine, and you just look where it's brought me."

Mulder lets out a sigh that sounds very much like surrender.

A disconcerting silence falls, during which we all feel guilty.

Deep inside, however, I have another feeling. Engineer Romolo Sesti Orfeo's understandable contempt for our society's institutions really grated on me. In part because he's been hammering home the concept for the past hour.

There was a young cousin of mine (the son of an especially idiot uncle) who had the same bad habit: whenever he found a reasonable argument to justify some whim of his, he'd hammer away at it until you wanted to throw him down a staircase.

In fact, one time I did. He hurt himself too, and I didn't really care much, truth be told.

"Perhaps I should stay out of this too, Engineer," I intervene, convinced I'm being witty, "but we get it that you have no respect for the Italian justice system."

He turns to look at me, closes his eyes and opens them again, with an aristocratic remoteness that makes me want to tell him, in great detail, exactly what I rather confusedly think of him.

"The facts are entirely on your side, okay? Your arguments are impeccable, there's nothing wrong with them at all, they're completely wrinkle-free, in fact *you're* completely wrinkle-free, it's as if you'd been perfectly ironed, you look like one of

Andrea Viberti's shirts, and none of us is capable of out-arguing you—there, are you happy now?"

I can see that he's a little bewildered by the mention of Andrea Viberti, but I'm not going to take the time to explain to him that he's a frighteningly well-dressed friend of mine in whose presence, as another friend of mine once put it, shirts seem to iron themselves; I just keep going full steam, by no means certain that the contents of my tirade are on a level with the vehemence that I display, as I convulsively pursue my various lines of argument, speaking at a breakneck speed to keep him from having a chance to think.

"And since that's the way things seem to be, let's just dispense with this whole farce: of the trial, of television as the ideal venue for a proper defense, and so on and so forth. Whatever you say you still understand perfectly that by pissing himself Calogero here, whatever the hell his name is, has just ruined your broadcast; otherwise you wouldn't have shot me that conspiratorial look a little while ago. Your reality show is finished, and we both know it. Go on, admit it. Porn . . ."

I stop and listen to the echo of this last word, which basically just tumbled out of my mouth, and I gaze at the look of horror on Engineer Romolo Sesti Orfeo's face, as he stands there wondering what the fucking hell I just said.

Out of the corner of my eye I register the cameraman's profile and see that his jaw has collapsed.

Even Mary Stracqua seems baffled.

It is in this exact moment that it becomes clear that I'm in the throes of a space-time trauma.

The fact is that I ought to avoid abandoning myself to these kinds of dialectical improvisations when I'm pursuing a complex concept. Because when that happens my thoughts and, as a direct result, my words tend to travel along at different speeds on two parallel tracks, whereby I wind up taking a little from here and a little from there, and expressing myself like someone with a dissociative personality disorder.

Let me explain: it's like when a friend comes over for dinner, and afterward you both take a seat on the sofa to watch TV, and you sort of doze off at a certain point, but since your friend keeps talking you answer him anyway because it seems rude to be sleeping while he's chatting away at you, so you come out with responses that are at first a little vague and then increasingly incongruous, because in the meanwhile you've started dreaming and, since you're being stimulated by the voice of your friend who goes on talking (because in these cases friends always seem to become inexplicably loquacious), what you do in effect is to reply with words from your dream (like, I don't know, "Let's take the boat, it'll be safer," after he asked you whether the actress who just showed up isn't the same one who played X's wife in film Y), until after a couple of these demented replies your friend shakes you by the shoulder to determine whether you're asleep or actually insane, so you wake up with a jerk, knowing with absolute certainty that you've uttered a string of nonsense, even though you can't remember a word of it.

"*Porn?*" asks Engineer Romolo Sesti Orfeo, aghast.

The collapse of my television quotes hits me like a cement pour.

At this point I have nothing left to do but bluff.

Which is what I do.

"Ah, you don't know *what* I'm talking about, do you?"

Note the filigree of sarcasm that I inserted into my question.

"No, I most certainly do not."

I'll bet he doesn't, and why should he? He hasn't heard my little treatise on reality shows that I jotted down mentally in the interval.

I counterattack, hoping to recover a bit of sense along the way. This time I do my best to remain lucid.

"I'm talking about the conceptual foundations of the format that you've created, that's what I'm talking about. I'm talking about television aesthetics, and the kinds of contrived emotions that should never be aroused on a reality show. I'm talking about controlling the contents of a program. The writing and the direction. I'm telling you that you can't sentence a defendant who's handcuffed and pissing his pants. If you'd taken him to your home, you could have done whatever what you wanted. But you put him on television, and here you have to watch out for sentimentality, because sentimentality tends to tear to shreds the finest intentions. I'm telling you that Cordiale's, or Caldore's, or whatever his name is's little potty accident here has practically disarmed you, and if at this point you shoot him you're handing him the audience on a silver platter: in other words, you're going to make him win the episode."

I instinctively shoot a glance at Matrix (what the fuck was his real last name? I still can't remember it), and he looks pretty bewildered, uncertain whether the bullshit that I'm spewing will lead to his ruin or to his salvation (which, I realize, must be one of the more unsettling dilemmas a person can encounter).

Engineer Romolo Sesti Orfeo remains confusedly interested for a few seconds, then he reorganizes his thoughts and answers me with the detachment of a driving instructor.

"Interesting analysis, Counselor. Truly refined. The only problem is I'm not here to win an Emmy, so your critique of my media presence leaves me entirely indifferent."

"Ha, ha, ha," laughs Mary Stracqua, spraying saliva in all directions through her ramshackle dentures.

No way! I can take anything, but to have that imbecile laugh at me is a step too far.

"Okay," I retort with mounting indignation, "then you need to stop wasting everybody's time with this charade of a television trial and your radical critique of the Italian judicial system. As far as I'm concerned, I'm sick and tired of standing around and being your stooge. Go ahead and pull that trigger, then we can all go home."

Matrix snaps his head in my direction, horrified at my provocation, which, however, as I'd hoped, causes Engineer Romolo Sesti Orfeo to immediately stop aiming his pistol at him and focus on answering me instead.

"I'm beginning to find this sarcasm of yours offensive, Counselor."

I can't believe that he said it. I don't think he's ever played the judge up to this point. Evidently there are forms of language that automatically snap into place once you take on a certain title and role, however arbitrarily.

"Hey, did you know you're starting to talk just like a prosecuting magistrate in court? What are you planning to do now, hold me in contempt of court?"

He pulls his head back slightly.

"If this is the best you can do on behalf of your client, I have to guess you're going to lose your case, Counselor Malinconico."

Matrix looks at me with understandable anguish, but I have no ambitions to introduce him into my meager portfolio of clients.

"And if you think you've done your son's cause a great deal of good, you're completely wrong," I retort.

"What did you just say?"

"You haven't done much for him, believe me. Except for making him famous, of course," and I gesture in the direction of the television monitors, dismissing their importance, "which doesn't strike me as much of an achievement, if you care to know what I think."

His eyes grow wide, betraying the sudden (and, to him, worrisome) suspicion that he may agree with me.

Let's see if I can persuade him entirely, in that case.

"This whole contrivance proves nothing. It doesn't prove that this man is guilty, nor that your son was innocent. We have no reason to believe you."

I hear another "Waahh," but this one drops a couple of octaves.

"Massimiliano was in no way at fault," he replies, with a perceptible crack in his voice, "he was just in the wrong place at the wrong time."

"Just like you are right now."

"What?"

"So you wanted television coverage? Well, fine, you got it. When you leave here, provided they don't take you straight to jail, you'll be giving interviews one after another. You'll receive a string of offers of free legal services from famous lawyers who will be so excited to sit at your side on *Porta a Porta*, where you'll certainly be invited to appear as a guest. They'll probably make a TV drama about this too. Tomorrow morning people having their morning espressos in cafés across Italy will trade their opinions," and I pronounce the word "opinions" with a dismissive emphasis, "about your son's innocence. They'll turn him into little more than a subject of gossip. They'll be moved by your tragedy as a father or they'll condemn what you've done with a shrug of their shoulders."

I take a moment to catch my breath, though this time I'm in no hurry, because I feel as if I know what I'm saying. And I think he knows too, judging from the silence in which he listens to me.

He's so attentive that he hasn't noticed that Mulder has vanished from the monitors.

A moment later I catch sight of Mulder in the monitor that alternates between views of the various aisles: he's sneaking along the shelves where the cookies are, like a large sewer rat on the prowl.

I pray that both Mary Stracqua's cameraman and the one from RAI keep their video cameras off that monitor and focus just on the three of us, because right now all it would take is for one hyena to sound the alarm to ruin everything.

I'm having heart palpitations, but I do my best to keep from giving away the game, and I go on talking quickly.

"But all of this adds up to nothing, Engineer. It doesn't prove that things went the way you say they did. It doesn't tell us anything beyond what we already knew about your son's murder. You wanted to simulate a trial, but all you've sent over the airwaves is your own despair. And you need to get it into your head that your despair is not a right. It doesn't give you any power (because that's what rights are: conditions of power), and certainly not the right to hand down a death sentence. You're just like a murderer shooting into a crowd. Except that instead of firing at those people you're throwing a corpse at them. And you expect gratitude in return. It's the worst contribution you could have made to preserving the memory of your son."

Engineer Romolo Sesti Orfeo's lips are quivering in agitation. His gaze is lost in the middle distance; I'd swear that what caught him off guard was that image of the corpse. He's stopped checking the monitor. Mulder was particularly cunning in choosing the moment to make his move. I wonder how far he's gotten by now.

You can't begin to imagine how hard it is to keep my eyes off the monitors.

The only thing to do now is to carry on with my *j'accuse*.

"You can tell us that you sent a message, that you set an example, if you like. But the problem with setting an example is that it doesn't prove anything. It's an end in itself. It demands a logic that it has no other way of attaining. It's pure ferocity. In even the best of circumstances, it leaves the question unresolved."

Have you ever seen someone's face, maybe in a movie, when he realizes that he's gotten everything wrong? Well, that's exactly the face I'm looking at right now.

I wish I could say something else to cap off this intolerable waiting game, but nothing comes to mind. Nothing at all.

Engineer Romolo Sesti Orfeo shakes his head as if to ward off a sense of dizziness, then he looks up at the monitor and sees Mulder, who at that exact moment is emerging from the aisle behind him.

He nods as he sees the game I've been playing.

He looks me right in the eye, disappointed and admiring at the same time: that is, if it's possible for those two feelings to coexist.

"Well played, Counselor."

He grips the butt of his pistol.

I recoil, imagining the executive session of the bar association voting to fund a handsome marble plaque with a phrase engraved on it, something along the lines of:

TO OUR COLLEAGUE MALINCONICO
WHO BRAVELY WORE HIS NOBLE ROBES OF THE LAW
EVEN OUTSIDE THE HALLS OF JUSTICE
TESTIFYING WITH HIS LAST LIVING BREATH
TO THE HIGHEST CIVIC VALUES
OF THE LEGAL PROFESSION

Oh go fuck yourself, I think.

"Drop the gun!" shouts Mulder, no more than ten or fifteen feet away from us.

I notice that he's spread his legs in a wide stance and is gripping his pistol with both hands.

A position of optimal balance when it comes to taking aim, probably.

You see the kinds of things that can pop into a person's mind at certain times?

Engineer Romolo Sesti Orfeo turns around, aiming the pistol right back at him.

Practically speaking, this has turned into a western.

"That's not a good idea, Engineer, believe me," Mulder advises him, with the confidence of an experienced sharpshooter. Which whether it produces an intimidatory effect on Engineer Romolo Sesti Orfeo I can't say, but it certainly makes me feel paranoid as hell, considering that I'm in the same line of fire.

I take one step to the side, unsure if it will even do me any good.

"I've come this far. I have no intention of stopping now," Engineer Romolo Sesti Orfeo replies.

Matrix curls up into himself and draws his head down between his shoulders.

"Put down the gun, Engineer," Mulder slowly enunciates, taking a step forward. "I'm not going to say it again."

Engineer Romolo Sesti Orfeo lets out a sigh and stretches his lips out into a smile of defeat.

First he lowers the gun, and then bows his head.

"Good," says Mulder. "Now get down on your knees and put it on the floor. Slowly."

Engineer Romolo Sesti Orfeo hesitates, his head still lowered.

"Engineer," Mulder calls out, implicitly repeating his order.

He lifts his gaze, looks at him, then suddenly rotates his wrist upward so that he's aiming the pistol at his own face.

Mulder leaps back.

We all watch, petrified.

Even Matrix seems alarmed.

"No!" shouts Mulder.

Then he lunges forward, but too late.

Truly, this was something none of us was expecting.

ADRIAAAN!

I t's not easy to shoot yourself. Otherwise there'd be no explaining why so many people try and fail. Who survive, let some time go by, and try again. And maybe fail again. Or do themselves permanent damage but still don't die.

Maybe it's because the close proximity complicates things. Maybe because the hand trembles. Maybe because when the time comes to pull the trigger, a part of us disapproves of the plan and does everything it can to sabotage it. Maybe because you have to be very accurate in choosing where you shoot yourself.

I wonder how the engineer is now. We were there, but it's not as if we really saw what happened.

And I have only the most muddled of memories from the moment of the gunshot to when I left the supermarket (receiving—this is a detail I can't leave out—an absurd burst of applause worthy of a TV star, which whether it woke me up or sunk me even deeper into my stupor, I can't say). A chaotic series of fragmentary scenes and more or less clear stills that surface of their own accord, sometimes fitting together, other times clashing, like morning dreams that to some extent seem to have a mind of their own but to another extent are clearly of your own invention.

The hooded members of the special operations team (the ones dressed like the comic-book antihero Diabolik if he had to leave the house in a hurry and didn't have time to put on his body stocking) bursting in a second after Mulder launches himself onto the inert body of Engineer Romolo Sesti Orfeo.

Me saying: "Already here?" but so softly that they won't hear me.

Matrix mumbling loudly as if his mouth were duct-taped shut. Maybe he's getting ready to fake an epilectic fit.

Two Diaboliks hurtling at him: whether to immobilize him or free him, it's unclear.

Him crying out that they're hurting him.

Me thinking to myself: Oh go fuck yourself.

One of the Diaboliks telling him to shut up.

And me thinking to myself: That's right, thank you.

Mulder holding Engineer Romolo Sesti Orfeo in his arms, propping his head up, his uniform smeared with blood, shouting something I can't hear—because suddenly everything's gone all muffled and my vision is even a little blurry—but I make it out (or at least I think I do) by reading his lips.

"He's still breathing," I think he's said.

Four paramedics, with all the latest equipment, super-synchronized.

Emergency resuscitation techniques.

Oxygen.

Engineer Romolo Sesti Orfeo lying on a modular four-piece metal stretcher that the paramedics have placed under his back and then reassembled so as to move the body as little as possible.

The monitors all suddenly switched off.

Matrix being led away in a different set of handcuffs.

Another Diabolik coming straight at me and then helping me to my feet (clearly I must have fallen).

An intense but strictly self-regulated traffic of professionals of various forms of expertise who are doing their busy best to take control of the scene of the hostage taking even as they disassemble it.

(And yet there's something violent about this frantic group effort to restore things to the way they were before: like a coercive return to normalcy, which needs to go back to its reassuring self as quickly as possible in defiance of whatever tragedy has occurred.)

The voice, in Dolby, of the Diabolik who's come to look after me, asking me with extreme courtesy if I'm okay, and repeating the question after I answer yes without much conviction.

Me looking into his eyes through the loose slits in the hood that conceals his face, two ovals of different sizes that seem to have been cut hastily and carelessly with a pair of scissors, and then and there I think to myself that the corps these guys belong to—they could be NOCS or GIS or whatever other paramilitary branch—really ought to do something to improve the look of their special agents, because from up close they seem like bargain-basement fetishists.

The Diabolik continuing to scrutinize me to determine whether I've been wounded somewhere on my body or I'm just an idiot.

"Are you sure you're all right, Counselor?" he asks again, and when I hear someone I don't even know call me that, and someone wearing a black hood to boot, my senses suddenly sharpen and I discover that I'm the beneficiary of a level of television fame that I could never have imagined was already so solid and so widespread, and so, even though this is the third time that he's asked me (and I'm actually pretty sick of being asked this question), still I reply: "Yes, I think I really am," and I even try to reassure him (astonished at myself and at the same time ashamed that I am already so willing to let myself by coddled by my public).

"You're covered with blood. Come this way."

And then that's it, we go *outside*, the smell of fresh air, real light, the insolence of the packed crowd outside the police barriers pushing and shoving to see us up close (to see things up

close, I think to myself: that's what audiences want). The roar
from the crowd is so overwhelming that I stagger, but Diabolik
steps in front of me, acting as a human shield (probably just a
conditioned reflex, I certainly hope so anyway, because I don't
think I actually need a bodyguard); there are shouts, piercing
whistles, and variously personalized vocalizations ("Mythical
Malinconico"; "Amazing!"; "Waaa!"; "Brother!"; "You're
incredible"), every one of them making me feel even more of a
poor fool than the last. Scully comes toward me, her face
wreathed in smiles. "You really were perfect," she says; I look
at her in disbelief and she says: "You okay?" "Thanks, fine," I
reply automatically as I realize that at least four national television networks are there with their vans and immediately after
that I say to myself: "Perfect at what? He shot himself in the
head, the poor guy"; after which a horde of journalists and
photographers assail me as if I owed them money, flashes go
off in my face, I feel a close-up surge of heat as if from a sun-
lamp, I'm blinded, Diabolik shouts for them to get back, they
all blithely ignore him, cascades of questions from right and
left, microphones and tape recorders just inches from my
mouth: "What does a person feel in moments like the ones you
just experienced?"; "In your opinion, would the engineer have
shot you if Captain Apicella hadn't arrived?"; "Do you entirely
disapprove of his actions or do you feel some degree of solidarity with him?"; "Do you feel it's safe to say that this has
been the most important case of your career?"; "Do you think
you won or lost?" I don't answer any of them because my head
is spinning and most of all because I can't fathom how anyone
could even think that a miserable wretch who's just emerged
from a situation of this kind could be sufficiently clearheaded
to answer such brazen questions, and, what's more, such theoretical ones, but there are certain reporters who'll take anything, they make no distinction between impulsive outbursts
and considered statements and they're certainly not about to

dismiss the former in favor of the latter: in fact if someone is speaking spontaneously and puts their foot in it, so much the better. If you want to know the truth, I've always been afraid of being taken literally, so you can imagine how I feel about being quoted or even worse, filmed. Wait a second, I think to myself, this is the last scene in the first *Rocky*, when Sylvester Stallone steps out of the ring all dinged up, ignoring the paparazzi who are blinding him with their flashguns and the reporters assailing him with questions and just starts shouting his girlfriend's name at the top of his lungs. It wouldn't be bad if I started shouting: "Adriaaan!!" over and over again, there's even a chance that the jackals would beat a hasty retreat. Speaking of which, I have an Adrian of my own: that is, I do in theory. Why isn't she here, why don't I see her?

Luckily I don't have time to focus on this dilemma, because Diabolik drags me away and shortly thereafter I find myself in an ambulance where a young doctor, courteous like everyone else (the nice part about being treated courteously again and again is that you feel like you're cashing a check with accrued interest), asks me to take my clothes off, and I reply that there's no need because I'm not hurt, I got some of Engineer Romolo Sesti Orfeo's blood on my jacket, but I'm fine, really, just fine.

"Please, Counselor," he insists, "it's standard procedure, let me examine you, I'll only take a minute."

Counselor, eh? I think; and I immediately take off my jacket.

The guy has a stethoscope pressed to my chest when, escorted by Scully and Diabolik, Alagia and Alfredo arrive, frantic and relieved at the same time.

God, how young they look.

They throw their arms around me and even knock the doctor aside, but he doesn't complain, in fact he seems pleased as he withdraws from the heartwarming family scene that we're offering him, something straight out of a Barilla pasta commercial.

There are times when I'm thankful I have children. This is one of them.

. "You can't even imagine what we've been through in the past few hours," says Alagia, her voice cracking with emotion, and she squeezes me so hard that I have to give her a tap on the shoulder to make her loosen her grip a little.

"Papà, really, does everything have to happen to you?" asks Alf.

Which is a little bit like the erotic filmmaker Tinto Brass telling the horror director Pupi Avati that it's time he started making some family films for a change.

So I limit myself to giving him a look with my eyelids lowered halfway. He does his best to cover his ass, just barely pulling it off.

"You enjoyed youself, eh?"

Let me tell you the last stunt Alf pulled, just to make clear what the young man I'm looking at right now is capable of. He requested an interview with the fascist squatter community CasaPound for some blog or other, I don't remember which; he busted their balls so relentlessly that they finally gave in and agreed to see him, and Alf, the minute he sat down, started the conversation by announcing that he was a communist. Those guys looked around, assuming they were on an episode of *Scherzi a parte*, then they tossed him out without even bothering to beat him up.

So you can understand.

Alagia, finally mastering her emotion at seeing me again, releases me from her embrace and starts winding up for one of her rants.

Let's hear how I've come up short this time.

"Do you know," she begins, already in a black fury, "that those idiots weren't going to let us through? We had to show them our ID, can you believe it?"

Whereupon I look at Scully, treating her to a display of paternal mortification.

She shrugs.

"And that's not all, when they saw mine they even gave me a weird look. I had to explain to them that Alfredo is my brother, can you believe it? I've never felt so humiliated in my life."

She seems to be blaming me. As if it were somehow my fault that she's the daughter of one of my ex-wife's exes and so she has a different last name from me. A tremendous lump forms in my throat on seeing how offended she is.

"Come on, that's enough now," I tell her. "Come here."

"Kids," the doctor breaks in, "I understand how worried you've been about your father, but right now it would be better if you let him . . ."

That's as much as he's able to get out before Alagia, just as promptly as I expected, barks in his direction, silencing him on the spot.

"What the hell do you know about it? Do you mind?!"

The poor guy grabs his stethoscope with both hands and puts his cervical transmission into reverse, astonished to find such an apparently amiable young woman to be capable of unleashing such a wave of unjustified bile (and make it seem so personal to boot).

I bring my hand to my forehead as my little girl tears into him.

"What do you know about how it feels to see your father trapped in such an absurd situation, glued to a disgusting television set without knowing what will happen to him, afraid that from one moment to the next that that miserable wretch might lose his head and start shooting at random, forced to accept the idea that at that very moment hundreds of thousands or maybe even millions of assholes are enjoying the show live, maybe even secretly hoping for someone to get killed. Sweet Jesus, you doctors are all the same, all of you believe that your words have the power to shed light on every tragedy, treating us ordinary mortals like so many imbeciles who just like to make things difficult for themselves for no good reason. Well, get this into your head: that's not the way it is!"

You should see the appalled silhouettes of those present when she's done with her tirade. The doctor, his face patchy and red, looks around at us frantically in the hopes of finding some fellow feeling, but no one comes to his aid. Scully, seized by an irresistible physiognomic impulse, looks at me, as if inspecting my features in search of the traces of some hereditary hysteria that I might have endowed upon my little princess.

Diabolik is a masterpiece. Without a doubt the most scandalized of all. The mask, oddly enough, makes his embarrassment even more unmistakable. If the cartoonist Andrea Pazienza were here, he'd draw him as a puppet or a doll: a sausage figure with stylized arms and legs, a black ball with tiny eyes for a head, and directly above a nice floating question mark.

As for Alf, he comes this close to laughing out loud.

I glare at him angrily, promising him a good hard smack if he doesn't put a lid on it.

"Ehm . . . What about your mother?" I ask.

Alagia replies, and the storm abruptly subsides. Whenever her mother is involved, the young Amazon suddenly discovers a talent for diplomacy.

"She stayed here until we were sure that nothing bad had happened to you," she recites, betraying a hint of shame that she unsuccessfully tries to dilute in the sugar water that follows. "She sends you her love and apologizes, but she just couldn't stay, it was all too emotional for her."

The rhetorical emphasis that she employs in reporting this pathetic justification is simply intolerable.

I know perfectly well how Nives likes to use calculated absence as a way of magnifying her own importance, especially in sensitive situations. I know even better how eager she is to regain the allure that she lost for me when I definitively chose another woman over her. And I would have willingly over-looked her present absence, since deep down her exhibitionistic strategies don't make me like her any less. But if there's one thing I absolutely refuse to tolerate, it's the emotional vassalage that our daughter shows by testifying on her behalf, spouting her mother's unrepeatable monstrosities like a trained parrot.

I delicately caress my face with my left hand as if to console myself, while also quelling the sudden surge of that recurrent rancor which the more identical it seems to the last time it washed over me, the more offensive I find it, mocking in its persistence, indifferent to my attempts to dismiss it; but the mitigating effects of my small autoerotic gesture are almost immediately shipwrecked, because I'm simply incapable of restraining myself.

"Oh, of course," I reply contemptuously, "if she'd come to say hello, she might have wound up drowning in her own tears, that much is obvious"—and here I take a very short pause before coming to the point I care most about—"but how dare you contribute to these miserable charades of hers. Aren't you ashamed of always serving as her spokesperson? What are you, her press secretary?"

Touché.

She flies into such a rage that it looks to me as if her face is swelling up. If she'd had anything in her hands, I'm positive she would have thrown it at me.

"Go fuck yourself, Vincenzo."

"Go fuck myself? Go fuck *yourselves*," I say, just to be fair and balanced, as long as I'm on the warpath. "You always take that bitch's side."

"Hey, what'd I do wrong?" Alf asks, justifiably.

I have to give that a few seconds' thought.

"Well, you were here as long as your mother was, unless I'm mistaken."

"Sure. So?"

"Then why didn't you tell her to stay?"

"Hey, stupid," he replies with an icy calm, "the two of you are divorced, in case you've forgotten. You live with another woman in fact. You want to tell me where *she* is?"

Oh, shit, I think to myself.

Then a maelstrom of slimy self-pity pulls me under, centrifuges me, and spits me back out in a para-vegetative state.

I've never been so completely silenced in my life.

What I need right now is a speech therapist.

It's true. Alf is right. I have a woman in my life, and she ought to be here right now. Forget about Nives. I may be taking it out on her, but the one I'm really angry with is Alessandra Persiano (or, perhaps I should say, myself).

"Alfre'," his sister scolds him rhetorically for punching below the belt: a solicitude that I would hardly have expected from her and that I certainly don't deserve, considering that I attacked her just a minute ago (she's a great lady, my little girl).

"No, sorry," Alf rebels, arguing back with understandable vehemence, "he's complaining that Mamma left and he even blames us for it; instead of worrying about his girlfriend, who ought to be here and isn't. I mean, what the fuck."

Such a solemn and definitive analysis that, after the concluding "what the fuck," we all plunge into a silence worthy of a university library.

Scully and Diabolik turn to look at each other for what must be the fifth time since we started putting on our show. If they keep this up, they're bound to fall in love.

The doctor seems seriously embarrassed. We must really have torn to shreds the pleasing picture of the happy little reunited family that he thought he was admiring until just a short while ago.

And then, no big deal: they take me to the hospital, I'd say basically just so they can release me, and there I learn that Engineer Romolo Sesti Orfeo is in the OR, where they've been working feverishly for some time now to remove the bullet. Half his body is paralyzed. No one knows if he'll ever emerge from the coma, and if so, in what condition.

While I'm there I run into Assistant District Attorney Garavaglia (actually, he comes looking for me), who feeds me a song and dance about what a fantastic job I did (way to go!) of maintaining control of that hostage taking "that aspired to become a trial." He says that if I hadn't been up to the cultural challenge that Engineer Romolo Sesti Orfeo threw at me with that "surreal courtroom process," right now they'd be about to declare the proceedings null and void due to the death of the the defendant instead of finally being able to bring mob boss Caldiero (right, *that* was his name!) to trial for his crimes; that what happened is serious because it could set a precedent for those who have lost faith in the justice system, etc. etc.

Now, I understand that a district attorney has to give certain speeches, especially in certain circumstances (though they could be a little less pretentious in the way they express themselves, truth be told); and I can't even say he's entirely wrong. But still there's something about it that just doesn't add up (something that, if anything, in fact, I find vaguely unsettling) in this attempt to condense events into a single narrative, using logic itself as a sort of packing tape. Maybe it's just that I've never liked potted histories.

I have no wish to get into an argument with him (in part because he really isn't a bad guy), but still I have a thing or two to say to him.

"Did you really find the 'courtroom process' all that surreal, Dottore?" I ask him. "Because as far as I could tell, we talked about a number of very matter-of-fact things: a fugitive from justice who, undisturbed, frequents a supermarket where he knows he can find his favorite yogurt; a young murder victim who's under a defamatory suspicion; a desperate father who's been pushed to the point of taking literally the example set by television of a criminal trial reduced to unbridled gossip . . ."

He nods, both while I'm talking and after I'm done, though I don't know whether he's doing it in preparation for arguing against my points or just as a way of making a mental note of them.

"What's surreal is the idea of being able to resolve these problems with a spectacular and violent act, Counselor," he objects politely. "Believe me, the engineer has all my human sympathy and understanding, but I cannot accept what he did. I say it as a citizen first, and as a magistrate second. Trials should be conducted by us, not by television. Your summation, Counselor, was an impassioned plea on behalf of the law and of the necessity to judge crimes according to jurisdiction. You dialectically demolished, one tile at a time, the entire inquisitorial arsenal that the engineer had erected to justify his plan. You conducted yourself as a genuine criminal lawyer, the kind I hadn't seen for a good long time."

"Oh, well," I say with a shrug.

I told you he wasn't a bad guy.

"Still . . ." the ADA says all of a sudden, narrowing his eyes slightly, as if from one moment to the next he'd been seized by an irresistible curiosity.

"What?"

"Odd, that the two of us have never met."

Eh, I think. Not really all that odd.

"Sure is," I confirm.

"Have you always practiced in this district?" he asks, making things even worse.

My forehead begins to perspire.

"Well, yes."

"Truly strange," he drills in. And he goes on staring at me.

Goddamn it all to hell, what do I need to do to escape the persecution of my own professional anonymity, change professions? I'm an unsuccessful lawyer, and that's that.

"I don't do a lot of criminal law," I toss out, in the hope that he'll leave me in peace.

"I know plenty of civil lawyers too," he notes circumstantially, confirming his ontological uncertainties concerning me.

Oh, sweet Jesus.

"Let's just say that I'm one of those lawyers who doesn't like to dally in the courthouse."

He must have liked that one, because he finally looks satisfied, thank God.

"Too right."

What is he doing, making fun of me?

Well, let him have his fun (if that's the case), as long as we can be done with this conversation.

He smiles, he extends his hand.

I happily shake it.

"It's been a real pleasure, Counselor."

"Oh, same for me."

You have no idea.

"I need you to come by my office, even tomorrow if possible. Just to take a few statements from you."

"If you think that would be best."

"I'll be expecting you, then."

At last, we declare the session adjourned.

At this point there's nothing I want to do so much as go home, but the carabinieri inform me that there's a fresh crop of reporters outside, and that the best way to avoid another attack would be to get a ride in an ambulance heading out on an emergency call.

I tell them that I'll take advantage of that suggestion and how, first of all because I don't think I could physically endure another beating from a crowd of question-asking, flash-popping journalists, and second because the prospect of fleeing the scene in secret, completely unbeknownst to the press, gives me a certain shiver of excitement, to be honest.

Whereupon they tell me that they'll inform me as soon as the ambulance is ready.

And while I'm sitting there waiting my phone rings.

With what delight I read the caller's name on the display.

"Mother-in-Law! I was just wondering when you'd go to the trouble to call."

She heaves one of her little sighs and replies:

"I always knew you'd come off looking smart, eventually."

I shake my head.

"Oh, how I love getting compliments from you."

"Really, you were great."

"Not you too? Listen, did you all get the part about how that poor wretch shot himself? God Almighty, he's under the knife right now, they're trying to dig out the bullet in his cranium, they don't even know if he'll pull through, and ever since I walked out of that goddamned supermarket (why on earth I ever set foot in there in the first place I couldn't say), no one says anything to me except how masterful I was, when I couldn't even stop him from doing it."

"Don't spout bullshit, Vince'. You found yourself in a situation straight out of the loony bin and you did what you could. That's it. You're not to blame for anything."

I assume a confidentially dramatic tone.

"My jacket is covered with blood, Ass. The engineer's blood, you understand?"

"You want me to get the stain out?"

"Don't try to be funny."

"What are you trying to do, make yourself feel responsible for a despairing man's attempted suicide?"

I heave a long sigh.

"I know it's hard to understand, but that's pretty much the size of it."

"Hey, try to calm down, okay? You didn't have any role in it, you can't consider yourself guil . . . Wait a minute."

"What?"

"God, I can't believe it."

"What are you talking about?"

"You're such a charlatan, Vincenzo," she says, with a caustic note in her voice that makes me break out in one of my sweats.

"Huh?"

"Go fuck yourself."

"Hey, what's come over you, have you lost your mind? Have you started drinking again?"

"You're playing the part of the failed hero. The one who's overcome by a sense of guilt for having failed to avert disaster. Christ, it's disgusting."

I turn as red as a field of tomatoes and my perspiration level skyrockets.

"What are you . . ." I stammer.

She doesn't give me the time to defend myself (that is, if I even could) and she overpowers me, tearing me to shreds.

"Who the fuck do you think you are, James Bond on her majesty's secret service, and now you're developing mission failure syndrome? Fuck off! And another thing, now that I have a clear picture of the vulgar little song and dance you just tried to put over on me: the pathetic detail of the blood on your jacket was really despicable. Shame on you."

"Are you out of your mind?" I try to counterattack, displaying high dudgeon. "How dare you come up with such a thing?"

It doesn't work.

"How dare I come up with such a thing, eh?"

It suddenly dawns on me how Nives must have felt when

she was a little girl and caught the dressing down that later turned her into a psychologist.

I wipe my forehead, smearing the cuff of my shirtsleeve with sweat, then I fan myself using my left hand as a paddle and raise the white flag.

"Okay, maybe I hammed it up a little, but I swear that I nev . . ."

"Now you listen to me," Ass interrupts me, "you so much as try and make a reference to this miserable cabaret of yours to the first journalist who comes along and asks you a question, and I swear I'll spit in your face."

I lick my lips.

"Hey, relax. I don't plan to. I'm just a little upset, okay? Right now I don't even know what I'm saying."

"No, you know exactly what you're saying. And you're not upset in the slightest. You're just turning into an idiot, that's all. You've caught a whiff of celebrity and you're wallowing in it."

"Hey. Hey. Mother-in-Law. Are you still there?"

Fuck.

I sit there motionless, cell phone in hand, humiliated and sweaty, staring at the picture of Alagia and Alfredo when they were small; then I hear, not far overhead, a horrendously familiar flap-flap, and guess who lands next to me a second or two later.

"Oh, just who I was hoping to see," I say. "What happened to you? I thought you'd been drummed out of the service, for, you know, poor guardianship."

"Funny," he says, one hand brushing his equipment. "Who knows where you find the courage to crack jokes, after the miserable display that you just made of yourself."

"Listen up," I reply, "while you were hanging out on a cloud scratching your balls, I was down here taking care of business on my own. And I think I did a mighty fine job too, if you don't mind my saying so. And, as usual, you show up when it's all over. Why don't you go back to collecting unemployment in the celestial heights, I already can't stand looking at you."

"Now that you're famous? Not on your life."

"I wouldn't have pegged you for such an opportunist."

"Ah! Of all the people to talk, after that pathetic performance with your mother-in-law."

At this point I don't even bother retorting: I just shoot him a glare so eloquent that he understands that this isn't the day for it and gets the hell out of there. The coward.

"Counselor," one of the carabinieri from before comes over. "The ambulance is leaving."

I look at him.

He looks at me.

"Counselor?"

"Eh?"

"The ambulance," he repeats, pointing at it, as if showing me what one looks like.

I f at this point you're getting the impression that there's
something missing, like an answer to a question, you aren't
mistaken: that's how it is. And the question is this: "Are
you planning to overlook the fact that Alessandra Persiano
hasn't gotten in touch with you, or do you think you have some
right to an explanation?"

So, since you seem so eager to hear about it, Alessandra did
finally show up. And it was just as I was heading for the ambulance, in slow motion, still catatonic from the telephonic brow-
beating I'd gotten from my mother-in-law.

Then and there, I swear, I was so stunned from my sudden
plunge in self-respect that I didn't even recognize her. She
must have thought I was still in shock or something, because
she took my face in her hands and told me to look at her.

"My love, it's me," I heard her say, and only then did I ask
her where she'd been all this time.

"I was right here, where would you expect me to be?" she
replied, adding a melancholy smile.

At that point I really would have liked to hear her explain,
but the driver hit his horn, practically sending the both of us
into ventricular fibrillation; so we hastened to climb in and the
ambulance took off, tires screeching, with the siren wailing.

After that, what can I tell you. We went home, where it
seemed that nothing had changed, except for the blinking red
light on the cordless phone that indicated that the voice mail
was full (I don't know about you, but to me there's something

fairly depressing about the consolation offered by the place you live, as if it were showing you the unmodifiable picture of your existence, and no matter what you do and how many resolutions you make, it still offers you the same living room on the right, the kitchen on the left, and your bedroom down at the end of the hall).

Alessandra Persiano was exactly the way you would expect a woman in love to be in a situation of that nature: sweet, considerate, proud of me and my televised performance, happy that nothing bad had happened to me, humanely showing concern for the tragedy of Engineer Romolo Sesti Orfeo, intellectually disturbed by the issues that the live televised hostage taking raised with regard to the inadequacies of courtroom trials and the media spectacle that's taken over the administration of justice.

As is always the case when you escape unscathed from a traumatic experience, we became frantically talkative, seized by the need to compulsively recount everything that happened without skipping a single detail, a single line of dialogue, comparing notes from our different points of view, as if by cross-referencing and juxtaposing them, taking turns interrupting each other and finishing each other's sentences, we were trying to come up with a shared, definitive solemn version of events, one that was our and ours alone.

And I was constantly filling in, completing, and adding every last minuscule detail that surfaced in my memory, giving in (this is the truth) to the presumption that I somehow knew much more about it than those who had seen the whole thing on TV (more or less like when you travel to see an away soccer match, and when you get home your friends, who watched the same match on TV, still pepper you with questions, as if you'd seen the real match and they'd only watched an imitation).

At a certain point, Ale latched on to the theory of the television lawyer that Engineer Romolo Sesti Orfeo had drummed into me so obsessively, treating me like some sort of cretin who doesn't know what world he's living in, and for a good half an hour that was all that we talked about.

"You know," she chose to confide in me, with a discretion that seemed to say: "This is just between us" (even though it was at least the fourth time that she'd repeated the concept), "I'm uncomfortable admitting it, but this idea that our profession, at the levels that really count, has moved from the courtroom to the television studios strikes me as frighteningly true. I know that I shouldn't say so, but the more I think about it, the more I realize that I'm in complete agreement with the engineer. That man, after all, with just a short speech confronted us with a very simple truth, a truth that we lawyers know very well but which we've never had the courage to admit."

"And that would be?" I asked, immediately regretting it, since, as I should have been able to foresee, a political harangue commenced forthwith.

"That talent no longer matters, Vincenzo. That a lawyer, these days, is no different from a realtor, someone who sells in theory, you see, who doesn't even sell but merely promises to sell units of real estate, without knowing precisely when and how they'll be built, who provides services that serve no real purpose and never gets his hands dirty with actual work, but instead mediates, channels, makes statements without structure or shape: pay close attention and you'll see that he never actually says anything, at the very most he limits himself to denying things, to contradicting the opposing side."

Christ, she sounded like Radio Radicale. Once she gets started, there's no way of stopping her. And heaven have mercy on you if you dare to let your attention wander. She's capable of grabbing your jaw and forcing you into position, making you stare her in the face until she's done. And if she's not convinced you're listening, she'll even ask you to repeat back what she's said.

"If you think about it, it's absurd, but that's how it is: the television lawyer offers nothing solid, he doesn't get results, he loses more cases than he wins, and yet he's on top of the world. His professional success is entirely independent of merit; the only defense he offers is the delegitimizing of the prosecution. And with this elementary system he reverses the burden of proof: de facto, you realize, he subcontracts his job to the legal institution, which almost seems to have to justify its reasons for wanting to put his client on trial. And yet this modern charlatan is successful, creates trends, pontificates whenever a reform is implemented and even then notice how he never says anything strictly technical but instead limits himself to broad, obvious, pragmatic considerations, dodging the real point, pushing the discourse into the realm of simplistic politics, and yet his opinion is the one the newspapers print, you get it? People like us, with years and years of hard work behind us, the ones who make the machinery run and do the dirty work of trial hearings, we're kept out of this circle, we don't count, even though professionally speaking we know a thousand times more about the actual practice of the law than they do."

And at this point she brought up the example of a, shall we say, *colleague* of ours, notoriously ignorant and conceited, who all the same is constantly featured on TV and in the newspapers (we have no idea how she does it) dispensing banal platitudes on the difficult conditions facing young people today, as if she knew something about it, and her law office is thriving even though she doesn't know the difference between a lawsuit and an appeal and in spite of the fact that, most important of all, she systematically ruins virtually all of the unfortunate clients who turn to her, thinking that she's every bit as talented as she claims to anyone who will listen.

I know at least a dozen fellow lawyers who've had to do triple backflips to make up for her colossal screw-ups (a couple of which would have justified lawsuits on the grounds of crass ignorance).

"The truth is," Ale continues, increasingly pessimistic, but finally coming to her (I hope) concluding statements, "that the world runs backwards, Vince'. We've watched this go on year after year right before our eyes. We realized, of course we realized what was happening: we talked about it, scandalized and concerned, but we were unable to do anything to stop it. And look where we've come to. But at least, perhaps, we can stop . . ."

"Listen, would you tell me why you didn't come to see me right away after I got out of the supermarket?" I asked her point-blank.

I'd been waiting for her to volunteer an explanation spontaneously ever since we'd gotten home, to tell the truth.

She scratched her elbow.

"You said you were there," I added.

"In fact, I was there. From the very beginning," she confirmed sadly. "I got to the supermarket as soon as I heard that you had been involved in the hostage taking."

"Well, then what?"

"Then . . . when I saw your children and Nives arrive, I decided I should wait my turn."

"Wait your turn?" I repeated, as if by repeating the phrase with a question mark at the end I could make it mean something (or, better yet, prove that it was sheer nonsense).

No answer.

"I didn't think you felt you came after anyone else. Not even my children."

"I didn't think so either," she said, as if the admission caused her a sense of discomfort she'd rather not show. "I only realized it in that instant."

Now, I'd like to open a parenthetical consideration. For what obscure reason, whenever you enter into a discussion of emotional import with the woman you love, do you eventually inevitably find yourself face-to-face with dogma? That is to say, you're presented with a fait accompli (obviously something that was done without your knowing about it; even better, when you were away), unproven and clearly illogical, but which she nevertheless places at your feet like a heavy stone, an irrefutable reason that, however, she refuses to explain to you even out of simple courtesy and which, in fact, you are even implicitly informed that you have already been given every opportunity to remedy? Whereupon you don't know what the fuck to say. You just sit there, feeling guilty without knowing why, while she limits herself to saying nothing.

So you ask her, in the kindest and most reasonable way you can think of, to tell you just what problems she feels the two of you have, since you're just not seeing them; but she's sick of explaining, and so she merely repeats under her breath that you just don't understand (the subtext being that you need to stop pestering her about it, since you ought to be able to figure it out for yourself); on top of which, the fact that she's forcing you to lean forward to hear what she's saying is something that has always driven you into a black rage.

Whereupon you try to ask a few questions, hoping to get some clue as to what's going on; and you even offer an array of simplified explanations on the fly, with the sole effect of making her become even more withdrawn, so that before long—obviously—you lose your temper and start shouting (but since you don't know what you're talking about you can't even get your thoughts straight, and you wind up muttering a series of offensive phrases that even you can't make heads or tails of), while she keeps her cool, and the fact that she remains as calm and collected as an Englishwoman while you go on ranting dementedly makes you lose your temper even more (because after all the most intolerable thing about all this is that you don't even know what you're fighting about), and so you start saying things that you don't think or exhuming issues from ages ago that you can't even remember all that clearly, and in the course of just a few minutes a fissure opens up with such force that you can actually hear the cracking sound.

So this time I decide not to bother to fall intentionally into the trap. I'll wrap myself in silence too; then let's see what happens.

She says nothing, I say nothing.

To get through it, we turn on the TV. We zap from one news program to another. The story is one of the first to go by in the crawler at the bottom of the screen.

After a while, we stumble on an entire story on RAI News 24. Seen on television, there is something at once banal and sinister about the images of the supermarket: that yellowish inexactness, that snuff-film-like lack of focus that makes them at once unsettling and ridiculous. Alessandra Persiano agrees with me that they are nothing much to look at.

"But you're not bad at all," she comments.

And I detect in myself a certain something, a twinge of pleasure at seeing myself on TV. It's probably the lack of focus, in fact.

At the end of the news report, we decide to have something to eat.

We make the food together. We're kind and helpful to each other.

Then we turn off our cell phones and go to bed.

We don't make love.

After we've been lying silent in the dark for a while, she tells me that the next day she has to go to Milan, because that criminal trial that she told me about is beginning.

I say I remember, but I don't remember.

"I'll be away for a few days," she says.

And it's clear that's not what's going to happen.

When did this all begin? What did we do to each other to treat each other with this level of hypocrisy? I shouldn't feel so obstinately mute in the presence of the woman I love when she feeds me a line like: "I decided I should wait my turn." Did I really make her feel so completely excluded or did she simply realize that I'm not the one she should be with?

I could ask her, certainly, but I don't. Because this truth belongs to me, and I refuse to receive it in response to a question.

And so, for once, I leave things the way I found them. I don't intervene; I don't try to rescue or save.

And she, in spite of the fact that she understands exactly what I'm doing, doesn't narrow the distance she's keeping from me by so much as a millimeter.

It might seem as if we've reached some sort of tacit understanding, but it's not true. We don't want the same thing. And the worst thing is that neither one of us is responsible for this heartbreak. The grand asshole who put us together just parked us here, waiting to make up his mind about what to do. He's acting the way he always does when he's unsure of himself, when he's fumbling, when he still doesn't know whether he should leap into the void or let himself die.

For us, right now, love is an exchange of blame.

THE MORTALITY OF YOUNG LOVES

Why is love so fragile in its first few months of life? Why so allergic, so vulnerable to chills and bad weather, such a victim of the pitiless law of natural selection?

Because of the conflicts of interest that have been tormenting me for the past few years, I've recently been speculating on the subject of the physiological death of love during the breaking-in period.

Now if in ordinary life (the kind without exceptional traumas or joys, which is after all the kind of life we all tend towards: an October-life, where you don't have to wear a heavy coat or gloves) death is a bit-part actor, in Young Love it plays the role of an unfair tax, an IRS of happiness. Like the little fish that swim along under a shark's tail, with the difference that the IRS-death doesn't attach itself to Love in order to free-load off it, but rather to crash into the nearest reef, taking Love along with it.

In other words, death, in Love, is essentially fucking bad luck waiting in ambush. Because, after all, Old Lady Death has this unfortunate tendency to make herself the center of attention, especially that of lovers. Lovers, that is, who are loved in return, lovers with a working relationship and all that. Because obviously if you are an unrequited lover and you haven't got a relationship going on, the problem doesn't even come up. In that case, the Old Lady won't even bother with you, with all the requited lovers there are out there.

In fact when you first get together and you're really happy, and the days and nights never seem long enough, it's typical to be assailed by the fear that from one moment to the next everything might end.

When those sort of thoughts come to you, don't waste a lot of time interpreting them: they're thoughts of death. They come to you because you've been doing well for yourself and death—which is always out chasing down tax evaders, and has a sterling record of catching them—has wasted no time in calling you in for an audit.

It is no accident that most love affairs come to an end shortly after they begin. That's when the insatiable Old Lady offers you a deal: "Give it all up," she says, "and you'll avoid a world of pain." A superstitious belief that's as old as the hills, but terribly effective. When all you really need to do is come to the realization that it's not necessarily better to break up sooner rather than later. In fact, if you ask me, e.g., later is better.

And that is why, when you are in love and that love is returned, you ought to do everything you can to avoid paying that abominable tax.

Lovers are all tax evaders. That is why, when they walk down the street, passersby turn to look at them as if they'd just stolen something from them.

THEN WHAT GOOD ARE FRIENDS?

D on't say a word: I bought ten newspapers this morning. Not all from the same newsstand, of course. I even disguised myself a little bit, truth be told (with sunglasses, a rasta skullcap with "Legalize" written on it that Alf gave me, a day's worth of stubble, etc.), just to see what it feels like to *want* to pass unobserved, unrecognized (if there's one thing I've always envied famous people for, it's the problems they face), but still all three news vendors told me very sincerely how much they admired what I'd done.

I got to the office especially early, to have a chance to work undisturbed on my press clippings for at least half an hour, and in any case before Espedito could burst into my room with his plans for getting lucky which (I'm willing to bet any amount of money) he'd certainly try to drag me into in order to take advantage of my, let us say, fame and strike while the iron was still hot (the first text message I got after the supermarket was from him; it said: "Now I think we're finally going to get laid"), but instead my potbellied office-mate, whose nameplate hanging on the front door I treacherously reproduce below (recommending in particular that the reader appreciate the disproportion in size between the characters):

Espedito Lenza, CPA
FINANCIAL ADVISER
was already there waiting for me.

"Hey," I say, with as much enthusiasm as I would have shown if the day before an SUV had run over his cat, "you're in early this morning."

"Come here, come here!" he exclaims, throwing his arms wide, eager to express to me in unmistakably physical terms his joy at seeing me safe, sound, and fungible as a close friend who's momentarily become a celebrity; then he rushes toward me, undertaking a lunge that makes him look like an overweight Ninja Turtle, and wraps me in a reckless and irresponsible hug, without a thought to either the stack of newspapers clamped precariously under my right arm or his own general heaving bulk. The next thing I know his protruding belly slams into me, I'm shoved backwards, six pounds of newspapers tumble to the floor, and to keep from following them down I desperately grab on to that idiot's shoulders. He pulls me toward him with virile promptitude, in a pathetic pantomime of a tango step.

I recoil in disgust.

"What the fu . . ."

"I swear I could practically kiss you," he says, taking advantage of our sudden proximity.

That line twists my mouth into a frown.

I finally twist free of his abominable embrace.

"Look at what you did," I protest, bending over to pick up the newspapers. "You think you're built like Carla Fracci?"

"Hoo-hoo!" he retorts mockingly, as I scrabble around on the floor for newspapers. "So we suddenly have an appetite for news this morning, do we?"

"Go fuck yourself."

"You're such a dope, I bought four or five papers myself."

"What's your point? Are you saying we usually take turns buying papers?"

"Well, not really. Still, you could have said something."

"What are you, my press office?"

"Is it just me," he replies, standing with arms akimbo, "or is someone here getting a swelled head?"

I look up at him, on the verge of saying something, but I'm too late. He's already turned his back on me and started off resentfully toward his office.

"Oh, come on, don't be an idiot, come here," I call after him, getting to my feet. But he doesn't even turn around.

I'm left standing alone in the entrance hall, my hands encumbered with the stack of newspapers. I heave a sigh, thinking to myself that pretty soon I'm going to have to go in and apologize to him, and I look at the door of what until recently was the office of the Arethusa cooperative, but which is now the pied-à-terre of the landlord's son, Alberto, a pampered heir-to-be who drops by regularly to smoke joints with two friends who are even bigger losers than him (and, let me point out, never with a girl: and to think that the kid's twenty years old, for Christ's sake), often putting us in awkward situations with our clients (who are admittedly few and far between) on account of the distinctive odor that fills the hallway. One time we even told him it might be a good idea to at least open the window, but he told us—I swear—that he catches cold easily; and he was completely serious.

Ah, the Arethusa. The married couple whose last names I never could seem to remember, and their freakish, demented little Italian spitz. The elevated heart rates we used to get from the furious barking fits that he'd break out in whenever someone rang the doorbell. We haven't heard from either of them in quite a while. Never laid eyes on them again: never even ran into them in the street. I don't think it was a coincidence that their office was vacated in the immediate aftermath of the sudden (and, to them, inexplicable) catatonia into which the dog fell one day, a transition from hysterical yapping to a serene contemplation of the empty air. I never walk past that door without feeling guilty (however indirectly) for the tragedy that befell them. One day I'll make a clean breast of things, and tell them how sorry I am.

"Okay, all right," I say to myself; then I shoulder the cross and trudge off toward Espe's office, if that's the right term to describe his cubbyhole.

The smartass is sitting at his desk, his back to the door, staring at the window. I stop at the doorway and emit a snort that falls midway between the argumentative and the conciliatory, but in his indignation he doesn't even give me the satisfaction of turning around.

Whereupon I try to break the counterfeit ice by improvising a stance, figuring I'll just give it a shot and whatever comes out comes out.

"Yes, it's true: there were a few moments there when I was definitely afraid for my life, but that's over now, there's no reason for you to be so upset."

That one doesn't work either.

Okay, you asked for it.

I step forward, I hoist the stack of newspapers high, and I slam it down on the desktop with all the strength my arms can muster.

The noise is so explosive that the poor idiot jumps straight up into the air, rebounding off his chair so violently that he comes this close to falling over (under the weight of his fat ass, the chair's upholstery emits a puff of air that's reminiscent of a city trash truck). He brings one hand to his chest, goes purple, and finally turns to look at me—and I'm already laughing.

He's tempted to laugh himself (I can see it in his face), but since he's too invested in his role as the princess with her pea to sacrifice his dignity, he merely raises his eyebrows and looks me coldly up and down.

I'm about to launch a Bronx cheer in his direction, but I change my mind and come to the point.

"Okay, let's be done with this," I cut in brusquely. "What do you have in mind?"

"What do I have in mind?" asks Espedito I-Have-No-Idea-What-You're-Talking-About Lenza, CPA, as if the question had dropped out of the clear blue sky.

"Oh come on, cut the bullshit. Talk."

He scrutinizes me, evaluating the risk that, by continuing the little charade, he might incur of seriously pissing me off, thereby ruining his plan once and for all, and finally decides to opt for a frank approach.

"Do you remember Anna Carena?"

I have no need to wrack my memory, since the mere mention of the name, by conditioned reflex, projects an embarrassment-inducing D-cup chest before my eyes.

Espe, in fact, looks me in the face and answers his own question.

"So you remember her. Well: last night she was at the Push-Up, with . . ."

"The Push-Up? What is that, a lingerie shop?"

"Oh, good one, that's the first time I've ever heard it. Now try and let me tell you the story without making me lose the thread: so there she was, so hot she could set your night on fire, in a turtleneck sweater that was at least two sizes too small, if you know what I mean, and the worst part was that she was standing next to a girlfriend who, and I swear my children's lives, could have been a body double for Jennifer Lopez."

"Oh, *really?*"

"I can see you're starting to get the point. So I go into the club, I pick her out along with that other specimen—I'm not even going to tell you how *she* was dressed—and just to keep from ruining my evening entirely I walk past them without even turning my head, since the bitch usually won't so much as glance in my direction. Instead, the minute she sees me she leaps to her feet, windmills both arms in the air, and asks me to come over and sit with them."

"How very odd," I comment sarcastically, crossing my arms.

In that exact instant I suddenly remember hearing or reading somewhere that crossing your arms while someone is speaking to you is a way of erecting a barrier, of manifesting disapproval; and even though the gesture I've just performed in fact does manifest disapproval, I continue to think—as I've always thought—that these alleged catalogues of body movements to be adduced as evidence of one's intentions are nothing more nor less than steaming piles of bullshit.

"You have no idea, Vince'," Espe continues, as euphoric as a pusher singing the praises of his merchandise, promising a shower of psychedelic sparks, "these two were glued to the television set from the beginning to the end of the live feed. They kept interrupting each other, ah, he was so brave, and so skillful, and what an interesting man . . ."

"No, eh?" I interrupt. "Don't even think about it."

"Oh, believe me, I didn't do anything. It was all their idea."

"Their idea?"

"Tomorrow night at nine thirty, at the Push-Up, like I told you," he adds without so much as a hint of shame; he even acts annoyed, into the bargain.

My head starts to spin a little as I grapple with my incredulity.

"Like you told me? Like you *told* me?!?" I shout, scandalized at his almost supernatural gall. "This is the first time I've heard anything about this fucking appointment from you!"

He heaves a sigh of annoyance.

"What the fuck, why are you so damned finicky? It's not as if the basic concept changes, whether you hear about it before or after."

"Holy Christ, Espe," I inveigh, slapping my legs (and to think that I've always despised the aesthetics of self-flagellation), "I knew it, and I knew it, and I knew it."

He stands up from his office chair in annoyance, as if he were the one who had had enough of me.

"Listen, let's just pretend like I never said anything, okay? I didn't think that something as trivial as going out with a couple of women would trigger this enormous crisis of conscience for you. I'll just give them a call and tell them nothing doing."

He reaches for his cell phone, but it's disgustingly obvious that he never intends for his hand to get there.

And that's when it dawns on me.

"What did you say, sorry?"

I don't add: "And how the fuck dare you make a date for me without even asking, you horny lunatic!" but it's as if I said it.

He looks at me as if he weren't wondering what planet I was from.

"Do you really think that I was going to leave two hot babes of that level waiting to see whether Father Malinconico would say yes or no?"

I smile at him in disgust, then I throw open my arms, let them drop heavily against my sides, and parade around in an apathetic little stroll from the desk to the door and back again.

"*Mamma mia*, Vince', since when have you become such a pain in the ass?" he asks me after, like, maybe, my third lap.

I stop in my tracks, and I look at him with new eyes. Because no matter how much of a con artist he is, I suddenly realize he has a point.

"Can it really be that you don't have any other outlets for your energy?" I ask, shifting into reverse.

"You're so right. Tomorrow I'm going to join Greenpeace and volunteer to go out on the next whaler-sabotage expedition."

"You're forty-seven years old."

"That's not a problem."

"Look at the gut on you."

"You see how little you understand? Women like it."

"Which explains that line snaking out the door."

"Listen, let's just get one thing clear, okay? No one's forcing you to go all the way. I know that you want to be faithful to your beautiful lawyer."

My eyes start to cloud over.

"What's the matter with you?" Espe asks.

I shake my head no, as if to say, "It's nothing," and he finishes laying out his plan for the evening's entertainment.

"All you have to do is come along, hang out with them for a little while, while I see how far I can get with one of them."

I lift my right forefinger, as if to ask if I can have just a few seconds to try to get the finer points of this concept straight in my head.

"All right then, if I've understood correctly, I'm supposed to play the clown and talk about how hard the whole thing was, while you go to work on one of them (the Jennifer Lopez look-alike, I'm guessing), and when we leave, and go over to your place, I imagine, I'm supposed to stay with Anna Karenina, or whatever the fuck her name is, and say to her: 'I'm so sorry, you're beautiful and I really like you and everything, but I don't want to cheat on my live-in girlfriend'?"

"There's no need for you to say those exact words."

"True," I catch myself saying.

"So you see."

"Eh. So I see," I confirm, like an asshole.

Then we both fall silent.

"Well?" he asks, understandably.

"Well, what?

"Christ, Vince'! Yes or no? You're lowering this fucking answer from Father Abraham's testicles!"

I go into a trance and the scene from this morning plays out again before my eyes: Alessandra Persiano pushing the last few items into her roller suitcase with just one hand because she's holding her cell phone to her ear with her other, as she repeats out loud the ID code of the taxi she's just called, and then she closes the suitcase and comes over to me, as I watch her passively from the bed, and she plants an insipid little kiss on my cheek and says: "I'll call you later."

"Give me twenty minutes, okay?" I say.

"That long?" he asks, as if he'd already done more than enough to meet me halfway.

"I'd like to read the newspapers, if you don't mind," I retort, picking the stack of papers back up.

"I can tell you what they say."

"Aaah!"

BLUES

I'm everywhere: *la Repubblica, Corriere della Sera, Il Mattino, La Stampa, il manifesto, l'Unità,* and *Il Messaggero,* not to mention the vast number of newspapers I never even knew existed, and others that I would never, ever have dreamed of buying.

My performance on television is unanimously hailed as an example of civil activism, a "celebration of the right to defense counsel as a value in and of itself, not a mere protection of one partisan interest" (*la Repubblica*); a "surprising demonstration of emotional clarity and talent for dialectical improvisation, powerful enough to reverse the situation when it seemed that all was lost" (*Corriere della Sera*); the "well-founded hope that it is through the unexpected discovery of one's fellow man that one arrives at a sense of belonging to a larger community" (*L'Unità*); and even an ethical model for the profession to which I belong: "Watch and learn how a real public defender does his job" (*il manifesto*).

There are even a few prominent bylines who go out on a limb in my favor: "Just this once, I feel like going overboard: Malinconico is the greatest lawyer now working, and he probably doesn't even know it" (Antonio D'Orrico, *Sette*); "I actually find his awkwardness sexy; the way he winds up digging himself into unlikely dialectical holes but always manages to work himself free, even winning extra points on difficulty" (Mariarosa Mancuso, *Il Foglio*); "He managed to defend simultaneously both the prosecutor and the defendant: how on earth did he do it?" (Massimo Gramellini, *La Stampa*); "The attempted suicide of this father is nothing more nor less than the symbolic murder, horrifically televised, of a justice system that no longer serves any real purpose. The outmatched Counselor Malinconico, who has all our sympathy, has defended a case that he could never hope to win" (Goffredo Fofi, *Il Mattino*); "He wore the wrong tie, but who gives a damn: Malinconico is the man that a great many Italian women would like to have ask them out to dinner" (Maria Laura Rodotà, *Corriere della Sera*).

Especially memorable, moreover, was the "L'amaca" column that Michele Serra dedicated to the trial (*la Repubblica*), and I feature the unabridged version here:

If the politicians (you can guess which ones) who give us today (too) our daily mantra of "Let's put an end to televised trials paid for with taxpayer money" (as if taxpayer money wasn't already used to pay for the salaries and countless privileges that those same politicians enjoy, the lucky ducks) only had a certain sense of proportion, they would acknowledge that the talk shows against which they hurl their preprinted anathemas are the equivalent of the Teletubbies in comparison with the grotesque, heartbreaking legal experiment that we witnessed yesterday, aghast and hypnotized, on the screens of our home television sets: undeniable proof of the degree to which a televised trial (a real one: in fact, as we saw, a narrowly averted tragedy) is driven by the largely ignored demand for justice, which politicans ought to give far greater consideration beyond the invective that they normally assail it with.

From this point of view, the improvised summation of the polymath lawyer Malinconico (a surname that—I confess—I envy him) did full honor to the adjective that he bears as a family crest: an authentic blues riff of justice denied, which no one, not even a despairing father (which is to say no politician or cabinet minister), has the right to stand in for. Justice, ladies and gentlemen, whether you like it or not, is above partisan politics and personal interests. Because it is there to give an answer to people who are afflicted by grief and (of course) injustice. And this is the moral that this remarkable reality show, at once horrendous and wonderful, has given us.

Predictably enough, there are also a few assholes (do I have a vested interest? of course I do) who accuse me of hogging the spotlight, claiming that "when the video cameras are running, even courage becomes suspect" (and the last thing I'm about to do is to provide publicity for him and his filthy rag of a newspaper by naming names), but I know perfectly well that in cases like this, smear jobs come with the territory.

I hardly need to say how squalid I feel getting my fingers smeared with ink from searching for my name in all this newsprint, ignoring all the other news as if the rest of the world's stories didn't exist, weren't worthy of my attention, but I do it all the same, because here and now I would rather be an imitation of myself than the original.

That's just the way I am: when I lose a sense of the pace of life (which—and you're free to disagree, if you like—kind of does what it pleases, more or less like the bodies we're all born in), when I'm broken and I don't know how to fix myself, when I'm missing pieces and parts and I can't even be bothered to find out where they may have fallen, the only option is to find something else to do, let it pass, like a bad cold.

However irresponsible it may seem (and it undoubtedly is), I find that practicing disengagement as a technique for solving various problems works reasonably well. The only real challenge is choosing your manner of disengagement. Because even disengaging is an activity, and it demands application and method. You can't fool around when it comes to disengaging.

It's vital to have something that catches your interest and keeps you (in point of fact) disengaged, otherwise your mind will always circle back around where it's not supposed to.

And what better way could I have found to disengage from my private concerns, in the kind of situation I'm in now, than that of contemplating the effects of my television debut (that is, remaining right there in that damned supermarket, in a certain sense)? The privilege of becoming a public personality consists in enjoying another life in which you start out with a clear advantage. In which you can make up for the failures that you collect in private.

Are you depressed because your woman has left you? Read about yourself in the newspaper and you'll see someone else who happens to have the same name as you but no signs of that inner torment. Who talks and smiles as if everything was going just fine. Who gets off funny lines. Who wouldn't bet a penny on himself but who is endowed with the esteem of others. Who knows perfectly well that he's not up to the things he says, but who goes ahead and says them anyway.

Well, to offer myself as an example, if for at least the past six months you've found yourself intolerable and haven't had the slightest desire to spend time with yourself; if your relationship with the woman you live with, after a grueling sequence of highs and lows, has come to the point where you stay in bed while she packs her suitcase; if your ex-wife has started asking for her alimony payments for the sole purpose of bringing you face-to-face with your inability to pay them; if your working life comes closer and closer with each passing day to straight-up unemployment (overlooking the minor detail that you're self-employed, at least in theory), it's clear that if you have the opportunity to live life with another identity, you're going to take advantage of it.

And so I thought that reading my name in the papers over and over again would have given me that distinctive sensation of dispossession that those who have experienced it describe: a destabilization, I imagined, similar to what happens when you think obsessively about a given word and after a while it seems to break apart and lose all meaning, all ties with its object, turning into a flavorless clump of letters (a virtual disintegration: that's what I was aspiring to). I thought that hearing myself referred to by authoritative editorialists would gratify me to the point that I'd be able to believe that *another Malinconico is possible*. That a vacation was finally coming my way.

But that's not what's happening. Because the more I see myself in the papers, the more I feel like myself. And the shelves of the Billy bookcase across from me warped months ago and I continue to have no earthly interest in replacing them. And it's not even nine in the morning and already I want a cigarette. And I don't feel as if I know anything I didn't know yesterday. And time, which I imagined would slow down a little bit, so that it would be—to quote that old song by the Rolling Stones—on my side, continues being the same old windshield wiper as ever, letting me watch as it ticks off the days before my eyes.

And so I start to wonder if it wouldn't be better for nothing ever to happen at all, for life to be nothing but monotony and repetition. If the changes that you spend your life sitting around hoping for won't prove to be gigantic frauds, when it comes down to it.

Well, you know what I say? I want to remain as I am. Broken as I am. I'm tired of the sense of guilt in the background, tired of always thinking that there's something wrong with me, something I ought to be doing that I'm not, some train I've missed, something important I still haven't taken care of. This is what I am, okay? This is what I'm like, and there's nothing I can do about it. No one can do anything about themselves; that's just how it is.

I don't like myself, but I don't want to change, okay?
Leave me alone.

"Guess what?!?" shouts Espe, bursting into my office and waving his cell phone in the air. "Jennifer Lopez just announced a change of plans: dinner's at her place!"

I register the news and decide to ignore it, for the time being.

"Could you possibly stop fumbling with your junk while you talk?"

He takes a quick look down at the mezzanine.

The hand, in fact, is still there.

He quickly pulls it away.

"Sorry," he replies, pretending to be embarrassed. "What am I supposed to do? It gets in the way."

I place my elbow on the desktop of the Jonas; then I stretch out the thumb and forefinger of my right hand and use them as stakes to support my forehead, which I set down on them a moment later, disconsolate.

"Well? Aren't you going to say anything?"

"Yes, one thing," I say, reemerging from my meditative pose, "I don't remember telling you to confirm the date with your, let us say, friends."

"You said twenty minutes, no?"

"Eh. So?"

"So look: it's been twenty-five."

"So how does that work? Once the deadline passes, silence equals consent?"

"You're not going to throw away the invitation now that Jennifer Lopez has invited us over to her place, are you?"

"Right, what kind of a fool would I look like, is that it?"

"Exactly. Help me say it."

"God Almighty, Espe, there's no reasoning with you."

"That's the story of my life, old man. Well?"

"*Yes!* Just get the hell out of here."

He puffs out his cheeks and waves his hands in the air as if to underscore how much I made him sweat to obtain my agreement, but now that he's achieved his goal, he doesn't so much mind getting the hell off of my back.

For a little while I contemplate the empty air, then I listlessly shift my gaze to the forest of newspapers covering the surface of the Jonas and I realize that I won't even be able to get rid of them for a whole week, since the recycling truck came by to pick up the paper products just yesterday.

And at the exact moment when I start to wonder whether, given the size of my, shall we say, office, it might not be better to take them home, I have a sudden flash forward: me opening the door, closing it behind me, and before I have a chance to set the bag of newspapers on the floor, I hear Alessandra Persiano's absence coming at me from the bedroom, roaring as it races down the hall, and a second later it overwhelms me, suffocating me in its coils like the black smoke on *Lost*.

At this point I ought to be having an anxiety attack, but instead I realize that the premonition is having a strangely familiar effect on me, even leaving me with a faint smile on my lips.

At first I don't understand.

Then, even though I do nothing to remind myself of it, a refrain pops into my mind:

Go out among the crowds, woman, go
out into the streets of the world and the cities . . .

"Diario!"

Jesus, how many years has it been since I've heard it.

My Favorite Song By Equipe 84

For the reader who might (possibly) not know it, Equipe 84 was an Italian musical group that was active in the sixties and seventies: to date, without question one of the finest groups we've ever had.

Contemporaries of the Rokes (the group that recorded "È la pioggia che va" and "Che colpa abbiamo noi"), they vied against Shel Shapiro's excellent band for the title of standard-bearers of Italian beat music.

I only chanced to see them on one occasion (I think it might have been in 1976), during a festival in the piazza of a small town outside Salerno. By this point they were at the tail end of their career, and yet, as soon as they got up on the stage, they took possession of it with such ease and class that all of us, down below and looking up, began to behave like a sophisticated audience out of sheer empathy, as if associating with longhaired hippies who played a different kind of music and traveled around with beautiful girls in short skirts were the most natural thing in the world.

I can still remember the wiry physique of the front man, Maurizio Vandelli, also known as the Prince (in absolute terms, one of the most original voices of Italian music), who played an imposing double-neck electric guitar (perhaps a Gibson EDS-1275 Double Neck Guitar like the one that Jimmy Page used to play, who can say; back then I didn't know much about guitars), which along with his bush of curly and gravity-defying hair gave him the allure of an international rock star.

Playing with him were Victor Sogliani on bass ("And on the cigarette," said Vandelli when he presented him to the audience at the end of the concert, since he hadn't put a single cigarette out the whole night), Alfio Cantarella on drums, and a keyboardist whose name I now forget.

Despite my extreme youth (at the time), I still remember how those songs rang familiar, even though I was hearing most of them for the first time (a kind of déjà vu that is typical of very good music: you've heard it somewhere before, even if you've never actually heard it at all, like when you fall in love at first sight and it feels as if you've met her before): "Io ho in mente te," "Tutta mia la città," "Un angelo blu," "Bang bang," "Auschwitz," "Pomeriggio: ore 6" (which was about adolescents having sex: a topic that paradoxically is more scandalous today than it was back then), and the memorable covers of Lucio Battisti's "29 settembre" and Lucio Dalla's "Gesù bambino."

That whole evening I waited for them to play the only song of theirs that I actually knew by heart, and the forty-five of which I had bought a few years earlier. That song, of course, was "Diario" (Diary), but they never played it.

"Diario" is a song from 1973, with lyrics by Vandelli set to music by Dario Baldan Bembo. It's about a guy who comes home from work at the end of the day, and as he performs the routine sequence of acts associated with that time of the evening he realizes that his woman has left him.

His discovery of her absence takes the form of a traumatic interruption of their domestic intimacy, an epiphany typical of mourning. It is a well-known fact that routine can anesthetize recent grief, projecting it into a fragile and provisional oblivion, which functions as a semi-waking state of despair.

And so a poor fool who's been freshly dumped comes home

from work and gives in to the leisurely flow of habit as if nothing had happened:

> It's six o'clock, time to head home
> I find the place exactly the way you left it
> I'd better get myself something to eat
> I grab a paper, I turn on the TV

At first, in other words, everything seems normal. Then, something happens. A moment of friction, a flash of insight, an epiphany, in short: a detail that stands out among the others and suddenly lacerates the reassuring surface of things, making concrete the loneliness and solitude that have been overlooked until this moment.

But notice the detail:

> How is it my fault if a little ash always
> Drops on the floor, you'll clean it up

You see the gesture that serves as the catalyst for his discovery that he's been abandoned? It's not like the narrator comes home, shuts the door behind him, and bursts into tears. Or, I don't know, goes into the bedroom, sees the dressing gown of the woman he loves, and folds over at the waist. Not at all: a little ash falls off the tip of his cigarette, he realizes that the woman who used to clean it up is gone, and his heart breaks then and there.

In fact at this point the song shifts into a different harmonic realm (corresponding to the change in the narrator's state of mind), and goes:

> I was forgetting, my love, that now you're gone
> I never gave you what you wanted

And from there it takes off in a lyrical and deeply noble refrain, in which the dumpee proves himself capable of a generosity worthy of a man with unbelievably broad views:

Go out among the crowds, woman, go
Out into the streets of the world and the cities
Go in search of greener pastures
Live out your fantasies in the real world.

After that, now that he's launched into it, he tells her not to "look back" (in case she ever happened to think she'd made a mistake), and that "among the stones that line the riverbank a white flower will bloom" that she once "dedicated to him before God."

Really, just unbelievable.

And in fact no one believes it, truth be told.

But as far as my own feelings go, if you want me to tell you, this male chauvinism, so ham-handed and at the same time so stupidly heartfelt and still free of the censorship that shortly thereafter Italian feminism would impose on the language, sort of does it for me.

After all, this man who refuses to blame himself for dropping cigarette ash on the floor (because anyway, as we say in my part of the world, *ci sta chi ci pensa*: there's someone whose job it is to take care of that) inspires a certain human compassion for the sheer ineptitude he shows in performing a basic task, which is to say, smoking a cigarette without leaving a trail of ashes behind him around the apartment.

This abstension from any and all responsibilities for household care, a right claimed by way of biological inadequacy, for that matter, is not all that distant from the lives we lead now.

I, for instance, can testify that I saw more than one male adult, when I was a child, who not only failed to even consider the question of where to drop his ashes, but who didn't even know the location of the laundry hamper, which tells you something.

To this day I clearly remember (it's a sort of mild childhood trauma) an uncle of mine, a conceited oaf and an idiot (certain, though reality had never provided him with anything in support of his belief, that his intelligence was well above average, that he was a refined man of letters and even something of a sophisticate), who, when he woke up in the morning, used to sit up in bed while his wife, who was even stupider than him, scuttled around putting on his socks and big-boy underpants and would then led him to the bathroom to help him wash up and get dressed (I'm not joking, this is all true; after witnessing this scene out of a porno I remember asking my grandmother if by any chance her son suffered from some debilitating illness that we were unaware of, and she replied: "What are you talking about. He's fit as a fiddle").

This lack of self-sufficiency, and the resulting total dependence upon the female gender, was a horrendously widespread condition among Italian men until not even all that long ago, a collective submission that made it so that male chauvinism took the form of a sort of de facto ideology of ineptitude (let's put it this way: men boasted that they didn't know how to do fuck-all), whereby they consigned themselves to the women in their lives like senior citizens to home healthcare workers, expecting them to wait on them hand and foot, in a way that more closely resembled volunteerism than love, conjugal though it was.

Now listen to the rest of "Diario":

If I go out for a while I'll get over it
My friends are down at the bar waiting for me
No, I'll stay here, after all I know
You still believe I'm seeing her

The former collector of cigarette ash, in other words, had also been cheated on. And the narrator, in his astounding sincerity, even admits it. Because he doesn't say, e.g. "You still believe I'm seeing *someone else*" (that is, some unspecified, generic lover, with reference to a sort of generalized jealousy on the part of his ex-girlfriend); no, his statement is specific: "You still believe I'm seeing *her*," that is, a woman with a precise identity, a repeat offender, well known to the long-gone cheated-upon partner described in the song.

The question that arises spontaneously at this point in the song (which comes before the second and last refrain and the conclusion, which involves another reference to the white flower before God), is this: you, my good friend and lyricist of "Diario," are by your own admission:

a) someone who never lifts a fucking finger around the house (because if you're at the level where you don't know how to use an ashtray, we can make certain assumptions about how helpful you are in the kitchen, and whether you do the dishes every once in a while or ever help to make the bed, just as an example);

b) someone who regularly goes out at night and leaves his woman alone at home ("My friends are down at the bar waiting for me");

c) someone who also has a steady lover on the side, of whom, moreover, his live-in girlfriend is fully aware;

and you're telling me that you come home and find her gone, and you're surprised? The surprising thing would be if you came home and she was still there, if you don't mind my saying so, eh.

This fresco, crude and possessed of a certain quality of grotesquerie, of good-for-nothing spoiled masculine debauchery—which demands extreme catering and tolerance of philandering while philosophically singing the praises of the woman's freedom when she finally hands in her resignation from her position as chambermaid and betrayed lover, exhorting her not to change her mind and look back, and reminding her that when a white flower blooms among the stones along the riverbank she must remember the dedication that she made to him before God—is, to my mind, anthropologically speaking, a masterpiece.

A brilliant transposition of the profile of the average Italian cheating male, opportunistic and whiny, and originally portrayed by the master himself, Alberto Sordi, into the form of a pop ditty.

DISGUSTING HEIGHTS

I'd never in my life experienced the problem of my voice mail being full.

It's not as if it makes you feel who knows what, when you come right down to it. In fact, after a little while it's a tremendous pain in the ass sitting there listening to all that talk. In part because the people who leave voice mail messages have a habit of winding up to it slowly, so that the recording cuts them off just as they're finally making up their minds to get to the point. And the amazing thing is that they don't call back, either. And there you sit, an even bigger idiot than they are, wondering what they might have been calling about.

At the very least, I'm over those nervous fits I always used to get when I watched those movies where the main character comes home from work (and not from a vacation, either) and listens to fifteen messages in a row while loosening his tie and unbuttoning his shirt cuffs as he parades around the room (super neat, decorated like a high-priced modern showroom, and almost invariably illuminated by designer standing lamps that emanate diffuse light; there's never a single ceiling lamp in movies), commenting with eloquent facial expressions on the indignant messages from female voices scolding him for not calling as he'd promised. Because obviously when you watch a scene of this kind you feel like a lonely coyote. And the thought occurs to you to leave yourself a message when you leave the movie theater, just so you don't have to howl at the moon.

But anyway it's unbelievable the sheer number of people who suddenly notice you exist after you come by a little television visibility.

First of all, the clients. When on earth has it ever happened that I received from fifteen to twenty requests for legal services in a single day? Such a sudden and daunting increase in demand that I felt compelled to make a quick subcontracting agreement on the spot with the associated law offices of two old friends, thus assembling an emergency stable of legal defenders (in practical terms, I offer them my clients and my brand and they do the dirty work of defending the cases—while I reserve the right to make the occasional stage appearance at the hearings—and the split is fifty-fifty).

Professional considerations aside, I received messages from (I'll just list them as they come to me): friends (damn, I never knew I had so many friends), acquaintances (a much smaller number than the friends), relatives and kin ranging from moderately close to the most far-flung, cousins I've never heard of, old schoolmates (one message in particular, from that huge idiot from Monteverde Marco Gettatelli, I found especially appalling; it said, in a practically impenetrable Roman accent: "I gotta tell ya, Engineer Sesti-the-fuck's-his-name, or whatever it was and still is, to hell with him, why couldn't he have fired that bullet into that fat dickhead of yours instead of trying to kill himself?"), an ex-girlfriend from my high school days who I definitely thought was dead (she says that her husband cheats on her; "Can hardly blame him," I commented internally), the chairman of the bar association ("You almost seemed impressive," he said), the mayor, my close friend Dalia (who took the opportunity to say that here and there she might have edited the summation down a bit), the head of my condo board (but just to remind me to pay my share for the work on the elevator), a woman who said she was my "aunt" something or other, Alf to apologize (and that filled me with sadness, because when your children apologize to you, you're the one who feels at fault), and some potty-mouthed creep who rattled off a seemingly endless chain of insults without giving his name.

I must have jotted down (even though I wasn't all that sure that I wanted to call them back) something like a dozen names and numbers for reporters from local and national publications who expressed just how tremendously urgent it was that I get back to them at any time of the day or night (oh sure, because they couldn't just call me back, right?).

The only one I called back with relative promptness was Paolo Di Stefano, whose questionnaire response column I read regularly in *Io donna* magazine, which comes with the Saturday edition of *Corriere della Sera*, loosely based on Proust's famous parlor game.

I already had my answers ready (I've always wanted to take Proust's questionnaire someday), and so when Di Stefano asked me if I had ten minutes to spare, I said yes without even pretending to think it over (the text of the questionnaire is on pages 286-289).

Even Nives got in touch (that one wasn't a message: I just answered the phone). A slow, disagreeable, shamefully hypocritical conversation that I transcribe here (supplying in italics, in the parentheses that follow the answers I gave her, what I was actually thinking):

"Vincenzo, it's me."

"How are you, Nives."

(You know, caller ID has been around for a while now, you idiot, why are you telling me that it's you? Just hurry up, because I have Paolo Mieli on the other line.)

"I thought you didn't want to talk to me."

"Why would you think that?"

(You're right, I didn't want to talk to you, but I'm hoping that if I'm nice you'll hold off on asking for the alimony payments for at least a couple of months.)

"The kids told me that you noticed I wasn't there."

"Yes. I did notice. But don't worry, I understand."

(Do you think I needed some kind of clue in order to notice such oafish behavior, driven entirely by a need to be the center of attention? You didn't like it, eh, having to share the spotlight for once in your life, right?)

"I just couldn't handle it. I'd have embraced you and started sobbing on your shoulder, I swear it on our children's lives."

When she got to the end of that one, I scratched my balls before answering.

"If it's any consolation, I'd probably have started crying myself."

(Sure, sure, of course. You crying: no doubt. You're going to try to foist this piece of nonsense off on me, of all people? Christmas 1996: you slammed a hammer down on your left thumb in an attempt to drive a nail into the living room wall— so you could hang, what's worse, a still life that was probably still because it was putrefied, done by a so-called girlfriend of yours who was a painter—and even then you shed not a single salt tear.)

At this point she took a break and sniffed piteously a couple of times (a performance so cringeworthy as to earn her an immediate nomination for the Golden Rotten Tomato); after which she uttered my name emphatically and melodramatically, as if I needed to brace myself for who knows what revelation that any second now would change my life forever.

"Vincenzo."

(The fuck is it, now?)

"Yes, Nives."

"The reason I . . ."

(Oh, sweet Saint Anthony. How much longer is this going to take? Here's another thing I can't stand about you: the way you break up sentences to heighten the suspense. We're not doing

*amateur theater here: just say it, for fuck's sake! The reason you
what?)*

". . . Yes?"

". . . The reason I couldn't bring myself to embrace you is
that I didn't think you'd let me. And even though I have no
right to say this, given that we're divorced, feeling rejected by
you still causes me a great deal of pain."

"I'm sorry to hear that, Nives. You know that you're the last
person on earth I'd want to hurt in any way."

*(Oh, really? And all the times that it was you rejecting me,
dumping me—when I did, in fact, cry—after we'd fucked like
rabbits between your sessions at work? And all the times that I
tossed and turned in bed like an obsessive at the thought of you
going home to that architect you were seeing? All the times that
I asked you, either directly or indirectly, to consider getting back
together—when I asked you indirectly your rejection was even
more painful—it didn't hurt you then, did it, you stupid, conceited, egocentric monster? You know what I say to you? That I
don't give a good goddamn if it hurts you to be rejected, in fact
I'm delighted to hear it; now maybe you'll understand what it
feels like to be the one taking it unwillingly up the ass, you who
never once in your entire life took it up the ass without wanting
it, if I remember rightly.)*

Uncomfortable pause, during which I dreaded that any second now she'd say what I hoped against hope she wouldn't say:
which is exactly what she promptly did.

"I . . . this conversation is becoming too difficult for me,
Vincenzo. I know that your . . . partner . . . wasn't there when
you got out of the supermarket, and . . ."

"I'd actually prefer not to talk about that, if you don't
mind."

*(Alagia and Alfredo: the minute I see you two again, I'll kick
your asses, you little bastards.)*

"Yes, of course. It was indiscreet of me, forgive me."

"No, it's just that we're going through kind of an awkward period, and so that's something that's, how should I put it, been on our minds."

(You can say that again, my dear psychologist, that that was indiscreet of you. I never expected you to sink so low. Of all the self-nominations that you've trotted out so far, that one is absolutely the most devious. Fuck you and your alimony checks. I don't have the money anyway.)

"All right, I don't want to meddle. But if you ever want to talk, I'm here."

"Okay."

(Of course, the only thing missing from my life is a regular session with you. What kind of idiot do you take me for?)

"And I want you to know that I really admired what you did in the supermarket."

"Thanks."

(Go fuck yourself.)

There followed a very short pause.

"Vincenzo.

"What."

(Aaah!!)

"I love you."

"Yeah, me too."

(Ooh, you can't imagine how much. Esepcially if you forget about those checks I owe you.)

I sat there in a trance for I couldn't say how many minutes, waiting for my disgust with myself to subside, until I realized that I'd left the window open.

"Do you think this buffoonery is going to do you any good?" the busybody angel asked me from the windowsill. I'd hoped he'd taken his leave, after the way I'd gone to town on him the last time.

"Now's not a good time," I told him.

"I heard word for word exactly what you were thinking."

"Then that means you can hear what I'm thinking about you right now."

He came over and sat down on a corner of the Jonas, as if I'd said, "Make yourself comfortable."

"Keep it up and you'll just be leading her on, you cretin."

"That's her problem. I have another woman; it's not exactly a secret."

And here I have to say that he surprised me, because he refrained from making comments of any kind. A display of generosity that I didn't expect from him.

"You know what your problem is? You let things take care of themselves through inertia."

"Excuse me?"

"But things develop and grow just the same—what do you think? And it's not as if, when you find them big and fully developed before you, you can just say, 'Oooh, lookee here.'"

"I don't . . . understand . . . what you're talking about," I stammered.

"I'm talking about you."

I dropped my head.

"She's the one who left," I whined pathetically.

"Yeah, exactly. You see what I'm talking about?"

"I couldn't move. I was there, she was leaving, and I sat there watching her."

"Well, what if that was the right thing to do?"

"Seriously?" I asked, astonished and beaming.

"Try and look at it from another point of view: for once in your life you were aware of what was happening to you."

I felt something like a gust of cool air rushing up from underneath me, like Marilyn on the subway grate in that famous movie. I was tempted to clap my hands, I was so enthusiastic about the idea of successfully reenvisioning my status from a dignified point of view—just like that, from one moment to the next.

"Hey, you know that you have a point?"

He nodded and shrugged (implying that this was hardly a new experience for him), then he hopped down off the Jonas and back up onto the windowsill in a way that I wouldn't exactly describe as athletic.

"Okay. I'm going, then."

"What?"

"Well, for today my work is done, I think."

"You're already taking off?"

"What do you think, it's fun to look after you?"

I could have answered in kind, but since he'd momentarily earned my gratitude, I let it slide.

Flap-flap.

Taking advantage of my sudden surge of enthusiasm I went to court, just to take a walk around and enjoy the situation a bit, if you know what I mean.

And in fact I have to say that I really enjoyed myself. Everyone turned and looked. Everyone said hello. Even the ones who'd never said hello before. Everyone congratulated me. Even the ones I didn't know.

The things they ventured to say as commentary on the hostage taking qua trial made me feel awkward and embarrassed, but to see them cluster around me was a joy, truth be told.

From behind my sunglasses (which I never took off once, and in fact I almost fell down the stairs a couple of times), I gave monosyllabic responses. When someone waved a newspaper in front of my face, as if to say, "You represent us all," I acted shy and self-conscious.

Just one, shall we say, colleague, an old acquaintance (and pretty old, himself), all things considered a perfectly nice guy, one of those people who could live a peaceful existence if only they didn't feel they were engaged in some perennial competition with the world at large, walked past me repeatedly, ostentatiously refraining from saying hello.

On what was maybe the fifth flyover he came up to me and extended his hand. His jaws were clenched so tight by the effort he was making that I expected him to crack a molar any minute.

I felt as if I could read the subtitles beneath everything he said to me.

"Very moving stuff, Vincenzo."

(Oh, how I wish a heart attack would strike you down at this exact moment, leaving you conscious just long enough to see me smile as I pretend to call for help.)

"Oh, gee, really?"

"You were very . . . powerful."

(My God, I hate you so.)

His gaze had taken on the strange fixed expression that is a premonitory sign of a stroke. His ears had even reddened. Any moment now, I swear, I expected him to collapse twitching on the floor.

Luckily, my old friend Massimo came over and frog-marched me off, in defiance of all the rules of etiquette, forcing me to down another expresso.

My sixth that morning.

Vincenzo Submits
to Proust's Mini-Questionnaire

The principal feature of your personality?
Did you get my last name?

The quality you appreciate most in another man?
A sense of humor.

And in a woman?
A warm welcome.

Your biggest defect?
I tend to brood. But my secondary defects are every bit as impressive.

When was the last time you cried?
Just a few days ago, while watching a seventies tearjerker, *L'ultima neve di primavera* (The Last Snows of Spring), on a local channel. Do you remember it? The tagline on the posters was just appalling: . . . *Papà, it's a shame I'll never see you again.*

I don't believe you.
That's smart.

Who's the one person you met who changed your life?
I didn't remember that this was going to be one of the questions.

*

Excuse me?
Nothing, forget it.

Recurring dream?
I'm in an old apartment, I relax and get comfortable, then suddenly I remember that I sold the place and I'm filled with anguish at the thought that the new owners may come back from one moment to the next.

The person you'd summon back to life?
Massimo Troisi.

Favorite singer?
Sting.

The song you whistle most often in the shower?
"Oh! Susanna."

Personal cult film?
The Accidental Tourist.

Favorite actor?
William Hurt.

Favorite actress?
Emmanuelle Béart.

If you had several million euros?
I'd be much better off.

Favorite dish?
Spaghetti with *spunzilli* and basil.

Spunzilli?
Cherry tomatoes.

Favorite drink?
Amarone.

Hardly an unpretentious wine.
Now that I have several million euros in the bank, what should I drink, Tavernello?

Favorite city?
New York.

Your first love?
A total bitch.

The television show you love most?
The satirical variety show *Magazine 3*.

The transgressions you're most inclined to forgive?
Misdemeanors and petty felonies.

That's exactly the answer a lawyer would give.
I didn't feel like coming up with a moralistic answer.

Favorite song?
Fabrizio De Andrè's "Verranno a chiederti del nostro amore."

What would you be doing if you hadn't become a lawyer?
I'd be a rock guitarist.

Why, do you play the guitar?
No.

*

In that case, sorry?
Will you stop making comments about my answers?

What's your motto?
If you can't seize the moment, just take a little extra time.

What kind of motto is that?
Listen, are we done?

I have the impression that you've given me a series of non-sensical answers.
Sorry about that.

Premature Capitulation

I'm heading toward Assunta's place when my cell phone starts vibrating, forcing me to slow my pace. Without stopping I pull it out of my jacket breast pocket, already resigning myself to have to answer questions from another journalist.

But it's a text message.

From guess who.

My heart starts playing a piece of speed metal music.

I stop and lean against the trunk of a Smart car parked sideways between a Fiat Panda and a glass recycling bin, and I hyperventilate.

A, shall we say, matron, who is dragging a wheeled checkered cloth shopping cart behind her, walks past me and stares at me with a lack of discretion that I could even forgive if that indiscreet stare weren't tainted with disgust. So I ball up my fist and shake it at her, as if to say: "You want to tell me what you're staring at?" and she keeps on walking.

I've had enough of those housewives who go around town expressing their opinions of their fellow man by squinting or rolling their eyes. Why don't you just stay home, if you find modern society so repugnant? What do you think, that you're so wonderful to look at?

I take another minute before reading, hating myself for the queasiness I feel at the idea of learning the content of the text message that just a moment from now is going to appear on my cell phone screen, and I finally make up my mind.

*

I'm here.
The flight went fine.
Kisses. Ale

Ah, the flight went fine, I think to myself.
Wow, what a piece of news.
I shut my eyes, reopen them, and reread:

I'm here.
The flight went fine.
Kisses. Ale

And then once more:

I'm here.
The flight went fine.
Kisses. Ale

The total absence of pathos so completely takes the beauty out of the experience for me that I'm ready to believe in magic: and so I go on compulsively reading and rereading this vapid text, as if I expected it to transform suddenly before my eyes into something else, like maybe:

How handsome you were, stretched out on our bed, so sad, resigned to the fact that what we have together is coming to an end. I was an idiot not to tell you how much I love you, in that moment, not to confess to you that I have no idea why I've been so stubbornly pulling away from you in the last few months, when you're the one thing in this world that I want. Forgive me, and wait for me, confident I'll come back to you. As soon as I can get away from this stupid trial we'll lock the doors and close the shutters and make love for three straight days (speaking of which, have I told you you're getting better all the time?).

Just saying.

Instead the text remains unchanged, indifferent to all my entreaties and/or utopian dreams, just like the objects in front of Massimo Troisi when he tries to move them with the power of his mind in *Ricomincio da tre*.

I take a deep breath.

What a distinctive flavor depression has.

I resume my stride with my cell phone in my hand, and all around me everything becomes muffled. I stop thinking entirely, I just move my legs and walk.

I feel very much like Alan Ford in an old comic book story in which Brenda, his not-quite-girlfriend, gives him his walking papers in a letter, and he wanders down the sidewalks of New York with an idiotic smile stamped on his face (the compositions of the great Magnus go on for two or three pages, with the same unaltered drawing of Alan in the foreground, with only the background of each individual panel changing, signifying the flow of life all around him, indifferent to the despair of the protagonist as he moves through it), until suddenly he stops and bursts out sobbing in the middle of the crowd.

I go on walking for I don't even know how long in this state of dazed self-pity until I realize I've long since walked past Ass's front door.

If there's one thing I can't stand, it's losing control of my mental faculties, so I decree that the time has come to rebel: I position my cell phone in front of me as if to take a selfie, I enter REPLY mode, I concentrate long enough to calculate the degree of resentment to inject into the text, then, accompanying myself with a malevolently satisfied smile (and even though I feel as if my thumb has developed a localized case of Parkinson's), I compose the following text:

Congratulations on your choice of airline.

It takes me a minute to hit SEND, but in the end I press the button. During the sending process I close my eyes, savoring a sensation of vaguely nauseating lightheadedness that is not entirely unpleasant. When I reopen my eyes, and the display confirms the message has been sent, I slip my cell phone back into my pocket as if it were a .44 Magnum with smoke still pouring from the barrel and I look around, ready for new opportunities.

As I head back toward the front entrance of Ass's apartment building, I compliment myself effusively.

The situation changes radically when, as I'm ringing the downstairs doorbell, I feel the vibration of an incoming text in my breast pocket.

My legs start trembling, but I act cool, calm, and collected, grabbing my cell phone at the exact same moment that Miorita (Ass's caregiver) answers the intercom saying, "Yes," without a question mark, in a tone that sounds a lot like, "Did you really have to ring this apartment, with all the surnames listed there?"

"It's me," I say.

She thinks it over for a minute.

I still can't tell if she's doing it intentionally.

"Ah, Vinshinzo," she says, in her accent.

"Yeah, Vinshinzo," I say (meaning: "Do you think you might open the door now or should we carry on this conversation a little longer?").

The lock clicks open, accompanied by a buzzing sound like a protracted Bronx cheer.

I shoot a distracted glance at Alessandra Persiano's reply as I push the front door open to go in.

Perhaps I'd have appreciated it if you'd called me to find out if I'd arrived safely. Do you think that sending me a sarcastic response is going to make things easier? Have a good day.

Shit, I think. And I bitterly curse the moment I let myself give in to my anger and send her that cutting text, from which I already disassociate myself.

How solid her point of view looks to me and how infantile my own viewpoint seems to me now. What I wouldn't give to be able to go back in time and simply chop off that damned thumb if I could.

After all, I say to myself: I had a reasonable position, founded on omissions and things left unsaid; all that was needed was a dry, terse response (like, maybe: "Good. Break a leg in court") and I would have seemed remote and austere, but instead I had to ruin my facade of indifference with that stupidly hostile sentence, which revealed my resentment and, with it, my weakness. Practically speaking, I handed it to her, as they say, on a silver platter (when really, for these kinds of offerings, a plastic plate would be more than sufficient).

This is what always seems to happen with text messages: they give you the illusion that you have all the time you need to make your move and foresee the reactions that you'll provoke, but instead the opposite is true. When you're texting you feel all strategic, but you're simply being impulsive in a whole new way.

When I engage in flame wars via text, all I ever do is step in dogshit. And having stepped in dogshit in permanent written form, the dogshit sticks to me as documentary evidence, Exhibit A for the prosecution.

But I'm not emotionally credible as a witness. I tend to have fleeting bursts of rage, and it takes next to nothing to make me see the opposing side's arguments, especially if the opposing side is the woman I live with.

In other words, I suffer from premature capitulation. I wonder whether this tendency of mine to capitulate so prematurely is the main cause of the emotional shipwrecks into which I periodically steer myself.

I find Assunta curled up on the sofa, wrapped in a double-faced wool cardigan, with the TV turned on. I don't like the look of her complexion, to tell the truth. How long has it been since the last time I saw her, three days, four? It seems like two years have gone by.

She looks at me sideways, like she's just read my mind. I barely have time to come up with some diversion before she can broach the subject.

"I didn't know you watched *Mad Men*."

"I like the guy who plays Don Draper."

"So he's the reason you watch it?"

"Why else would I watch a show full of depressed people?"

I'm left speechless for a couple of seconds, as if I'd found the compressed review irreverent somehow, then I realize that I endorse it in the most unconditional terms imaginable. I've been watching *Mad Men* from the first season, and I can't wait to watch the next one, but I don't think I would have been capable of coming up with such a stark and essential critique.

How I admire the nonchalance with which some people can take an unprejudiced look at a book, a movie, a painting, a concert, whatever it happens to be, and capture its essence. Me, I don't know how to do that.

"Hey, that's true," I say, "these guys are all unhappy, each one more miserable than the next. You're absolutely right."

"So why do you watch it?"

"Because I like the actress who plays Joan, obviously."

"Ah, the busty one. Eh, well. Of course."

I sit down next to her as Miorita goes back and forth

between the living room and the kitchen, clumping around in her beat-up Crocs almost as if she were deliberately trying to annoy me (I'm starting to wonder if she's jealous of the fact that I'm Ass's favorite).

So nothing special, we chat, as usual. I try to wangle her forgiveness for making a fool of myself by motormouthing on the phone after the supermarket, she is courteous enough not to touch on the subject again, then we move on to the press coverage, she asks me what it's like to see myself in all the newspapers, I say, "No big deal," she says, "Suuure," then she asks me if anyone's recognized me on the street, I say, "A few people, yes," whereupon she asks me, with a provincialism that I'd never have expected from her, "Really? You can't really remain completely indifferent to a stranger's lack of discretion, tell me what it was like" (so odd how people tend to ask you to tell them about sensations more than events), so I concentrate for a few seconds and then I say to her, "I've got it," and she says, "What?" and I say, "Do you remember in school when the teacher would be lecturing and at a certain point he'd mention a historical figure, say King Ferdinand, and since there was a Ferdinand in our class, we'd all turn around smiling and look at him, and suddenly he'd take on a new light in our eyes, and he'd smile back at us as if he somehow deserved the attention, because he was now the beneficiary of a renown and notoriety that obviously had nothing to do with him and yet he was gratified by the coincidence?" And she says, "Of course, of course, I like this analogy, bravo," and I say, "There, now you see, that's how I feel"; after which she confesses that she got a certain thrill out of hearing me mentioned so frequently on the news in the past few days, whereupon, taking advantage of this unexpected softening on her part where television is concerned, I confide to her that I've been invited to appear on both *Annozero* and Daria Bignardi's show and that I'm thinking about picking

Daria Bignardi, and she asks me why, and I tell her that since Daria Bignardi's studios are in Milan, I want to go there, because Alessandra Persiano is in Milan and it's there that I'm planning to see her, convinced as I am that if we meet up in neutral territory we might be able to fix whatever it is that's gone wrong between us, because if you think about it, I add, you always need neutral territory to talk and come to an understanding, and sure enough at corporate and professional offices of a certain level there's always a room specially designated for this called, in fact, a meeting room, furnished with a long, usually oval table, chairs, and at the most a bookshelf, usually half-empty, and what else could a room so designed and furnished be but a neutral territory? And she says (the asshole), "In fact, you don't have a meeting room, do you?" And I say, "Thanks for reminding me, what would I do without you," and she says, "But, excuse me, do you have to go on Bignardi's show to go to Milan? Can't you just plain go to Milan, call Alessandra, and say to her, 'Hey there, guess where I am?'" And I say to her, "'Why, I'm surprised at you, are you really trying to compare going up there just to see her—giving her such an inordinate satisfaction, practically crawling at her feet, or even worse, giving her a chance to accuse me of having gone up there to check up on her (I can already hear the speech: 'So this means I'm not even free to travel for work without your feeling you have the right to follow me and see what I'm doing? Thanks a lot for the vote of confidence')—with going up there for an independent and admirable reason like being the guest of honor on a popular talk show." And she says, "Vincenzo, you amaze me, what an idiot you are, but how old are you, twelve?" And I say, "How much do you want to bet that it works?" And she says, "Certainly, you must really respect her a great deal, this woman," and I say, "It's not how you think," and she says, "Obviously you'll have to tell her that you're going to be on

Bignardi's show, otherwise how can you be sure that she'll see you?" And I say, "Clearly." And she says, "Wow, what a brilliant plan."

We stop for a minute to watch Don Draper angrily climbing the staircase in his home with his wife at his heels, scolding him for never taking responsibility for what goes on in the family (I'll take this opportunity to note that in a moving matrimonial quarrel—a classic trope—it's always the wife pursuing the husband, never the other way around), and from a certain way that Ass has of settling back into the sofa I foresee an imminent transition to a much more serious topic of conversation than that of using my television appearances to win back my girlfriend.

A moment later, in fact, as Betty (Mrs. Draper, as lovely as Grace Kelly) shouts at her husband: "It's not her job to raise our children!" she puts a hand on my shoulder and says:

"Now there's something I need to tell you."

I pick up the remote control, lower the volume, set the remote control down next to me, lean forward, place my elbows on my knees, and interlace my fingers.

Assunta follows the entire sequence with her eyes, as if she found my intricate preparations to be a bit much.

"Wednesday I have my first session of chemo."

I take a few seconds, then I realize that the time has finally come to get down to brass tacks.

"Listen, Ass, till now I've never really talked to you about it, but I think you ought to let Nives . . ."

She shakes her head, stopping me from finishing my sentence, and shoots me the off-kilter glance you normally concede to the completely discredited, when denying them the faculty of arguing their case.

The next thing she says to me makes me feel like a complete and utter boob.

"Look, don't think for a minute that I haven't known all along you were here to see me on a mission, please."

I suddenly feel a surge of feverish heat.

"*On a mission?*" I reply, pretending to be scandalized.

"Come on, now don't make that face. I've been treating my daughter like shit for weeks now, I barely even answer the phone when she calls, I measure out my visits with my niece and nephew with an eyedropper, so now they've sent you, obedient minion that you are, to scope out the situation: what could be simpler. Why shouldn't they have? It's exactly what I would do myself."

"Obedient minion that I am?" I repeat in my mind something like five times in a row.

If the mortification-induced outbreak of rosacea that has just swept over me is stamped on my face, I must be a ridiculous sight to behold.

The only thing that keeps me from telling Ass to go to hell in a handbasket (together with her lovely daughter, it goes without saying) is the affection I have for her.

So I say nothing, limiting myself to opposing a rhetorical resistance to the subcutaneous vascular dilation that continues to inflame my cheeks.

"Are you offended because I called you an obedient minion?" she asks when I don't react.

"Oh, don't be silly, why should I be?"

"In fact, why should you be? It's the truth."

"You're right, it's the truth," I say indignantly. "In that case, my scouting expedition ends here."

I get to my feet, but only because I can no longer bring myself to remain seated.

"Are you leaving?" she asks, with an edge of hostility.

I peer around nervously, as if I were looking for something, or I were having an attack of claustrophobia, what the fuck do I know.

No, I have no intention of leaving. And I already know that even if she asked me to go, I'd try to stay. But since I say nothing, she moves the conversation forward on her own.

"So tell me, is the only reason you've been coming to see me to reconcile me with Nives? And now that you know you've failed your task, you're leaving?"

I fill my lungs with air, then I let my shoulders drop as an exasperated sigh escapes my lips.

"Holy Christ, Ass!" I exclaim, nauseated with myself and with this unexpected dispute.

She sits back and blinks twice, realizing that she's been taking it out on someone who is not at fault.

"Sorry," she says. And she turns her gaze away from me.

I can't stand to see a pained expression on the face of someone I love; it reduces me to despair in a way that nothing else on earth can do. I'd do anything to wipe the pain from their features. When I see a mouth twisting in mortification, a gaze lost in the middle distance, a stab of pain that takes form and disfigures a face I adore, it just kills me.

And so I sit back down next to her and take her hands in mine, as if I were about to pop the question.

"Hey," I say in a whisper, "I *may* be an obedient minion, and in fact I most certainly *am* one, but I haven't been coming here as Nives's informant, I swear to you. If I've been coming to see you, it's because I wanted to."

She slowly raises her head until her eyes line up with mine, with the air of mocking defiance I know all too well.

She's already over it.

"Oh, you really don't understand a thing. You've been coming because *I* wanted you to."

I snicker.

"You know what your real forte is? Modesty, without a doubt."

"I was just trying to explain to you that I've finally decided to allow myself the freedom to decide who I want to spend time with and who I don't."

I close my eyes; I shake my head. I gently squeeze her hands.

"Listen, Ass, being the chosen one flatters me, it really does. But you also ought to understand that declaring an embargo on your own daughter at this juncture is, how to put this, kind of . . . *nasty*, that's the word."

Her eyes open wide and then she whinnies in amusement.

"And you know what your true forte is? Finding exactly the right word."

"Which word, 'embargo'?"

She laughs.

"What an idiot you are."

"Am I your pet or not? That ought to give me the right to speak my mind."

"And in fact it does. You said it and you're still here, if I'm not mistaken."

"So am I right?"

"Of course."

"Oh, my God," I comment, stroking my forehead.

"It doesn't happen to you often, does it?"

"Ha, ha, funny lady. In that case, if I'm right, would you tell me why you're behaving this way?"

"Because I want to know what it feels like to be an asshole, for a change. It's not like I'm necessarily going to die the day after tomorrow; I have a little time left to earn her forgiveness."

I try to collect my thoughts before answering. It's no easy thing when you're dealing with someone who formulates such solid ideas.

She's a little bit like Engineer Romolo Sesti Orfeo, now that I think about it. Demanding conversationalists.

"Think for a second about what you just said, would you? A minute ago you scolded me for behaving like a twelve-year-old: does this strike you as a grown-up way to act?"

"I've been acting like a grown-up since I was fourteen, Vince'. Imagine how little I care, considering how long I have left to live."

"Jesus Christ, Ass, this is your daughter you're talking about. Your daughter and your grandchildren: which is to say my children, not to put too fine a point on it. Did you really have to experiment with being an asshole on them, of all people?"

"What do you think, that a person always wants to see their children? To have them in the house at all hours, with the right they seem to have to butt into everything and nitpick everything you do, including the way you dress when you go out and the clothes you wear around the house, to let you know about everything in their lives that isn't working, from their vacuum cleaner to their marriage, as if you possessed limitless energy, and had no life of your own, with things you lack and things you need, as if it were your duty to always take out your scissors and clip away a little bit of space for yourself, because three quarters of your time they eat up for themselves? A time must come when you can stop taking care of your own children, am I wrong?"

Jesus, she's right. She's so right that I wouldn't argue with her even if I knew what to say.

"You can easily imagine how much I adore Nives. And I feel ridiculous even saying it, it's such a given. Probably she's the only thing I ever did that I don't regret; and you know how much it cost me to raise her. But my daughter is a tremendously self-centered person. She's a power-monger. A winner. Capable of manipulating people in a way no one else seems to be able to do."

"You're telling me."

"That's right, I'm telling you. Because you know what I'm talking about."

"And how."

"For once in my life, I'd like to show her that everything can't always go according to her plans. That I had a right to know about my illness, that she should have told me right from the very start and not left me to figure it out on my own."

"So that's it."

She gently frees her right hand from the fragile grip of both of my mine and fans herself with it. Then she answers me with an edge in her voice, as if she were doing it unwillingly.

"Yes. No. I don't know what it is, Vincenzo. All I know is that I no longer have any desire to understand anyone else. To behave like an adult, as you say. And that if right now I don't feel like seeing Nives, I have no intention of feeling guilty about it. Period."

I pull my head back, and it dawns on me that her unwillingness to engage in a give-and-take, for some reason that I can't quite explain, moves me.

"Okay. Okay. You're right," I say, pulling back the hand she'd taken away from me and wrapping it once again in mine.

"Really?"

"Yes. I can't see how I can disagree with you."

"Thank you. It does me good to hear it."

We sit for a few seconds without speaking. When I'm pretty sure that she's over her inner turmoil, I go on.

"Hey."

"What is it."

"Do you want me to go with you on Wednesday?"

"That's what I was trying to tell you before. I don't think I'll go."

"Excuse me, what did you just say?"

"I just can't do it, Vince'. Chemo is exhausting and demoralizing, and it takes real determination to take it on."

I certainly wasn't expecting this. And the worst thing is that I can't say a single word. Because it's clear to me from the expression on her face when she tells me this that any argument would sink like a stone—*plunk*.

My speechlessness must inspire a certain tenderness in her, because she immediately changes her tone.

"Hey. Don't look at me like that. Today's Thursday. I might very well change my mind."

I nod sadly, pretending to believe her.

She looks at my hands, which are still holding hers captive, and then smiles at me.

"Now, unless you're about to pull out a ring, you really ought to give me back my hands, because I need them."

W hat do you mean?"
That's the question that arises automatically when you're presented with a fait accompli. More than rhetorical, it's a polemical question: it contains the illusion that by talking about what's happened you can still do something to prevent it. And that's the question Alagia slaps me in the face with when I answer her call to my cell. I'm on the street, with a nervous haste prodding me on, unjustifiably, because no one is expecting me where I'm going.

"Your grandma doesn't want to do the chemo."

"You already wrote that to me in the text."

"Exactly."

"But that's bullshit. It doesn't make any sense."

"That's what I think too."

Actually that's not exactly what I think, but it's what I say.

"Vincenzo, don't try to be telegraphic, for Pete's sake. Do you think this is the kind of news you break in a text?"

I find her point so stupid that I abruptly stop where I am.

"In effect, I'd been planning to say it with flowers, but I've been so busy lately."

Come to think of it, my retort is stupid too.

A guy with a dog that looks exactly like him walks past, looks me in the face, and snickers.

"What an asshole you are."

"Among other things."

Alfredo must be close by; he's just asked her in the background: "Why?"

I start walking again.

"Go on, you talk to him," I hear her say with a tone of disgusted superiority.

As I wait for her to hand the phone to her brother, I'm hypnotized by a flier stuck to a stoplight pole with packing tape, as if in a picture frame.

PUPPIES FOR SALE
BORN TO A PUREBRED GERMAN SHEPHERD
EXCELLENT PEDICURE
FOR INFORMATION: (348) *******

Generally speaking, when I run into a gem like this one, I immortalize it with my cell phone. Only right now I can't, seeing as it's pressed up against my ear. But since I wouldn't dream of missing the opportunity to capture and archive this masterful display of extemporaneous illiteracy, it occurs to me that I'll have to stay right here until the end of the phone call and then take the picture immediately thereafter.

"Papà?" says Alf.

"Tell that neurasthenic of a sister of yours that she's an uncouth oaf," I promptly reply.

"Sure, okay, I'll tell her. But what's all this about Grandma?"

"What can I tell you, Alfre'. She won't go in for the chemo. She doesn't feel up to it."

"But she'll die."

"Yeah, I know that."

God, it's so frustrating.

"Did you try reasoning with her?"

I say nothing.

"Papà? Hello?"

I take a deep breath and prepare myself for the line of bullshit I'm about to hand him.

"Sure, I tried," I say, stroking my forehead in shame, "but you know your grandmother, she doesn't talk, she issues decrees."

He heaves a helpless sigh.

"Now how are we going to break the news to Mamma?"

I have nothing to say, so he goes on, as if talking to himself.

"Plus, in this whole thing, Grandma keeps refusing to see her. And she's pretty remote with us too. What is she thinking? Not only do we have to fight Grandma's cancer, we actually have to fight Grandma who's decided to stop fighting cancer. Why are we all so twisted, Papà? Why do we always make everything more complicated? Why can't we just deal with our problems the way normal families do?"

I don't feel I have much to add on this topic either.

"Papà?"

"Eh."

"Holy Christ, why don't you say anything?!"

"I was just listening to you, Alfre'."

"Well, okay," he says, fuming, "but at least emit a sound, moan, just so I know that we're still connected, for Christ's sake! I feel like I'm sitting here talking to myself!"

"You see?" I hear that jerk of a sister of his say in the near background.

I'm mortified.

"Come on, Alf, don't be that way. The first session is in a week. She still might change her mind."

"So in the meantime you're not planning to do anything?"

For a moment everything around me goes blurry.

"Could you repeat that, please?"

My lips are quivering.

"Listen, Papà, we need to . . ." he says, trying to backpedal, sensing the storm bearing down on him, but I don't let him finish.

"No, you listen to me, young man: who the hell do you think I am, your man in Havana?"

He tries to reply but I'm all over him.

"It's not my fault if your grandma decides not to seek medical care, you understand? Just as it's not my fault if she doesn't want to see her daughter."

I stop for a second and look around, because I've just realized I'm shouting.

Alf doesn't dare to answer me.

Which just winds me up for the rest of my rant.

"Instead of calling me on the phone and delivering these indignant and insolent lectures, why don't you get your asses in gear and go see your grandma and give her one of these lovely self-righteous speeches?"

"Papà, wait just a se . . ."

"You know what's changed? What's changed is that I'm sick and tired of being your scapegoat. I have problems of my own, and I certainly don't come around and weigh you down with them, neither you nor your sister, much less your mother, get it? Why don't the three of you learn to do the same, and leave me in peace!"

And with that, I hang up.

In the instant that follows, I realize that I've applied Ass's lesson, exactly as imparted. Which not only offers me a chance to experience the liberating sensation that she had described to me, it makes me feel closer to her than ever before. If I weren't already setting up the phone in camera mode so I could take home with me the flier advertising German shepherds with excellent pedicures, I'd call her and tell her just how right she was.

I get to the bus stop and take the first one that pulls up. If I felt like it, I could check the routes shown on the map posted on the pole, but I don't feel like it. I'd rather leave it to fate and maybe ask later along the way whether I'm heading in the right direction or not.

It's crazy, and I know it. But that's how I've always used public transportation. As long as a bus isn't actually going in the opposite direction I just get on board and then figure out how to get where I have to go.

There must be a reason that I tend to be a repeat offender when it comes to intentionally getting lost this way, but I don't have the slightest idea what it could be.

I take a seat, giving myself up to vague, listless thoughts made up for the most part of regrets already equipped with justifications, and by the time we're well outside city limits (those stretches where, almost from one moment to the next, the landscape slips into a depression, and all you see are shuttered restaurants, gas stations, car repair shops, and half-built apartment buildings), I walk up to the driver and ask him if this bus goes to the hospital.

He turns around as if he suspects I'm trying to make a fool of him, but then he looks me in the face and asks me despairingly why I didn't ask in the first place.

So he explains to me more or less where we are (I nod and pretend I understand), then he pulls over and lets me out (even though, he specifies, it's not a stop on his route) and recommends I take another bus, but on the opposite side of the road.

I thank him and cross the road, without even slightly understanding where the hell I am, then I wait for almost forty minutes, buffeted by an inexplicably cold wind, until in the distance I see a bus appear, marked with the number that the driver told me to look for, and at that moment I feel so euphoric that I actually consider the possibility that it might be a mirage.

When I finally arrive at the hospital, I do some quick addition and realize that it took me exactly an hour and twenty-five minutes to get there.

I walk into the ward and speak with the chief nurse. She tells me that she saw me on TV and compliments me lavishly before telling me that Engineer Romolo Sesti Orfeo is in stable condition, and that in any case she can't let me go in because right now the chief physician is making his rounds, but that if I'm willing to wait, I can get more information from him.

So I head over to the waiting room.

It's awkward to find yourself in the same room as a very pretty girl, especially if you don't know her and above all if the room in question is empty except for you and her. Because you immediately begin to act as if you'd done something wrong. It's as if she knew something compromising about you and could tell everyone who cared to know anytime she chose. You act indifferent, but you are in fact acting, and it shows. Among other things, the unnatural effort you're being forced to make puts you on edge in a way that comes very close to crossing the line into downright rudeness, so that if it happens that the girl asks you what time it is (which she does, with the utmost non-chalance and without any ulterior motives) you're likely to bite her head off in response.

All of this, whether we like it or not, derives from the fact that beauty is a form of truth, and it doesn't like having liars around it.

Personally I try to avoid this kind of embarrassment (because in the presence of great beauty I become terribly provincial: I blush, I stammer, I stand up and sit back down, I fan myself with my bare hands, and so on), but the problem is that when I wind up in a situation of this sort, I don't know how to get myself out of it (even though right now, for instance, I could simply pretend that I need to make a phone call and take refuge in the hallway, or perhaps go straight home, since I don't really even know what I came here for), and I behave in a variety of very odd ways.

In fact, when out of the corner of my eye I notice that the girl (who by the way looks a little like Cameron Diaz in *There's Something About Mary*, and is emanating a wonderful scent that is vaguely reminiscent of caramel) has looked at me once, and then again, and then a third time, and I begin to fear that before long she's going to try to start a conversation with me (though why she would want to do so, of course, I can't figure out to save my life, unless perhaps she's seen me on television), which is in fact exactly what happens, because she gets up and comes trippingly over to me and says, "Excuse me?" dominating me from above with her ineffable beauty, not only do I remain in hiding behind the pages of an issue of *Marie Claire* from, I think, six months ago that I picked up from a chair on my way in, but I don't even answer her.

"Excuse me," There's Something About Mary repeats at this point, speaking a little louder and tilting her head to try to look into my face, understandably confused by my indifference.

So I'm forced to emerge from behind my *Marie Claire* shoji screen, like a tortoise from its shell.

"Oh. I'm sorry. I was just focused."

She shoots a baffled glance at the magazine, then decides to ignore my answer.

"I apologize if I'm intruding. I've been hoping to meet you. I'm . . . or, rather, I was Massimiliano Sesti's girlfriend."

As she says this, she looks me right in the eye, without any uncertainty, like a person who has no fear of being taken the wrong way.

Her face remains smooth: she hasn't granted me a ceremonious smile, or blinked hesitantly, or shown even a hint of awkwardness. This paragon of dignity, so compactly homogeneous, immediately extinguishes my shyness. I close my copy of *Marie Claire* and stand up, extending my hand.

"It's a pleasure. Vincenzo."

"Irene," she replies.

She seems so tired. I'm very tempted to ask if she got any sleep last night.

"I remembered your last name, but not your first," she adds, and at last she smiles.

Jesus, it's as if the sun had just come into the room.

"I believe that," I say. "It's the only thing about me that people tend not to forget easily."

The smile spreads until it narrows her eyes. I couldn't say just what color they are, by the way (I don't really know how to tell what color eyes are; but I do know how to drown helplessly in them).

"For what it's worth, I wanted to tell you that I really appreciated what you did."

"Believe me, I didn't do anything," I reply, and I say it with sincerity. "I don't even remember exactly what I said. I was just feeling my way, hoping the mayhem would come to an end as soon as possible. I don't even know whether I should feel guilty or not for what happened to the engineer. Maybe that's why I came here today."

"There's no reason for you to feel guilty."

"How can you say that?"

"Because he would have done it no matter what."

I look into her eyes in search of some kind of sign that confirms the confidence with which she makes this statement, but once again she offers me nothing.

And so I go on.

"I was the one who distracted him so that the carabiniere could take him by surprise."

She shakes her head. Once, decisively.

"That doesn't count. In fact, I don't think it's an accident that he allowed himself to be distracted."

"Why are you so sure?"

"Because I know how he felt."

I say nothing.

We study each other, reciprocally.

"Would you tell me something?" I ask, adopting an indiscreet tone of voice.

"Sure."

"How long has it been since you got any sleep?"

She seems happy that I asked, judging from the way she looks at me.

The Future Is a Repressed Past

If only I'd gotten it right in my flash forward: my return home is much worse than I expected. Forget about the killer smoke from *Lost*, forget about "Diario" by Equipe '84: the loneliness grabs me by the throat before I even get my key into the lock. And when I close the door behind me, the way I miss Alessandra Persiano becomes a quality of the air, an impoverishment of the meaning of things, the wear and tear of the walls, a crumpling of the apartment's floor plan.

From the front door to the bedroom is all uphill.

Miming (without even consciously meaning to) a sequence of absolutely filmic gestures, I take off my jacket, I toss it toward the Foppapedretti valet stand (the only piece of non-Ikea furniture I possess, a Christmas gift from Alagia and Alf), miss it entirely, then stand with my back to the bed (the old Ikea Hemnes, but with a new Sultan Finnvik polyurethane memory-foam mattress selected by Alessandra Persiano along with the Gosa Klätt pillows specially designed for side-sleepers like us), throw out my arms, and let myself fall back onto the Astrakhan bedcover, which puffs gently as I land.

And as I perform a series of exercises in self-pity while contemplating the ceiling in this Christlike position, I think (speaking of the cinematic nature of this moment) how nice it would be if I could just make time dissolve, skip the present entirely, and go directly to the after, to when I'll be over this moment of pain. If my image could shimmer out and then reappear in another scene, e.g., an Exterior Day, and superim-

posed at the bottom of the shot there could be a caption reading "Six months later," and there I'd be, I don't know, strolling
past a café, ideally in Paris, waiting for a woman who bears a
striking resemblance to Emmanuelle Béart in Claude Chabrol's
L'Enfer, or even better, not someone who looks like her, but
her, and she'd show up a little later, late and out of breath, and
after kissing me sweetly on the lips she'd ask me (in French,
which of course I'd have learned to speak fluently in the last
six months) whether I've been waiting long; then we'd walk off
arm in arm down the Boulevard Saint-Germain as the credits
begin to roll.

If there's one thing that drives me crazy in movies, it's the
therapy of grief. The suppression of unhappiness. The censorship of the long hard slog out. Life resumes only when it
becomes tolerable. What I wouldn't give to be able to put up
a sign saying "Six months later" in my own non-cinematic life.

Oh, I know what you're thinking. I can already hear the
objection: "Sure, okay, but even that time between is part of
your life: if you skip it, it's as if you died in the meanwhile."

Then try this one on for size: "Better to add life to your days
than days to your life."

Nice, eh?

And do you want to know who said it?

Rita. Levi. Montalcini.

That's who.

So to hell with the two-bit rhetoric of life being worth living even when it involves suffering. If I possibly can, I avoid
suffering.

And in any case, in the interest of covering all our bases, let
it be said that in literature too it's possible to pull a "Six months
later": e.g., by closing one chapter of a novel with a separation
or a death, without telling what happened next and then moving on to the next chapter; but the reader, who is alone with the
book and therefore has to do everything for himself (without the

assistance of lights, locations, bodies, voices, and music playing in the background), will internalize that unnarrated interval and drag it with him into the next chapter in the form of pure melancholy; while film, which possesses an array of tools of mystification and above all enjoys the privilege of light, doesn't give the viewer time to self-flagellate, assaulting him with all the biting intensity of its toolkit, centrifuging his emotions and hurling him bodily into a possible future, to fill him with a new hope.

An illusion, no question. But isn't it a great one?

I'm so astounded by the sheer intelligence of these thoughts that I don't hear my cell phone until the third ring. I jump to my feet in the grip of anxiety. I know it's her calling me, I just know it.

I gather my jacket up from the floor but I can't find my cell phone; it must have fallen out of the pocket when I threw the jacket on the Foppapedretti valet (or perhaps I should say, *toward* the valet).

I get down on my knees and scan the floor.

When I finally spot the phone, on like the twelfth ring or so, perfectly camouflaged between one leg of the bed and a leg of the Hemnes nightstand, it's too late.

With my heart in my throat I look at the caller ID for the missed call.

I knew it, I knew it, I knew it.

I immediately call back, praying that it won't go the way I'm afraid it will.

No such luck: it goes straight to the "can't be reached" message.

I grip my phone tight, I lift my arm, and I hurl it straight forward, aiming at the wall and practically dislocating my shoulder (I don't release, obviously, I only pretend to throw it; the last thing I need to do right now is break my cell phone just so I can feel like I'm in a movie).

I try calling back: same as previously.

Of course; it went straight to the "can't be reached" message just a moment ago.

I ought to have figured it out by now, right? Nope, I press CALL for the third time (thereby giving the witch a gift of three consecutive records of my clinging psycho-affective dependency), and for the third time the prerecorded female voice informs me that the number I've dialed cannot be reached for the moment, in a peremptory tone that I'd swear has just a hint of annoyance lurking beneath the surface.

I listen to it in English too, as long as I'm at it.

Once I hit the bottom of my helplessness, and the bedroom begins to take on a murkiness that seems to foreshadow the grayish-yellowish hue that will tinge all my returns home from this moment forward, I start pacing back and forth in the apartment, trying to convince myself that a person would have to be terribly cynical to call for the sole purpose of making an incomplete attempt, to prefabricate an alibi as vulgar as it is threadbare.

The message she's sending, I tell myself out loud, is clear: "I tried to call you. You weren't there (or you chose not to answer). I am therefore authorized to do whatever the fuck I want until the next time we speak; that is, if we ever do."

I wish that that busybody guardian angel who was assigned to me were here right now. Then at least he could tell me that this is not the way these things are done. That if Alessandra Persiano had really wanted to talk to me, she would have called back. Most important of all, she wouldn't have shut off her phone after the first attempt. And that therefore, in fact, she really is a bitch.

I really need this kind of reassurance, because to think badly of your own girlfriend is a little like thinking badly of yourself. It's not something you can handle alone. But he's never around when you need him; so I decide to set aside my resolution to be discreet and I do what I have until now wholeheartedly intended not to: I call Espe and tell him the whole story.

Contrary to my expectations, he lets me confide in him graciously and with admirable sensitivity. He starts by categorically ruling out the hypothesis that this constitutes a definitive separation, and to support this belief he describes a couple of personal experiences that have absolutely nothing in common with my own, and in fact I forget them in real time (it's typical of friends to offer examples that don't have anything to do with anything when you ask them for advice); then he remains silent for a few seconds (but as we all know, on the phone, seconds are converted into minutes the way that lire are converted into euros) before asking me a direct question that, I confess, really catches me off guard.

"Do you think she's pissed off at you for any specific reason?"

"Sorry, what do you mean?"

"I mean do you get the impression that there's something that she just can't forgive you for?"

Fuck, I think to myself.

"I'm not following you," I lie.

Pause.

"Have you been faithful to her, Vince'?"

"Come again?"

"Did you fuck someone else?"

"Ah, I see," I say to myself. "He's beating around the bush."

"I don't see what that has to do with anything," I reply, starting to fan myself with my free hand.

"Okay, let's move on from there. Just one woman?"

"Espe, please."

"Two? Three? Twenty-three? Believe me, there's a big difference."

"Only one, I swear."

"That's exactly the difference: one is the worst."

"What?" I say. But I know exactly what he means, and I couldn't agree more.

"Is this affair still going on?"

"There is no affair."

"How long did it last? And don't lie to me."

I unbutton my shirt.

"Two months. Three, maybe. But I might have seen her four or five times in all."

"Hmm."

"What are you ruminating about now?"

"And Alessandra doesn't know a thing."

"Of course not."

"And you're sure."

"Sure of what?"

"Of that."

"Of *what*?"

"That she doesn't know."

"Yes. I think so. I mean, no. Fuck, no. She doesn't know."

He withdraws for a moment. Probably to chambers, to deliberate.

"Now I have to ask you a tough question. But you have to answer me on the spot."

"Good lord, Espe. I don't know what I was thinking when I decided to confide in you, really."

"Ready?"

I take a deep breath.

"Ready."

"Did you pull some bullshit move, by chance?"

"Some bullshit move?"

"That's right, some blunder. Like Alessandra was about to catch on and you had to cover your ass at the last second."

Sudddenly I can't see; I lose my twenty-twenty vision all at once.

Then out of nowhere I feel a compelling need to unburden

myself of the truth. This is why people cave under questioning and confess.

"Yes. Goddamn you. Yes."

"There," he says with satisfaction.

"But it went off without a hitch, Espe, I swear to you," I hasten to justify myself while talking in machine-gun bursts, as if I were trying to stall before he could file the verdict and make it official. "That idiot, I mean the other woman, sent me a text message calling me Filippo on purpose just to make me jealous, and Alessandra and I ended up laughing about it, just think, Alessandra wanted to call her and ask for this Filippo's phone number and . . . Oh, Christ."

And that's where I break off, because justifications (as you realize right in the middle of trying to justify yourself) need to be brief in order to be convincing.

Espe picks up on my discomfort, and meets me halfway.

"There's no reason for you to explain it to me, Vince'. If you say that she didn't put it together, I believe you, okay? But it's just that when a woman pulls away from one day to the next without telling you why, and your conscience isn't absolutely spotless, then the first question to ask yourself is whether she knows something that you thought she didn't."

"Ah, I see," I reply in terror.

"We need to think like guilty men, understand me, Vince'?" he says, shifting into the first person plural just to make it clear how close he feels to me at this moment. "Because if we are the first to be suspicious of ourselves, just imagine how suspicious they are."

"But I really believe there's no way she could have figured it out."

At this point I'm answering without even thinking about what I'm saying, as if I'd signed some diabolical pact with Espe and I automatically set out in bad faith, converting that bad faith into actual sincerity.

"Well, in that case, you're ahead of the game," he says, becoming more tractable; as if my answer had convinced him and, therefore, reassured him.

"Really?"

"Suuure. And remember not to fuck up by bringing up the subject yourself or offering her the slightest pretext for thinking you lied. Stick to your story, play the moron, and flip the problem on its head. Go on acting as if you can't wrap your head around why she would want to treat you this way. If that's the reason she left you, that is, if she's convinced you took another woman to bed, then you'll see: she'll come back."

I look around, bewildered by the professional approach that Espe has taken to my personal drama. It's as if he's scaled down my romantic sufferings to some lesser stage of trauma, delivering me a version of myself that I find frankly repugnant.

The truth is that this, shall we say, criminologist's approach unsettles me because it appeals to the more ignoble part of my personality; and it does so directly, without hypocrisy. As if he were saying to me: "I'm not going to sit here and play the sidekick to your pretentious moaning about how complicated you are and the fact that you think you're losing your woman for who knows what untranslatable motives. Let's take it down a couple of levels. Let's start out from the basic assumption that you're a filthy male pig who likes to screw the first piece of female flesh that comes within reach. I'm not going to treat you like an overwrought intellectual, I'm going to treat you like a male hypocrite who wants nothing more complicated than to have sex and get away with it. So why are we wasting our time and our breath, just tell me that you didn't leave any embarrassing evidence at the scene of the crime, right?"

However much I value his good intentions, I'm filled with a powerful need to disassociate myself from such a materialistic (or perhaps I ought to say flatly material) version of my suffering.

"I think that you're looking at things from a rather narrow point of view."

He hesitates, as if he were tempted to laugh in my face, or emit a Bronx cheer in my direction, or possibly both; then he retreats to a more open-minded point of view.

"Maybe so. But if it turns out I'm right, I want you to let me know."

"Okay."

"But another thing: dinner with the hotties is still on for tomorrow night. You're not going to come up with some excuse at the last second, eh?"

"No, don't worry, I'll be there."

"You'll see, you'll feel better."

I suddenly visualize a picture that chills my blood.

"Tell me something: are you already envisioning, like, a big old orgy?"

"Are you joking? I'm an old-fashioned gentleman."

"Listen, I'll ride along. Nothing more."

"Eh. I know. How many times are you going to tell me?"

"You don't believe me, eh?"

"Oh, good lord, why shouldn't I believe you? Your heart is broken, you're proof against temptation. What kind of effect would I expect two gorgeous babes who are dying to spend the evening with you to have?"

"Oh, go get fucked, Espe."

"Sure, but I want to be in the driver's seat. Oh, and I'm picking you up at eight. Wear a nice suit. Come to think of it, do you *have* a nice suit?"

I hang up on him, then I go back to my tour of my apartment in an attempt to recover my noble state of anxiety in order to cleanse myself of the horrendous discomfort that this not-exactly innocent conversation between old friends has left me with. But it does no good: I already feel like I don't know myself.

At that point I delve into the archive of Happy Moments, exhuming a couple of truly unforgettable ones dating from the first six months of my affair with Alessandra Persiano; then, without any collateral effect much less a direct link, I find myself singing the refrain "E mi manchi amore mio" by Laura Pausini (which just yesterday, wafting out the windows of a Fiat Cinquecento as it went past, practically brought me to tears), then I try to break the bank with the evergreen "Se bruciasse la città" by Massimo Ranieri (which even fits in perfectly with the condition of separation aggravated by geographical distance), but nothing happens at all—zero.

The failure of this last experiment really worries me. Because "Se bruciasse la città" is a neorealist song. It contains a faithful description of the fantastical scene that's inscribed in the genetic code of any male who's been dumped, and it's therefore an ideal test bench. You can't be insensible to the power of "Se bruciasse la città" if your woman has just left you.

In the song in question, as many of my Italian readers will remember, the narrator, who has just learned that his ex is getting married in May (people always get married in May, in songs), wishes he could make his way through the smoking rubble of the city devastated by some unspecified cataclysm to rejoin his beloved (love being reborn in the ruins: who hasn't daydreamed about that fairytale, at least in response to your first brutal dumping as an adolescent?).

This is the refrain:

If the city were on fire
To you
To you
To you I'd run
I'd even beat the fire just to get back to you
If the city were on fire
I know

I know
You'd come looking for me
Even after our farewells
I am love
For you

Then, as long as he's at it, the apocalyptic dreamer makes a quick reference to the location that the two former lovers preferred for their intimate encounters:

That meadow on the outskirts of town
Saw you become mine so many times
It's been too long since it knew
Where my happiness lies

Which is not exactly a gentlemanly thing to go around telling the whole world, but if a guy's girlfriend is about to get married to someone else, we can overlook a stylistic misstep, I think (and in any case the choice of a meadow as one's trysting place is a classic, to be found in many popular songs: let one serve as an example among many, "L'uva fogarina," which, after an extended series of "diridindindins," hails the act of love during a grape harvest, in fact, in the midst of a meadow or field, "*in mezzo al pra'*").

And so, in short, I sing the song again from beginning to end, in a mumble, but there doesn't seem to be any way of getting back to my suffering. In fact, if you want to know the whole truth, I'm not the least bit interested in burning Milan to the ground (because that's where Alessandra Persiano is right now) and sacrificing all those innocent lives just for the sake of making peace with her.

As much as it annoys me to acknowledge it, Espe has corrupted me. And I even suspect that I'm enjoying the infection.

It's at this point that I receive the phone call that I absolutely shouldn't be receiving. Of course, I know with total certainty who it is. I'm so certain that when I see the name on the display I'm not the least bit surprised.

When this kind of thing happens, I start to think that the future, at least the near future, consists of nothing other than the least opportune thing that we can imagine happening to us.

"Hello."

"Counselor?"

"Yes?"

"It's Irene," says Cameron Diaz.

I close my eyes and open them again.

"Oh, hi. Sorry, I hadn't saved your number."

"That's all right, I just wanted to talk to you."

"Ah," I say, flattered. "But where are you calling me from? I hear a lot of noise around you."

"I'm at a bar, with some friends. We're just having some drinks. What about you?"

"Me? At home, much more prosaically."

She says nothing, as if my answer had made her feel somehow indiscreet. In the background I hear a clinking of glasses that makes me yearn for a margarita.

"I'm sorry. Maybe I shouldn't have called you."

"No, it's fine," I reply, hoping she detects the faint sigh of resignation that I inserted into my voice.

What on earth are you doing? I ask myself.

"You know, it's been a long time since I've gone out."

"Really?"

"Yes. I wanted you to know that. It did me good to talk to you."

"I'm overjoyed to hear that."

"I'm overjoyed"? What the fuck am I saying?

"Listen, maybe it's late," There's Something About Mary resumes, "but I was wondering if you wouldn't like to come join me. My friends are really nice, you'd like them."

"There, that's exactly what you need," I say to myself. "A nice extemporaneous evening out with a group of kids young enough to be your children. Maybe you'll run into Alagia at this place, and it'll be a full house."

"Thank you, you're very kind. Maybe some other time."

A moment's silence.

"I overstepped my bounds. I apologize."

"No, it's just that it's a little late, and tomorrow morning I have a lawsuit."

"You don't have to explain. I wouldn't want to spend an evening in the company of people I don't know either. But will you save my phone number now?"

"Yes. As soon as we hang up."

"All right then, let's hang up."

"All right," I say, with some embarrassment. "I certainly hope you enjoy the rest of your evening."

"'Enjoy the rest of your evening'?" I say to myself. "What are you, the TV weather girl?"

"I hope the lawsuit goes well, Vincenzo."

I'm so struck at hearing her say my name that I trip myself up like a genuine moron.

"What lawsuit?"

"Didn't you say that you have a lawsuit tomorrow?"

"Ah, the lawsuit. Certainly, of course I do."

Jesus, what an asshole I am.

"Good night," she says, without a hint of irony in her voice. The girl has style.

"Good night, Camer . . . Irene."

"What are you looking at?" I ask that busybody of an angel, who of course has decided to show up right now.

"Me? Nothing."

"I didn't go, as you saw, no?"

"Hm-hm," he says sardonically.

"And besides, she was with her friends, right? That shows that it was nothing but a friendly invitation."

"A woman who gets out her phone and calls you while she's spending the evening out at a bar, and with plenty of company, is definitely not making a friendly invitation, Vince'."

An impeccable observation. And in fact it gets on my nerves.

"Listen, why don't we just drop this topic now, okay? I-didn't-go-and-that's-that dot com. Now quit bugging me because I'm hungry."

He lifts one hand and opens and closes it backwards, like an old-fashioned gent: "*Addio core.*"

I ignore him.

"No question though, the resemblance is startling, eh?" I say.

He rolls his eyes.

I grab my phone again to order a pizza, even though I don't even know what number to call.

Huffing and puffing as if doing so were an intolerable sacrifice, I get out the phone book from wherever it was (you have to admit that it's always, and I mean always, a 2 x 4 to the forehead to find a number in the phone book), and as I flip to the page with the pizzerias I'm reminded that right around the corner they've just opened a fast-food place called (I swear) *Luncho Espress.* And so I pass the motion by acclamation to try out the food from a placed called *Luncho Espress*, an experience that should not be missed.

So I look up the number and dial it.

The phone is answered by a guy who clearly doesn't give a shit. When I ask what they have that's hot and above all whether they deliver, he says nothing for, like, twenty seconds, and then, as if he were under some kind of duress, he asks where I live, and he does it all with such patent rudeness that I wait for him to get ready to take down my address before hanging up on him in a rage.

"Go take it up the ass, Luncho," I say, and at that point I opt for a quick plate of spaghetti with Buitoni Fior di Pesto.

I put a pot of water on to boil, I turn on the TV, and I run through the list of channels available thanks to digital cable (which is to say a technological innovation that really was needed, one of those useful innovations that, really, once you have it you ask yourself regularly: "How on earth did I live without this, until just the other day?").

A local TV station is playing a commercial for the impending concert of an Italian band whose name I've heard many times without understanding what it means. Three skinny guys dressed in a style that's a hybrid of Armani and Sears, Roebuck, all of them with their faces ravaged by the business of living (one of them is clinging so hard to a semi-acoustic guitar that he looks like he's afraid somone's going to come along any minute and confiscate it: and perhaps that would be for the best, all things considered), looking straight ahead as if urging the photographer to hurry up because if there's one thing they hate doing it's posing for pictures.

Meanwhile the voice-over of someone who's clearly mentally unhinged gallops along repeating the name of the group and the date of the concert, panting and flushed as if he were announcing the imminent apparition of the Virgin Mary, and a cell phone number appears superimposed on the screen, preceded by one of the most chilling commercial names of modern times ("Infoline"), and the presale prices of tickets.

Balcony seating 35 euros, concert seating 50 euros.

I look at those numbers as a sort of personal affront. I feel like such an anachronism. It's not like I just discovered how much concerts cost these days. It's just that when confronted with examples of this sort, I'm seized by a nostalgia for the days when no one would have stood for those kinds of prices for a concert by a group with that level of aesthetic incompetence.

WHEN YOU WAKE UP AND REALIZE
YOU DIED IN YOUR SLEEP

At the beginning of the eighties, in fact, right in 1980, that is, when politics (I don't mean professional politics, but rather the kind of self-taught not-for-profit politics that marked those youth movements that based their reason for being on a contempt for the Italian Chamber of Deputies, Senate, mass media, free market, and religion) was dead and its body was cold, all that survived, for just a short time, was the practice of proletarian self-discounts at concerts.

The practice of self-discounting, in the second half of the previous decade (the late seventies, in other words) had been imposed with the caustic savagery of a political right, self-evident, requiring no theoretical justification. The message (or perhaps it would be more accurate to say the lesson) conveyed by the act of self-discounting was inhibitory in its nonnegotiable self-righteousness: we don't pay to get into concerts because it's right not to pay. Full stop. Nothing more need be said. And if the security team tried to do its job by defying that diktat, bim-bam-boom, bricks and bats would fly.

And it wasn't as if, when faced with the arrogant practice of self-discounting (which was actually more of a self-exemption, because these people weren't demanding a discount so much as they were saying: "Let us in or we'll wreck the place from floor to ceiling"), anyone was willing to provide explanations.

In those years, if you asked why, then you just looked like a fool (in which case you'd be banished with a smack to the back of the head or a chorus of insults such as: "You're out of it,"

"You're freaking out"—that one had almost exactly the same value as "You're freaking me out"—"Ouch, you're bringing us down," "You're harshing our mellow," etc.; and then you were mocked for at least a semester as the political equivalent of the Lampwick character from *Pinocchio*, as much as if you'd said "between you and I" at your high school final exam) or, at the very worst, you'd be taken as a political know-nothing (in which case you became the target of derisive whistles and spit, as well as possibly being physically attacked by some aspiring, homegrown Che Guevara, beet red with fury for the occasion, who actually had no intention of hitting you at all, but just planned to be stopped in the nick of time by a couple of volunteers and thus still come off looking like an implacable leader unwilling to brook dissent).

The movement, in other words, was unwilling to tolerate uncertainty, much less debate. It treated you like a mental defective if you failed to understand. So what happened was you went along with it. Okay, you said, intimidated by the thought that someone might suspect you didn't know what you were talking about. So you behaved like Obelix in that old comic book where his friends, the other Gauls, are readying a military expedition, and they spend days and days arguing about attack strategies and battlefield conditions and finally, without understanding a word of what they're saying, he screams: "I don't know why, but I'm coming with you guys!"

But it should also be said that in those days there was also a degree of self-interest in obtaining self-discounts (or I should say, self-exemptions), truth be told. Though it wasn't clear why the same principle didn't apply to pushers. Did anyone ever get a joint through proletarian self-discounting, I wonder?

In other words, for a good long while in Italy self-discounting was the nightmare of musicians from around the world, but especially Italians, who were often subjected at concerts to genuine authentic people's trials in addition to the self-discounting. The self-discounters would climb up onto the stage, take the singer prisoner, and subject him to the third degree. They'd ask him: why did you go on TV, what the fuck kind of song did you write, what kind of bourgeois smart-ass lyrics are these, look at your cute little fashionable shirt, where do you think you're going to wind up with this music, at the Sanremo Music Festival?

This was militant cultural criticism—forget about the number of stars and smiley or frowny faces at the beginning of reviews in the local newspapers. A musician (especially an Italian musician, because a foreign musician, as soon as he got a whiff of what was happening, would turn around, leave the country, and not come back until things began to improve) was not allowed to act like a rock star. He couldn't treat the audience with disdain or superiority, make money, screw fashion models, appear on television, or give autographs. Music was a political matter, a way of making a statement; you couldn't sell out or be a whore or catch the syphilis of success. It was brutal, back then, to climb onto a concert stage.

At the beginning of the eighties, though, all that was finally coming to an end. And the astonishing thing was that the end came with a velocity that verged on the technological. It came, moreover, with such a discretion, a silence, an absence of warning signs, that once the results became evident it seemed as if it had all happened without the protagonists themselves being aware of it—as if they'd discovered they were dead while still walking, meeting, organizing, and making a ruckus in the general conviction that they were actually still alive.

At concerts the practice of self-discounting still continued, but there was no mistaking the fact that by now, after the most violent and criminal elements had been pounding on the gates and doors of stadiums and theaters to be let in, nobody really cared that there was a slice of the public that did their talking with their fists, using tough manners to impose an antagonistic vision of popular art.

The message of self-discounting, practically from one morning to later that same day, had lost all its critical value and had become, paradoxically and unconsciously, a demand for things to be free, for no reason other than self-interest. The ones who continued to practice it with the mindset of the political action, once they'd burst into the stadium or theater, realized that the audience didn't give a clenched fist about the fact that they'd gained free admission after the show had started ("Okay," the audience in the concert seating seemed to say, "they let you in for free? Now be good and let us watch the show").

The musicians would only stop playing long enough to leave the now-obsolete radicals enough time to get comfortable and then they'd start playing again, as if they'd stopped for station identification and a word from the sponsors. It was the most depressing thing, a loss of meaning, live, that gave you an unsettling hunch about the tragic drift that was going to characterize the continuing deterioration already under way.

I remember once, at a concert by the band AreA—Demetrio Stratos was already dead, and the group had started playing jazz-rock (in fact, they just strummed and bored their audience after a while)—a band of self-discounters threw an oversized M-80 outside the stadium. It made such a huge roar that the musicians all exchanged glances and stopped playing. Inside the stadium we were all more surprised than afraid. After a couple of minutes Giulio Capiozzo stood up from his drum set and went over to the microphone.

"We'd like to know what just happened," he said.

That's it. Nothing more. A sincere, completely nonrhetorical question, which in its simplicity provided a pathetic depiction of the state of affairs.

The fact that anyone would ask to know what had happened in the aftermath of a loud explosion from outside the stadium during a concert pointed to the end of a shared experience, the definitive undermining of a political act that had by now lost its original identity. A couple of years earlier, it would have been obvious to everyone that a mass concert-break-in was under way.

The security crew didn't make an issue of it, they just let in the rioters who'd set off the M-80. A total of four or five minutes, all told.

"If we're done with the fireworks, then we'll start playing again," Capiozzo wrapped up, slightly annoyed, and went back to his drums and quietly sat down.

The concert started up again, and in the meanwhile the bomb-throwers (there might have been a baker's dozen of them) were admitted into the empty space between the bottom tiers and the hurricane fencing along the field. While AreA was playing, the radicals who had thrown the M-80 all looked at each other and started chanting their old battle chant: "Workers' autonomy, organization, armed struggle, revolution." And the effect was devastatingly pathetic. Both because they were unable to interfere even slightly with the music being played (which, after all, since it was jazz-rock, wasn't even particularly loud), and because they were just a tiny knot of people, and not particularly robust individuals, either: the last holdouts of a battle that, as you could easily see, had long since lost touch with reality and was already firmly rooted in the past, a melancholy low-budget remake of itself. Like Vittorio Gassman's line in the final scenes of *C'eravamo tanto amati*: "The future is now past, and we didn't even notice it happening."

After that point, what happened is what happened. And we all know what happened. It all came to an end: the self-discounts, the armed struggle, the revolutions, the workers' autonomy. Nowadays, people pay for their concert tickets, and they pay through the nose. Musicians have all become rock stars, or at least they've all tried to without being shy about it. They've lined up to get a spot playing on TV, they've all gone to the the Sanremo Music Festival and even to the Festivalbar. And while formerly they were forced to defend themselves at their concerts against people who indicted them and tried them as criminals, now they whine about their albums being downloaded online. They warn against drugs, sex without love, political views that don't speak the language of the *ggente*—the ordinary people courted by the populists in Rome. They get married (some of them even get married in church), they raise families, rediscover old-fashioned values, quit drinking, quit drugs, and advise young people not to waste their lives.

In the end, the marketplace triumphed. The audience evicted the people. We're freer now than we were then. Free to buy anything we want.

But it's no accident that, when all is said and done, as time goes by, we have less and less music worth buying.

I Have a Dream

The audience applauds as if operated by remote control when Daria Bignardi, beautifully dressed, walks onto the set and reaches the center of the stage, positioning herself with her back to the megascreen, which is showing scenes from the hostage taking in slow motion. She greets the spectators and announces the title of this episode: "Do-it-yourself Justice."

We guests are seated facing each other in two rows of three.

I'm sitting between Giancarlo De Cataldo and Ambra, wearing a sky-blue suit and my old down-at-the-heels Blundstone 500 slip-on boots, which give just the right touch of slovenliness to my overall look. I have three days' worth of stubble and I'm not wearing a tie.

Across from us sit Emanuele Filiberto, Vittorio Sgarbi, and Fabrizio Corona (who can't seem to stop looking at my Blundstones, though I can't figure out whether that's because he likes the fact that they're so beat up or because he's disgusted with them for the same reason).

Bignardi introduces us to the welcoming applause of the studio audience while the TV cameras archive one face at a time (the first—I'd like to see them try any other order—is mine), she summarizes in a few evocative lines the whole dizzy adventure at the supermarket, then she asks the control booth to run a few sequences (in particular, the one in which Engineer Romolo Sesti Orfeo scolds me for having an antiquated conception of the legal profession, reiterating the theory of TV as the sole forum for the only kind of trial that really counts anymore), and then opens the dances, starting (and I would have put money on it) with Ambra.

"I don't know about you," says the TV host and actress, "but I haven't been glued to any television the way I was to this in a long, long time. Aside from the principles in question (televised trials, the question of why you can't take the law into your own hands, etc. etc.), I believe that the live feed from the supermarket has been one of the most gripping and tragic television spectacles that we've witnessed since 9/11."

Silence falls over the audience in place of the applause that one might expect but which doesn't come.

Daria Bignardi is caught off guard. When a guest beats the clock in terms of the time assigned to them to speak, it's as if the program has just suffered a heart attack. Which means that it runs the risk of stagnating, unless there's an urgent and decisive intervention.

I immediately look at Sgarbi, who nods progressively, showing that he approves—if not of the content, then at least of the aesthetic—of the opinion that Ambra has just expressed.

"Right," he breaks in, seizing the floor, "very good. I think that's the one sensible thing we can say on the topic."

Ambra preens, satisfied that she's dodged the bullet of cynicism that she knows she risked.

Emanuele Filiberto blinks twice in succession, as if he can't quite see why Sgarbi found her observation so exhaustive.

"Could I ask you," Bignardi asks Ambra, starting to take a step forward but then stepping back (which is her way of battling against the basic immobility of the role of moderator without going for a stroll around the set the way some colleagues of hers like to do, for instance Giovanni Floris, who does so much traveling around the studio during his show that sometimes no one even seems to know where he is), "whose side were you on?"

"Well, not on the Camorrista's side, that's for sure," Ambra replies.

A wave of laughter, followed by applause.

Daria seems put out.

"Have you noticed," I break in, speaking to everyone and no one in particular at the same time, in an attempt to undercut the irritation that seems to hover in the air, "that a second after the laughter comes the applause? It's a little bit like a second sneeze, don't you think?"

Everyone turns in my direction, baffled.

I wait.

It takes a while to get this one.

The first one to get it is De Cataldo, who unleashes a hearty slap to my leg. The others follow in rotation, nodding and snickering, showing their approval of my subtle juxtaposition.

So now I get a round of applause myself.

Fabrizio Corona intercepts a roving TV camera and shoots it a ferocious glare.

"The second sneeze, nice work, Malinconico: they both come in pairs," Daria acknowledges.

"Right," I confirm with some satisfaction.

"In any case, you have a point, Ambra," she resumes, putting things on a personal level, "I should have been more explicit. The choice was between a despairing father who was demanding justice and a lawyer doing his best to stave off tragedy by insisting that trials should be conducted in a courtroom and not on TV."

Sgarbi snorts impatiently and brushes his hair with his hand, as if he'd suddenly had a hot flash. No question that Daria's clarification, unobjectionable though it was, did have the ring of rhetoric, truth be told.

"Oh, I was rooting for Malinconico, obviously," Ambra replies, playing the fool. And she flashes me a big smile which I return without especially wanting to.

"As we were preparing this episode," Bignardi says, overcoming her momentary disgruntlement to return her focus to the program with admirable professionalism, "we conducted a broad survey of people from various walks of life, and what we found was that everyone, and I mean *everyone* we spoke to, was rooting for Counselor Malinconico during the live broadcast. Does this mean that the country is much more concerned about the protection of civil rights than we imagine? That lawyers are actually more popular than is widely thought? Or is this consensus limited strictly to Malinconico? De Cataldo?"

"Well," replies the judge/author, shifting around in his seat to get more comfortable, clearly caught off guard by the question, "as much as I may find Malinconico likable, I'm not sure I'd go so far as to name him Italy's favorite son."

"Why not?" I object.

Laughter.

"Because you have a very different style, *caro mio*," he replies.

Hey, I think. He's right.

"Does that mean you'd like to have him as a character in one of your novels?" Bignardi cuts in, quick on the uptake.

"Sure," says De Cataldo.

"As long as we can work out an agreement on the royalties," I retort promptly.

Applause. Not sure if it's for me or for him.

"In any case, coming back to your question," De Cataldo resumes, speaking once again to the moderator, "I suspect that it is precisely the division between judicial hardliners and civil rights advocates that constitutes the aberration that has ensured the spread of a generalized mistrust toward the administration of justice in this country. For that we should be grateful to our Counselor Malinconico, because he has reiterated a statement of values that we should all be able to agree on: trials should be held in courtrooms. With all their shortcomings and all their flaws, there is no better place for them."

"You think?" Corona breaks in, ready for a fight.

"Why, yes. I most certainly do," De Cataldo confirms.

"Bah," he retorts, shooting another sour glare at the camera. ("What on earth did those cameras do to you?" I think).

He doesn't seem to want to say anything else; but the next thing you know he's back on the subject, challenging the judge/novelist and actually pointing a finger in his face.

"Go tell that to someone who's been taken hostage by an absurd trial for a crime he was eventually acquitted of."

"Well, Corona," De Cataldo replies, unruffled, "the fact that a person was acquitted shows that criminal trials aren't a form of persecution but rather a system subject to an effective oversight process, don't you agree?"

"Vittorio," Bignardi cuts in, calling on Sgarbi even before Corona has a chance to reply, "is De Cataldo right? Do we live in a country split between judicial hardliners and civil rights advocates? And how would you explain the massive groundswell of support for Counselor Malinconico?"

"Hm," the critic begins his reply, squirming uncomfortably in his chair, "I think that what happened in the supermarket is an episode that can be analyzed without having to bring in pro-justice topics that I don't think our viewers are any too interested in hearing about."

"Ah, I see," says Daria.

As if to say: "Thanks for informing us that up until now nobody's said anything interesting."

"The engineer and would-be judge, jury, and executioner had, in fact, an iconoclastic plan," Sgarbi harangues. "That hostage taking and intended execution, offered up to the eyes of an audience practically forced to watch and wonder what it all meant, almost resembled an art installation."

And at this point he accompanied the statement with his hands, sketching out two imaginary half-moons in the air, as if he were giving form to the concept.

Whereupon everyone (with one exception) nods.

The critic comfortably pockets our attention, and continues.

"By kidnapping the alleged murderer, claiming to put him on trial on a live broadcast, without any legal due process, that desperate father leveled a radical critique at the justice system. Malinconico, on the other hand, by dismantling his artwork, behaved like an authentic intellectual: by defending the supremacy of the jury trial in a court of law, in a certain sense, he prevented the collapse of the hall of justice itself."

We all sit in hopeful silence, looking at each other as if to convey the impression that we understood what we were hearing.

"Malinconico?" Bignardi finally calls on me.

"Eh," I reply.

As if to say: "The question being?"

"What do you think?"

"What do I think of what?"

"Of Sgarbi's analysis."

"Well, I don't know if I understood it all, but I liked it."

Laughter/applause.

"That's always a good sign," Sgarbi comments.

"This may strike you as a provocative question," the moderator says, suddenly turning more serious, "but how about *you*, Malinconico—whose side were you on?"

"You know, I'm glad you asked me that, because the truth is that I don't know."

She smiles at me, at the same time intrigued and satisfied that I appreciated her question.

"To put it briefly," I add, "when you find yourself dealing with a man in that state, it's difficult not to feel a certain degree of solidarity."

At this point I get an applause without laughter.

"So tell us, are they going to make a movie out of this?" Ambra unexpectedly asks me.

"Oh, please," I reply.

"Well, why not? There are plenty of TV dramas being made in Italy all the time based on actual events taken from the news: why shouldn't they make a movie, or at least a TV movie, based on this story?"

"Because it would never stand up to the original, which we all already watched live," Corona tosses out.

"An impeccable observation," says Sgarbi. "Bravo."

"Thanks," Corona replies.

"You're right, Fabrizio," says Bignardi. "But let's say a producer decided to go ahead anyway and offered you the part of Malinconico, would you take it?"

"Why not," he says (but it's obvious that he doesn't mean it). "I have something to offer."

It's not clear what that has to do with anything, but whatevs.

"Oh come on," Sgarbi breaks in, "Corona is too tall, too muscular, too scandalous, too macho. He wouldn't be believable as Malinconico."

"He says that because he's never seen me in a Speedo," I say.

Laughter.

"But have you watched many Italian TV dramas, Vittorio?" Ambra interjects. "Do you really think that they worry about that kind of thing when they cast actors?"

There's a moment of awkward silence, but no one seizes the opportunity.

Emanuele Filiberto looks around, bewildered. Hostage takings, judicial hardliners and civil rights advocates, casting for TV dramas based on televised trials . . . This is a ship of fools and madmen, he seems to be saying to himself. What on earth am I doing here?

"Excuse me, Daria," he volunteers. "But what do I have to do with the subjects of this conversation?"

"What kind of question is that?" says Corona, visibly disgusted.

The prince looks at him, nonplussed, and Corona, in response, does nothing but shake his head as if he were having trouble believing what he has just heard.

"In any case, I'd like to thank the audience for giving me such a warm round of applause earlier," says the prince.

"So would I," says Ambra, probably sarcastically.

"Hey, people," De Cataldo pipes up, "why don't we try to to restore some civility here, okay? We're deteriorating to the level of farce."

"Malinconico," Bignardi suddenly asks me point-blank, practically giving me a heart attack, "did you end up making that phone call before coming on the show?"

It must be a joke, I think. I didn't hear her right.

"Excuse me?" I reply, or rather, I ask.

"What do you mean," she says sarcastically; and she shoots a couple of glances at her staff, who flank the set like so many vultures, "are you trying to tell me you don't know what I'm talking about?"

"No, I have no idea," I reply, turning beet red at the very same instant that the cameraman aims his lens at my face, taking an obscene closeup.

Audience and guests all chuckle.

"Was there someone you should have alerted to the fact that you'd be appearing on this program, by chance?"

I'm left speechless. I stare at her, in horrified confusion, still doubting my own ears.

"Come on, Vince', it's all right, you gave it a shot," De Cataldo says to me affectionately.

I look at him. Then at Ambra. Then Bignardi. Then Sgarbi. Then the prince. Then Corona.

All of them dead serious.

What is this, a conspiracy?

I get to my feet, swiveling my head back and forth, as if I were searching for the nearest emergency exit.

"I want to see the *Candid Camera* banner. Come on, let's see it."

"Sit down, Vince'," Giancarlo advises me, taking me by the arm.

I do as he says, dazed.

"We have a little surprise for you," says Bignardi. "Something you weren't expecting; part *L'Isola dei Famosi* and part *Carràmba!*, if you see what I mean."

And she looks up with a coy smile, as if inviting us to notice something in the air itself.

When the voice of Alessandra Persiano echoes through the studio, I'm stunned into disbelief.

"You're an idiot, Vincenzo."

There ensues a moment of silence, after which the audience doesn't just start laughing: they're rolling in the aisles. A couple of really stupid women in particular howl in a disgustingly vulgar manner, attracting everyone's attention and encouraging copycats.

"But how . . ." I ask, in a state of panic.

"Of all the pathetic machinations you could have come up with to get my attention, this is the most childish by far. What did you think, that if I saw you on television I'd come crawling back to you?"

"Heyyy!" I shout, leaping to my feet once again, to a another burst of laughter from the audience. "What the hell is going on here??"

"And another thing," Alessandra Persiano resumes, her voice turning even grimmer, "submitting to the advances of a young girl who happens to like older men does you no honor, just so you know."

"*Whaaat?!?*"

"What, now you act all surprised?" she drills in. "Next

you're going to try to tell me that you believed her story about being the son's girlfriend, aren't you? You may be an idiot but you weren't born yesterday. Come on, you knew it all along."

"Eh, that's pretty serious, Vince'," De Cataldo says to me, with the tone of an expert.

I'm about to implement the decision I've just reached, to rip off the microphone and the transmitter that the sound technicians clipped to my jacket before this miserable program got started and take to my heels toward the exit when, thank Heavens, I wake up. Drenched with sweat, by the way.

With a twinge of horror I realize that I'm already on my feet, which makes my return to reality all the more laborious. I eagerly reach around for the light switch and flip it on, blinding myself. I cover my eyes with both hands and sit down on the bed, waiting for the cardiac tempest to die down.

I've always had a gift for nightmares, but this one blows them all out of the water. I remember that as I was falling asleep I tried to imagine how Bignardi's program might go (I think I did the casting while still wide awake), but I never would have believed I could drag it down with me and script it in such detail during full-on REM sleep.

When, after a short while (but a short while that seems to last a long time), I start breathing more or less regularly again, I put on my slippers and I shuffle into the kitchen. I get a mineral water out of the fridge, I drink right from the bottle, and then I carry it with me around the apartment, chugging on it like a bottle of vodka, thinking over and over again about the bloodcurdling perfection of my nightmare and finally concluding, though with a cold sweat, that things can't get much worse if even my subconscious has decided to start mocking me.

ÉGOÏSTE!

When the intercom buzzer sounds I look at my watch and pray that it's not who I think it is. Then and there I consider pretending not to be home, but he must have read my mind from down on the street because he leans on the doorbell.

"Cut it out," is my opening line.

"Are you alone?"

"If that's a joke it isn't funny."

"Open up."

"For God's sake, Espe, you're an hour and forty minutes early."

"Open up, I need to take a shower."

"A *shower*?"

"Holy shit, Vince', what do I have to do, kick down your front entrance?"

"Okay, okay, fuck you, I'm buzzing you in."

When Espe walks into my apartment, brushing past me as he enters through the front door, I come dangerously close to suffocating.

"Ahh," I moan as I rub my eyes, which are already burning.

"Don't say a word, okay?" he raps out impatiently, infesting my entryway with the overpowering stench of cologne. "Just get me a fucking clean bathrobe, if you have one."

"Have you gone stupid?" I shout at him, coughing. "How much of that stuff did you put on, a whole case?"

"Okay, I might have overdone it a little."

"'Might have overdone it a little?'" I retort, chasing after him into the bathroom, where he has gone without asking me. "Holy Christ, you're a bacteriological weapon!"

"I didn't notice it before I left home, what am I supposed to do about it."

He pulls open the towel cabinet. He pulls out a couple, choosing the longest ones and rumpling all the others.

"Ah, really?" I say, my voice muffled by the hand I'm using to cover mouth and nose. "And when did you notice it, when you emptied that bus of passengers?"

"Something like that. Are you going to give me a bathrobe or am I going to have to make do with these?"

I yank them out of his hands and clutch them to my chest, though I have no idea why.

"But couldn't you have just gone home, damn you?"

"Are you nuts? I was already halfway here."

He unties his shoes.

"But it's almost two hours till we're supposed to be there, *Madonna mia!*"

"Exactly," he replies, unbuttoning his trousers, "so we have plenty of time, no?"

At that exact moment I realize that my cell phone is ringing, though I couldn't say in what room.

Terrified at the thought that I might miss another call from Alessandra Persiano, I throw the towels into the surprised face of a by-now seminude Espe and run at full speed into the bedroom, which is where I think the Boccherini minuet that I've chosen as a ringtone is coming from.

I'm practically sure that I'm going to be picking up on the last ring when I finally manage to get my hands on the phone. The position that I find myself in as I raise it to my ear isn't even worth describing, it's so ridiculous. Moreover I've inhaled so much poison from that idiot's musk fumes that my voice has become a pathetic croak.

"Hetho, who ith thith . . .?"

"Vincenzo?" Alessandra Persiano says my name hesitantly.

"A . . . the."

"Hey. What's the matter with you, are you okay?"

"No, it'th jutht that I wath . . ."

"Who else is there with you? I can hear someone singing."

In fact, Espe is belting out "Con te partirò."

"Es . . . hh . . . pedito," I reply, doing my best to recover a minimum level of understandable pronunciation. "And you'll never guess where he is, at this very moment. If I tell you you won't believe me."

"Why, where is he?"

"In the shower."

"In the shower? At our apartment?"

"That's right," I reply, comforted by the thought that she still considers this "our" apartment. "Apparently his water heater suddenly broke down," I invent freely.

"Oh."

An "Oh" that could just as easily mean "I understand" as "that's odd."

A substantial pause ensues.

"Ale."

"Yes," she says dully, betraying an absolute lack of interest in following me down the conversational path I'm about to start on.

"If I hadn't been fast enough to answer this time you would have turned off your phone again, wouldn't you?"

"I . . . No."

"Yes, you would. That's what you did yesterday."

"I was . . . in a meeting."

"At nine o'clock at night?"

"Let's not talk about this right now, Vincenzo, please. I need to focus on the trial."

This cunning answer, such a patent postponement of the issue, makes me simply furious.

"Would you be terribly offended if I tell you that I don't give a flying crap about your trial? And that this attempt of yours to put me off until some later date so that you don't have to waste an ounce of focus strikes me as truly oafish?"

She sighs.

"Vincenzo, I asked you nicely."

"Okay," I tell myself. "I tried to keep my cool."

"Asked nicely my ass, Ale! Ever since you left you've erected this ambiguous partition between us. If you think that you can cleanse your conscience with your texts about the weather forecast and the occasional pro forma two-minute phone call, you're dead wrong. We're talking about the two of us, and there's no need to hold a conference on the topic, the question is perfectly simple: are we still a couple, or not?"

"Don't shout."

Oh my God. Why did she say it? Why?

What is it you're supposed to do in this kind of situation? Count to ten? I try, but I don't even make it to five.

"Who do you think you're talking to, a misbehaving school-child? Go fuck yourself, you and your fucked-up affectations! Better yet, since it costs you so much just to answer me, why don't I just do your thinking for you: *no, we're no longer a couple!* There, did you hear me? I even shouted it, just think."

Hoooold it right there.

I take a long pause. Long enough that I have all the time to cough, pant, think back over what I just said, listen to an entire verse of Espe's rendition of "Con te partirò" coming from the shower.

"You know what, Vincenzo?" Alessandra Persiano finally

says decisively (though she's already a little less high and mighty than before). "I don't think I want to put up with your vulgarity anymore."

If I had my druthers, I'd start shouting again, but I collect myself and try to refine my argumentation.

"Ooh, I beg your pardon with my face pressed down in the dirt, baroness. So you find curse words repugnant? Has the trip to Milan already disinfected your language? Well, now I'm going to give you a tip when it comes to vulgarity: putting your man on standby without even taking the trouble to let him know whether or not you've dumped him is much, and I mean much more vulgar than merely invoking cocks and asses with accompanying instructions as to their use."

Another very long pause.

Hey, even though I feel culpable for the disaster I'm provoking, I'm proud of myself.

"Okay, thanks for the lecture," she resumes once she thinks that I might have cooled off enough to listen to her retort. "You were brilliant. Now if you'll excuse me, I have other things to do."

And with that, she hangs up.

Whinnying with rage, I immediately dial her number, ready to rattle off a machine-gun burst of insults, but just as I expected the coward has already turned off her phone. Maddened by frustration, I hurl the phone against the wall at the very instant that Espe, barefoot and dripping wet, one towel wrapped around his head and the other around his waist, appears in the door.

The cell phone smashes into the wall, the back panel detaches, the battery flies spinning out of its compartment, shooting to one side and smacking into the floor.

It's not broken, I think to myself.

"What's gotten into you?" Espe asks, raising his gaze from the scattered phone parts to me.

"What's gotten into me is that Alessandra is an asshole!" I shout into his face, forcing him to recoil, gripping the bath towel to his waist. "An arrogant asshole. And she's spoiled too. She can go fuck herself!"

I pick up the pieces of the phone.

"Hey, calm down. Just tell me what happened, okay?"

"To hell with my guilt complexes, Espe. Do you remember all the whining I did over the phone? Well, I take it all back. I'm not sorry I screwed another woman; in fact, you know what I say? It's a good thing I did."

I slip the battery back into its slot.

It fits.

Let's see if it turns on.

"So she wanted to pull the sly move of taking off and leaving the idiot here to wonder if she'd ever come back? Well, the idiot answered his own question: we're finished. *Game over.*"

It won't turn on.

Shit.

"And let me tell you something else: if after this remarkable piece of performance art from a stuck-up blue-chip grande dame she thinks she can change her mind and go back in time with a snap of her fingers, she's miscounted her cards. Because if she dares to call me ever again, even if it's just to apologize, she'll come face-to-face with the most resounding fuck-you of her life. Why on earth are you looking at me like that?"

Wait, wait, it's turning on.

"It's just that right now you're too pissed off to keep any of the promises you make."

"No, I assure you, Espe, look at me, I've never been so clearheaded in my life. I'm tired of this subalternate status, this kowtowing to women, I mean it. I want to regain my dignity, I won't let myself be treated like some pathetic asshole anymore, I've had it I tell you, I've had it!"

"What can I tell you? If you're really so convinced . . ."

"You know what I say to you? That I'm grateful to you for pushing me into accepting this invitation to dinner tonight."

"That's my boy."

"Fine. Then I'd better get ready."

"Just one thing."

"What."

"I need you to lend me something to wear."

Reality Never Outstrips the Imagination, It Just Brings It Down to Its Level

As I take a shower myself while Espe plunders my Aspelund wardrobe, I review the reasons for my tirade against Alessandra Persiano, since I'm already beginning to fear the moment when—once my post-screaming-fight excitement subsides (that typically fleeting confidence destined to crumble to dust over the course of no more than four, maximum five hours)—I'll be overwhelmed by the knowledge that our affair is now irremediably finished, in the aftermath of the charming compliments I saw fit to bestow on her.

In the angel's absence, I'm on a first-name basis with myself.

First of all, don't feel guilty. Sure, you flew off the handle and told her go fuck herself. There's really nothing surprising about that, you behaved like a human being. In fact, you want to know what I think? It was about time. Because if there's one mistake you've made, especially lately, it was agreeing to abide by this sort of romantic standby state in which she, with glaring impunity, accorded herself the unilateral right of rescission at any moment of her choosing. Don't you think that in a lion-vs.-lamb arrangement like this one you were bound to get fed up sooner or later? It's just a good thing you still have some small shred of personal dignity.

Second, did you hear how she was treating you? "Don't shout," "Let's not talk about this right now," "I need to focus on the trial": who the hell does she think she is to talk to you like that? Fuck her, you did the right thing, absolutely.

Third, the fact that she hung up on you proves—leaving

aside any questions about her complete lack of manners—that she didn't know what to say. Because it's obvious that if someone has a point to make, they don't run away from the argument: they argue. Too easy to think you can get away with just hanging up. Far, far too easy.

Fourth (and here we come to the point that's got you most upset): okay, it's over, so what? The irreparable can actually be a great source of relief, if you look at it from a different point of view. You'll suffer for a while, sure, you'll have your year or so of self-pity and pissing and moaning, and when you're done complaining you'll make peace with yourself and you'll start your life over. I'm not saying it will be easy. But we're also not talking about moving mountains. Alessandra isn't indispensable. You don't need her to go on living. There, say the name: Alessandra Persiano. Say it again. Repeat it until it becomes the mark of a woman no better or worse than any other. Can you see how the edge of drama and tragedy is already blunted?

Fifth (and here we're taking a step back, or actually, a step down): free yourself of your miserable little fear of loneliness. Stop clutching feverishly at broken relationships. Cut it out. You're absolutely fine without a woman at your side, okay?

Eh, I say. Okay.

Bah.

As long as I'm at it, I try to come up with a preview of the evening that lies ahead of us. And so I close my eyes, bow my head, flatten my hands against the walls of the shower, abandoning myself to the cleansing force of the gushing water, and I mentally jot down a quick treatment and outline.

Jennifer Lopez's apartment is bound to be one of those places where every room is a different color. As soon as we walk in, we'll be handed Martini. I'll look around for an ashtray in which to discard my olive pit without finding one. The table will be set in an ocher-yellow lunch nook, lit—and I'm not sure that's the right term—by a few guttering candles about to give up the ghost. A subtle, pungent scent of incense will be in the air, designed to create—along with the partial darkness—that fake mystical atmosphere that as soon as you recognize it you think: "Okay, tonight I'm getting laid."

Next to the window there'll be a little corner den with a small desk, an iMac, and a Billy bookshelf displaying the spines of the entire library of *la Repubblica*. One wall will probably feature a Kandinsky poster. The lady of the house will probably have put on a Brian Eno CD that no one likes (especially not her or her girlfriend) but which is a must for these kinds of dinners. We'll eat sushi, sashimi, and skewers whose flavor will be impossible for me to figure out. I won't like any of it because I don't like Japanese food.

Jennifer Lopez (and since I haven't yet met her, I'm going to have to just stick with the original, her namesake) will probably have loosened her long blonde-chestnut hair over a T-shirt that's not even tight but still sufficiently snug to accommodate her curves in a way that can't be ignored. She'll have full lips and will laugh at anything you say. She, as the lady of the house, will be the one to make sure everything's ready and will bring the food to the table. Espe will no doubt follow her on her frequent trips to the adjoining kitchen, helping her with every task and investing everything he's got into the objective of ending the evening sprawled between her legs.

Anna Karenina will certainly wear a pageboy cut, light makeup, and a black sheath dress that gives an embarrassing prominence to her, ehm, balcony. She'll display a detached, meditative interest in me. She'll put on an attitude of open indifference to her friend's obliging hyperactivity, taking it for granted that she will take care of everything. She won't bother to take a single dish to the table and she'll loiter listlessly between the dining room, the kitchen, and, from time to time, the bathroom, with the nonchalance of someone who feels very much at home. This openly avowed layabout ethic will make me dislike her, and I'll speak to her only in monsyllabic grunts, especially at first. She'll look me up and down as if to say: "Well, just take a look at this asshole," and by so doing she'll immediately drive up my stock quotations, because there's nothing like rudeness to stir the flame of a woman who's already interested in you. During dinner we'll bicker constantly over any and all subjects while Espe and Jennifer Lopez cheerfully get drunk, methodically preparing for the ensuing diversions.

Later, Anna Karenina will ask me to see her home. I'll pretend to resist but make it abundantly clear that my implicit consent is unmistakable. As soon as we're in the car we'll stop being so argumentative. When we get to her place she'll ask me if I want to come up for one last glass. I'll point out to her that she's just committed one of the most persistent film clichés of the past thirty years and she'll reply: You imbecile, you're the one who's writing the screenplay; and I'll say: Ah, right, that's true; and she'll say: Well, what are you going to do, you coming up or not coming up? And I'll say: Are you kidding? There's nothing I like better than clichés.

At this point I abandon the story, I turn off the water, I step out of the shower, I put on my bathrobe, and I go into the bedroom, where I find Espe, who is once again dressed in his cologne-reeking clothing and is standing with his shoulders slightly bowed.

"Well?" I ask, briskly drying my hair and massaging my scalp with the hood of my bathrobe.

He doesn't answer. The look on his face.

"Hey. What on earth's wrong?"

"Those sluts called me," he slowly enunciates. "Dinner is off."

"What? We were just about to leave."

"Yeah."

"But why?"

"I can't even remember the excuse, that's how ridiculous it was."

"That's nuts."

"The part I found most humiliating is that they wanted your cell phone number."

"I don't understand."

"Well, it couldn't be any clearer. The one they wanted was you. One of them had to give right of way to the other, and neither of them was willing to yield."

I hold up my forefinger, like I'm trying to orient myself.

"So you're saying that . . ."

"If one was for you, the other was for me."

"Well, of course," I say. I look at Espe and I fall silent, drawing the obvious conclusions along with him.

"Am I that unattractive, Vince'?" he asks me, depressed.

"What are you talking about? All you do is pick up girls."

"The decline has begun, Vince'. I've suspected it for some time now. I've never been flunked so resoundingly. These are very clear signs."

"Hey, cut it out now, okay? I'm already complaining all the time, and I'm not looking for competition. As for those two, they're just ignorant bumpkins, and it's not worth wasting another word on the subject."

"You'll get no argument from me."

In the moments of silence that ensue, I sense the urgency of goading my old friend into doing something before he relapses into his depression.

"You know what we're going to do now, you and me? We're going to go out anyway."

His face lights up.

"Yeah, you're right. You're absolutely right. Let's go have some fun. And those two harpies can go fuck themselves."

"Oh, now that's the Espe I know."

"Come on, get ready," he says, galvanized.

"Okay."

I pull some clean underwear and socks out of the drawer of the Leksvik dresser, and then I have a moment of, how to put this, hesitation.

"Ah, Espe."

"What."

"You didn't by any chance *give* them my cell number?"

"Of course not."

"Thanks. You're a pal."

Casual

The evening out with Espe is, without exaggeration, tragic. A couple of losers in a *birreria*, one of them reeking like an aging whore, exchanging their respective states of depression practically without uttering a word the whole time.

It's not as if the other clients of the place (those who are our age and over, I mean to say) are much better off, in fact, quite the opposite seems to be true. Just to tell you: it's stunning to see how many men aged 50+ enter and exit on a hunt for pussy. Because there's no mistaking the fact that that hunger is stamped on their faces and, most particularly, on the clothing they wear. There are lots, and I really mean lots and lots and lots, of men well along in years and pathologically obsessed with youth. It's stronger than them, and they all want at least a taste of it. They throw on the attire of youthfulness however it happens (and it generally happens badly), abdicating any personal sense of the ridiculous. They wear torn blue jeans and Hogan shoes, their hair is thinning but still long, they wear hip glasses, sky-blue or off-yellow, with BlackBerrys blinking in the pockets of their unbuttoned shirts, revealing white chest hairs and jutting bellies.

The tragedy of these latter-day monsters is not that they feel young: it's that they want to seem young. My opinion is that this sort of conscientious objection to the facts of the registry of vital statistics implies a sort of desperate yearning to grab a few crumbs from the surrounding banqueting table of sexual abundance, as if, by disguising oneself as a young person, it was possible to fool the world into giving up some of its treasures without realizing it.

By the time I can no longer stand sitting there wallowing in the act of expiation, inhaling (though by now I'm inured to it) Espe's pestiferous scent, and wandering off into zooanthropological speculations concerning the surrounding bestiary, I finally suggest to my office-mate that we give up the long-since shipwrecked idea of having fun and simply make our separate ways home.

And so we emerge from the *birreria* to immerse ourselves in the youthful throngs (with the exceptions mentioned above) swarming along the long line of clubs, pubs, and bars that remain open and jumping until dawn along this thoroughfare, the site of the city's *movida* (as the local press likes to call it), and those throngs seem to part for us, opening immediate and generous gaps for us to pass through, thanks to the filthy and bestial scent my friend is emanating.

It is just as we're breaking up one of those many groups of merrymakers bivouacking on the sidewalk that I feel someone tug at my arm. I turn around as Espe is being swallowed up by the next surge of humanity, vanishing from my sight. The exact words that come into my head when I lay eyes on There's Something About Mary just inches from my face, are: "Now you tell me, doesn't she look like the girl from the hospital?"

"Ciao," she says, bestowing upon me a faintly embarrassed smile. I have the impression that her eyes are glittering, and I also get the feeling that it's more than just an impression. Here and now, I couldn't describe the clothes that she's wearing, but I know for an absolute certainty that I find her fabulously elegant.

I'm going on instinct there, obviously.

"Oh, ciao," I say, reciprocating her informal tone and deafened by the roar of voices around us.

"I'd never have expected to find you here."

"You'd be right," I shout. "I never come here."

I get up on my tiptoes in search of Espe, but I don't see him anywhere.

"Why not?"

"Do you have any idea how old I am?"

"No, none at all."

I raise my right hand, fold over my thumb, and flash four twice. Once for forty and and once for four.

"Really?" she says, startled. "My compliments."

Jesus, I'd forgotten how much noise people can make just by talking. More than hearing what she says, I read her lips.

"Compliments for what?"

"What did you say?" she asks, putting her ear next to my mouth and letting me inhale the scent of her hair.

"FOR WHAT?" I shout.

"For the way you look at your age."

"Oh, thanks."

"Are you here alone?"

"Actually I was with a friend, but I think I've lost him. What about you?"

"With them," she replies, pointing to a couple nearby, both of them more or less her age.

They both nod at me with a sort of approval (which I return) and then, as if they'd (not so much understood as) sensed the direction things were taking, they shoot a quick look of agreement at There's Something About Mary and slip away into the crowd, hand in hand.

"Why are they leaving?" I ask.

"I'll catch up with them later, don't worry. Besides, we're not going anywhere."

"Ah," I comment.

We look each other in the face.

"At this point, I ought to ask if you want anything to drink, I guess," I say.

"What?"

"AT THIS POINT, I OUGHT TO ASK IF YOU WANT ANYTHING TO DRINK, I GUESS!"

"Well, why don't you?"

In the "American bar" we just entered you practically can't see a damned thing. Okay, the idea of reproducing *night* in a place known, in fact, as a nightclub is a very *cool* effect; and I understand that semidarkness facilitates intimate interactions, makes the people you meet seem that much more interesting, and all the rest, but when a person walks into a nightclub to get a drink, it seems reasonable to expect that they should at least be able to spot the bartender.

We flutter like bats to claim a table that Cameron Diaz, who knows how, has already homed in on. I let her lead me, trusting her instincts as we glide through the crowd that occupies the center of the upper level. In here, it seems that the prohibition of smoking is honored more in the breach than the observance. The one positive is that the music being played up here is jazz, which I don't much like but which at least makes it possible to exchange a few words without having to shout.

Once we're seated I do my best to get my eyes used to the partial darkness, using the dim light of a votive candle set in a small glass cube at the center of the tiny table where we've taken a seat.

The beauty of Cameron Diaz from the elbows up is enough to make anyone blush. Every time she smiles, it's as if a stapler had just punched a staple into my crotch.

"You like it here?" she asks.

"Here where?" I reply.

She gives me a blank look, then gets it and laughs.

A waiter shows up, ripped, wearing a sleeveless T-shirt and leather pants. He hops in place and blows his bangs out of the way as he talks.

"A sweet evening to you," he says.

Oh my God, I think.

"Ciao," says There's Something About Mary.

The waiter shoots her a gigolo's come-hither look that makes me want to light his bangs on fire.

"What can I bring you?"

"A Negroni for me," Cameron orders.

"Margarita for me," I say.

"You want that normal or *frozen*?" the aspiring male model asks me, tapping his pencil on his order pad and leaning on the pretentious English *frozen*.

I'd have to guess that, in his imagination, the fact that he addressed me in the informal is quite an honor.

"*Frozen*."

"Negroni . . . Margarita," writes the bangs-blower, dictating the order to himself.

At this point he ought to clear out, but he seems to have something else he wants to tell us.

"All right. Well then, I'll leave you two to your synergy. Have a nice evening."

I'm so disconcerted by the unholy obscenity that this mental defective with the cascading bangs has allowed to escape his lips that I can't help but track him with my eyes as he moves off, as if I somehow found the fact of his earthly existence to be an inexplicable mystery at this point.

When I turn back to Cameron Diaz, she's already laughing.

A text comes in for me.

"Excuse me," I say.

"No worries," she says, wiping away her tears.

I read it.

It's from Espe.

WHERE THE FUCK ARE YOU?

"Is there a problem?" asks There's Something About Mary.

"No, it's my friend from earlier, he's looking for me."

She gives me a confused look as I slip my phone back into my breast pocket.

"Well? Aren't you going to text him back?"

"No, I've had enough of him for today, believe me."

We look at each other. We're both pretty uncomfortable, which is a worrisome sign.

"You know," she says, "my friends recognized you. I hadn't even spotted you."

"Go on, get out of here."

"Really. They said 'Isn't that Malinconico?'"

"Of course, when you think about it, it's just nuts."

"Why?"

"I'm not a successful lawyer, Irene. It's odd that I'm at risk of becoming one thanks to this whole business."

I answered instinctively, without thinking. Something must be happening if this girl can make me speak sincerely just by sitting across from me. The same thing that happened at the hospital, now that I think about it.

"Yeah," she says, a note of sadness entering her voice, as if my observation had reminded her of the inescapable nature of the grief that she was doing her best to outsmart.

"Hey," I say, taking her hand. "Hey."

"It was all wrong, all of it. From the start," she whispers, talking to herself.

I shyly reach my other hand toward her and try to stroke her face.

She squints her eyes as if to stave off a tear; she bites her lip and smiles at me, with a need to reassure me that touches me in a way I'd rather not have been touched.

"Don't worry, it's nothing."

"Listen, I'm sorry, I didn't think I was . . ."

She rubs her cheek against my hand and squeezes the other hand tight.

"It's okay. Really. I'm over it."

I look at her as if to ask her what to think about the fact that we're here doing what we're doing. I ought to change the subject, and right away, withdraw from the intimacy that is growing between us, move the conversation to topics of no particular importance so that I can bring this interaction to an end as quickly as possible and get my ass out of here before it's too late. Instead, once again, I wind up following my atavistic instincts to do everything I can to ruin my life.

"Do you know who you remind me of?" I say to her, point-blank.

She rolls her eyes to the ceiling, as if I was about to say something that she'd heard billions of times.

"Cameron Diaz."

"Wrong answer. An old song by Dik Dik."

"What?" she says, astonished.

"'L'isola di Wight.' You know it?"

She shakes her head.

"One verse, in particular. Want to hear it?"

She smiles.

"Does that mean you want to sing it to me?"

"What am I supposed to do, recite it? Songs aren't poems, after all."

"Right. Okay, go."

She turns her ear to me, all curious, as I lean toward her, clear my throat, and intone:

Without a suitcase you and I
Set out one Thursday
In our eyes was the word yes

Here I pause briefly, both because that's how the song goes and because I want to gauge her reaction.

Her eyes are closed. A way of concentrating, probably. So I continue, moving on to the part that in my mind has the most to do with her:

A rain of butterflies all around us
You gave me your youth
And no one's stopped me since

I lean away, announcing the end of the performance.

She waits a few seconds before opening her eyes. When she does, she looks upset.

"Let's stop here, Vincenzo," she says, avoiding my eyes.

"Sorry, I didn't mean to make you uncomfortable."

"You really don't get it. Stop."

"Why?"

"Because otherwise, we'll keep going."

"Ah."

"As long as he's in that condition, I can't bring myself to, I'm not able to, I . . . Oh, how stupid, forgive me forgive me forgive me."

She's on the verge of breaking into tears. She puts one hand over her mouth.

I look around, dreading some indiscreet observer (I'm blessing the darkness we're sitting in), then I stand up, bring my chair over next to hers, and sit down.

"Hey," I tell her, stroking her head, "don't worry, nothing's happened. Let's just start over from the beginning, okay? I'm an emotional mess myself right now, and . . ."

I'm about to finish my sentence but I can't because, darting like a cobra, she grabs my face with both hands and pulls me toward her, dragging me into a desperate, ravenous kiss. When we're done, she pushes me away.

I sit there, astounded and vaguely enthusiastic, while There's Something About Mary stands up and adjusts the strap of her purse over her shoulder.

"Please, Vincenzo," she says, leaning over me.

"Eh."

"If I call you, don't answer."

I look at her and say nothing.

She kisses me again: no tongue this time.

I start to stand up.

She presses her hand gently down on my shoulder, and when she's sure I've gotten the message, she leaves.

"I can take the Negroni back if you want," the bangs-blowing waiter says to me, materializing out of the darkness at that exact instant with the tray with our drinks.

What an ass I've just made of myself, I think.

THINGS CHANGE

E ver since Alessandra Persiano left, I sleep with my cell phone turned on. Since I no longer hear all that well out of one ear, I keep it under my pillow, and I rely on the vibrate mode, in case any updates come in overnight.

This ignoble practice has ensured that my sleep is automatically interrupted at preset intervals so that I can check the possible arrival of calls and/or texts: 2 A.M., 4 A.M., 6:30.

It goes without saying that every time it takes the hand of God to get me back to sleep, so in the end I get a terrible night's sleep, and my face only starts to reassemble itself around two in the afternoon.

But last night, as I returned home from my surreal tête-à-tête with Irene, something very strange happened to me. I pulled my phone out of my jacket pocket; I looked at it; it occurred to me as if it were the most natural thing in the world that there was no rule written anywhere that I had to ruin another night of sleep, and then I *turned it off*, triggering an exquisitely political sense of relief at the realization of how little it takes to set a caged man free.

That's not all: when I brushed my teeth I moved the toothbrush correctly (up and down, rather than scrubbing horizontally like an ignorant donkey the way I usually do), then I switched the light off, I turned my nose up at the small angry mob of guilt complexes that usually gathers in my bedroom when I lay myself out flat on my back and recapitulate the events of the day and the state of my life in general, then I simply closed my eyes and I *slept* until nine the next morning.

Absolutely unbelievable.

I turn my cell phone on at ten (an unthinkable time for a person to get up who is a vassal to his loved ones, and has therefore long since sentenced himself to be available around the clock, 24/7/365), while I spoil the pleasure of my morning espresso waiting for a slow-moving tree sloth of a man to finish reading the one copy of *Corriere della Sera* offered free of charge to the customers of this café.

There are three missed calls: two from Assunta and one from an unknown number.

I'm just calling Ass back when I'm interrupted by an incoming call (the number seems to be the same one I read just a moment ago). I want to reject it, but I'm always getting the commands muddled (for someone who's used to doing one thing at a time, the multifunctionality of modern cell phones is pure avant-garde) and so instead I take it.

"Yes," I answer. As if to say: "No."

"Am I speaking with Counselor Malinconico?"

I'm so frustrated at having postponed the phone call I wanted to make in order to answer an incoming call from I have no idea whom that I have a sudden urge to be rude.

"No."

Pause.

The guy on the other end of the line is probably trying to make up his mind as to whether or not to believe me.

"Actually, I wrote the number in my agenda book . . ." he replies, without the slightest argumentative edge.

"Nice work, Vincenzo," I say to myself. "You're such an oaf."

And an idiot to boot.

"You're right. Forgive me."

"In that case, I'm speaking with Counselor Malinconico?"

"Unfortunately, you are."

"Then that's taken care of. *Buongiorno*, this is Simone, I work with Daria Bignardi, do you remember me?"

God, what an ass I just made of myself.

"Oh, of course, how are you? I was just thinking that I needed to hear back from you about the trip. I'm coming on Friday, right?"

"Actually," he says, somewhat embarrassed, "well, that's why I was calling you. There were some unexpected developments during the preparation of this week's program and the topic we'd invited you to discuss has been, ahem, crossed off the list, I'm afraid."

"Ah," I say, "why is that?"

"Well, you see, it's by and large a thematic issue."

"A thematic issue."

"Yes, you see, we do our best to offer a minimum of continuity in terms of the subjects that make up the broadcast. Unfortunately, when, as in this case, more than one of the guests drop out before air time, we're forced to restructure the program around another theme."

"Okay. Maybe if you give me half an hour or so I'll be able to figure out what you just said."

He laughs.

"In any case, we'd be delighted to have you on the show some other time."

Sure, I think.

"Of course."

"Daria sends her best."

"Thanks, please give her mine. And forgive me for earlier, I'm not usually so rude."

"Don't give it a second thought. Please forgive us, rather, for this last-minute change."

370 - DIEGO DE SILVA

After we end the call, I enjoy the surprisingly sweet sensation of lightness that this cancellation in midstream has brought me.

I don't know if I've told you this, but I basically adore cancellations. They suddenly free you of all responsibilities, all expectations. Above all, they reconcile you with boredom.

Another call.

This one at least comes from a number I know: it's Assunta.

"Who were you talking to?" is the first thing she says, without even giving me the time to say "hello."

I give a start.

"Hey, who do you think you are, my girlfriend?"

"I try calling you for almost two hours and find the phone turned off the whole time, then I try again and this time it's busy: with your kind permission, I'm going to go ahead and be irritated, okay?"

"What's gotten into you, if you don't mind my asking?"

"Where are you? I need you to come over here for a minute. Right away."

"Do you know what time it is, Ass? Ten thirty in the morning. You know where I could very well be at this time of day? In court. And you know what I could very well be doing? Arguing a case."

"But instead you're wasting time in some café, right?"

Shit, I think.

I hold the phone away from my ear, then I bring it back.

"I hereby inform you, my dear mother-in-law, that the countdown has begun for the mission to tell you to go fuck yourself, and I've already reached the number four. Three, two, one . . ."

"Go fuck yourself, Vincenzo."

"Hey, wasn't I supposed to be the one saying that to you?"

"Get your ass in gear and get over here, I want you to do something."

"But what?"

"I'll tell you when you get here."

"Oh, Jesus. But why is it so urgent?"

"It's not actually that urgent, but I want to do it before I stop feeling like it. Come on, enough with this debate, just swing by here, now, Christ!"

"Okay, okay, I'm on my way, fuck off."

That she's decided to undergo chemo, even if it sounds absurd to say so, is good news. That she's decided to put an end to her reprisal against Nives, likewise. Also because that means we can put an end to my clandestine visits, and she can finally accept the assistance of the person who really ought to be there at her side in the challenging period that lies ahead of her. But it's not as if I'm really all that eager to take credit for these fine decisions, as she wants me to do.

I tell her that I have no need of rehabilitation in Nives's eyes, and in fact I'm not comfortable with the idea of informing her of the fact that all this time I've been—let's go ahead and put it in these terms—taking care of her mother behind her back, but Ass doesn't want to listen to reason, she demands that her daughter know that if she's changed her mind, it's thanks to me.

"But I didn't do anything, Ass."

"You came to see me in secret and you put up with the ravings of a bitter old woman, Vincenzo. And in spite of all that, you made me laugh."

This, I have to admit, I am pleased to hear.

"You certainly don't expect me to deliver this whole lovely little speech to her?"

"There's no need. There's just one thing I need, and it's very simple."

She tells me what it is.

"Okay," I tell her when she's done.

"Thanks," she says.

"A quick shot to celebrate?" I ask teasingly.

She smiles.

"Your Jack Daniel's is long gone."

"You're not the one who's been drinking it, am I right?"

"Let's just say that Miorita really enjoyed it."

"I knew it."

"But you can't even begin to imagine how much good it did me to see you walk in here with that bottle in your hand."

Alagia? Alfredo? I wish you were both here right now. Ears wide open.

I pull out my cell phone, I dial the number.

She picks up on the second ring.

"Vincenzo," she says, happily surprised.

"Ciao, Nives. Do you have a minute?"

"I . . . yes, of course, why not. I'm happy to hear from you, I wanted to . . ."

"We can talk later. Right now there's a person here I want you to talk to."

"A . . . person?"

"Yes."

And I hand the phone to her mother.

As I leave Ass's building, I catch myself thinking how odd it is that a person who feels damaged deep inside can still be deserving of someone's love. Whether it's a terrible father sleeping in an oxygen tent or a sad sack like me who does nothing but rack up one failure after another doesn't much matter. We're all the same. Unhappy in different ways, doing what we can to make sure that not everything is a dead loss.

I never asked love to save my life. All I wanted was for it to be there when I felt its absence, to never abandon me entirely. Even when it was ramshackle and ridiculous, I never gave up on it.

*

My phone rings.

I glance at the display.

It's Alessandra Persiano.

For a second my heart leaps up into my mouth, then it sinks back to its proper location unassisted, without my having to do anything to persuade it. Perhaps it simply no longer cares that much.

That's what I would have said to Paolo Di Stefano, if he'd asked me, "How do you want to die?" during Proust's questionnaire.

I look at the phone in my hand as it squeaks and vibrates. It's like holding a mouse. Alessandra Persiano's name keeps blinking, like a cry for help.

I put the phone back in my pocket, I start walking again, and for perhaps the first time in my life, I avail myself of the right not to answer.

NOW, THEN

This is a work of fiction (it's odd that novels so often point out this fact: have you ever purchased a couch and found a notice, perhaps on the consumer safety label, informing you that "This is a very wide upholstered seat with a backrest and armrests"?). Events, names, characters, and places are all imaginary. Any resemblance to actual events, real persons, and mothers-in-law is purely coincidental. Not so for real persons mentioned in this book, whom I fictiously enlisted in what I hope is the most respectful way possible as far as their public images are concerned.

I thank Prof. John Spanish for his advice on the subject of video security.

I also wish to thank Ernesto Franco, because he knows what a writer is and what he does; Paola Gallo, who knows how to point out a novel's better qualities and shortcomings with the same tact and delicacy (and who wears boots with all the flair of an authentic cowgirl); and Maria Ida

Cartoni, who has an unmatched talent for describing a book in a sentence or two at the most, and nailing it every time.

My special thanks to Dalia Oggero, who has been following me since I took my first literary steps, and who after all these years still lets me know whether I'm keeping up the pace or just scampering on all fours.

D. D. S.

(The chapter "When You Wake Up and Realize You Died in Your Sleep" appeared in the February 2008 issue of *Rolling Stone Italy*, in a slightly different version.)

About the Author

Diego De Silva was born in Naples in 1964. He is the author of plays, screenplays, and six novels. *I Hadn't Understood*, the first book featuring Vincenzo Malinconico, was a finalist for the Strega Prize, Italy's most prestigious literary award, and winner of the Naples Prize for fiction. He currently lives in Salerno.